Aileen Armitage is half-Irish, half-Yorkshire by birth. She began writing when failing sight forced her to give up work in the outside world and in 1988 she was the winner of the Woman of the Year award. She is also the author of *Hawksmoor*, *A Dark Moon Raging*, *Touchstone* and *Hawkrise* and the 'Chapters' series of novels, *Chapter of Innocence*, *Chapter of Echoes* and *Chapter of Shadows*. Her most recent novel, *The Jericho Years*, was also published by Corgi. She is married to Deric Longden, journalist, broadcaster and author of *Diana's Story*, *Lost for Words*, *The Cat Who Came In From the Cold* and *I'm a Stranger Here Myself*.

D1470991

Also by Aileen Armitage

THE JERICHO YEARS

and published by Corgi Books

CEDAR STREET

Aileen Armitage

CORGI BOOKS

CEDAR STREET
A CORGI BOOK : 0 552 14229 8

Originally published in Great Britain by Bantam Press,
a division of Transworld Publishers Ltd

PRINTING HISTORY
Bantam Press edition published 1995
Corgi edition published 1996

Set in 10pt Adobe Times by Kestrel Data, Exeter.

Corgi Books are published by Transworld Publishers Ltd,
61–63 Uxbridge Road, London W5 5SA,
in Australia by Transworld Publishers (Australia) Pty Ltd,
15–25 Helles Avenue, Moorebank, NSW 2170
and in New Zealand by Transworld Publishers (NZ) Ltd,
3 William Pickering Drive, Albany, Auckland.

Reproduced, printed and bound in Great Britain by
Cox & Wyman Ltd, Reading, Berks.

In memory of my ancestors
who have lived and worked in Huddersfield
for some 400 years.
They played their part in its history
and bequeathed to me
a legacy of love and pride in the town.

ONE

1910

In the long, high-ceilinged workroom in the back of Rose's furniture store machines clattered and whirred, punctuated every now and again by a muttered swear-word from one of the seamstresses when the cotton snapped.

May sewed on, oblivious. She enjoyed her work, taking infinite pains to make sure every detail was exactly as it ought to be. Over the last three years she had learnt her craft well, taking delight in the intricacies of frilling heavy brocade cushions and fringing elaborately pleated and tucked sofa covers.

Miss Openshaw's curt nod of approval was all the reward she needed. The tight-lipped overseer wasn't the easiest of women to please but she hardly ever had cause to rebuke May nowadays for a stitch out of line. That was why Mr Rose had selected her to go up to Thornleigh Hall.

'Only the best is good enough for Sir Joseph,' Mr Rose had beamed proudly as he told his staff. 'That's why he comes to the firm with the best reputation in Hawksmoor. Furniture, curtains, cushions, bedcovers – we're to supply the whole lot. And like I said, only the very best work is good enough.'

And out of all his seamstresses he'd picked May to be responsible for all the soft furnishing at the Hall. The bigger items would be made in Rose's workshop but she would be in charge of the final details. It was thrilling to think that, before Sir Joseph's family moved in, she would actually be living in and sewing at the Hall to make sure every detail was complete.

Mam would be so proud of her. She was proud enough

already – May had overheard her boasting to their neighbour Mrs Boothroyd over the yard wall as they both hung out washing on the zig-zag of lines slung between the house wall and the privy down at the bottom of the yard.

'She's a grand lass is our May. Not been a minute's trouble since the day she was born, she hasn't. I only wish our Cassie were a bit more like her.'

Mr Rose bustled in again with the same air of enthusiastic eagerness he'd worn ever since he'd learned he'd won the Thornleigh Hall contract. All day he'd been in and out of the workroom, talking to Miss Openshaw, a thing he rarely did as a rule. Normally Miss Openshaw was left to queen it in her own domain down here while Mr Rose sat in state upstairs in his grand office.

May eased her foot off the treadle and looked up. He was outside the glass door now with Miss Openshaw again, and the girls were whispering to one another. There was definitely an atmosphere of suppressed excitement in the air.

She frowned. Whatever it was, the girls seemed to know something. If they did, they wouldn't tell her. Snotty-nosed, they called her behind her back, stand-offish and aloof. She knew, she'd heard them, but it didn't worry her. They didn't talk about things that interested her. But right now, she wished she knew just what was going on.

'I assume he'll be working upstairs in the office with you, Mr Rose. I wouldn't like to think he might unsettle my girls.'

Henry Rose spread thick, capable hands. 'Not at all, Miss Openshaw. Aaron's settled down a lot, and even if he's in and out of the workroom they'll soon get used to him. He'll be like part of the furniture, so to speak.'

He waved his arms to indicate the three floors above stacked with expensive furniture and smiled at his own joke.

Miss Openshaw interlocked her fingers tightly. 'You don't know these young women like I do, Mr Rose. Mr Aaron is a very presentable young man.'

Henry beamed. 'That's true, my boy is a handsome lad but he's growing into a very shrewd business man. He hasn't spent all this time learning the trade inside out in that big London store only to waste his time dallying with shop girls. You've no need to fret on that score.'

Miss Openshaw grunted. 'Happen so, but I'll have my work cut out trying to keep their minds on the job.'

Mr Rose patted his spreading stomach. 'Ah well, that's what you're paid for, Miss Openshaw. I've told Aaron he starts tomorrow.'

'Mam – I've lost a button up me nose!'

Ada Turnbull ignored the panic in her small daughter's voice. She lifted the flat iron from the fire and spat on it, watching the droplet of spit hiss along its surface and slither off the edge.

'What you on about, our Elsie?' she demanded, slapping the iron down on a folded sheet. 'What button?'

The seven-year-old wriggled down off her high stool and pointed to an array of multi-hued buttons laid out in long lines and circles on the sideboard.

'One of them little ones, like them off me dad's nightshirt. I had one too many for me pattern. I shoved it up me nose and now it's gone.'

Ada sighed and up-ended the flat iron on the table. 'You do talk some rubbish at times, lass. Come here, let's have a look.'

Turning the child to face the fading light from the window, Ada tilted the fair head back and peered up the small nose. 'Nay, I can't see anything,' she pronounced at last. 'There's nowt up there.'

She glanced up at the clock on the high mantelshelf. 'Oh, just look at the time!' she exclaimed, snatching up the iron again. 'The others'll be home before I've done. Why don't you make yourself useful, cut them newspapers up into squares for the privy?'

The little girl came to stand beside her, tugging at her apron.

'But what about me nose?' she said fearfully. 'What if it's got stuck up there for ever?'

Ada propped the iron back against the red coals then stood looking down at the child, hand on hip. 'Happen it'll do your brains good – stir 'em up a bit. Nay, don't look so worried – it fell on the floor, most likely. We'll find it later. Now look sharp, get the scissors and a bit of string out of the drawer.'

She bent down, the folded piece of felt in her hand, to lift the second iron off the fire. A sharp thud overhead made her straighten up.

'Hey up – your dad wants summat,' she murmured. 'Go on up and see what it is, love, and take the bucket with you. Happen he needs a pee before the others get home.'

Elsie put the bucket down on the floor and straightened. Her father's gaunt face lay level with her own in the big high bed, covered with the patchwork quilt May had made out of the remnants she brought home from work. His eyes were open, but they wore their customary vacant, far-away look. It was the pain that did it, Mam said.

'Want a pee, Dad?' she asked. 'Shall I help you?'

He grunted and blinked, and she understood. 'I'll leave it by the bed then. Shall I shut the curtains for you now it's getting dark?'

The rings made a loud rattle as they slid along the pole. She heard him groan and she turned and waited. He rolled his body with difficulty onto his side then levered his weight onto one elbow, and in the gloom she could just make out his haggard smile.

'You're a good lass,' he muttered. 'Fetch us a cup of tea, will you?'

'The kettle's not on yet – me mam's got the irons on the fire still. Give us a bang with your stick when you've done and I'll bring up a drink of water.'

Ada stood back from the stone sink to let the child fill the cup. Another thud reverberated on the floor above and she watched Elsie carry the cup, carefully clasped between chubby fists, towards the scullery door.

'How's his back?' she asked.

The child shook her head, then bit her lip as she steadied the cup. 'He didn't say.'

'Never mind. I'll see to it later. Tell him his supper'll be ready very shortly.'

She watched the straight little back as Elsie left the room. What a pity it was that the child would never know her father the way he used to be in the old days, sturdy and cheerful, bringing a smile to everyone's face with his light-hearted ways. Nothing had ever got Jim down; he'd always see the bright side of things.

But not any more. Not since the day the mine-shaft collapsed and a pit prop smashed his spine. It was emblazoned on her memory for ever, the day there'd been a thumping at her door and she'd opened it to find the grimy-faced men carrying the shattered body of her barely-living husband on a yard gate.

She wasn't going to let him die, not with his child in her belly. She'd nursed him fiercely back to life – of a sort. Steeped in his own agonizing pain, he'd barely been aware of hers as she gave birth in the next room to his third daughter. But at least, thank God, he'd lived to see her.

But try as she might, she hadn't been able to mend his back; even the best surgeons in the world couldn't do that, the doctor had told her. He was lucky to have a heart that still beat and lungs that still breathed. Maybe, with luck, the hole in his back would heal over in time . . .

But it never had and now, nearly eight years later, it was clear it never would. The best she could hope for was that the festering could be kept at bay. Right now it wasn't too bad, not like last winter when for months it had been too icy-cold to open the bedroom window to sweep away the smell . . .

So Elsie knew him only as a helpless thing lying up there in the bed, needing to be washed and dressed and fed like a baby. Only May and Cassie were old enough to remember the laughing, loving father he used to be.

Ada sighed and, dipping her hands into a bowl of flour, began rolling the dumplings to drop into the mutton stew.

May Turnbull turned quickly off Fountain Street into the shelter of Cedar Street's tall terraced houses just as the Manchester express came clattering over the viaduct. Every night at this time she tried to beat the train so as to avoid the soot-flecks which came fluttering down, making ugly marks on the collar of her white blouse. Mam could wash them out but she had enough work on her plate already with all the washing she took in, without having to get her one good blouse clean again for morning.

She walked on, head bent and deep in thought, not taking in the familiar row of identical stone houses punctuated at intervals by a narrow entry to the back yards. Saturday tomorrow, she thought. Pay day. As always Mr Rose would lay a small brown envelope on each table beside the sewing machine on the dot at half-past five. Under the eagle eye of Miss Openshaw not one of the girls would touch the tempting package until the bell shrilled at six.

It gave May pleasure to think of handing over those precious shillings to Mam. Life hadn't been easy for her since she'd been forced to become the breadwinner after Dad's accident. Hopefully things would look up now Cassie too had started work up at the box factory.

'Evening, May.'

The unexpected voice startled her out of her reverie. A plump backside protruded from an open doorway. A woman was busily donkey-stoning the edge of the doorstep till it gleamed dully white in the dusk.

'Evening, Mrs Tandy.'

The older woman straightened and gave an apologetic smile. 'Daft time of day to be doing it,' she murmured, 'but there'll be no time in the morning, what with all there is to be done before his relatives come over from Wakefield for high tea. How's your dad these days?'

'Fair to middling, thanks.'

At the far end of the street a lamp flickered slowly into life. May saw the lamplighter heave his pole over his shoulder and trudge on to the next lamp post.

Mrs Tandy shook her head. 'Aye well, I reckon it's too much to hope for any better. Still, give your mam my regards.' She wagged the donkey-stone in May's direction. 'She's a good woman, is your mam.'

'Yes,' agreed May quietly, turning to go. 'She is.'

Mrs Tandy's voice followed her in the half-light. 'Many a woman would have pushed off long ago. Not even a bit of compensation from them tight devils to help her through.'

Mam was waiting on the doorstep, arms folded. 'I heard,' she said briefly. 'There's nowt private, is there? Everybody gets to know everybody else's business in this street.' She stood aside to let May pass. 'Did you see our Cassie on the way home?'

May moved on from the tiny lobby into the living room and shrugged off her coat. The air was heavy with the mingled aromas of stew and wet washing steaming on the rack.

'You know she comes the other way from me.'

'Aye, I know, but I thought as you might have seen her hanging around by the corner shop again. You know what she's like.'

Elsie lay on the hearthrug. Her mother pushed her gently aside with her foot so that May could warm her hands at the fire.

'You could do with a pair of gloves, lass,' she remarked.

May smiled. 'I'm saving up. I'll have enough to get some before winter comes on.'

Ada shrugged. 'There's nowt to stop you knitting yourself some and save your brass. There's that grey wool left over in the cupboard.'

May rubbed her hands together and turned. 'I know, but I've a fancy for a leather pair, like Miss Openshaw wears.' Her fingers slid slowly up and down the back of her hand, caressing the imagined luxury. 'Kid, they are, all soft and lovely. That's what I'm saving for, Mam. I can wait.'

Ada was ladling the mutton stew out of the big iron saucepan when Cassie came home, her pretty face flushed and her eyes glowing. She dropped her bag and coat on the rocking-chair and came to sit down at the table.

'That smells good, Mam,' she smiled. 'I'm starving.'

Ada sniffed. 'Where have you been till now?' she asked.

Cassie reached across to slap Elsie's hand down from her face. 'Come out of your nose, you. What you doing? Looking for your brains?'

The child scowled. 'No, me button. I lost it.'

Ada wasn't to be side-tracked. 'I said, where were you? You should have been home half an hour ago.'

Cassie gave her a dimpling smile. 'I would have been, only I met Eunice down the road – I haven't seen her since we left school. She was telling me about her job at Whitfield's. I said I'd go round to their house tonight for a bit.'

Her mother slapped a steaming plate in front of her. 'Did you now? And is that good-for-nothing brother of hers still sniffing around after you?'

'Mother!' said May, her fork pausing halfway to her mouth.

Ada folded her arms. 'It needs saying plain to our Cass. I thought I'd made it clear as day, them Fairchilds aren't the sort I want you going with. And I'll not have you hanging about on street corners at night like some trollop.'

Cassie flushed and put down her knife. 'I'm not a trollop. I just like talking to folk, that's all. I'm not like our May, all quiet and not a word for anyone.'

Her mother drew a long strand of gristle out from her teeth and laid it on the edge of her plate, then wagged a greasy finger. 'Never you mind about gossiping – you can do that all day in the factory. At night you just come straight back here and do your share of the chores instead of leaving it all to May.'

'What's a trollop?' asked Elsie.

Her mother ignored her. 'And you can forget about going out tonight, Cassie. Soon as supper's over you can bathe your dad's back for him.'

Cassie looked stricken. 'Oh Mam – do I have to? It fair makes me back teeth chatter, does that.'

'You'll do it and like it,' said Ada firmly. 'We've got to keep it open, I've told you often enough, otherwise if it closes over all that putrid green stuff will go into his insides and poison him.'

Cassie pushed her chair back and folded her arms defiantly. 'Let May do it – she won't mind. She's got much more patience than me – she'd make a wonderful nurse. Let her do it.'

'You heard me,' repeated Ada. 'May does more than her fair share as it is.'

'Happen it'd be best if it did poison him,' Cassie muttered angrily.

May saw her mother's face redden and her fist tighten into a ball. She laid her knife and fork neatly side by side on the empty plate.

'I'll do it, Mam,' she said quietly. 'It's no bother.'

Her mother's fist thumped down on the table. 'I've said it's Cassie's turn, and that's all there is to it.'

May set the bowl of warm salt water down on the dresser and turned up the oil-lamp. Dad lay face-down, his head twisted to one side, half-buried in the depths of the pillow. He opened his eyes, saw the bowl and groaned.

She dipped the lint pad in the water and bent to draw back the sheet and pull up his nightshirt. In the hollow of his back the hole gaped dark and angry. Slivers of his backbone gleamed white between the raw red flesh, and the edges of the wound were showing tell-tale signs of yellow. If it started festering again and turned back to the revolting ulcer he had had last winter . . .

'Grit your teeth, Dad,' she murmured. 'I'll be as gentle as I can.'

She gritted her own teeth as she touched the pad to the open wound. Despite the number of times she'd done this task before, it still nauseated her. No wonder Cassie rebelled.

Her father was holding his breath, trying hard to beat the pain. As she wrung out the lint pad once more she heard him mutter. 'Nay, lass, I don't know why you bother,' he said weakly. 'It would be best for us all if I were dead and gone. A merciful release for everyone, I reckon.'

'Don't talk so daft,' she said angrily, and then bit her lip. 'It'd break Mam's heart to hear you talk like that. You mustn't give up.'

He twisted his head a fraction to catch her glance. 'You're a good 'un, May,' he said sadly. 'Pity your sister's not more like you.'

May's hand faltered. Could he have overheard Cassie's outburst in the room below? She dabbed gently at the wound.

'She's all right, Dad. She just isn't really up to this – she can't help it if it turns her stomach.'

She heard the hiss of his indrawn breath, saw his face contort. 'Aye, and yours too, lass. I remember how it made you sick first time.'

'That's a long time ago,' she murmured soothingly. 'I'm well used to it now.'

Why did she lie to him? Touching that rotting flesh nauseated her now just as much as ever. She looked down on the shrunken body in the bed. Somewhere within that emaciated flesh lay the cheery, fun-loving father who used to fill her childhood days with stories and adventures. He was squinting up at her thoughtfully.

'Nay,' he muttered, 'that weren't what I meant. I fear our Cass'll come to no good, having no firm hand to guide her.'

May patted his shoulder. 'Nay, I shouldn't fret, Dad. Mam keeps a strict eye on her.'

'Aye, but she doesn't know I've heard the lass through the window, giggling out there with some lad or other. Nowt good comes of that sort of carry-on.'

'There's no harm in her, Dad. She's buckling down well at the box factory.'

May drew the pad firmly down the ragged yellow edge of the wound, watching the pus ooze from under the flesh. Her father groaned and closed his eyes tightly, and his voice came in a strangled whisper.

'Aye, happen. But at least we'll never need fret over you.'

Ada was clearing the table when May came downstairs. She held out the saucepan and ladle in invitation.

'Any more for any more? There's just a bit left.'

May shook her head, Elsie patted her stomach and blew out her cheeks, and Cassie took no notice as she rooted in her bag.

She pulled out her purse and peered into it. 'I'm skint,' she announced. 'May – can you lend me sixpence till I get paid?'

'No she cannot,' said Ada. 'What you want it for anyway?'

'I'm going out. I told you.'

'That you're not. No self-respecting girl of fifteen ought to be out in the dark.'

'I'm nearly sixteen!'

'No matter. You can just take that snap tin of yours off the sideboard and go out in the scullery and make up your sandwiches for tomorrow. You never leave yourself time in the morning and I always get lumbered with it. Go on, and polish your shoes while you're about it.'

'Mine are all nice and clean,' said Elsie smugly.

'And you can get your nightie out of the drawer,' said her mother, 'and put it round the brick in the oven to warm. Bedtime.'

Elsie growled and did as she was told. Ada lifted the curtain to look out into the street. It was starting to drizzle and the glow of the lamplight glistened on wet cobbles. She saw a black-coated figure passing through the pool of light thrown by the lamp on the far side of the street. It was Mr Jordan, the undertaker, on his usual nightly stroll.

Behind her in the kitchen she could hear the clatter of dishes in the stone sink as May started on the washing-up, and Ada smiled to herself as she let the curtain fall. She'd miss that girl if she left home, and it was surely only a matter of time before some bright young man spotted her qualities and came courting. She mightn't be as pretty as Cass but she had a nice way with her, dainty in her habits and just as ladylike as Mrs Jordan up the road.

It still puzzled folk why the Jordans had chosen to live in Cedar Street. They couldn't be short of a bob or two, both of them always smartly dressed – Mrs Jordan even wore a hat and gloves just to pop down to the corner shop. But she never spoke to a soul beyond a polite 'Good morning'.

Jordan's must be a thriving business, the best-regarded undertakers in Hawksmoor this many a long year. Folks died every day, and all self-respecting folk made a point of putting by enough for a decent burial.

'I'd like to think of being carried out by Jordan's men,' they said. Only the other day old Mrs Boothroyd had said as much over the yard wall.

'Only I'm not planning on going just yet a while,' she'd added, 'not before I've got it all written down who's to have what, once I'm gone. I want no squabbling like there was among them Bottomleys. Scandalous it were, the way they carried on.'

Elsie's mouth gaped in a huge yawn.

'Come on, let's be having you,' said Ada, bending to pull the child's pinafore up over her head, 'else there'll be no time to put the rags in your hair.'

No-one noticed a small shirt button fall out of the pinafore pocket onto the lino and roll away under the sideboard to settle beside a startled cockroach.

TWO

Harold Jordan stepped down off the tram and watched its lights recede into the distance as it rumbled on its way uphill towards Lindley. He stood on the pavement edge and drew a fob-watch from his pocket, peering at it under the lamplight. Twenty-eight minutes past seven. Mr Lucas had said half-past was always a convenient time.

As he neared the house he adjusted the angle of his bowler hat and straightened his tie. It always paid to present the right image of prosperous efficiency. No-one must ever suspect that nowadays every penny counted.

Conducting business with the recently-bereaved was never easy at the best of times. Mrs Lucas's funeral was barely three months ago, a simple, restrained affair with a plain coffin, no satin lining, no brass. Still, the schoolmaster's approval was important to him. And he had just settled the bill.

Pushing open the wooden gate and composing his features, Harold walked circumspectly up the path to the door of the semi-detached house, noting the overgrown lawn and the lace curtains hanging awry. Not so long ago Harold had owned a house like this, but he would never have let this happen. Marchmont Avenue had been the pride and joy of his life. That flower-bed would have been immaculate, ablaze with peonies. Fanny too sorely missed her beds of herbs and fruit in the back garden now they'd moved to Cedar Street and the only vista from the kitchen window was of a cobbled back yard and the peeling paint on the privy door.

He composed his face into solemn, dignified respect and rapped the brass knocker. There was a sound of distant barking. Moments passed before he heard footsteps hurrying on an uncarpeted floor and the door opened and Mr Lucas's flushed, distracted face appeared.

Harold removed his hat. 'Good evening, Mr Lucas. I believe you'd like a word with me.'

The schoolmaster made an uncertain step back. 'Oh yes, of course – come in.'

Harold followed his attenuated frame as he hurried into the parlour. Grief seemed to have shrunk the schoolmaster's already spare body. As he entered the parlour Harold could smell its musty air, a mingled scent of dust and wet dog.

Mr Lucas grabbed up a pile of books from the sofa and pushed them on to the already overloaded sideboard.

'Forgive me,' he murmured. 'I'm afraid the house lacks a woman's touch these days. Dorothy used to keep it so nice. I really must see about getting someone in. Please sit down.'

Harold sat, clasping his hat on his knees. 'A sad loss, Mr Lucas. The church choir sorely misses Mrs Lucas's fine soprano voice.'

The schoolmaster trailed his fingers along the piano. Harold could clearly see the lines left in the dust. 'Ah yes, she had so many talents,' the schoolmaster murmured. 'Singing, embroidery, jam-making. Funny how one doesn't truly appreciate another's qualities until too late.'

He turned briskly to face Harold. 'That's what I wanted to talk to you about – a memorial to my dear wife. I'd like very much to have a headstone erected on her grave and I'd welcome your advice, Mr Jordan.' Then he added with a touch of embarrassment, 'Something tasteful, something which would do credit to her memory, but it would have to be reasonable—'

'Of course,' Harold cut in. 'I understand.'

Lucas spread apologetic hands. 'Schoolteaching doesn't pay very handsomely, I fear.'

Harold made a deprecating gesture. 'I know the very man,' he said. 'Thaddeus – he's a master stonemason, getting on a bit now and fond of his tipple, but there isn't a finer craftsman in the whole of Hawksmoor.'

Harold saw the dubious look. 'Do you know if he charges a great deal?'

Harold shook his head. 'Not if I have a word with him, he won't. And by the time it's done the grave'll be just about settled enough. You just leave it to me, Mr Lucas – I'll put a word in for you.'

'I'd be very grateful,' said the schoolmaster. He glanced sideways at Harold. 'You never had children either, did you?'

'No,' said Harold, twisting his hat between his hands. 'A source of great regret to both Mrs Jordan and myself.'

The schoolmaster sighed. 'To us too. Dorothy always felt she'd let me down.'

Harold rose to his feet and cleared his throat. 'Don't you fret about that headstone, Mr Lucas. I'll put in a word with Thaddeus – I'll see you're all right.'

Fanny Jordan laid a pair of kippers on her husband's plate and sat down opposite him. 'I hope your indigestion's up to eating supper this late,' she remarked. 'So what did Mr Lucas have to say, love?'

Harold shook out the napkin the way he'd seen Mr Chadwick of Chadwick's mill do it so often at the Conservative Club, and laid it across his lap. It afforded him pleasure the way Fanny still set the table like she used to when they lived in Marchmont Avenue, the silver always sparkling, the black-leaded range gleaming as if it had just been delivered that day from the foundry, and the room smelling of carbolic and wax polish. Whatever her shortcomings in some directions, and however reduced their circumstances, she still kept a gratifyingly clean and comfortable house.

'He wanted a favour of me,' Harold replied, tucking into his kipper. 'Do people like him a favour and they bear you in mind later.'

'What did he want?'

'A headstone for Mrs Lucas on the cheap. I promised to

talk to Thaddeus. As it happened I saw him coming out of the Fleece so it's all arranged.'

'That's not going to earn you anything, is it?'

Harold shook his head. 'I'm to get 10 per cent of what he charges Mr Lucas,' he mumbled round a bony mouthful. He pulled a long, silvery spine from his mouth. 'Happen that's not a lot,' he said, 'but I've done 'em both a favour and it'll pay off sooner or later.'

Fanny sighed and reached for the teapot. 'It'll cover the coal bill with any luck. That's you all over, thinking of other folks first.'

'That's business, love. That's the way it works – you scratch my back and I'll scratch yours. Thaddeus wouldn't have got the job but for me.'

Fanny handed him a cup of tea then leaned her elbows on the table, cupping her chin in her hands. 'What's his house like?'

Harold tried to evade the question, knowing it could only bring regret. 'Whose? Thaddeus's? How the devil should I know?' he joked.

'No, Mr Lucas's. It's on Thornhill Road, isn't it?'

Harold frowned as he chewed another mouthful of kipper. He was aware of the wistfulness in her tone. She still pined for Marchmont Avenue, but she'd never reproach him that it was all his fault.

He shrugged. 'It looked nice enough when Arthur and me went up with the coffin but it's going to rack and ruin now, it is.'

He tore a piece of bread and, mopping up the last of the kipper juice, stuffed it into his mouth. He didn't want to pursue the subject. He'd done his best, finding this house. It hadn't been easy tracking down somewhere he could just about afford and which had a decent-sized back yard large enough to house a workshop, his hearse and the horses. He couldn't help it if Millsbridge was crammed with back-to-back terrace houses spilling out dogs and cats and squealing children onto the narrow pavements.

Outside he could hear the children now, yelling and shrieking as they played under the lamplight.

'Noisy kids,' he muttered. 'Decent folk ought to have 'em in bed by now.'

It wasn't that their noise really irritated him. Many of the poor little devils seemed to have no shoes to their feet and only their father's cut-down trousers on their backsides. Too many children, that was the problem, with feckless fathers like that Irish tinker Tim Nagle. All the Irishmen seemed to be either work-shy or had found work in Chadwick's mill only to drink their wages away in the Fleece. Irresponsible, the lot of them, breeding like flaming rabbits.

Fanny seemed to sense his thoughts. She gave a sad smile. 'At least there's only us two to worry about, love,' she murmured.

He swallowed the last of the bread. 'Aye,' he muttered. 'We'll manage.'

'Of course we will.'

Fanny looked fondly at her husband and he permitted himself the briefest of smiles. 'Now did you remember to iron my best shirt?' he asked. 'I've to see that architect's widow first thing in the morning. With luck she'll want a right good send-off for him.'

Elsie was taking the short cut home from school, past the smelly gasworks and down Archer Street. Mam wouldn't like it if she knew.

'Hey kid, what you doing in our street?'

A red-haired girl, a couple of years older than herself, leaned her skinny body against a lamp post. Two other girls stood near by, eyeing her with suspicion, and a younger boy squatted on the pavement. Elsie sensed the hostility in the air.

'What's it to you?' she said truculently.

She moved to pass by, but one of the girls barred her way and pointed a finger. 'You live down Cedar Street, don't you? You think you're better'n us.'

'No I don't. Let me get past.'

23

'What you doing in our street then?'

There was a charge in the air, their faces eager for battle. Elsie tried to sound calm.

'I've got a friend lives down here.'

'You haven't,' the big girl sneered. 'We don't pal up with Cedar Street kids. You're telling whoppers.'

'I have – she's called Mary.'

The girls were clearly not appeased. 'You got a wagon in your street,' the small boy sang out. 'I seen it. You have dead bodies in it.'

One of the redhead's satellites gave a mock-shudder and they both moved closer. The nearest peered into Elsie's face.

'Is that right? You have dead bodies in your street?'

'Do we heck. Not in the street.'

'Our Dennis says you have.'

Elsie saw the movement as one of the smaller girls hastily crossed herself.

'Don't you get frightened?' the girl whispered.

Elsie gave a brave shrug. 'They're dead,' she said airily. 'They can't harm you.'

The small boy rolled over and lay on the pavement looking up. 'I can see your drawers,' he sang out. 'They're navy.'

'Shut up,' said Elsie. 'That's rude.'

The red-haired girl uncurled herself from the lamp post. 'Hey, who are you telling to shut up?'

Elsie jutted her chin. 'Him – he's rude.'

'He's my brother, and nobody don't tell our Dennis to shut up.' She came close, so close Elsie could smell the onions on her breath. 'So you say sorry,' the redhead said softly. 'Now.'

Elsie felt a shiver of apprehension. 'No I won't. He's the one ought to say sorry to me.'

'Ooh, listen to Lady Muck!' the girl jeered, and the others began to laugh. There was a harshness in the sound that she knew spelled trouble. The redhead pushed a finger into her chest.

'Go on, say sorry to our Dennis.'

'Won't!'

'Then I'll have to make you.'

Elsie felt panic rising. 'You and whose army?' she yelled, and started to run, but Redhead snatched hold of her wrist, swung her round and pinned her against the house wall.

'You ever had a Chinese burn?' she hissed.

Elsie tried to wrench her arm free but the bigger girl was too strong. She was aware of searing pain, of Dennis sitting cross-legged beneath them, of the other girls laughing raucously. The pain was terrible. She could feel tears starting to sting her eyelids. She pulled hard, straining every muscle. Redhead grinned, and the closeness of her smug, evil face gave Elsie strength. A hand came close to her mouth, and she sank her teeth into it.

Redhead shrieked and jerked her hand away. Elsie snatched her chance and ran as fast as her legs would carry her. Voices yelled, feet started pounding after her. She could hear the racing footsteps as they closed on her.

Archer Street had never seemed so long. The only break in the long row of terrace houses was a wide archway, and she ran blindly into it. Heart slumping, she saw only an enclosed yard with no other way out.

Cornered, panting, her wrist burning with pain, she turned, feeling something under her feet. She looked down – a fence post. Her frenzied brain was quicksilvered into action by sheer panic. Next moment she found the post up-ended between her hands as Redhead raced round the corner. Elsie saw the look of triumph on that hated face dissolve into astonishment as the post thudded down on her head and she sank to the ground.

Three more faces appeared around the corner, turned pale as mouths fell open, and melted away. She could hear Dennis wailing for his mother.

Redhead got up slowly, rubbing her head, and gave Elsie a baleful look.

'You rotten shit,' she muttered. 'I'm going to get you for that.'

'Oh aye?' said Elsie with a strangely quiet feeling of superiority. 'You and whose army?'

This time it was deliberate. With all her force she swung the post round, catching Redhead a fierce thwack at the back of the knees, and she stumbled.

Redhead howled and swore again, biting back the tears as she limped away into the street. Elsie's arm was still stinging as she listened to the retreating footsteps. She'd wait a little while before going out again into Archer Street, just in case. And she wouldn't tell Mam about the Chinese burn or she'd cop it anyway for disobedience.

Leaning her forehead against the cool stone of the archway she waited for the thudding of her heart to slow . . .

Thaddeus squatted back on his haunches and wiped the sweat from his cheek with the back of a grimy hand. It had been pleasant working outside the shed on a warm afternoon but now the sun was going down and it was thirsty work chiselling. He reached for the brown jug lying on the cobblestones at his side and lifted it to his lips. Damn, it was empty again.

Out in Archer Street he could hear children's voices. It must be gone four and school had loosed out.

Suddenly he became aware of a strange tingling sensation on the back of his neck as the hairs stiffened, and he knew eyes were watching him. He craned his head round. At first he could see nothing; then he noticed the small figure leaning against the blackened stone of the archway leading out into the street. He screwed up his eyes as it moved forward.

He recognized her with her long blond hair and her bright eyes. It was poor old Turnbull's little lass, pretty as a picture she was in her neat print frock. She was a credit to her mother and no mistake.

She came close to his shoulder, looking down gravely at the inscription he'd been chipping in the stone. He could hear her quick, deep breathing as though she'd been running. She stood silent, rubbing her arm, and he saw her lips move silently as she read the words.

*'In loving remembrance of Dorothy Lucas,
died April 13, 1910, aged 46 years.'*

Thaddeus picked up his chisel again. 'Stand back a bit, love. We don't want no chippings going in your eyes.'

He raised the hammer and chisel to start again, then bethought himself. Over the years he'd learnt to spell most words people chose for their epitaphs, but this . . .

'Pass us that bit of paper, will you, lass?' He pointed the hammer to where it lay, lodged under a pebble of marble. She picked it up and handed it to him. He peered closely, then held it out to the child.

'How many l's in that long word there?'

She frowned as she read slowly aloud. *'A lass unparalleled.* There's two and then one more. What does it mean?'

He began chipping again, slowly and with care while he thought of an answer. It was easy work cutting the stone from the local quarry, not like the Aberdeen granite he'd laboured so hard on last week.

'It means she were special, love – there weren't nobody else quite like her.' He gave her a mischievous sidelong glance. 'Summat like you.'

She looked back at him solemnly. 'Am I special?'

'You're asking me? Hasn't your dad told you?'

He saw the quick flicker of her eyelids and knew he'd embarrassed her. 'I'd better be getting off home now,' she said quietly.

'Aye.' He peered at the piece of paper again. 'Two l's, did you say? And then one?'

The small figure was walking slowly through the archway. 'If you see our Christine,' he called after her, 'tell her to fetch us a jug of ale, will you, lass? Or our Eddie either – from the Fleece – they'll put it on the slate till tonight.'

As the little figure vanished from his view Thaddeus turned back to his work. Pretty little thing she was, face just like a cherub. She'd have made a wonderful model for an angel. Pity of it was, nobody wanted angels these days . . .

*   *   *

The little angel poked her head round the corner and peered along Archer Street. There was no sign of Redhead or her gang. It looked safe enough. Just to make sure she went back and picked up the fence post.

Fanny Jordan made her way round to the back door. She didn't want her outdoor shoes marking the linoleum in the front lobby she'd polished so lovingly this morning.

Arthur, Harold's young apprentice, was hanging about in the back yard, whistling as he kicked a pebble around the cobbles. She could see the dark splotches where his shirt clung to his back. He stopped whistling when he saw her and she tried to hurry past him up the steps into the house. He was a nice enough lad, but it embarrassed her the way he was always kept hanging around on pay day.

He grinned. 'I'm still waiting,' he said. 'Mr Jordan always forgets.'

Harold didn't forget. He'd told her, more than once, that it didn't harm to keep the lad waiting a while. That way he'd learn respect both for money and for his employer. Harold would be sitting in the parlour now, the money ready on the table, while he drank his cup of tea and read the afternoon paper. He wouldn't make a move till six o'clock.

Harold lowered the newspaper and laid aside his pipe as she came in. 'Give us a kiss then,' he said.

She gave him a peck on the cheek and drew back quickly. He didn't like hugs and she didn't care for the prickle of his whiskers on her lips and the smell of tobacco on his breath.

He folded the newspaper with care and laid it on the table. 'Did I see you coming out of the corner shop just now?' he asked.

He'd been watching from the window again. 'Yes,' she answered quietly. 'I needed some washing soda.'

He shook his head. 'You know I don't like you going in there.'

Fanny didn't point out that it was a long walk to the shops

in town, heavy work carrying home a week's shopping. Instead she gave a patient sigh.

'It's all right, Harold, I didn't talk to anybody.'

She saw the colour rise to his cheeks and knew she'd been clumsy. 'It's not gossip that bothers me,' he muttered. 'They can't possibly know anything. The Committee promised, but even so . . .'

'You're afraid I might let something slip.'

He gave a faint smile. 'It's not you, love – it's them. They mean well but they can't help being nosey.' She saw the weary shake of his head. 'They're not your sort, Fanny. I'm sorry, I wanted better for you. If only I hadn't been so daft—'

She reached down to touch his hand. 'We'll be all right, love. We just have to be patient.'

He straightened and snatched up the newspaper again. 'Go on,' he muttered gruffly, 'go and get the tea ready.'

As she turned to go the clock on the mantel chimed six and she heard him growl, 'Tell Arthur if he kicks his boots off in the back porch he can come in now and sign for his money.'

'How did you get that bruise on your arm, our Elsie?'

Ada's fingers paused as she twisted rags into the long fair hair to prod at the purple weal. Elsie shrugged.

'It's nowt. One of the lads in the school yard were having a go at me, that's all.'

Ada's lips tightened. 'Were he now? We'll have a word with the teacher about that.'

The sturdy little body stiffened. 'No you won't, Mam. I can stand up for meself.'

Ada smiled to herself. Whatever else her girls might go short of, they certainly didn't lack for spirit. They were made of the right stuff, all of them.

THREE

May could sense the shiver of excitement trembling in the air of the workroom even before Mr Rose breezed in, his remaining grey hair plastered across the top of his head in Macassar-oiled stripes. Behind him stood a tall young man. The treadles whirred to a stop as Mr Rose held up a hand, the eyes of every girl fixed, for once, not on him, but on his handsome son.

May eyed him speculatively as he stood to attention at his father's elbow. In his early twenties, he was taller than Mr Rose by a good six inches, with a head of thickly curling black hair, but his nose was just as prominent and his eyes just as dark as his father's, and as his gaze came to rest on her she felt a flutter down her spine. He had his father's way of looking right through you to your very backbone.

Embarrassed, she looked away quickly and missed Mr Rose's first words. He was smiling broadly, gesturing with his hands the way he always did.

'So whatever Mr Aaron tells you, do it same as if it were me,' he concluded, and turned to go.

'Any time,' muttered Mabel at the next bench as the two men vanished through the door. Miss Openshaw flashed her an angry glance.

'Get on with your work, girl,' she snapped. 'You've better things to do with your time than fill that feather-brained head of yours with silly notions. Mrs Haigh wants them cushions delivered by teatime so you'd best get cracking.'

By dinner-break the girls were exploding with eager anticipation. They piled out of the workroom to sit in the sun on the low stone wall at the back of the building, then opened their snap tins to start munching thick sandwiches. May sat a little distance away, nibbling Mother's tasty meat pasty alone, pretending not to listen to their chatter.

'I wonder if he'll come in the workshop much – I do hope so,' Mabel murmured dreamily. 'If he's holding the steps I'll gladly climb to the top shelf in the stock room for him any time.'

The other girls jeered and shrieked.

'Don't forget to put some scent behind your ears, then.'

'And put your Sunday drawers on, just in case!'

Their ribald laughter echoed round the cobbled yard.

'Tell you what,' said another girl as the merriment subsided, 'Mr Rose sometimes gets the number twenty-seven home, same tram as me. Now if I get chance to sit by Mr Aaron . . .'

May sat silent, licking congealed gravy from her fingertips. It was all very well to joke like this about Joe, the saucy-looking youth who drove the firm's delivery wagon, but Mr Aaron looked far too refined a gentleman for that sort of thing.

A whistle sounded. The girls sighed and snapped their tins shut, and as they filed back through the narrow passageway into the workroom, Miss Openshaw tapped May on the shoulder and drew her to one side.

'I noticed from the window – you never sit with the other girls,' she commented crisply.

'No,' May replied quietly. 'I like being on my own.'

The older woman cocked her head. 'You don't let them bully you, do you? You mustn't let them walk all over you. You have to stand up for yourself more.'

May met her gaze levelly. 'Nobody walks all over me, Miss Openshaw. I'm just different from them, that's all.'

The overseer nodded. 'Aye, you're different all right. That's why you've been picked to do Thornleigh Hall. Now go on back to your machine before you're missed.'

The overseer watched as May squeezed her way between the benches to her own place and sat down. The girl was decidedly

31

different from the rest of the mob, quieter and more meticulous, both in her work and in her person.

She took a pride in her work, that one, not like the others. One day perhaps, when Miss Openshaw was obliged to retire at last after a lifetime's dedication to the store, it could well be May Turnbull who took her place. Pity she had such a timid air about her. If only the girl could learn to be a bit more forceful . . .

Miss Openshaw cast a watchful eye along the rows of bent heads, seeing the specks of dust thrown up from the fabric and caught in the sun's rays. They needed a stern hand, this lot. On the whole they turned out good work, but they needed discipline. A mere glimpse of a man – other than Mr Rose, of course – and they went all daft. It wasn't going to help having Mr Aaron continually in and out of her workroom, setting their silly hearts in a flutter with his good looks and his captivating smile.

No, Mr Aaron had been a bit of a handful before his father sent him off to London. With luck he'd have quietened down now, learnt a bit of sense.

Anyway, Mr Rose had said he'd be sending him up to Thornleigh Hall to supervise the work so that would keep him out of her way for some weeks.

'Oh heck!'

Miss Openshaw's head jerked round. Mabel was scowling down at the broken needle dangling from her machine. With a sigh Miss Openshaw hurried over to her bench. If Mrs Haigh's cushions weren't delivered by teatime there'd be hell to pay.

The sun was still filtering through the branches of the trees when Aaron Rose came out of the store and stretched his shoulders. They were aching from crouching over the desk for so long. It would do him good to walk home along Halifax Road instead of catching the tram.

It had been a pleasant enough day despite all the paperwork, far less onerous than working in the London store, but then he had Father's proud indulgence to thank for that. He wouldn't be so easy on any other assistant manager.

He had good reason to be proud. Rose's was a good shop, well placed in a side-road just off Hawksmoor's high street, spacious and well stocked with a fine selection of high-class furniture. And Father's list of regular customers was quite impressive too. Not many provincial stores could boast the titled gentry among their clientele.

A good shop, yes – but it could be better still. One day Aaron would be in a position to bring his own ideas and London expertise into play. Father didn't want to hear of any newfangled notions, as he called them, but Aaron could wait. One day Rose's would be his, a chain of furniture stores spanning the whole of Yorkshire, maybe even beyond, selling elegant, sought-after goods to the high-born and wealthy.

Plans and ideas bubbled in his head, but he must be patient. Softly, softly, step by step. He would utilize the time to sow the seeds. No need for any drastic changes yet.

He'd keep Father's present store staff, a pretty decent bunch on the whole, capable and conscientious. And loyal too. Many of them would remember Aaron's early days in the shop, before he went off to London.

Only the girls stitching away in the back room were different. They hadn't the sophisticated air of the London girls but some of the younger ones were quite pretty, with bright, lively faces. And he'd noticed one in particular, the dark-haired, quiet girl with graceful movements sitting at the corner bench who held an air of keeping herself aloof. She looked interesting, that one, with her dignified grace, her slow, thoughtful gaze which suggested subtle depths within, waiting to be uncovered. She could be an interesting diversion to lighten the working hours. That girl had an enigmatic air about her, certainly someone worth watching.

Aaron turned into the laurel-bordered drive and strode up towards the house. Father was just as proud of Birkby Lodge as he was of the shop. It was a substantial house built of solid stone, impressively double-fronted and ornately decorated with wrought iron and shutters, a far cry from the two-up and two-down terrace cottage in Leeds where he had been born. He'd worked hard, done well for himself. One day soon Aaron too would own a house like this, complete with a wife and children.

When he married Adele Rabin. He knew it was the dearest wish of his mother's heart, and Father too would not be averse to the idea. He and old man Rabin had started out from the same humble roots in Bramley Yard in Leeds fifty years ago and both had made their pile, and the prospect of uniting his fortune with Rabin's would be sure to tempt Father.

Then, in time, Aaron would inherit Birkby Lodge and the shop, and then he would buy a far grander house, with a sweeping gravel drive and his own carriage drawing up at the flight of steps leading up to the double front door.

He smiled to himself as he crossed the oak-panelled hallway towards the parlour where Mother would be waiting, silver teapot at the ready. She'd be sure to bring up the subject of Adele again, probably in some roundabout way, but he wasn't going to appear too eager. Adele was a nice enough girl, pretty and intelligent, but she had a slightly dominating air about her, as if she were already practising to be the stern, matriarchal figure that Mrs Rabin had become. She would run Aaron's household with genteel efficiency, the velvet glove concealing the iron hand.

There was no hurry. At twenty-three he should still have time for a little freedom. Marriage would put a stop to all that, and marital restraint would come all too soon . . .

He heard a loud sneeze as he pushed open the parlour door. Mother was seated on the sofa, handkerchief in hand and a tray of tea before her. She glanced around with a welcoming smile but he could see her reddened eyes. She always got hay fever at this time of year, and she seemed to revel in it.

She dabbed at her nose with the lace-edged handkerchief. 'Ah, just in time for a nice fresh cup of tea,' she sniffled. 'Come sit with your mother.'

He stood by the sideboard. 'Actually, I quite fancy a drop of Scotch,' he murmured.

She gave a damp smile and poured tea through a silver strainer into a second cup. 'I keep telling you, whisky is not good for your stomach before dinner. Listen,' she said, putting down the teapot and patting the cushion beside her, 'you'll never guess who I ran into today while I was shopping in Leeds . . .'

Aaron took the cup from her outstretched hand, set it aside and poured a glass of whisky before he sat down. 'No – who?' he asked.

His mother threw up her hands. 'Mrs Rabin, no less, on her way to Silver's for a new costume. The poor woman, she is getting so fat these days.' Mrs Rose gave her son a sidelong glance. 'Not like her daughter,' she added. 'That girl has the figure of Venus, I swear, and such manners! I should be proud to have such a daughter.'

She chattered on, little finger jutted elegantly as she took quick sips from her cup. Aaron smiled into his glass. Mother's persistence was incurable. She'd got round to the subject in double-quick time tonight.

'So I invited them to come to dinner on the tenth,' she concluded, setting down her teacup and folding plump hands around the handkerchief. 'Eight in all, four couples with the Chadwicks as well, just a nice number.'

Aaron shook his head and said nothing. His mother cocked her greying head to one side and regarded him quizzically.

'Nice girl that Adele has grown into, don't you think? Nineteen years of age now and very pretty.'

He shrugged.

'The apple of her father's eye,' Mrs Rose went on wistfully, dabbing her nose once more.

A brick wall could read her gist. Added to her other attributes and the possible heiress to a fortune, it couldn't be long before some young man snapped her up. Aaron put down his glass and walked over to the window, conscious of his mother's rheumy eyes on his back.

'Anyway,' she said equably, 'I'll seat you next to Adele at dinner, so be sure to be charming to her.'

Aaron stood silent. He could hear the silken tone in her voice as she added, 'You might even suggest taking her out, to the museum perhaps. I'm sure she would welcome a pleasant outing.'

He smiled out at the lawns where dusk was creeping in from the shadows under the trees. Mother was becoming decidedly less subtle in her campaign these days.

'Yes,' he agreed quietly. 'It could be very pleasant.'

Ada held the corners of a large linen tablecloth between her teeth as she attempted to fold it. Suddenly the door burst open and Cassie flounced indignantly into the kitchen.

'Just look at me blouse,' she wailed, pointing to her chest, 'all covered with muck from that dratted train. Now I've nowt to wear in the morning.'

'What's wrong with your other blouse?' her mother enquired. 'It's washed and clean.'

'There's a button off, just where it shows.'

Ada nodded towards the cupboard in the corner. 'Well, you know where the needle and thread is. Get it sewn on.'

Cassie threw her coat aside and looked around. 'Where's our May?'

'Upstairs, seeing to your dad. Sew it on yourself.'

Cassie snatched the sewing box out of the cupboard and flung herself into a chair. 'I hate bloody work,' she growled. 'I wish I didn't have to work.'

Ada gave an ironic smile. 'We all do, lass, but it has to be done if you want money.'

'I get that rotten paste all over me hands and me clothes. I can smell the bloody stuff in my sleep.'

'That's enough,' Ada snapped. 'I'll have no swearing in this house.' She laid the tablecloth on the pile of ironed laundry and turned to her daughter, hands on hips. 'Any road, now I think on, why would you be coming home by the viaduct? You come from the other direction.'

Cassie's needle quivered and she looked up quickly. 'Ah – private business,' she murmured.

Ada eyed her severely. 'What's so private you can't tell me?' she demanded. 'What you been up to?'

Cassie bit through the thread and bent her fair head, busying herself putting the needle back into the pincushion. 'Ah well, sometimes a body can be too nosey for their own good,' she murmured. 'Best leave well alone.'

Ada flowered. 'How do you mean?' she snapped. 'Now just you look here, my girl—'

Cassie looked up with a sly smile. 'I hadn't meant to say owt but – hasn't somebody got a birthday coming up?'

Ada's mouth dropped open. 'You mean me? Oh, love, I'm sorry, I wouldn't for the world—'

'Never mind,' said Cassie with an airy wave of the hand. 'No harm done, is there? You still know nowt.'

Harold Jordan climbed the ladder, panting a little as he emerged into the sweet-smelling air of the hay-loft. He could still hear the horses below him snuffling in the trough as he counted the remaining bales of hay and then sighed. He'd very soon need to order more feed, and in this fine weather not enough people were dying. Come the harsh winter, picking off the old folk like flies, business would surely pick up again.

God knew, it needed to improve if he was to get the last of his debts paid off. But every penny seemed to be spoken for almost as soon as it came in, what with more elm to buy, more brass fittings and satin linings, not to mention Arthur's wages and the casual men. Time was when he employed half a dozen men full-time, a coachman and four pall-bearers as well as a cabinetmaker. Now there was only Arthur.

He glanced down through the trapdoor. Beyond the glossy black of the horses' backs he could just glimpse the edge of the big black hearse, its paintwork gleaming in the half-light. It was beautiful, the object of his fevered desire for many years, and it was the cause of all his misery.

If it hadn't been for that hearse he'd still be a prosperous man, still living in Marchmont Avenue, a respected pillar of Hawksmoor society. He wouldn't have had to drag Fanny from the comfortable home she loved to the dismal seediness of Cedar Street, to live among people she couldn't begin to understand.

It wasn't that she considered them beneath her, just that she'd never had cause to mix with the curt, roughly-spoken sort. No, it was more than that. Harold hung his head. The truth was that she feared they might find out what had happened, and she just couldn't bear the shame. It was wisest, perhaps, if she kept her distance.

He gazed out of the tiny loft window. From here he could see the rows of cobbled back yards spreading into the grey distance, the squat privies backing onto the dingy alley. Whatever speculation went on over those back-yard walls, he consoled himself, thanks to Fanny's reticence, the worst the neighbours would think was that Mrs Jordan was a snob.

From out in the night came the sound of raucous singing. Harold recognized the powerful, if tuneless, voice of Nagle, the Irishman who lived at the far end of Cedar Street, the one who staggered home from the Fleece every night singing and calling out cheerily to passers-by. Only the Lord knew how he managed to father his ever-increasing brood of children when he spent all his time in the pub. The singing died away as a loud slam indicated that he'd evidently found his own doorway at last.

Along the street a light glowed in an upstairs window. Harold stood on tiptoe to peer. That was the house where the family lived whose father had been crippled down the mine. He remembered well how the Misses Bottomley had poured out the tale with relish that time he'd called to arrange the interment of their aged mother. Simple deal coffin, no embellishments, no black plumes.

'You never saw owt like it,' the elder Miss Bottomley had told him. 'Carried home on a gate like he was a dead dog picked up out the gutter. Smothered with blood, he was – I were stood on the front step and I saw it all. His back were gaping wide open, and it's never healed up since, they tell me.'

'Never left his bed after that,' chimed in the younger Miss Bottomley, the long black hairs in her nose quivering in excitement. 'And that poor Mrs Turnbull nursing him with them three young lasses to bring up and all. Never a penny compensation neither, I heard tell.'

Harold stared out into the gathering gloom, watching the light in the Turnbulls' house. It could be in that very room that the poor man lay suffering. Harold sighed. Immersed in his own problems it was easy to forget that other folk as well had their crosses to bear.

He was about to turn away from the window when he saw the shadow cross the light and he paused. Someone was moving in the bedroom. He screwed up his eyes, fishing in his pocket for his spectacles. The shadow came into view again, and stopped. He put his spectacles on his nose, and almost stopped breathing. The shape of a woman stood silhouetted against the light. It wasn't Mrs Turnbull for the woman was high-breasted and slender, and though he couldn't swear to it, it seemed as though she was wearing no clothes.

Harold stood transfixed. He couldn't recall how many years it had been since he last saw a naked female figure, but he could recall very well the sudden fire which leapt in him, deep in his stomach, because it was happening again now, and his spectacles were steaming up.

By the time he had whipped them off his nose, given them a quick rub with his pocket handkerchief and replaced them, she was gone. As he watched, willing her to return, the dull glow of the lamp was suddenly extinguished, but the glow in the pit of his stomach remained.

The outline of the Turnbulls' house melted into the surrounding darkness. With a sigh Harold turned away and, easing his girth through the narrow trapdoor, he lowered himself carefully down the ladder. Dolly looked round at him with big, liquid eyes and whinnied. He laid a hand on her smooth flank as he passed by and, murmuring words of comfort, caressed its warmth, welcoming the trusting response to his touch.

Retracing his steps across the unlit yard towards the house he could see that lights no longer glowed downstairs. Fanny would be in bed asleep, and as always her ice-cold bottom would be turned towards his side of the bed.

Elsie lay curled up, fast asleep and her thumb in her mouth, in the big bed in the back room. Beside her Cassie lay stretched, her eyes screwed tightly shut as she tried to recall every delicious detail of the kiss.

It was her first proper kiss. For over fifteen years she'd been brushing her lips against her mother and sisters' cheeks to say goodnight, but never once had she dreamed that kissing a boy could be quite like this. It had been thrilling, sending shudders of delight surging through her entire body, and she wanted desperately to relive every exciting second of it.

Mother would be furious if she knew. She'd have a fit if she knew it was Donald Fairchild. For some strange reason she had it in for the Fairchilds, Eunice too. Eunice was nice, had always been her best friend, but her brother was out of this world.

He was gorgeous, far more handsome than any of the lads at the factory, with his tall, spare frame, his wavy brown hair and teasing blue eyes. And he had a wicked laugh which made her tremble as they stood together in the shadow of the viaduct.

'Come in under the arch with me,' he'd urged her, and when she'd hesitated had said, 'Come on, I dare you.'

And then he'd dared her to let him kiss her. It was magic, those arms tight about her, his lean body pressed against hers, his mouth hard against her lips. Cassie shivered at the memory.

And he wanted her to meet him there again. Somehow she'd have to keep Mother in the dark. She'd managed it tonight all right, but now it meant she'd have to find a way to buy her a decent birthday present. Cassie groaned. How the devil was she to find the money?

Might Donald be willing to lend her a shilling? What was another kiss worth to him? She had a sudden recollection of the bawdy rhyme the lads in the schoolyard used to chant, round the back of the rubbish bins.

> *'Penny a peep, tuppence a look,*
> *Threepence a feel and fourpence a—'*

With a giggle Cassie rolled over and buried her face in the pillow. Elsie groaned and stirred in her sleep but Cassie took no notice. Tonight had been the most exciting night of her life, and this was only the beginning.

FOUR

Early on Friday morning Miss Openshaw adjusted her week-day hat, pinned it firmly to her head, took a final look at herself in the mirror then went out into the street, locking the front door carefully behind her.

As she walked down to the tram stop she pulled on her gloves, the kid ones she'd found in Mother's drawer after she died. Mother had never worn them, saying she was waiting for a really special occasion, and it never came. It was Miss Openshaw's one concession to luxury, wearing them to work.

Today was going to be even busier than usual, what with everything having to be packed and sent up to Thornleigh Hall ready for Monday. Mr Rose – Mr Henry, that was – had been like a cat on hot bricks, fussing in and out all week over the order. What a relief it was having a girl like May Turnbull she could rely on.

She stood primly at the tram stop, trying not to notice the youth who'd recently joined the usual knot of daily travellers. Judging by the smell of fish around him he must be either working at the poulterer's or be newly apprenticed at the glue factory at Longroyd Bridge. As the tram came in sight she moved forward to the pavement edge and Mr Harris nodded and touched his hat the way he always did, and as always Miss Openshaw granted him the briefest of smiles.

The tram rumbled on its way downhill. For over twenty-five years she'd done this journey down from Newsome into town, ever since the days of horse-drawn buses when Mr Rose was still a slim young man and Rose's was only a quarter of its present size, a small shop down by the Beast Market. It was going to be a strange world when Mr Henry finally pensioned her off and there was no longer any need to come out in all weathers to catch the tram. She tried to convince herself that she would enjoy the freedom, but she knew in her heart that it was going to be lonely in that little house now there was no-one left but herself. A house full of memories, all Mother's embroidered tablecloths and antimacassars and her aged cat, Oscar, but even he was too creaky these days to come and meet her at the gate.

In town she alighted from the tram and walked along the high street to the store. To her surprise Mr Aaron was already inside, dangling a bunch of keys in his hand.

'Morning, Miss Openshaw,' he said breezily, and turned to head for the office. 'When that girl arrives who's going up to the Hall,' he added over his shoulder, 'send her in to me, will you?'

Miss Openshaw sighed as she unlocked the workroom door. She hoped Mr Aaron wasn't going to mess May Turnbull about. Life was hectic enough without complications like that.

When the parish church clock struck eight the girls started to trickle in. May was among the first. Miss Openshaw beckoned her over.

'Mr Aaron wants to see you in the office about Monday. I've arranged for your machine to be sent over on Sunday so it's up to you then. You just mind you do your best to please – they might well change their minds from time to time but you just remember that nothing's too much trouble. Do whatever you're ordered. Now go and see Mr Aaron.'

She watched the girl leave the room. She wasn't the sort to let attention go to her head, Miss Openshaw reassured herself. And she wasn't all that pretty either. She'd be all right alone with him up at the Hall. Now if it was that feather-brained Mabel it would be different.

Mr Aaron sat behind the big desk, smiling as he fingered his shirt cuffs. May stared at him in disbelief.

'A new skirt and blouse?' she echoed. 'Both at once?'

He rose and came round the desk towards her, seating himself on the corner and folding his arms. 'It's important that you look smart if you're to represent Rose's,' he said quietly, 'but I appreciate it could be difficult for you to buy these items at such short notice—'

'It's impossible!' said May. 'So much money!'

'—so that is why I've decided that Rose's should bear the cost, since it's to our benefit. I want you to take this.'

He unfolded his arms and held out a slim-fingered hand. In his palm gleamed two golden sovereigns. May stared at them, and then looked up at him.

'You – want to pay for a new outfit – for me?'

'Why not? I set great store by appearances, and I'm sure Sir Joseph does too.'

Seeing she made no move to take the money, he took her hand and pressed the coins into her palm, bunching her fingers together. The black eyes bored into hers as he went on, his hand still tight around her fingers.

'You want to look your best, don't you? Don't misunderstand me, it's not that you don't look splendid the way you are, but you want to be a real credit to the firm, don't you?'

The pressure of his hand on hers sent a tingle running through her. 'Oh yes,' she breathed. 'Indeed I do.'

'Then take an hour off this afternoon – tell Miss Openshaw I said so – and go and buy yourself that blouse and skirt. Good stuff, mind you, none of your cheap market stuff. Tell you what, go to Harris's, tell them I sent you and they'll give you a discount. I'll come to the Hall myself and have a look at you on Monday.'

He stood back, letting her hand fall. 'I'll be sure and bring you the change,' May murmured.

He waved a hand. 'There's no need for that. Get yourself some stockings. Just make sure you're well turned out.'

She stared down at the gleaming sovereigns, more than a month's wages, and felt dizzy.

'I'm grateful to you,' she murmured. 'I don't know what to say.'

'Say nothing. Just go and do as I tell you.'

She nodded and backed towards the door. 'I'll show you what I've got tomorrow,' she said, 'then you can be sure you like them.'

He shook his head. 'Not tomorrow, I won't be here. It's the Sabbath. Show me on Monday. Now be off with you and tell Miss Openshaw what we've arranged.'

May frowned as she told the overseer. 'He must have got his days mixed up though. It's Saturday tomorrow. Sunday's the Sabbath.'

'Not for Jews, it isn't,' Miss Openshaw said with a shake of her head. 'Haven't you noticed they never come in on a Saturday? It's their holy day, same as our Sunday. Jews have their own laws, different from ours. Now you'd best get cracking if you're off out this afternoon.'

Ada carried the bucket from the bedroom down the yard to the privy. It was chilly tonight and the cobbles were slippery underfoot after the rain, but the night air smelled fresh and sweet, free of the pungent smell of soap and washing soda.

That reminded her – she must get some more Sunlight grated. It should be well dried out now in the cupboard next to the range and she needed it ready for morning if she was to make an early start and leave time to do a bit of baking. The last of the bread in the crock was so stale it was beginning to get green bits round the edges. Still, scraped off, it would do to make toast for breakfast.

She lifted the seat and emptied the bucket into the lavatory, then paused. She might as well pay a visit herself now she was down here.

The wooden seat felt damp to her backside but it was a relief to sit for a while, easing the weight off her aching feet and the throbbing in her shoulders from hours of winding the mangle.

It was quiet out here, a moment of peace with only the plaintive sound of a cat mewing. Over the serrated top of the privy door she could see the stars glittering in the sky. Like those nights long ago when Jim used to take her courting in Grimscar Wood, when the air smelled sweet with the scent of bluebells and the sky looked like velvet and young hearts thought that bliss like this would never end . . .

Stop it, you can't go back. You wouldn't change anything if you could. You'd still wed him, bear his children and care for him, no matter what. And hang it all, things were picking up – the older girls were working now and being a great help.

Life goes on. Go on, wipe your backside before the night-soil men come clattering down the alley to empty out. Ada reached for the newspaper Elsie had cut neatly into squares. It felt soggy from being up against the damp stone wall. Better use two sheets tonight, else your fingers would go straight through, then pick up your bucket and get back indoors and start grating that soap.

Harold Jordan had made a point of grooming the horses himself tonight instead of leaving it to Arthur.

'Special do, Councillor Mayhew being such an eminent man in Hawksmoor,' he explained to the lad. 'Not that I don't trust you – I just want to make sure, that's all.'

Fanny had made no bones about him staying down in the stable so late. She was delighted that Councillor Mayhew's widow had seen fit to come to Jordan's after all.

'You just take your time, love,' she'd urged him. 'You do what you think necessary. I've a new book from the lending library to read anyway.'

He wondered if she realized how nervous he was about tomorrow. To her it meant that he'd got a decent burial to do, a chance to earn good money for a change. The fact that he would have to face once more all those men who'd shunned him for so long seemed to be lost on her.

He'd have to brazen it out. Luckily his role at the ceremony called for an impassive face which might be taken for stoic calm. But inside he'd be trembling. It wasn't every day a convicted man was called upon to confront his accusers and jury once again.

But Mayhew's funeral wasn't the only reason Harold came down to the stable tonight.

His legs were getting stiff now, reaching up on tiptoe for so long to look out of the small, high window of the hay-loft. It was getting late and still no light had come on in that bedroom down the street. Maybe she wasn't at home yet, or maybe she'd gone to bed early. Or undressed in the dark the way Fanny insisted on doing.

Pain shot through his left calf. Dammit, he was getting cramp. Harold bent to rub it vigorously for a few moments, then as he straightened he caught sight of the glow.

She was there! Cramp forgotten, he inched himself up as high as he could, wishing he'd pulled a bale of hay under the window. Yes, it was the same room, the soft glow from the lamp casting a pale sheen on the wet roof of the outhouse. He could feel the eagerness balling in his stomach as he waited for a shadow to cross the light.

There it was! And then his spirits sank. For only the briefest of moments he saw a girl's slender shape cross the square of light, graceful and willowy, as though she was wearing a nightdress, but then she was gone. Minutes passed and Harold clung eagerly to the window-sill, willing her to reappear.

But then suddenly the light went out. The gleaming roof of the outhouse vanished again into the misty night. There was nothing at all now to be seen. She wasn't going to reappear tonight.

Bitterly disappointed, Harold limped over to a straw bale and sat down to rub away the last of the cramp.

Ada stood looking down at the gaunt-faced, shrivelled man lying asleep in the big double bed. She still found it hard to believe that this was the same man she had married twenty years ago. It seemed only yesterday that she stood before the altar in St Thomas's, looking up at her handsome, broad-shouldered bridegroom beside her and saying, 'I, Ada Mary Senior, take thee, James Turnbull, to be my lawful wedded husband . . .'

He didn't move or open his eyes as she straightened the sheets and turned back the cover on her side. The bowl of milk sops lay still only half-eaten on the chest of drawers. He couldn't be feeling well, but he'd never grumble.

She could have fed the sops to that hungry cat out there in the night, she thought as she drew the thick curtains and bent to blow out the lamp and then started to undress in the dark the way she always did. As she unlaced her stays she heard Jim's breathing, quick and erratic.

'You all right, love?' she whispered.

He groaned. She climbed cautiously into bed, inching herself down beside him so the movement would not hurt his back. He lay as always face-down, his head turned away towards the door, so his words came to her muffled and indistinct in the darkness.

'It's no use, lass. I'm neither use nor ornament to any of you.'

'What you on about?' she said sharply. She couldn't bear to hear him talk like this.

'What I said,' he murmured. 'I'm no use to anybody the way I am. I only disgust you. You'd all be far better off if I were dead.'

Ada couldn't help the curtness in her tone. 'Don't talk so daft. Don't you think I've enough to worry about without you moithering?'

'And I'd be better off and all,' he muttered. 'I spend my life just staring at the pillow and the window, knowing things'll never change. I'd be out of this stink, out of pain – you'd be doing me a favour.'

Ada sat up sharply. 'Me? You expect me to—'

'Like I said, lass,' he cut in quietly, 'you'd be doing me a favour. Cut all this short, else it could drag on for years more. You wouldn't want that for me, would you?'

Ada sat open-mouthed in the dark. 'Me – help you on your way? Oh Jim, I couldn't!'

He turned his head towards her and she could feel his breath on her arm. 'Nobody need know. A drop more laudanum than usual—'

'No! It's wicked even to think it! Kill my own husband? What do you take me for?'

There was pain in his quiet words and it tore at her heart to hear him. 'It'd be easy – no-one would ever guess. Please, lass, if it gets too bad—'

She lay back on the pillow. 'If it ever comes to that, happen I'd do summat,' she said uncertainly. She wanted desperately to give him the assurance he needed, but this . . .

'You'd be rid of a burden,' he whispered. 'You and the girls.'

'You're no burden!' Ada bit her lip. Self-doubt was beginning to creep in. Could she possibly be so selfish? She yearned to be free of the never-ending round of drudgery and worry over money, but it had never entered her head to want to be free of a crippled husband.

She touched a finger to his shoulder, felt its work-roughened tip catch on the fibres of his nightshirt, and beneath the fabric she could feel the flaccid flesh of an old man. Time was when she used to bathe that body in the old tin bath in front of the fire every night when he came home from the pit, caked with grime, and she'd savoured the texture of his muscle-hard back under her touch . . .

'I'm sorry, love,' she murmured. 'I'm doing the best I can, but you've got me fair flummoxed now. I don't know what to think.'

She felt his lips brush the back of her hand. 'I know, lass, I know. I'll not vex you again with daft notions. Get some sleep now.'

For a long time Ada lay awake, probing the velvet darkness of the room for an answer, but none came.

FIVE

Harold stood alone in the corner of Mrs Mayhew's oak-panelled parlour, his top hat tucked under one arm and his black gloves clasped between his hands. It wasn't often he was invited back to the deceased's home, but Mrs Mayhew had insisted.

There'd been the usual kind of funeral tea, ham or egg and cress sandwiches followed by Madeira or ginger cake, but he'd eaten nothing. He was far too apprehensive about having to face the late Councillor's colleagues, make small talk with them as if nothing untoward had ever taken place. He'd been safe enough at the ceremony itself, occupied as he was with his official duties as mute pall-bearer and ushering mourners to their pews.

But he might have guessed they'd cold-shoulder him. They hadn't made it evident, but somehow they had all contrived to nibble their tea, give their condolences to the widow and bid farewell without apparently noticing his presence.

It still baffled him why he was here, attending to the last rites of his chief accuser. Clearly Mrs Mayhew could know nothing or she'd never have asked him to officiate. She was in the vestibule now, showing the last mourners out. He could hear their voices as they bade farewell and promised to call again soon, the sound of the front door closing, and then Mrs Mayhew's quick, light step as she came back into the parlour.

She sank into one of the armchairs with a sigh. Harold stood silent, waiting dutifully for her to speak. She looked small and fragile in her widow's black, the jet beads at her throat contrasting starkly with the pallor of her cheeks.

50

After a moment she seemed to remember he was there and looked up with a faint smile. 'It was a splendid funeral, Mr Jordan. You gave my husband a wonderful send-off.'

Harold inclined his head. 'Thank you, ma'am. We aim to make life as smooth as possible at what we know is a very difficult time.'

She gave a slight nod. 'You certainly did that. You did a grand job, and I'm grateful to you.'

'The whole Committee turned out to see him off,' murmured Harold. 'Every last one of them.'

She was gazing into the distance, twisting the gold ring on her left hand. Harold felt she'd forsaken him now; it was time for him to go and let her grieve alone.

'I'll bid you good day then, Mrs Mayhew.'

He turned to leave. As his hand touched the doorknob he heard her voice behind him, soft and musical as a distant bell.

'You can send the bill just as soon as you like, Mr Jordan.'

He gave a slight cough. 'There's no hurry, ma'am. All in good time.'

'He was a hypocrite,' she said dreamily, still staring into the distance. 'They're all hypocrites, the lot of them.'

Harold stared, unable to believe his ears.

'Oh yes,' she went on, 'they were all in it together, tipping each other off about shady deals, greasing each other's palms.'

She turned to look up at him with a smile. 'I tell you this, Mr Jordan. If he wasn't dead already it would have killed him to know you did his funeral today.'

Cassie stared at the packages in growing disbelief as her sister unwrapped them.

'A new blouse, a new skirt, and a pair of stockings as well?' she gasped. 'And you had all them things new at Whitsun – it's not fair. I had to make do with your cast-offs.'

Ada ignored her. 'They're lovely,' she said to May. 'Real good quality. Eeh, love, you're going to look a fair treat.'

May unfolded the last sheet of tissue paper with a smile. 'And that's not all – with the change I got these.'

She held out a pair of gloves for her mother's inspection. Ada took hold of them reverently.

'Leather,' she breathed softly, caressing the palms. 'Real leather. By heck, they must think a lot about you at that shop.'

'Yes,' agreed May. 'And so they should.'

Cassie gave her a sour look. 'And you're to live in at the Hall as well? My, my, we are the lady, aren't we?'

'That's enough,' snapped Ada. 'We can do without your sarky remarks, miss. Now if you was to take a leaf out of our May's book then maybe you'd get somewhere.'

'Instead of working at sticky Whitfield's, you mean?' retorted Cassie. 'Anywhere's better than mouldy old Whitfield's.'

Ada gave her a severe look. 'Less of your lip, lady. You're lucky to have a position at all with your cheeky tongue. Now come on, shift yourself. Get out of me road so I can get the table laid for supper. We'll have all on tomorrow getting our May packed and ready to go.'

Early on Monday morning Ada stood on the doorstep watching her eldest daughter until she rounded the corner into Fountain Street. For the next few weeks she'd see no more of her.

'I'll have Sunday off,' May had said. 'I'll come home and tell you all about it then.'

'That you won't,' Ada had retorted. 'I want to see neither hide nor hair of you till this lot's over. No point wasting money on train fares when you can tell me all about it for the price of a stamp.'

Ada turned back into the house. No time for fretting, she told herself as she set about sorting the mountain of soiled linen lying on the scullery floor. Poke up the fire under the brick sett pot, get busy mixing the starch and dolly blue.

Steam swirled about her head as she lifted off the lid and began lowering in the first of the laundry. Be glad for the lass, she told herself. It was a wonderful opportunity for her, a chance to see how rich folk like Sir Joseph lived. And who knew – there could be useful contacts to be made, maybe a good recommendation to other rich folk. This could be the start of something big for May.

Ada glanced round at the clock, then hurried to the foot of the stairs.

'Cassie!' she called. 'Get a move on else you're going to be late for work.'

From upstairs came a muffled reply.

'You what?' demanded Ada.

Elsie's tousled head appeared over the banister rail. 'She says she doesn't want to go to bloody work,' she said primly. 'She said that, not me.'

'You mind your own business – go and see if your dad's ready for a cup of tea. And Cassie—'

'What?' The voice was sleepy and irritable.

'You get your backside down here this minute, lady, if you don't want me to take the posser to you.'

Clicking her tongue and shaking her head Ada went back to pour into the sett pot the soap jelly she'd made by boiling up the left-over bits. Just about now May would be climbing aboard the paddy-train along with all the miners on their way to the pit, like that big Irishman Nagle from up the street. Just like Jim used to in the old days . . .

She was going to miss May, no doubt about it. The house wasn't going to feel the same without her placid presence. She might be the quietest of the three, but she was solid and dependable. You could rely on May. Never a moment's bother since the day she was born, she'd never bring trouble home like Cassie.

'*I want to see neither hide nor hair of you till this lot's over.*'

As she heard the train rumble slowly over the viaduct Ada was already beginning to regret the hasty words.

May tramped along the leafy lane towards Thornleigh Hall, her wicker box under her arm and an eager lightness in her

53

step. She hadn't minded at all the speculative stares of the miners on the crowded train. She felt so stylish in her new outfit, with her Sunday hat pinned with Mother's best beaded hat-pin, that she could hold her head as proudly high as any lady.

As she reached the wide gates with *Thornleigh Hall* carved into the stone pillars, she could feel the quiver of excitement give way to apprehension. There'd be a Mrs Gabbitas waiting for her, she'd been told, Sir Joseph's long-serving housekeeper whose word would be law. May walked up the long drive, feeling her stomach starting to tie itself in knots. Would she be able to live up to Mr Rose's and the housekeeper's expectations?

She rounded a clump of elm trees and the Hall suddenly came into sight, taking her breath away. It was enormous, stretching as wide as the castles in her favourite fairy-tale book, with colonnades and turrets, overlooking vast lawns and rippling fountains which glittered in the morning sun. It was beautiful. It was paradise.

She shied away from the porticoed front door, making round the back for the servants' entrance as she'd been told. There seemed to be several doors, but from one she could hear the sound of voices, and she knocked timidly.

The door was opened by a pretty, buxom girl. She smiled, and May could see one of her front teeth was missing.

'You the seamstress?' she lisped. 'Mrs Gabbitas is expecting you – come in.'

May followed her inside, through a vast, stone-floored kitchen. 'I'm Cora,' the girl said over her shoulder as she led the way. 'There's just Dolly and me here till the family move in. And Mrs G, of course.'

'Mrs G? The housekeeper, you mean?'

'Mrs God, we call her. You'd think she was, the way she carries on, so don't say you wasn't warned. This is her room now.'

Cora led the way in and announced May. Behind a large table sat a middle-aged woman with neatly coiled grey hair, slim hands fondling a pen as they rested on a pile of papers. She spoke crisply to the maid.

'Thank you, Cora. You may go.'

The housekeeper put down her pen and arched her hands elegantly under her chin. May stood silent, box under her arm, as the older woman's grey eyes scrutinized her thoughtfully. Cora was right, thought May – she did have an imperious manner about her. At last the housekeeper nodded.

'You'll do,' she said curtly. 'Come, I'll show you the sewing room.'

It was a small room on the top floor, not so high-ceilinged as the housekeeper's room but flooded with sunlight and piled high with all the fabrics and cottons Mr Henry had promised. By a large table under the window her own treadle machine already stood waiting.

Mrs Gabbitas wiped a critical finger along the window-ledge, inspected the tip, then turned to May.

'This is where you will work, and you will sleep in a room near by which I will show you later. There will be no need for you to go downstairs while the men are still at work.'

'Very well. Shall I start with the window-seat covers for the upper rooms then?'

The housekeeper inclined her head. 'And the curtains. I've had them hanging ever since Mr Rose delivered them so they should have dropped sufficiently by now. They are to be hemmed by hand, of course.'

'Of course.'

'And you will take lunch with me – a light lunch, since Cook still hasn't moved in. The village girls will see to the workmen and eat later.'

May juggled with the heavy box under her arm. 'Thank you. You're very kind.'

She was aware of the woman's appraising look before she turned to go. 'Yes, I think you'll do,' Mrs Gabbitas said quietly. 'Come, I'll show you to your bedroom now.'

*   *   *

The room was a delight. Clearly a maid's room, small and tucked under the roof, it was nevertheless sheer luxury after Cedar Street. May lay on the bed, savouring its downy softness and staring up at the thirteen different surfaces of the ceiling between the criss-cross of beams and joists.

Twisting the folds of the sheets between her fingers, she lay revelling in the rich texture of the linen and breathing in the sweet smell of the pot-pourri on the dressing chest. No, home was never like this, with the ever-pervasive smell of wet washing and the stink of Dad fouling the air.

May sat upright, feeling a sudden spurt of guilt. She shouldn't think like that. After all, it wasn't Dad's fault. She rose and turned to empty out the contents of her box onto the flower-sprigged counterpane.

The morning passed quickly enough, and after the lunch Cora brought in trays for May and Mrs Gabbitas in the house-keeper's room, May returned to her sewing. The heavy brocade curtains and bed hangings in the master bedroom weren't easy to hem, with the thick, heavy texture resisting her needle, but she looked forward to making the matching covers for the window-seats.

She sewed in silence, savouring the peaceful stillness of the stately old hall. She could hear no sound of servants or workmen. For all she knew she could be completely alone. It was so different from the noise and squalor of Cedar Street, so unlike it that she could be in another world.

It was a new experience, having space and peace to think her own thoughts uninterrupted, with no harassed mother fussing around, no petulant demands from Cassie, no pleading for treats from Elsie. No need to go upstairs and minister to Dad's needs.

The sun through the high windows fell warm on her back, fostering pleasant dreams of what-might-have-been. But for an accident of fate she could have been born into a family like Sir Joseph's, accepting all this luxury as her birthright. May stretched her neck and inclined her head graciously towards the imaginary maid standing at the door. Given the chance she could behave with the dignified decorum of any lady in the land.

She heard a knock as the door opened. May turned her head with genteel grace. Mrs Gabbitas was ushering in two men, and with a sudden return to reality May recognized Mr Henry and Mr Aaron.

The housekeeper excused herself and left. Mr Henry came up close to where May sat, rubbing his hands together.

'Just called to see how things are getting on,' he murmured, glancing round at the curtains and bed hangings. 'Anything else you need?'

'I don't think so, sir,' May replied.

She was aware of Mr Aaron smiling at her over the top of his father's head, and she looked away quickly, feeling the colour leap to her cheeks. It was a conspiratorial sort of smile, almost as though he had read her mind and glimpsed her flights of fantasy. As Mr Henry fussed about the room examining each hem, she bent her head to her work, studiously declining to meet Mr Aaron's disturbing gaze.

It seemed an age before Mr Henry decided it was time to leave. He nodded goodbye and hurried from the room, but Mr Aaron lingered by the door. May could feel his eyes burning into her back.

'You did well, May,' she heard him murmur. 'In your choice of clothes. You look great.'

'Thank you, sir,' she said, without looking up. 'I should have remembered to thank Mr Henry for his generosity.'

She heard his soft chuckle. 'Why thank him?' he murmured, and his voice was coming closer. 'It was my idea, not his. He knows nothing about it. It's our secret, May, yours and mine.'

He was standing close behind her now, and his nearness flustered her. She let the treadle slow to a halt but didn't look up.

'You're very gratifying, May,' he murmured. 'You do your best to please, don't you?'

There was a soft touch on her shoulder. Startled, she caught

57

her breath, but by the time she looked round, the door was already closing behind him.

Cassie was in a filthy mood as she stamped along Cedar Street towards home. Donald Fairchild was a total waste of time. He'd just said he wouldn't give her sixpence – not unless it was in return for 'the works', as he crudely put it. He could go choke himself on those bloody humbugs he kept offering her.

Mam wasn't home when she stomped in. She wouldn't be far away – she never left Dad on his own for very long. Elsie wasn't around either – she must be playing out with the other kids, probably on the cutting where Mam forbade her ever to go. All the kids loved the excitement of the cutting, laying a halfpenny on the line and dodging out of the way before the express came steaming through. Cassie could remember herself, not so long ago, claiming her halfpenny once it had been flattened to the size of a penny. The trouble was, the shopkeeper at the corner had soon grown wise to the game.

She drew the kettle on the fire and flung herself down in the rocking-chair, staring gloomily into space. Money. That had always been the problem in this house. Never enough of it. Mam worked her fingers to the bone, May and she both surrendered most of what they earned, and still Mam said there wasn't enough to pay the bills and leave anything over for treats. If it wasn't for Mam getting a bit from the Provident – and even then she had to pay the tally man every week. That's why she had all them tins on the mantelshelf, to sort out the coins and put them in, week by week.

Cassie's gaze wandered up to the mantelpiece. There they were, all ranged neatly in a row, one for the rent, one for coal, one for the tally man . . .

She sat upright. Two days to go to Mam's birthday. She never tipped out the coins to count them until it was time to pay out. And Donald Fairchild was obviously not going to come across, not now she'd slapped him hard across the face . . .

SIX

'Elsie, out,' said Ada sternly.

The child looked up in alarm. 'What have I done?'

'Nowt,' replied her mother. 'I want a word with our Cass, that's all. On us own. Go round and see if Mrs Boothroyd wants any messages done.'

Elsie's eyes gleamed with curiosity as she made for the door. 'Has she been talking to the lads again?' she asked.

'No, I haven't then,' snapped Cassie. 'Bugger off.'

Elsie sidled out slowly. Ada waited for the door to close. 'Shut it,' she called out. 'Properly.'

The door closed, and then the front door banged. Ada waited for a small head to pass by the window, and then turned to her older daughter.

'There's a shilling gone from the rent tin,' she said succinctly. 'What's happened to it?'

Cassie's blue eyes widened in aggrieved innocence. 'How should I know? Have you asked Elsie?'

Her mother pointed to the mantelshelf. 'You know damn well she can't reach that high unless she put the stool on top of the chair, so don't come the innocent with me. I know exactly what was in that tin, and now it's a shilling short. What I want to know from you is, where is it?'

Cassie's wide-eyed righteousness gave way to a pout. 'Why do you always think the worst of me? You never talk to our May like that. It's always my fault if there's summat wrong.'

'Because it's always you who's at the back of it, that's why. Come on, I'm waiting.'

Cassie's face crumpled into tears. 'You always pick on me, never our May. It's not fair. She's your favourite.'

Ada glowered. 'And what's that supposed to mean?'

'Well,' said Cassie sulkily, 'she's the one always get new clothes and everything. Never me.'

Ada drew herself upright, hands on hips. 'Is that a fact? Well, I'll tell you this for nowt, lady. May deserves everything she gets. She works hard, she hands over every penny without complaint – not like you. You're the bane of my life with all your moithering and whining. I know for a fact it was you took that money, and I'll have it back – now.'

She held out a hand in demand. Tears trickled down Cassie's cheeks. 'I can't,' she sobbed. 'I haven't got it.'

'Why? What have you done with it?'

'Spent it,' the tiny, miserable voice replied, 'on your birthday present. I've only twopence of me own left.'

The demanding hand fell away. 'On my—? Oh Cassie, you might have known doing that would only end in tears. Whatever possessed you?'

Cassie's voice was barely audible behind the handkerchief. 'I had to – or else sell Grandma's brooch and you wouldn't want me to do that. She give it me just before she died.'

Ada felt robbed of argument. Cassie was a cunning little devil all right. How was it she always managed to turn the tables?

Clearing her throat she turned away to pull out cups and saucers from the cupboard.

'Well, I'll have no more of it, do you hear?' she muttered. 'No more pinching without asking, else I'll never know where I am. And you can put back twopence a week till you've paid off, you hear?'

Cassie gave a watery smile. 'Yes, Mam. Sorry.'

Dammit, thought Ada, she wasn't going to relent just because the girl knew how to turn it on like a tap. To hell with the little-girl-lost act. 'Starting now,' she said firmly, stretching out her hand once more. 'I'll have that twopence in your purse.'

May emerged from the sewing room, stretching her arms above her head to relieve the ache in her shoulders. It had been yet another tiring day, but she felt an enormous sense of satisfaction that it was all coming together so beautifully. Sir Joseph's lady would have a home to be proud of. Mr Henry himself had said so only yesterday. It was disappointing that this time the handsome Mr Aaron hadn't come with him . . . Without thinking she reached to touch her shoulder.

A warm September sun reached in through the tall windows. It was a pity her work was nearly done. She'd enjoyed handling those wonderful fabrics and she'd grown used to the comfort of the hall, to eating unusual and exciting meals, sometimes with Mrs Gabbitas but more often than not alone. The housekeeper's cool poise was giving way to barely suppressed excitement now that the final preparations were almost complete.

'There's only the last bit of mosaic to be finished off now,' she told May, 'and on Sunday I shall go back to supervise packing up the last of the linen and kitchenware. You'll be all right here on your own, won't you?'

'Of course. Don't worry about me.'

Truth to tell, she enjoyed being alone in the place. She could roam about the beautiful rooms as she chose and admire the Italian mosaic-layers' handiwork, watching the expanse of tiny coloured tiles growing wider day by day. Alone, it was easy to imagine that she was the lady of the house, mistress of all she surveyed, queen of a fairy-tale castle.

It was bigger even than she'd dreamed a castle could be but she'd grown accustomed to its spacious splendour over the past few weeks. She walked slowly down the wide staircase, trailing her fingers on the smooth surface of the mahogany balustrade, listening to the swish of her skirts on the deep carpet underfoot. Below her in the spacious hall she could visualize a swarm of guests awaiting their hostess. She held out a gracious hand in greeting, and a handsome young gentleman took it and together they crossed the hall to the high windows. It was Aaron holding her hand, and she smiled at him before she let it fall, then laid her cheek against the thick velvet curtains, luxuriating in their opulence.

From here she could look out over the grounds and see the smooth lawns sweeping away down to the ornamental lake in the hollow. From here she and Aaron would be able to watch the gardeners bending over the flower-beds as they worked, and the nanny supervising her children as they frolicked in the sunlight . . .

May sighed and straightened. It was going to be hard to wrench herself away from the idyllic beauty of Thornleigh, to go back to the seedy poverty of Cedar Street. Here, surely, was her natural home. She felt born to this world, to space and grace and privacy, not to that noisy, smelly street where the houses were packed so tightly together that you could hear the Nagles fighting and quarrelling four doors away.

She hated the idea of going back to all that, and fought hard to quell the feeling of resentment which burned in her.

'I've told you, I'm fed up to the back teeth with that rotten place,' growled Cassie. 'Paste in me hair and ruining me clothes – I'm getting out of there just as soon as I can find summat else.'

Her voice was truculent but adamant. Ada eyed her daughter's back as she sat on the doorstep, stiff with defiance as she scraped trickles of hardened glue off her skirt.

'Leave Whitfield's?' echoed Ada. 'Give up a good job with good wages when you've nowt else to go to? Don't talk so daft, lass.'

'I'm not – I mean it. It's so boring I could scream, the overseer's got it in for me, and they pay me peanuts. Why shouldn't I look for summat better?'

Ada considered for a moment. 'Any road, what else are you fit for?' she asked. 'You're not trained for owt.'

She saw the careless shrug of Cassie's shoulders silhouetted against the sinking sun. 'I could go to Rose's same as May – she'd put in a good word for me.'

'That you can't,' retorted Ada. 'She's well thought of, is our May. That's why she was picked out of all of 'em to do Thornleigh Hall. It'd do her no good at all to fetch in a sister who's not got her heart in it. Nay, you leave our May alone.'

Cassie turned to face her mother. 'There's other things I could do.'

'Like what?'

'I could go into service.'

Ada stared in amazement. 'You – in service? Mopping and cleaning for others when you can't stand even to wash the dishes? Who'd have you?'

Cassie pouted as she stood up. 'Somebody. I could do owt if I was paid for it.'

Ada chuckled. 'In that case you'll be able to stick with the box factory and be grateful for what you've got. And when the time comes, happen you can put in a word for our Elsie.'

Jim Turnbull strained his neck to look up at his wife when she came up to bed.

'What was that all about tonight?' he asked sleepily.

'All what, love?'

'You and Cass. I could hear your voices in the lobby.'

'Oh that. Nowt. She wants to leave the box factory, get more money.'

Jim groaned. 'Doesn't everybody? Common enough complaint hereabouts. She'll have to get used to it same as the rest of us.'

Ada sighed as she pulled back the curtain to look out into the darkened street. 'Aye,' she murmured. 'I reckon she will.'

'What's that noise out there?' Jim asked weakly. 'Cats, is it?'

Ada shook her head. 'There's only that Nagle fellow staggering home again. Wonder how he manages to get drunk so often, earning what he does and with all them kids to feed. I see Mrs Nagle's expecting again and all.'

She let the curtain fall and turned away from the window.

Jim's eyes were closed. Ada blew out the oil-lamp and began to undress.

Tim Nagle clung to the lamp post, staring down at the pool of vomit in the gutter, illuminated by the light. His knees felt rubbery and his head swam, but he hadn't expected that sudden uprush. Bracing his knees to steady his legs, he started off again towards his own door. Cedar Street had never seemed so long, so winding.

His shin collided with yet another lamp post. Nagle swore and stumbled on. Who the devil kept putting those extra lamp posts there when he wasn't looking? It was all some damnable plot to confuse a poor, simple fellow.

Like the doors. His key didn't seem to fit the lock. Somebody overhead was shouting to him to go away. Dammit, it was a green door, wasn't it? Like his own. How was he to know?

At last he found a door that fitted his key and went in. Maureen was sitting by the low fire with young Thomas on her knee.

'In heaven's name, what's the child doing out of bed at this hour?' he asked, holding down the kitchen table which was wavering in the air.

Maureen held the boy close. 'It's his teeth again, I'm thinking – I couldn't stop him crying and he was waking the others.'

Nagle waved a magnanimous hand. 'Give him a drop of the ould stuff – that'll quiet him.'

Maureen shook her head. 'We have none. 'Tis all gone, and 'tis food he needs. They had only gruel for their supper.'

Nagle let go of the table and moved unsteadily towards her. The toddler looked up at the huge figure of his father, then turned and buried his face in his mother's breast. The movement irritated Nagle.

'Get him away out of here,' he muttered. 'Get him to bed.'

'He'll not sleep. I'll give him a drop first.'

She began unbuttoning her blouse. Nagle watched as she

drew out a full breast and offered it to the child. Thomas clamped eagerly onto it and the little mouth began sucking vigorously.

Nagle felt a sudden leap of fire in his guts. 'Away out of that,' he muttered, pulling the child's head away. 'Put him down.'

Maureen looked up at him, alarm glowing in her pale eyes. 'Not tonight, Timmy, please – not the way I am.'

The breast hung in front of his eyes, temptingly full and rounded. 'You heard me,' he roared, curling his hand into a fist. 'I'll not have a wife who denies a man his rights, you hear me?'

Maureen scrambled to her feet, the toddler under one arm and pulling her blouse together with her free hand. 'I'll just take the child up to bed—'

'Leave him be,' yelled Nagle, 'on the chair, and come here to me.'

From behind the shelter of his newspaper Harold peered anxiously at the clock. Half-past ten already. Would she ever make a move? Usually she was in bed long before this.

Fanny pulled the wooden mushroom out of the sock then stuck the darning needle back into the pincushion.

'You know, Harold, these socks are almost past mending,' she remarked. 'I could buy some wool, now Mrs Mayhew's paid the bill – you'd like me to knit you some new ones for winter, wouldn't you?'

Harold yawned. 'That would be very nice, dear.'

She wound up the ball of mending wool and tucked it into her sewing basket. Harold watched every movement. Get a move on, he thought irritably, else it'll be too late.

Fanny looked up at the clock. 'Heavens – is that the time?' she murmured. 'Time to wend my way up the wooden hill to dream land. What about you, love?'

He lowered his newspaper. 'Gracious me, that late already?' he said in tones of mock surprise. 'Yes, you go up – I'll just pop down to the privy and then I'll be up directly.'

*   *   *

It took only seconds to slip out of the back gate into the alley. Harold could feel his heart thumping under his waistcoat as he hurried quickly down the cobbled lane towards his goal.

This was it, the Turnbulls' gate. He stretched up on tiptoe to peer over the top. A light glowed in the scullery and above it another glowed in the bedroom. The thumping in his chest grew louder.

Yes, she was there! She was standing framed in the window, looking down. He ducked instantly, feeling the flame colouring his cheeks. What if she'd seen him? For long seconds he crouched there, but no sound came from the house, no indignant cry or rattle of an opening door. No-one must have spotted him in the unlit alley.

Eventually he plucked up courage to peep over the gate once more, and his heart almost leapt into his throat. The girl was still there, her slim arms upraised above her head as she peeled off her chemise.

He stood transfixed, mesmerized by the sheer beauty of her, the tumble of fair hair about her shoulders and the outline of her young breasts as she leaned over. Then suddenly the light went out.

He turned away, unable to reconcile within himself the confusing torment of delight and embarrassment. It was the younger Turnbull girl. She was only a chit of a thing – she couldn't be more than sixteen years old.

Opening the gate with great caution so that it did not creak, he slunk into his own back yard and made his way noiselessly into the house. As he climbed the stairs the image of the bare-breasted girl in the window would not leave his mind. Shame burned his cheeks. They had an unpleasant name for men like him who lusted after young girls like her.

As he began to undress he heard Fanny stir in the darkness. 'You took your time – where've you been?' she murmured.

Harold turned away from the bed in case his state of excitement became apparent. 'Oh, just looking at the stars,' he said.

Fanny grunted. 'I thought it was cloudy tonight.'

'Only in patches,' said Harold, sitting on the edge of the bed. 'I was trying to find the evening star.'

He heard the tired yawn. 'I've never heard of the evening star.'

He pulled off his socks and dropped them on the bedside rug. 'It's Venus – you've heard of Venus.'

Her voice was thick with sleep. 'Oh that. And did you see it?'

'Oh yes,' he said dreamily, hauling his legs into bed. 'Quite clearly – for a moment or so.'

SEVEN

Sunday afternoon lay still and peaceful over Thornleigh Hall. The village girls had the day off and Mrs Gabbitas had gone back to Sir Joseph's other home to help with the move. For today May was the sole occupant of the house.

She finished packing up the last of her sewing materials. When Mr Henry had called yesterday he'd said that he would arrange to have them collected tomorrow morning.

'Oh, and by the way, May,' he added in slightly apologetic tones, 'apparently my lady has changed her mind about the cushions in the conservatory – she'd like them piped in green instead of the pink she originally chose.'

It had taken until late last night to unpick and re-sew them all. Thank heaven it was for the conservatory and not a curtained room, thought May, or it would have meant unpicking all the tarlatan-stiffened tie-backs as well. She stood now in the sewing-room window, gazing out over the sunlit lawns towards Hawksmoor.

There was no sign of the town, lying in the hollow of the Colne Valley between the folds of the hills, no sign of the thick pall of smoke which clung perpetually around the forest of blackened mill-chimneys. For all she could see, it might just as well not exist.

If only it didn't. If only she didn't have to go back there. If only she could stay in this magical fairy-tale world for ever . . . Still, for one last day she could play the lady. The housekeeper had seen to it that cold chicken and salad had been left ready on the cold slab in the pantry, with pink blancmange and jelly to follow – she could take her last meal in the dining room, sitting in state at the long polished table. She'd use a silver knife and fork and a damask napkin out of the sideboard drawer, light the candles. No-one would ever know.

She left the sewing room and, with queenly grace, swept along the landing to the staircase. On the top step she paused to look up at the array of portraits on the wall, a row of Sir Joseph's glassy-eyed forebears, then turned to descend. From below came the sound of a door closing, and she stiffened.

Footsteps rang out on the newly-laid mosaic floor. She held her breath, wondering who on earth it could be. A workman, completing a task? Or an intruder?

She held her breath as a figure appeared in the hallway, the tall figure of a man, and with a leap of relief and pleasure she recognized Mr Aaron. For a moment she felt confused, recalling how she'd dreamed about him in her fantasies.

He looked up and saw her. 'Ah, you're still here,' he said with a smile. 'I was hoping I'd catch you.'

His words gave her a thrill of pleasure. 'You startled me,' she said reprovingly. 'I thought I was alone.'

'I'm sorry.' As she reached the last step he held out a hand, just as she'd day-dreamed. As she let her hand lie in his it felt utterly natural, like a gentleman leading his lady partner out into the dance.

He smiled down at her. 'Have you had lunch yet?' he asked, and from behind his back he produced a bottle. 'I hope not, since I've brought a bottle of Father's very best French wine specially to go with it.'

May was entranced. Dreams could come true. He was treating her as if she were a real lady. 'There's cold chicken and salad in the pantry,' she said. 'I'm sure there'll be enough for two.'

He offered her his arm. 'Then what are we waiting for?' he said, and the teasing light in his eyes sent ripples of pleasure through her. 'Lead the way to the dining room.'

*   *   *

As they sat at either end of the long polished table May began to gather her wits. What was she doing here, a humble seamstress dining with her handsome young employer? Mr Aaron seemed to see nothing unusual in it at all as he poured out the wine and brought the glass over to her. Her fingers trembled as she took it.

'I'm a very lucky man,' he murmured, 'to have such charming company for lunch. It beats Sunday dinner at home any time.'

She watched as he went back to his seat, flourished his napkin and draped it over his lap. 'Now what shall we talk about?' he asked amiably as he picked up his knife and fork. 'The weather? Politics, perhaps? No, you don't seem the sort to be interested in what the Suffragettes are up to. What else is there? Crime? They've caught Crippen, you know – no, that's too sordid over lunch. What are you interested in, May?'

She hoped he wouldn't notice that her hand was shaking as she tried to spear a piece of chicken. 'I don't know really – my work, mainly.'

He waved his fork dismissively in the air. 'Let's not talk shop, not today. Have you enjoyed staying at Thornleigh?'

'Oh yes,' she breathed. 'I can't tell you how much.'

He nodded. 'It's a wonderful house,' he agreed. 'One day I intend to have one like it.' He picked up his wineglass. 'And I hope I shall have a lady as charming as you to grace my table. I drink your health, May.'

She felt the colour rush to her cheeks. She laid her knife and fork down with deliberate slowness. 'You're mocking me, aren't you, Mr Aaron? I'd rather you didn't try to make a fool of me.'

He threw up a hand, his handsome face registering shocked innocence. 'Mock you? Why should I mock you? I admire and respect you, May. Why else would I be here?'

'Just because I come from a wretched place like Cedar Street,' May went on levelly, 'there's no reason for you to make fun of me.'

He looked astonished. 'I'm not making fun of you, or Cedar Street – I don't even know Cedar Street.'

May wasn't going to be deterred. 'You think we know nothing, but from what I hear your background is just as humble as mine.'

His face broke into a smile and he held his glass aloft again. 'You're absolutely right,' he said. 'My father was born in a slum yard in the most wretched part of Leeds. I drink a toast to you, May. In fact, tell you what,' he went on, rising and picking up the bottle, 'let me fill up your glass and we'll drink a health to Cedar Street.'

She inclined her head. He filled the two glasses to the brim. 'To Cedar Street,' he declared. 'Long may it flourish.'

She gave a short laugh as she raised the glass to her lips. 'That'll make a nice change,' she said drily. 'It never has up to now.'

Lunch over, Aaron pushed back his chair and stood up.

'Come on, let's take a turn around the gardens,' he said, holding out a hand. 'They're well worth it.'

It was lovely, she thought contentedly, the way he talked to her as if they were equals. She laid aside her napkin and rose. He pushed open the french windows and stood aside to let her go through. She caught the scent of pomade on his hair. He smelled so clean, so fresh, and she felt the fleeting touch of his hand brush her waist as she passed him. A shiver of pleasure ran through her.

They must have sat over the meal far longer than she'd realized, she thought as they walked along the terrace, for the sun was dipping low over the hills, its amber light spilling over the rose garden and drenching it with vibrant colour. The scene was magical, putting her in mind of one of the wonderful illustrations in her fairy-tale book. It was a magical world, with a handsome young prince at her side.

The heavy scent of the roses was overwhelming, so intoxicatingly beautiful that it almost drowned her senses, numbing them into drowsiness. Or was it the wine? She'd lost

71

count of how many times Mr Aaron had refilled her glass. Or was it the nearness of this devastatingly beautiful man with his silken voice and his fingers burning hot on her arm?

'We could sit in that pretty little arbour over there,' he suggested as they strolled, pointing towards a shady corner. 'We could watch the sun go down. I bet the sunset is magnificent over those hills.'

She made no protest as he led her into the leafy shadow of the arbour and watched her settle on the iron seat before sitting beside her. Long moments passed in silence, then she heard him take a slow, deep breath, a sound like a sigh of contentment, and May felt enraptured. If only the girls in the workroom could see her now . . . If only this could go on for ever . . .

'I ought to be making a move,' she ventured at last. 'I've got to get home tonight.'

He must have heard the reluctance in her tone for he slid his arm along the back of the seat and she could feel the warmth of his forearm against her back. 'There's no hurry,' he soothed. 'Stay a little longer – I'll see you get home safely.'

The prospect was tempting, but she had to be firm. 'No, really, there's no need,' she said, scrambling to her feet. 'Only I must be getting back.'

'Very well.'

He rose obligingly. 'Let me take your arm,' he murmured as they walked, the gravel crunching under their feet. 'I wouldn't want you to trip in the dusk – it's not easy to see the steps in the half-light.'

The pressure of his touch sent shivers running through her entire body. The last thing she wanted to do was to leave him . . . As they entered the gloom of the hall he turned to her.

'Which is your room?' he asked.

'You've seen it – where my machine is,' she answered.

'I mean your own room,' he said softly. 'I'll come up and carry your bags down for you.'

She hesitated. 'I can manage perfectly well on my own,' she said in a small voice, but there was no conviction in her tone. His hand was already taking her arm, urging her towards the stairs. Her head was swimming and her heart thumping so loudly he must be able to hear it. She wanted to be close to him, feel his touch just for a little while longer . . .

As she turned she stumbled. His arm slid around her waist to steady her. The steps seemed to be melting into one another as they made their way upstairs, and she leaned her head against the smooth, soft fabric of his shoulder.

'Dammit.'

Ada swore under her breath as she unpegged the last sheet from the line. She'd left the washing out too long and now it had soot smuts all over it.

It was all Jack Smedley's fault, keeping her talking for so long. He'd come to visit Jim, not her, but he'd taken the best part of an hour to drink a cup of tea in the kitchen before he left. Just when she could have used the time to get ready for May coming home too – she should be here directly.

Ada scrutinized the blemished sheet in the half-light. It was Mrs Cooper's best linen, the one she'd turned ends-to-middle last year, and now it had black specks all over it. Even if she scraped them off with her fingernail it would leave smudgy brown stains. There was nothing else for it – the damn thing would have to be washed all over again. As if she didn't have enough on already. With a sigh Ada lifted the overflowing wicker basket and turned to go back indoors.

A sound caught her ear, a rustling behind the rubbish bin, and then a thin, mewing sound. Hungry cats again, no doubt, scavenging for food. Or maybe rats. She dropped the basket and grabbed up the yard broom to chase them off.

Behind the rubbish a small white face stared up at her in the gloom, and with a start she realized it was a little boy, his eyes wide in fear.

'Gracious me, what are you doing there?' she asked, letting the broom fall.

In answer he only whimpered. Ada bent to take his arm and draw him out. He pulled away, terror in his eyes.

73

'Don't hit me! I meant no harm!'

'Nay,' soothed Ada, 'don't be frightened, lad. I won't hurt you. Come on out of there.'

Reluctantly he let himself be drawn towards the light from the scullery door. She could see the grimy tear-tracks down his cheeks.

'What you doing here, love?' she asked him gently. 'Where are you from?'

He shook his dark head and began crying loudly again. From over the yard wall came the sound of metal scraping and Ada looked up. She knew the sound of Mrs Boothroyd's tin bath being dragged over to the wall so she could climb up on it whenever she wanted to talk.

A head swathed in rag curlers appeared over the coping stone. 'What's going off? What's all that racket?' her neighbour enquired.

Ada spread her hands. The boy cowered against the house wall, huddled and crying. 'I found this little lad hiding down behind the rubbish,' she said, 'shriking his eyes out. I don't know who he belongs to.'

Mrs Boothroyd peered into the gloom. 'I know him – he's one of them Nagles. What's your name, son?'

The voice was as tiny and pathetic as the child. 'Dominic.'

'Well, hadn't you best be getting off home?' said Ada. 'Your mam'll be fair worried out of her wits, you out in the dark on your own at this time of night.'

Dominic wiped a dirty hand across his cheek. 'I can't. Me dad says he'll flay the hide off me if he gets hold of me.'

'Why? What you done?'

He shook his shaggy dark head. 'I don't know,' he snivelled. 'He never says.'

Ada peered at his thin arms, mottled with dark blurs. 'Is that muck,' she asked, 'or are them bruises?'

The boy hugged his arms about him, trying to hide the marks. 'It's nowt,' he moaned. 'Never heed. Can I go now?'

Ada steered him towards the yard gate. 'And just you make

74

sure you go straight home,' she admonished him. 'I don't want it on my conscience if owt happens to you.'

She watched him scuttle away up the lane then turned back with a sigh. Mrs Boothroyd's curlered head still peered over the wall.

'You look fair whacked, lass,' said the old lady. 'Why not come round for a nice hot cup of tea?'

Ada hesitated. 'Nay, I shouldn't. I'll have all on to get done before our May gets home.'

'Five minutes,' urged Mrs Boothroyd, 'that's all. Do you good.'

Ada sat in the old lady's candle-lit kitchen, warming her hands around the cup of hot tea laced with brandy and pouring out thoughts she'd barely voiced even to herself.

'I don't know,' said Mrs Boothroyd, shaking her head sadly, 'it never rains but it pours. If it's not one you're fretting about, it's another. You've enough on your plate waiting on him hand and foot.'

'Our Cassie's never been any bother before,' Ada said defensively. 'She's just getting restless, that's all. Wants to be grown up before her time.'

Mrs Boothroyd snorted. 'What's the hurry? They've no idea, these youngsters. Time passes a damn sight faster than we want and before you know it, you've one foot in the grave already.'

'She wants money and be free to do as she likes,' explained Ada. 'I tell her we all do but it's not that easy. She reckons she's different, born to better things.'

'Oh aye,' agreed Mrs Boothroyd, 'she tells a good tale, does the lass. Tell her not to wish her life away. Before she knows it she'll be racked with rheumatics like me. I was telling our Hilda only last week. I said, old age isn't for sissies, you know, but I don't think she were listening and she's nigh on fifty herself now.'

Ada was only half-listening, one ear cocked for May's quick, light step in the street outside.

'No, old age is no joke;' said Mrs Boothroyd, then added philosophically as she emptied the dregs from the teapot into her cup, 'still, it's not that bad when you consider the alternative.'

May looked tired and pale when she came home. She must have been overworking up there at the Hall, thought Ada, for she didn't seem at all inclined to answer Elsie's excited questions.

'Is it a big house, May? Bigger than chapel?'

'Yes, it's huge.'

The child's eyes rounded as she tried to visualize it. 'And do they have loads of servants to do all the work?'

May nodded. 'They will have, when they move in.'

Elsie's gaze fell on May's wicker box and she pounced on it eagerly. 'What you got in your box, May? Anything for me?'

'No. Only some scraps for Mam's patchwork.'

'Oh.' Elsie's face fell, but she pulled the lid off and began to peer inside. May grabbed her arm.

'You just leave that be. I told you, there's nothing in there for you.'

Ada noted the alarm in her tone. It wasn't like May at all. She took hold of Elsie's thin arm and drew her away from the box. 'Now what about bed, young lady?' she said quietly. 'It's school for you in the morning. Come on now.'

Having tucked the child in, Ada went to peep round the door at Jim. His eyes were closed and he seemed to be sleeping so she pulled the door to and crept away.

Downstairs May had kicked off her shoes and was leaning back in the chair, her eyes closed.

'Weary, love?' asked Ada. 'Hard work, was it?'

May's voice sounded slurred. 'Bit of a headache, that's all,' she murmured. 'I was up till midnight last night unpicking some cushions.'

No wonder the lass looked worn out. Ada reached into the cupboard for her sewing basket. 'I reckoned as much,' she said. 'Best get off to bed then if you're to be up for work in the morning.'

'I've got the day off.'

Ada paused, startled. 'You what? On a Monday?'

'Mr Aaron was very pleased with me. He said I could, seeing as I'd done so much overtime.'

'Well, that was very nice of him,' said Ada reflectively, 'very nice indeed.' Such a thing had never been heard of before. Her work must have been very satisfactory if he was so impressed.

May's lips curved softly as she spoke. 'Yes, he's a nice man,' she agreed. 'Very appreciative.'

By the time May had washed her face with the cold water in the jug on the dressing table her fuddled brain was beginning to clear and the feeling of excitement was starting to melt into embarrassment.

She could hardly believe what had happened. Nice girls didn't do such things, not before they were married, at any rate, and she'd never even so much as flirted with the lads at work. But somehow it hadn't seemed wrong; somehow it had seemed so natural, so right, not the shameful thing folk said.

Even so, Mam must never know just how appreciative Mr Aaron had been or for what reason. She'd be bound to scold and talk about the disgrace however hard May tried to explain, and the last thing she wanted was to be made to feel guilty. It had been so thrilling, so pleasurably intimate, upstairs in her candle-lit room in Thornleigh Hall, his whispered words in her ear, his gentle hands on her body awaking sensations she'd never dreamt of.

She'd often wondered, of course, lying in her single bed at night, just how it would be, trying to conjure up a man lying next to her, how he would touch her, how it might feel. But the man had always been vague, a mysterious, faceless stranger. And it had been hard to imagine his actions because she knew so little.

But that was before this wonderful man had awakened her to the truth. Had he found her stupid? He hadn't seemed to; he'd guided her gently, coaxed her with the utmost tenderness, a knight wooing his cherished lady . . .

'Our secret, May.' She could hear his throaty whisper still, and she'd revelled in the conspiratorial closeness between them, swirling in ecstasy in their beautiful fantasy world. Their world, their secret, just the two of them.

Was it the wine or was it enchantment which made her forget for the moment that she was May Turnbull, seamstress, and he the son of her rich employer? It hadn't mattered then, it didn't matter still. He'd treated her like an equal – he wasn't just trifling with her, she knew. He'd made it clear that she was special – hadn't he spoken of owning a house like Thornleigh one day, and having her to grace his table? Hadn't he promised that this was only the start? A whole new vista spread before her now, the chance to become the woman she'd always known she could be. The lord of the manor and his lady . . .

But it must remain their secret, at least for the time being. No one must guess, especially down at Rose's, or it could make life extremely difficult for them both. He was right, of course. Not a word would pass her lips. Not yet, or it could ruin everything . . .

'Aaron, my boy, where on earth have you been till this time of night?'

Mrs Rose's big watery eyes fastened accusingly on her son as he entered the room. 'You missed dinner,' she reproved him, 'and you think nothing of your poor mother worrying that you could be lying dead in a ditch somewhere – what have you been up to?'

Aaron came up behind the sofa and planted a kiss on the top of her head.

'Working, Mother. I was up at the Hall, seeing that everything was in order and that the place was locked up securely. I had to wait for the girl to finish.'

'Ah yes,' said Mrs Rose. 'She's the one your father thinks so highly of, isn't she?'

Aaron seated himself beside her. 'She's not bad,' he murmured. 'She's got a lot to learn – but she's not bad.'

'She's done the job very well, your father says. There weren't any problems, were there?' his mother enquired.

'Just a few small things,' replied Aaron equably, picking up the newspaper, 'nothing of importance. It was all quite simple really. It just took a little time to organize, that's all.'

EIGHT

Elsie slammed Mrs Boothroyd's front door and put the huge mint humbug into her mouth which the old lady had just given her for fetching a pound of butter from the corner shop. Mam hardly ever bought sweets – they were a wicked luxury, she said, when there was hardly enough money for food. The smoothly rounded shape of the humbug seemed to fill her whole mouth, it was so huge, and it tasted like heaven.

Further up the street a small boy about her own age squatted on the pavement edge, staring into the gutter. She recognized him, one of the noisy Irish family, the Nagles. Curious, she sidled up to him. He didn't look up.

'Lost summat?' she asked.

There was only a growl for an answer. She squatted down beside him, peering into the mud and litter in the gully.

'Marble, was it?' she asked. 'I won four off a kid at school today – you can have one if you like.'

Dark eyes rose slowly to look suspiciously into hers and she saw tears hovering on his lashes. 'Hey, what's up?' she demanded. 'I told you, you can have one of my hollies.'

He shook his black head dolefully. 'It's me dad,' he muttered.

'What about him?' A fearful thought struck her. 'He's not dead, is he?'

It was a common enough event in the street, an accident at work like her own dad, an illness brought about by hunger or winter's cold. Folk were always dying.

Again he shook his head and made a brittle sound like a

laugh. 'Wish he was,' he said savagely. 'Then he'd stop hitting us.'

Elsie stared. 'What you done wrong then?'

'Nowt,' came the miserable reply. 'You don't have to do nowt and he belts us, me mam and the little 'uns and all. Look.'

He rolled back a ragged sleeve to reveal a mass of purple bruises mottling his forearm. 'And that's nowt to what he's done on me back. He just seems to like doing it.'

He spoke the words almost with pride and Elsie stared at him in disbelief. 'My dad doesn't belt us,' she muttered. 'He can't anyway 'cos he's poorly, but he wouldn't if he could. Dads don't do things like that.'

The boy glanced back at the house. 'Mine does, all the time. Sometimes I think I'll run away and never come back. He's worst when he's had a drop.'

'Drop of what?'

He gave her a surly sneer. 'Ale, of course. Don't you know nowt?'

'Course I do,' she flashed back. 'I know how to stop folk belting me, which is more than you do, seemingly.'

'You do? How?' There was interest in his dark eyes now, respect even. Elsie confided the story of the redhead down Archer Street while the dark eyes devoured every word.

'You hit her – with a fence post?' he repeated in admiration. 'Where did you get it?'

'Found it. I'll lend it to you if you like.'

He got up slowly, kicked a pebble and watched it bounce along the cobbled street. 'What's your name?' he asked.

'Elsie. What's yours?'

'Dominic. Sometimes they just call me Nick.'

She watched him disappear into the entry alongside his house. Poor Dominic. Fancy having a rotten brute for a father. He needed to be able to defend himself, and his little brothers and sisters. Now if that wooden post was still under the archway into the stonemason's yard . . .

Gathering up her courage, Elsie made her way up the street

and, jutting her chin and marching with purposeful step, turned the corner into Archer Street.

'My, my, now what might you be doing with that lump of wood, eh?'

She'd seen him coming towards her, the big, black-coated figure of Mr Jordan, but he'd never spoken to her before. Elsie looked up with a shy smile.

'I'm taking it to my friend,' she said.

He had a nice pink face, all round and chubby and smiling. 'I see,' he murmured. 'You're one of the Turnbull girls, aren't you? What's your name?'

'Elsie.'

'Haven't I seen you at church, you and your sisters?'

The fence post was getting heavy. She stood it on end on the pavement and shook her head. 'We don't go to church – we go to chapel. Cassie sings in the choir.'

'Does she now? Is she the fair-haired one?'

'Yes, like me. May's got brown hair like me dad.'

'And do you sing in the choir too, Elsie?'

'Not likely. I hate hymns. Anyway, me mam says I've a voice like a corncrake, whatever that is.'

She could hear him chuckling as he walked away and she levered the post up on her shoulder again. Mr Jordan seemed a nice, happy man. Not like that bad-tempered Mr Nagle.

It hadn't been as bad as she'd thought, going down Archer Street. That snotty-nosed kid Dennis had seen her and gone running into his house, and for long seconds Elsie had held her breath, waiting for his sister to appear, but Coppernob hadn't come out to tackle her.

Still, she'd take the post home for the time being and take it round to Dominic later. She'd had enough heroics for one day.

Harold Jordan was feeling pleased with himself. He pushed his empty plate away and patted his ample stomach with a smile.

'That was very good, my dear,' he said to his wife. 'You've never lost your touch with apple pie.'

She smiled to see his good humour. 'We used to have them lovely apple trees up in Marchmont Avenue, remember? All we had to do was go out in the garden—'

'And the day will come again,' he cut in quickly. 'The way business is picking up we'll soon have all paid off. Do you know, Mrs Mayhew has recommended me to two of her friends so that's more high-class trade coming our way. It won't be long now.'

He saw the glow in her pale eyes. 'Do you think we might ever go back there, Harold? That lovely garden—'

'Or somewhere very like it, love. We're starting to be recognized again by those who shunned us. I've been thinking, we might start going to church again.'

'Oh, Harold, that would be nice.'

'Not the old church – I couldn't stand them eyes on me. Maybe we could try the Wesleyan chapel. There's a very nice class of folk go there.'

He saw her look of surprise. 'But we've always been church, love, not chapel.'

He shrugged his shoulders. 'What's the difference? They all worship the same God, don't they? And like I say, there's some very classy folk round there; I've seen them.'

'Well, if you think it would be good for business—'

'I do, love, I do. And I'm very glad you see it my way. We'll make ourselves known to the minister this very Sunday.'

On Tuesday morning Miss Openshaw watched her girls filing into the workroom and hanging up their coats. As soon as May Turnbull came in she hurried over to meet her.

'Nice to have you back, May,' she smiled. 'Did you enjoy working at the Hall?'

'Very much,' May replied quietly as she peeled off her gloves and stowed them away in her coat pocket. Leather, Miss Openshaw noted with approval. The girl had taste.

'Good. Mr Henry tells me you did well. If her ladyship is

as pleased as Sir Joseph then we're sure to get a lot more work from her. Well done, May.'

'Thank you.'

She didn't blush or simper, only made her way over to her bench and sat down. If only the others were as serene and reliable as she was. Miss Openshaw scowled at Mabel who was giggling to her neighbour.

'Quieten down now,' she snapped. 'The clock's struck and you should be working. Mr Aaron will be here before you've even got started.'

May sat head bent over her work, feet busily rocking the treadle and her hands guiding the fabric under the needle, but her mind was buzzing with thoughts.

How would Aaron behave when he came in? He'd urged discretion, but surely he'd cast some look, some glance her way. After what had happened he couldn't just ignore her. Some time he'd have to speak to her, to arrange to meet her again – he'd said he would, but he hadn't said how or when.

She mustn't react, though, if he did chance to smile at her. Miss Openshaw's keen eye monitored every look and movement in her domain, and the girls never took their covetous eyes off him. No, she must be discreet, try not to meet his gaze, keep her attention on her work when he came in.

Ten minutes passed, twenty, half an hour and still the door had not opened. May tried hard not to peer through the glass to see what was going on outside.

Then at last she heard the creak of the door, heard the rustle of movement as the machines whirred slower and the sound of Miss Openshaw's footsteps tapping towards the door.

'Ah, good morning, Mr Aaron.'

It took all May's strength to keep her head bent and carry on sewing, but even so, the skin on the nape of her neck tingled and her whole body was aware of his closeness. She was conscious too of his moving about the room, speaking a few words to the girls as he came closer.

She willed her neck to stay stiff, not yield to the temptation to look up as, out of the corner of her eye, she caught sight of the dark serge of his trousers beside her bench. For a brief second he hesitated, as though uncertain or maybe waiting for her to acknowledge him, but she remained resolute. Discreet, he'd said. Don't look up, don't blush, or you'll give the game away!

The blur of his suit receded out of sight. One moment more and he'll be gone. As she heard his footsteps move towards the door May's determination faltered and she glanced up.

She was just in time to catch a glimpse of his broad shoulders and glossy black hair before Miss Openshaw closed the door behind him. With a sinking feeling of disappointment May bent back over her work. Still, why worry? She had a wonderful secret to hug to herself, and that was consolation enough for a queen.

The two Misses Bottomley stood outside their front door, listening to the racket from the Nagles' house.

'Just hark at that, Nellie,' said Agnes, wiping bony, flour-dusted fingers on her print apron. 'He's at it again, not five minutes after coming home.'

Nellie's plump face creased into a worried frown as she looked anxiously up at her sister. 'Who is it he's bashing this time, do you think? Is it his missus again?'

Agnes scowled malevolently at the green, peeling paint of the Nagles' front door. 'Time somebody gave him a bashing if you ask me. He oughtn't to be allowed to get away with it, hitting a nice, quiet little body like her, and with all them kids to see to and all. He ought to be locked up, he did.'

'But what can we do, Agnes? He's a big man, is Mr Nagle.'

Agnes pursed her thin lips. 'There's nowt we can do, more's the pity. I only hope he gets his comeuppance some day, the brute. She deserves better than that.' She laid a scrawny arm around her sister's shoulder. 'Come away inside, love. Let's get on with peeling them onions else us pasties'll never get made.'

From the end of the street Harold Jordan saw the Misses Bottomley go indoors, the short fat one waddling in front of the tall thin one who was ushering her ahead, and was relieved he hadn't been obliged to speak to them.

On the far side of the street the little Turnbull girl was playing hopscotch alone on a patch where someone had roughly scratched out squares on the flagstones with a pebble. She looked up, saw him and waved, then skipped away along the street and he saw her pause outside the Irish family's house. As he drew nearer he too heard what had caught her attention.

A man's voice was bellowing, a woman's high-pitched voice protesting, and as a background to the cacophony a child's thin voice wailed in descant. Harold snorted to himself in disgust. Typical Irish bog-peasants, he growled. Noisy, drunken layabouts, the lot of them. They knew nothing of hard work and thrift. They ought never to be allowed into the country.

He strode past quickly towards the sanctuary of his own house.

Elsie stared helplessly at the green door, wishing she could stop the angry voices. Poor Dominic was getting bashed again, she felt sure of it, and it was all wrong. He was her friend. She'd promised to help him. Without a second thought she ran through the entry into the back alley, then rushed into the back yard to grab up the fence post and rush out again into the lane.

The Nagles' back gate swung drunkenly on its hinges. She pushed it open and ran in. The back door stood open, and through the doorway she could see Mr Nagle's shirt-sleeved figure bending over Dominic who crouched, whining, on the floor.

'Leave him be, Tim, don't hit him again, please!'

Mrs Nagle's pleading voice whimpered somewhere out of sight. Elsie planted herself, panting, on the doorstep, fence post clenched tightly in her fist.

'Don't you hit him any more, you big bully,' she yelled. 'You're much bigger 'n he is, you coward.'

Mr Nagle looked round in surprise, his jaw sagging. 'And who the devil might you be?' he demanded.

'I'm Elsie, his friend. You ought to be ashamed of yourself, you did, picking on a little lad like him. You're loads bigger 'n him – why don't you pick on someone your own size?'

'Well of all the—' Mr Nagle's bewildered stare moved slowly from the angry little red face to the wooden post in her hand. 'What's that you have there?'

'My fence post, for belting bullies with,' Elsie said stoutly. 'Here, you have it,' she added, holding it out to Dominic. 'You can have a lend of it as long as you want.'

Dominic, unheeded, crawled aside and scrambled to his feet, staring open-mouthed at his rescuer. Seeing he made no move to take the post, Elsie laid it on the floor and glared accusingly at his father.

'I'll have no more of this, do you hear?' she said firmly, speaking the way Mam did when she'd had enough nonsense. 'Dads aren't supposed to hit kids. They're supposed to love 'em.'

Mr Nagle stood, feet astride, and planted his hands on his hips. 'The devil they are,' he muttered. 'Who told you that?'

She curled her lip. 'No-one has to be told, you just know. My dad wouldn't bash me about, but he'd give you a hiding for what you done. I mean,' she faltered, 'he would if he could.'

The big man was looking down at her with amusement in his eyes, and Elsie felt embarrassed. She shouldn't have said that about Dad.

Mr Nagle lifted a huge hand and she tried not to flinch as he dropped his fist on her shoulder. 'Seems to me your dad ought to take his belt to ye, having such cheek,' he muttered. 'Away home with ye, child, and don't be tempted again to meddle in other people's business. If ye do ye'll know the weight of me hand too, so ye will. Away with ye now.'

The brawny arm turned her about and gave her a hefty shove. Elsie didn't stop running until she reached the safety of her own back yard and she locked the gate behind her.

Jim Turnbull lay listening to the sounds from downstairs. It was the only way he knew what was going on in his house, listening and evaluating each sound. He knew when supper was under way by the rattle of pans, knew when the girls came home by the banging of the door, when Ada was labouring over the washing by the rattle of the old mangle.

He'd also learnt to recognize the silences. There were the still ones which meant Ada was dead beat, too exhausted even to talk to the girls. And sometimes it was a heavy, oppressive silence when she'd quarrelled with Cassie again. Rarely nowadays did the old, familiar stillness lie over the house which they'd savoured in the old days when he went out to work like other men, the tranquillity of quiet, unspoken trust and love.

He groaned and turned his head to face the window. He'd left Ada to cope with it all on her own, and she never grumbled. A man was indeed blessed to have a wife like her, but the thought of it going on like this for possibly another forty years . . . It was unthinkable. They hardly knew him now, none of them. He was little more than a lump of flesh upstairs that needed seeing to, not a human being. On the fringe of their lives he was, not the central, manly character other fathers were. He was a drain on them all, especially Ada. No-one would miss him if he was gone . . .

A door slammed down below and footsteps came running up the stairs, small, light footsteps. It was Elsie, his baby, and he turned his face on the pillow so he could see her as she came in.

The door burst open and she flew across the room, and he winced as she hurled herself on the bed.

'Hello, love,' he said softly, lifting his head. 'What's up?'

She took his face between her hands and plastered a big, wet kiss on his lips, then sat back.

'Hey up, what's that for?' he said with a smile.

'I love you, Dad,' she said firmly.

He curled his hand round a grubby little fist. 'Well, that's very nice to know. I love you too.'

She smiled contentedly. 'I know you do. You wouldn't hit us, would you?'

'Of course I wouldn't.'

'Not even if we were little boys?'

He smiled. 'What's brought this on?'

'Nowt. You wouldn't, would you, even if you could?'

NINE

Harold Jordan couldn't sleep, and it wasn't just because Fanny was snoring. He lay as still as he could so as not to disturb her but it wasn't easy to relax when visions of that angel kept invading his mind, tumbling it into turmoil.

He'd seen her the moment he went into chapel, his hand cupping Fanny's bony elbow. The three sisters were sitting together in a pew near the front, little Elsie ensconced between the dark and the fair older sisters. But Harold had eyes only for the blond one, her hair rippling in a golden cascade down her shoulders. He'd steered Fanny to a seat where he could watch the angel's profile, the soft curve of her neck, the lashes lying dark on her cheek as she looked down at her hymn book.

Now and again he saw her glance up under her lashes to cast an eye around her, and he'd looked away quickly in case she caught sight of him staring. Fanny sang on in her thin, reedy voice, unaware of the delight surging in him.

And it wasn't only delight which pulsated in him still. There was a fierce, yearning fire in his belly, the way he used to feel in those days long ago when he first courted Fanny. Fanny. He could feel her backside now against his thigh, cold as ice as it always was, and wondered how it came about that that fire had died.

Maybe it had never burned for Fanny. Maybe it was his fault that he'd never managed to kindle it. Given the chance now to school a virgin it would be so different. He'd make certain of it this time.

He closed his eyes tightly, capturing again the seductive image of the naked figure in the window, the beautiful fair-haired maiden who would be anxious to learn, to please. He visualized himself brushing out that long, silken hair while he murmured soft, persuasive words, soaping down that lissom body in the bath . . .

God, how he hungered for her! It was stupid, senseless, a man some thirty years older than she was . . .

But he could not chase the fantasy from his brain, nor did he want to. He yearned for her, longed to possess her . . . Be sensible, man, he told himself. Put these wild notions from your head.

But if I could get to know the girl, talk to her . . . He could take such pleasure in just gazing upon her, admiring . . . Like when he'd followed her down the path to the chapel gate, watching her proud, erect bearing, the way she tossed back her long hair, the way she smiled demurely to the minister . . .

'Harold?'

Fanny's voice in the dark made him start. 'What, love?'

'You're shivering – you're making the bed shake. Are you all right?'

Caught out, he felt his cheeks redden. 'It's nowt. I'm a bit cold, that's all.'

She wriggled round to face him. 'It's standing around in that cemetery in the rain today. I don't want you catching owt. Shall I make you a nice drop of whisky in hot water? Bit of sugar in too?'

'Nay, I'm fine.'

'Or I could put another blanket on the bed – there's a spare one in the drawer.'

Irritation prickled in him. It was typical of her, spoiling his beautiful thoughts with prosaic words. 'Don't fuss, Fanny,' he muttered. 'You get back to sleep.'

Within minutes she was snoring again. Harold returned to his fanciful idyll. Some day, somehow, he had to contrive a way to get to know more about Cassie Turnbull. Maybe if he were to follow her, unobtrusively, of course, and find out where she worked, where she went in her spare time, who her friends were . . . He had to do something. He needed more information for his imagination to feed upon. One brief hour in chapel on Sunday morning was not enough, and next Sunday was still four days away.

It was Friday night again. Ada put the flat iron down on the hearth and went out to lift the big tin bath off the hook in the back yard, then carried it in and placed it in front of the fire. There was plenty of soapy water still hot in the sett pot for the girls to have their weekly bath, and more in the range to top up when May took hers last.

Time was, she thought as she ladled the water in for Elsie, when the bath used to come in every night for Jim when he got home from the pit. He'd strip off his coal-dust-covered clothes and step in, lowering his lithe, muscular body gingerly into the steaming water.

'By heck, it's hot, lass,' he used to say.

'The way you like it, love. Give us the cloth and I'll scrub your back for you.'

She used to savour those moments alone together, rubbing the dirt away vigorously yet with tenderness. He would smile up at her, and all was right with her world.

But that was in another time, long ago. Ada ran the flannel over Elsie's thin little body, soaped the back of her ears and heard her squeal.

'You're wetting my hair!'

'What if I am? It hasn't been washed this fortnight and we don't want it running alive with lice, do we, like you was that time your mucky friend Eunice was running alive with 'em?'

'She's not my friend, she's Cassie's. And she's not mucky.'

'She never stopped scratching, that's for sure. Where is Cassie, by the way? She's due for her bath now.'

Thin shoulders shrugged, gleaming wetly in the firelight. 'How should I know? She never tells me nowt.'

'Me neither. Come on out now, the towel's all nice and warm.'

*   *   *

Clutching her laden shopping basket tightly Nellie Bottomley hurried home along Cedar Street as fast as her legs would carry her. It wasn't easy when childhood rickets had left you with little legs bowed like a croquet hoop and hurrying made you walk with a stutter. The faster she travelled the more she swayed from side to side like that metronome thing Mr Draper, the music teacher, kept on top of his piano.

But dusk was closing in fast now; no-one would notice her. She couldn't get back home quick enough to tell Agnes the news.

Her sister was sitting in the window to catch the last of the fading light, painstakingly sewing a patch on her red flannel petticoat. She peered over the top of her spectacles as Nellie waddled in and slapped her shopping basket down on the table.

'Whatever's the matter?' she demanded sternly. 'And where have you been till this time?'

'I took me books back to the lending library,' Nellie explained eagerly, 'and you'll never guess who I saw.'

'The library's only a cockstride away,' retorted Agnes, pursing thin lips as she snipped the cotton thread. 'It doesn't take all this time.'

'No, listen,' said Nellie. 'I took a short cut down the back of the library—'

'Down that dark lane?' Agnes looked shocked. 'Whatever for?'

'Taking a short cut to that new cobbler's. And who do you think I saw? Mr Jordan, and he was talking to a young woman.'

'How much?'

Nellie frowned. 'How do you mean?'

'Your shoes – to have them mended.'

Nellie waved an impatient hand. 'I don't know – I didn't like to ask. Listen what I'm telling you – I saw Mr Jordan with this young lady.'

Agnes took off her spectacles. 'And what if he was? Young

folks have deaths in the family too – he were probably doing business.'

'Down a back lane, in the dark? Nay, never.'

Agnes laid her sewing aside, a flicker of interest now in her pale eyes. 'A young woman, eh? Have you any notion who she were?'

Nellie came round the table, her plump face alive with excitement. 'I couldn't be certain, mind you – I didn't have me glasses on – but I could almost swear it were that fair-headed lass of Turnbull's – you know, Cassie.'

'It shouldn't be more than a shilling,' said Agnes, rising stiffly from the chair. 'Ninepence, more likely.'

Nellie looked at her sister in bewilderment. 'What are you on about?'

'Them shoes. If they're any more than that you've been robbed.'

Ada was aware of the glow surrounding Cassie the minute she came home but she couldn't ask the reason while Jack Smedley was still there. Whenever he called to see Jim he always lingered over a cup of tea with her long after he came down from the bedroom. He meant well, she knew, but he seemed unaware that he was holding her up.

So her curiosity about Cassie had to wait until he finally pulled on his cloth cap and made for the door.

'And don't forget, Ada, if there's owt you want, owt I can do for you, any time, you've only to ask,' he said as he was leaving, one calloused hand on the door-jamb. 'It's a poor do if a chap can't look after a workmate who's had bad times.'

'Thanks, Jack. I'll bear it in mind. Good night to you now.'

Cassie wrinkled her nose as the door closed behind him and flicked the chair seat with a tea-towel. 'I do wish he wouldn't come here in his work muck,' she said icily. 'Wouldn't you think he'd have more sense? All that coal dirt on the furniture.'

Ada smiled. 'Since when have you been so house-proud? Any road, he means well. He's all right, is Jack.'

'I'm not so sure. I think he's got his eye on you, coming here that often. It's not me dad he wants to see.'

'Cassie!'

'Well, how long does he spend upstairs? And how long down here with you? I know I'm right. I'm not daft, even if you are.'

'That's enough,' said Ada sharply. 'You keep a civil tongue in your head or else.' She turned away to busy herself with the saucepan.

Cassie spread her hands and sat down at the table. 'I'm just warning you – he's up to no good. I know these things.'

'That's for me to decide. Anyhow,' said Ada in a quieter tone, 'what's been happening? I can tell there's summat.'

Cassie gave a broad smile. 'I'm leaving Whitfield's.'

The back door burst open and Elsie raced in. 'You know when I cut me knee last week, Mam? Well, the scab's come off.'

Her mother didn't look at her. 'You mean you've got the sack?'

'No I haven't,' protested Cassie. 'I've given me notice.'

'And it's bleeding,' said Elsie. 'Look.'

She held up a grubby knee. Ada ignored it. 'You mean you've just walked out – with no other job to go to? You're mad.'

'But I have another job,' said Cassie proudly. 'That's just it. I've got a position as maid up at Chadwick's house – him as owns the mill. And I'll get more money.'

'I see. And how did you come by this job?' asked Ada.

Cassie tossed her head proudly. 'Being in the right place at the right time. Mr Whitfield came in the factory and picked me out to go down the bank for some change. Mrs Chadwick were in the bank – I didn't know it were her – and she was complaining about how her maid was leaving and how hard it was to find good staff these days. I told her I was looking for a job.'

'You spoke to Mrs Chadwick, just like that?'

'Why not? She'd only to look at me to see I was bright and

clean. She asked me a few questions and said she'd give me a trial. I start two weeks on Monday.'

'I'm bleeding to death,' wailed Elsie, 'and nobody cares!'

Ada looked down at her. 'Go and wash the muck off,' she said curtly, 'and then I can have a proper look.'

By the time supper was over and Mrs Cooper had called to collect her washing, the tally man had collected his weekly sixpence and Elsie had been despatched to bed, it was growing late. May sat reading by the fire and Cassie was humming as she made up the sandwiches for her snap tin.

'You've not said you're glad for me, Mam,' she remarked. 'Our May is, aren't you?'

'If it's what you want,' murmured her sister without looking up from the book.

'Of course I am,' said Ada. 'I'm just wondering whether it's good for a lass to be living away from home at your age.'

'I'm sixteen, old enough to be wed.'

'Old enough, aye, but wise enough, that's another matter.'

'Wiser than you give me credit for. I know what Jack Smedley's up to even if you don't.'

Ada glanced sharply towards her elder daughter. May appeared to be engrossed in her book. 'Right, if your snap's done, off to bed with you now, Cass. Just ask your dad if there's owt he wants.'

When Cassie had gone May laid her book aside. 'Will you miss Cassie, Mam?' she asked quietly. 'Would you miss me?'

'You?' echoed Ada. 'Why, you're not thinking of packing up Rose's, are you?'

'No, of course not. I just wondered.'

Ada watched her rise, stretch, and gather up her book. That girl was a real puzzle and no mistake. So much went on inside that dark head. No-one ever knew all she was thinking.

Cassie was at the top of the stairs in her nightdress when May went up. 'I feel that excited I don't want to go to bed,' she whispered. 'Two more weeks and I'll never get that rotten glue on me hands again, just think of it!'

'I'm glad for you,' said May. 'I just hope it's what you want.'

'Of course it is – it's freedom, don't you see? Do what I want, when I want. No more Mam asking where I've been, who I've been with. Don't you wish you was going too?'

May smiled. 'You never know. I could be off too one day. You just take care of yourself, that's all.'

Cassie snorted. 'I can do that all right, you just see. There'll come a time I can take care of you and all.'

May squeezed her arm. 'You're all right, you are, even if you are a pain in the neck at times. Be happy, Cass.'

Cassie returned the squeeze. 'I am. I've got an admirer.'

'What? Who?'

The younger girl gave a mischievous smile. 'Can't tell you – he's never actually said anything but he follows me everywhere. He doesn't think I know, but I do. I could twist him round my little finger if I wanted.'

May's face showed her concern. 'Oh love, be careful. It doesn't do to fool around with people's feelings. It's dangerous.'

Cassie patted her arm and turned away to the bedroom door. 'Don't you worry, love. I know what I'm doing. No-one will get hurt.'

May lay in bed staring at the light of the street lamp on the ceiling. She was happy for Cassie – she'd been longing to get out of Whitfield's since the day she started there – but like Mam she worried whether the girl was mature enough to cope without a guiding hand. Still, the Chadwicks would be sure to keep an eye on her. They wouldn't let her stay out late, nor would they encourage admirers around the premises.

For herself, though, she was not quite so happy. Weeks had gone by now since she came back from Thornleigh Hall and still Aaron had made no plans to meet again. True, he darted her secret smiles whenever he came into the workroom, smiles

97

of which only she could read the meaning, but she hungered for more.

Only once in all this time had he actually spoken to her, and then only when he came across her by chance in the stock room. He'd looked surprised, glanced behind him and laid a warning finger to his lips, then asked aloud how many reels of red cotton were still in stock since they had to be certain there were plenty for the new big order from the George Hotel.

She'd told him, he'd smiled and said, 'Thank you,' and left. That was nearly two weeks ago. How much longer would it be before he found the opportunity for them to meet? He must be growing as anxious as she was by now, so surely it couldn't be long . . .

No matter what, she mustn't allow splinters of suspicion to start to fester in her mind.

Fanny Jordan looked out of the bedroom window on the wet, cobbled street below. Harold was still out. He'd taken to having his evening stroll later and later these days. She wished he'd come back by their usual bedtime.

There was a rumbling sound on the far side – a stringy old man was pushing a handcart along the pavement, and Fanny could see legs protruding from it. Under the lamp he paused and tilted the cart, and a stumbling figure lurched against the door of the house opposite. It was the Irishman, coming home drunk again.

'You're home now, Tim,' the old man said, turning his cart about. 'You all right?'

'Ah, I'm grand altogether,' she heard the big man rumble. 'Good night to ye.'

He'd gone indoors before a movement in the gutter caught her eye and she strained to see, in the gloom, something small and shadowy. Rats again, scavenging after the rubbish? The thought made her shudder. She must talk to Harold about getting a cat, a good mouser. It was the least he could do if they had to live in this awful street infested with rats and drunks . . .

The shadow moved again, into the arc of light from the street lamp. It was a child, the little boy from the Irish house. He was scrabbling in the gutter, picking up something and putting it in his mouth. Poor little mite, he must be cold and wet, and fancy having to eat rubbish from the gutter! For two pins she'd bring the little fellow in and give him a bowl of soup left over from supper and a bit of bread, but how could she? It would be an insult to his mother, that poor beaten-down little thing who looked as if she was having another.

It hurt to think of that couple over there, breeding children like it was easy and then not taking care of them. Now if that little boy had been hers . . .

A distant clock struck eleven. Fanny turned away from the window. If only Harold would come home. It was a desperately lonely life here in Cedar Street.

TEN

No matter what she did, Miss Openshaw could not bring herself to like Oscar. In fact, to be truthful, she hated the damned animal. Only cats had that baleful, accusing way of glaring at you as if you continually failed them, just the way Mother used to do. He'd probably learnt it from her – after all, he was Mother's cat, Miss Openshaw's only by inheritance. And for the last two years since Mother died she'd felt those malevolent eyes on her back and begrudged every saucerful she put down for him.

He was an ugly animal into the bargain, with his black fur all spiky and matted from scratting around in the field behind the workhouse, one ear tattered as a result of losing one of his many fights in his youthful days. Nowadays he spent most of his time by the fire, watching and waiting for the next meal.

Even now, on a bright September Sunday afternoon when any self-respecting cat should be out luxuriating in the sun, he squatted, sphinx-like, on the hearthrug watching her with unblinking eyes. Damn you, she thought savagely, why should I let an ugly brute like you ruin my one day off? Suddenly she could stand it no longer. Pinning her hat on her head she set off to walk in Beaumont Park, anywhere away from those reproachful yellow eyes.

It was beautiful under the trees. A slight breeze sent crackling leaves swirling about her feet and strolling along under the canopy of bronze and gold she felt peace beginning to steal over her. It was good to be out of the house, not only because of Oscar but because the whole place seemed saturated in Mother. Her dominating presence still permeated the place, exuding like a miasma from her furniture, her knick-knacks and pictures and ornaments. Nothing of Miss Openshaw's stamped her personality on the house.

She hadn't had the heart to change anything. The little house was like a shrine to Mother's personality still. It was as though she could still feel Mother's steely eyes on her, forbidding her to change a thing, monitoring and dictating her daughter's life the way she did when she was alive. Miss Openshaw felt as much a prisoner in the place now as she always had, servicing it, cleaning and maintaining it out of her own limited purse, and it rankled.

A couple of small boys shrieked happily as they bowled a hoop across the grass. Under the trees a gentleman sat on a bench, listening to the lady beside him in a Bath chair. She wasn't old, thought Miss Openshaw – in her fifties, like herself, and the gentleman by her side was probably her husband. He was looking at her with gentle concern as he tucked a rug over her knees. How wonderful it must be, thought Miss Openshaw, to be cherished like that.

She couldn't help the surge of loneliness which swept over her. For her there was no-one, no-one who would be distressed if anything happened to her. How tragic to leave this world unnoticed, unmourned . . .

She thrust the fleeting self-pity aside. It was a weak, self-centred thought, unworthy of her. She was recognized as a strong and capable woman, wasn't she? Then anger swept in, washing away the sadness: if it hadn't been for Mother's unwanted intrusion there would have been someone, long ago. Mother just refused to hear of it.

'A stonemason? Whatever are you thinking of, Grace? And he lives down that dreadful street near the gasworks? We'd never be able to look folks in the face again. He's not to come courting round here, you tell him. He can find a lass of his own sort.'

Miss Openshaw clenched her gloved fists as she recalled the words. 'Damn you, Mother,' she muttered under her breath, 'my life's my own now, and the house is mine too and I'll do with it as I please – sell it, even, if I feel like it! I don't have to bow to your decisions any more!'

Yes, she thought defiantly, why not? Sell up and move to the seaside as soon as she retired. It would be something to look forward to. Or the country. They said Harrogate was nice.

'Good afternoon. Lovely day for a stroll.'

The quietly-spoken words startled her and Miss Openshaw looked around sharply. A man was just about to overtake her on the gravel path, and she recognized Mr Harris, the gentleman who always caught the same tram as herself every morning, the owner of the draper's shop in King Street. She flushed with pleasure as he raised his hat the way he always did at the tram stop. He'd never actually spoken to her before.

'Good afternoon. Yes, it's beautiful for the time of year.'

He fell into step beside her, shortening his stride to match hers. 'It's good to feel the sun on your back,' he remarked genially. 'Makes a pleasant change from weekdays in a dusty office, doesn't it?'

'Ah, well, I don't actually work in an office,' she admitted shyly. 'I'm the overseer in Rose's workroom.'

'Are you now?' His dark eyebrows rose in surprise. 'My old friend Henry's place? We've done a deal of business together over the years, Henry and I. And to think that for all this time I took you for a lady who ran an office of some kind. Do you live near the park?'

'Just over there, in Minerva Street.'

She pointed back towards the house. Mr Harris glanced back. 'With your family?' he asked.

She looked away. 'On my own, I'm afraid, since my mother died.'

'I'm sorry. My wife died two years ago. I know how you must be feeling.'

You don't, she thought privately. You wouldn't think me a lady if you knew.

'I found it worse when my daughter married a clergy-man last spring,' Mr Harris went on, 'and went to live in

Kirkburton. The house felt very lonely after she'd gone. So I like to get out where I can see people.'

'How odd, I hate staying indoors too,' said Miss Openshaw. 'The house gets to feel so oppressive.'

She wondered whether she'd made a mistake in being so frank to a stranger. But he wasn't really a stranger, not when she'd seen him every morning for the best part of twenty years.

He looked down at her with a slow smile. 'Then perhaps we could take a turn around the park together. May I know your name?'

'Grace Openshaw,' she said shyly. She hardly ever had cause to use her first name these days.

'Grace,' he repeated thoughtfully, and the word sounded beautiful on his tongue. Whenever Mother spoke it, it had always sounded like a reproach. 'What an appropriate name for a lady of such grace,' he murmured. 'My name is Edward Harris. Will you take my arm?'

And for the first time since she had walked out with Thaddeus as a young girl, Miss Openshaw slipped her hand through a gentleman's arm.

All too soon they'd walked the full circuit of the park and reached the gate again. Miss Openshaw stopped and withdrew her hand.

'I've enjoyed our little walk,' she said diffidently. 'But I'm afraid I must go home now. I've lots to do. Goodbye, and thank you very much.'

She held out her hand. He took it and held it for a moment. 'Perhaps I could look forward to meeting you here again next Sunday if the weather is fine?' he said gravely. 'I'd very much like to.'

She nodded, feeling her cheeks redden with pleasure. 'I'd like that too,' she said hesitantly, shocked at her own forthrightness. Maybe it wasn't ladylike, but it was true.

When she reached home again, Grace Openshaw felt strangely heady and there was a curious fluttering in her chest. She peeled off her gloves, finger by finger, and fancied they were still warm from his touch. She wondered if Mr Harris had noticed as he held her hand that the gloves were the finest leather from his own shop.

She was still quivering slightly as she draped her Sunday coat carefully over the hanger and gave it a brush-down. Oscar rose from the hearthrug, stretched, and sidled towards her, rubbing his arched back against her ankles.

'Now don't go trying to soft-soap me, you ugly old thing,' she murmured. 'You know as well as I do it's only cupboard love.'

Even so, she bent and gently stroked his matted head.

Despite herself, Ada found she was relishing the quiet about the house since Cassie had gone. And at least she was spared her acid comments about how often Jack Smedley had taken to calling in after work.

'I were telling your Jim just now, they've sentenced that Crippen fellow to death,' he told Ada in the warmth of the kitchen.

'So they ought, murdering his wife like that.'

'Huh. Some wives seem to ask for it,' Jack muttered.

Ada cast him a quizzical glance. Was he having trouble with Brenda again? Years ago Jim used to tell her the latest episode in the fiery romance between the two, how they quarrelled and made up, breaking off and starting over again until no-one believed they'd ever marry. After all these years their relationship still seemed like a volcano, liable to erupt again at any moment.

She refilled Jack's cup. 'You haven't been squabbling again, you and Brenda, have you?' she asked. 'Beats me why one of you doesn't run off with somebody else.'

'That's just it,' she heard him mumble. 'She has. Taken the kids with her.'

Ada sat down suddenly. 'Oh no! Who with?'

He shook his head mournfully. 'You don't know him. Fellow who works up at Sykes's.'

Compassion filled Ada. He looked so lost, so helpless. 'I'm sorry, Jack,' she said softly. 'I really am.'

He gave a rueful smile. 'I knew you'd understand. I've told nobody.'

'I won't tell a soul, I promise. But how will you manage?'

He shrugged. 'Same as I have done this past fortnight. Soldier on, that's all I can do.'

Ada searched for words of comfort. 'Happen she'll come back sooner or later. The grass on the other side always looks greener but she'll find out.'

He stood up slowly, reaching for his cap. 'Not this time, she won't. She's threatened before, and this time she's done it. Brenda's not a lass to go back on her word.'

Ada stood up. He mustn't give in without a fight. 'Can't you go and tackle this fellow?' she said firmly. 'Teach him a lesson, make him give her up?'

'What's the use if she doesn't want me? Nay, it's too late, Ada lass. I've got to make a life of me own now somehow.'

In the doorway he turned. 'You won't tell Jim, will you? He's enough on without my worries.'

'Not a word,' said Ada. 'You can trust me.'

He eyed her thoughtfully for a moment, then pulled on his cap. 'I wish I'd had Jim's sense. He knew what he were doing when he wed you. You're a good 'un, Ada, and no mistake.'

'Go on with you,' she said lightly. 'You could turn a woman's head with flattery like that. Be off with you now before our May gets home for her tea.'

November clung heavily around the slate roofs as May turned into Cedar Street, and in the lamplight she could see a damp mist swirling slowly as it mingled with the smoke and soot drifting down from the viaduct. Droplets of mist oozed darkly down the grimy glass of the street lamps, and the sulphurous smell of the gasworks choked in her throat.

A scrawny dog ambled ahead of her down the street. In the lamplight she could see Mrs Tandy sitting with her bottom out on the ground-floor window-ledge, busily trying to clean the panes.

'Don't know why I'm bothering,' Mrs Tandy said cheerfully as May passed. 'Only it'll be the last time now until spring seeing as winter's setting in.'

May gave a faint smile. Window-cleaning seemed a trivial matter compared to the anxieties on her mind. Nearly three months now and still Aaron had made no move. Whether she liked it or not, she had to admit to herself that as far as he was concerned, she'd been only a passing fancy, but recognizing it hurt like hell.

Where now the fanciful dreams of becoming mistress of his home? She'd been a stupid, gullible girl even to believe it might have been, even more stupid to think he could have loved her.

Face it, my girl, you were a momentary plaything, nothing more. You'd heard the rumours about him at Rose's, you should have guessed. You've only yourself to blame.

But being made a fool of was only the start. Another anxiety was now beginning to take its place . . .

'I hate winter,' said Elsie crossly, chin cupped in hands as she sat at the table after tea. 'You won't let me play out in the dark – I haven't seen Dominic for ages. There's nothing for me to do.'

'There's plenty to do,' said her mother. 'Grate some of that dry soap for me.'

'Cassie used to talk to me,' Elsie went on, 'but May never does with her head stuck in a book. Everybody stays indoors – even the old Misses Bottomley don't sit out on the step now like they used to. Everybody's vanished. I'm bored.'

'Why don't you make a dolly with one of Mam's pegs?' suggested May absently. 'Dress it up with some of her scraps.'

'I've got five in the cupboard already,' retorted Elsie. 'Just think, all along the street people are stuck indoors, bored stiff 'cos it's winter. It's like a row of doll's houses – wouldn't it be funny if you could lift the roofs off and see all the people inside, see what they're all doing?'

Her mother sniffed. 'I reckon it's a good job you can't.'

'Why not?' asked Elsie.

'Soap,' repeated her mother. 'The grater's in the drawer. I've to take this bundle round to Fountain Street and I'll expect it grated by the time I get back.'

Ada gave her eldest daughter a glance as she pulled on her coat. She wouldn't ask May to take the washing round – the girl looked paler today than usual. She never talked much, never complained, so it was hard to guess what was troubling her. Maybe they were overworking the lass at Rose's. Whatever it was, she wasn't eating much and was getting to look decidedly peaky. Maybe after Elsie had gone to bed she could try and find out what was bothering her, but Ada didn't hold out much hope. It had always been May's way to keep her thoughts to herself and she wasn't likely to change now.

Grace Openshaw looked out of her bedroom window, out over the darkened street. A drizzling mist lay over the cobblestones as it had done for days. It was no longer fit for a walk in the park, and she felt sad.

She'd learnt so much about Edward Harris during those walks, about his beloved wife Elspeth who'd died and his son who lived in Dewsbury. She'd learnt how his daughter broke off her engagement to a well-to-do mill owner in order to marry the curate she loved, and how happy she was with him in Kirkburton.

And despite her normal reticence she found herself telling him about Mother, in strong, vituperative words which surprised even her. He'd listened without attempting to judge, and it had afforded her relief to be able to get it off her chest. She looked forward to Sundays, to walking and talking with him, to feel at last she could speak her mind without fear of rebuke. It made her feel whole, a woman in her own right instead of Mother's shadow.

She'd found herself doing things she'd never done before;

sewing a bit of Nottingham lace from work on her Sunday bloomers and on the hem of her best cotton petticoat. No-one would ever see, but it made her feel feminine and dainty, and just a teeny bit racy.

Then that day it came on suddenly to rain he'd asked her in to have a cup of tea and shelter with him until the rain stopped. He'd even lent her his umbrella . . .

She'd have to invite him back to tea one day, if only out of politeness after he'd entertained her so charmingly. But that parlour, still reeking of Mother's taste – those cushion covers would have to go. There were some lovely remnants of satin brocade at work left over from the George Hotel job.

But something would have to be done about Oscar. She'd already made a start. The first time she took Mother's hairbrush to him he started violently and scratched her wrist, but after a while he hadn't objected too much. His black coat was beginning at last to show some sign of gloss. She'd battle on with the tangles in his fur until he began to look halfway decent, something like a cat ought to look. And when that day came she'd pluck up courage to smile at Edward at the tram stop and ask casually if he'd care to come to tea . . .

May left Elsie grating soap in the kitchen and grumbling to herself about her scraped knuckles while she went upstairs to fetch down Dad's supper pots. He watched her from the bed.

'Quiet now our Cassie's gone,' he remarked.

'Yes,' she agreed.

'I miss the lass. I hope she's all right.'

'You know she is. She was home the other Sunday.'

'Aye,' he muttered, 'but she'd no time to talk. Not to me, any road. I hope she's not making a fool of herself.'

'She'll be fine, don't you fret.'

He shifted slightly, groaning. 'She'll not come back, you know, not now she's in Edgerton. She wants no more of Cedar Street. She's out of it now. It'll be you next.'

She gave a weary smile. 'I don't think so, Dad, not me.'

'Happen,' he grunted. 'All this talk about female

emancipation, it only unsettles women. Jack tells me they've arrested more than a hundred of them Suffragettes for attacking the House of Commons. Whatever next, I wonder?'

May felt a rush of concern. Jack must have told him his wife had left him after all. Dad felt vulnerable, helpless. 'I'm here, Dad,' she murmured softly. 'I'll always be here, and so will Mam.'

Later that night May sat miserably on the edge of her bed. She'd always be here all right, she thought, now that Aaron had clearly forgotten her existence. She'd be here till she was an old maid.

That's if they'd have her here still. If what she was beginning to suspect was true, even those who loved her might well want to cast her out of their lives. The prospect was terrifying.

But it was no use trying to duck the issue any longer. Somehow she had to contrive to see the doctor – not Dr Evans who knew the family well – it would have to be a stranger . . .

ELEVEN

Harold Jordan was distraught. He hadn't seen his Venus for weeks now. All those freezing nights in the back lane and not once had she appeared at the bedroom window, not even a light. Nor had she turned up to Sunday morning service at chapel. The other two sisters were there, but not Cassie. If only he had the courage – or indeed the opportunity, with Fanny always at his side – to enquire of the dark-haired Turnbull girl how her sister was.

Desperation was gnawing at his brain like a famished rat. Was she ill? Had she gone away? Left Hawksmoor, even? The thought filled him with despair.

He could still hear the honey tones of her voice, the one time he'd ever spoken to her. It had been pure good luck that he'd walked along the lane behind the lending library that night. He'd been so startled at the unexpected sight of her that he'd dropped his glove and she'd bent and picked it up for him.

'Thank you,' he'd managed to stutter.

'Don't mention it. My pleasure,' she'd replied with a dimpling smile.

They'd exchanged a few words, he hardly remembered what, but he'd soaked in the sheer beauty of her, drawing it in deep like a sponge, to squeeze out and enjoy, drop by drop, later when he was alone. That meeting had been the high-point of his life, but it wasn't enough; he yearned for so much more.

'Harold, are you listening to me? I'm trying to arrange about Christmas.'

Fanny's querulous voice jangled into his thoughts. He

clicked his tongue in irritation. 'Don't bother me, woman –
that's your department,' he snapped.

Fanny stared at him in shocked surprise. 'I only asked if
you wanted me to drop a line to Beatrice, arrange for us to
go over and see her on Boxing Day. We usually do.'

'No, I don't,' said Harold shortly.

'She'll be expecting us.'

'Let her expect,' Harold snapped. 'My sister has no more
time for me than I have for her.'

Fanny shook her head sadly as she put her writing pad away
with the blotting paper. 'Whatever's got into you, love?' she
murmured. 'You've been that snappy lately – anyone would
think that things were going badly with you. You've almost
cleared your debts.'

Harold gave an impatient sigh. 'I've more to think about
than that. Just you see to what you have to and leave me be.'

She rose to leave, and as she passed his chair she tapped
him playfully on the shoulder with her pen. 'Dearie me, we
are a crosspatch, aren't we?' she said brightly. 'If I didn't
know you better I'd think you had a guilty conscience about
something. Oh!' Her fingers flew to her lips. 'I'm sorry, love
– I didn't mean that other business, I just didn't think.'

He wasn't listening to her prattle. Already his mind had
raced off again in search of Cassie. Nothing else concerned
him these days. Even major events in the world outside passed
him by. He'd vaguely taken in that the General Election had
resulted in a deadheat between the Liberals and the Tories,
but what did it matter if Asquith was still Prime Minister?

Nothing mattered but her. He had to find her again.

Jack Smedley wasn't alone when he called a few days
before Christmas. Ada could see the tension on their blackened faces as she stood back to let him and Charlie Andrews
into the house.

'What is it?' she asked. 'What's up?'

'You've not heard about West Houghton then?' asked Jack.
'About the explosion?'

111

'Oh no – when?'

'Last night. They reckon there's two hundred and fifty dead. Worst pit disaster in years.'

'Oh my God! The poor souls! Isn't there a chance they can still get to them, see if there's any survived?'

Charlie shook his head as he pulled off his cap. 'No chance, seemingly. There's only one lad they've rescued alive. He reckons as somebody struck a match below ground.'

She knew it happened, despite orders. Jim had often told her how some of them couldn't wait for the end of the shift to have a smoke. He'd had nightmares from time to time about explosions.

'You're not going to tell him,' she muttered as the men headed for the stairs. 'He's enough on as it is without fretting about summat he can't do nowt to help.'

'Nay,' said Charlie. 'Wouldn't dream of it.'

'There's some as would,' retorted Ada, glaring at Jack. 'Pity some folks just can't keep their troubles to theirselves.'

Life was ironic, thought May bitterly as she tramped home from the doctor's surgery on the far side of town. Not so long ago she'd been hugging a secret to herself, a secret which filled her with joy until she realized she'd been duped. Now she had another secret to conceal, an appalling dilemma which threatened to overwhelm her.

And the worst of it was, she had no-one to whom she could confide the awful news. She couldn't just go home and say, 'Mam, I'm pregnant.' Mam's whole world would collapse. She had enough problems on her plate without this. She couldn't spring this shock on her, on Christmas Eve of all days.

She'd said as much to the doctor. He hadn't been taken in by the young Mrs Smith. He was a kindly man, his keen blue eyes assessing her shrewdly over his spectacles as she made up a tale about being on her own, her husband away from home for some time on business. As she made to leave he'd touched her arm.

'I'd tell your mother if I were you, my dear,' he'd said mildly. 'I'm sure she'll see you right.'

'Beg your pardon?'

A gentle smile. 'You'd be surprised how many Mrs Smiths come through that door. I tell them all the same – trust your own folk. Once they've got over the shock they won't want to see you come to any harm. They'll help you arrange an adoption or some such solution. Trust them.'

Easier said than done, thought May, and she felt she could kick herself for her own stupidity. Of all the people in the world, the last one she wanted to hurt was Mam. And Dad too – how would he take it? He'd always believed her to be the trustworthy one, the one least likely to do anything silly. Now if it had been Cassie . . .

Cassie. She was coming home tonight to spend Christmas with the family. Surely if anyone could understand, it would be her.

Cassie swept in like a whirlwind, clutching an armful of parcels.

'No-one's to look until morning,' she pronounced proudly. 'Get your hands off, Elsie.'

'I'm only feeling.'

'You'll feel the back of my hand if you don't do as you're told. Why aren't you in bed?'

'She's all right,' said Ada. 'She'll not sleep if she goes to bed. Let me have a look at you.'

She turned her daughter about to face the lamplight. 'My, but you're looking grand,' she murmured. 'You're filling out into a real bonny woman.'

'Like me frock?' asked Cassie, twirling around to show off the dark green worsted. 'Mrs Chadwick said Miss Cecily won't wear it no more.'

'It's lovely,' said Ada, touching the fine cloth reverently.

'You look like a proper lady,' said Elsie. 'Can I just have one little feel?'

Cassie turned to her older sister. 'Like it, May? Happen I

113

could get one for you if you like. Miss Cecily's that faddy over her clothes.'

May smiled. Cassie dropped on her knees in front of her. 'Hey, what's up with you? You look terrible,' she said. 'Thin as if you'd just come out of the workhouse.'

'I'm tired, that's all,' said May.

'Been working too hard to eat properly,' said her mother. 'Good dinner of capon tomorrow and you'll be right as rain.'

Elsie squatted on the rug, her nose to the pile of parcels on the hearth. 'Can we open us presents before we go to chapel – please?'

Cassie stuck her hands on her hips. 'Now if someone was to go to bed now without grumbling and never a muff out of them till seven o'clock tomorrow morning—'

Elsie was already halfway up the stairs.

Grace Openshaw had fretted for days whether it would be seemly to send Edward Harris a Christmas card, and had finally decided against it. The last thing in the world she wanted when they'd been getting on so well was for him to think of her as forward.

So on Christmas morning she was startled to find a small packet on the doormat. Her fingers trembled as she read the message.

'My dear Grace, May I wish you the happiest Christmas ever now that you are freed from the past. Spring is not far away, and I look forward to our continued walks in the park. In the meantime, I enclose a little memento of me. Sincerely yours, Edward.'

Inside a folded sheet of tissue lay a lace-edged handkerchief of finest linen, embroidered on one corner with forget-me-nots. So he hadn't forgotten her. She smiled happily as she laid it to her cheek.

But what could she give him in return? Perplexed, Grace bit her lip. There was nothing in the house to suit a man's taste. Then suddenly an idea came to her. That batch of mince pies she'd baked last night – this was the opportunity she'd been looking for.

Carefully she wrapped one mince pie and enclosed a brief note.

> *'Dear Edward, If you like the taste, why not call round for tea this afternoon at four and sample a few more? Yours, Grace.'*

Then, quivering with anticipation, she hurried round to his house, placed the package down on his doorstep and rang the bell. By the time he opened the door she'd already hastened away out of sight in the direction of Minerva Street.

Even if Fanny was thick with cold and preferred to stay in bed, Harold was determined not to miss the Christmas morning service. It wouldn't be Christmas without a carol or two, and though he'd just about given up hope of seeing his angel again, you never knew . . .

And suddenly there she was! He could scarcely believe his eyes, and put his spectacles on to make certain. Yes, it was Cassie! God must have listened to his prayers after all! She looked even more beautiful than he remembered, as sleek and groomed as a well-fed cat. He was so overjoyed that he put a whole half-sovereign on the collection plate in place of his usual shilling.

And this time he wasn't going to waste such a God-given opportunity. His heart lumbered around uncomfortably in his chest as he waited, hat in hand, outside the door for her to emerge.

'Good morning, Cassie. Happy Christmas.'

A sudden smile lit up her face. 'Oh hello, Mr Jordan. And a very happy Christmas to you too.'

She paused beside him and her sisters walked on towards the gate. He plucked up his courage to ask what he wanted to know.

'I haven't seen you around for ages,' he remarked, as casually as he could. 'I thought perhaps you'd left Hawksmoor.'

'Oh no. I got a new position in Edgerton, that's all. Living in.' Then she added shyly, 'I get most evenings and some Sundays off, of course.'

His heart quickened. Was this meant to be some kind of encouragement? Oh no, the girl was too naïve, too innocent. 'What do you do then?' he asked. 'Do you go out much?'

She shook her head, the fair hair rippling in the light, and turned to walk towards the gate. 'Not much. It's not safe for a woman alone at night. Such a pity.'

He hurried after her. 'Surely you've no need to be on your own – aren't you walking out with anybody?'

She looked up at him under her lashes, and his heart turned somersaults. 'Good Lord no!' she said softly. 'There's no-one there who'd suit me.'

They were nearing the cluster of people at the gate now, and he could see the dark-haired sister holding the hand of the little one. He had to find out more before it was too late.

'Where?' he asked. 'Where is it you work?'

'Mr Chadwick's,' she said with pride. 'It's a very good position and a lovely place to work. I'll be going back tomorrow.'

Chadwick. One of the officers on that Committee. Harold bit his lip. At Chadwick's she'd be beyond his reach, but at least he knew now she was only in Edgerton. And for tonight she'd be in Cedar Street.

'Merry Christmas, Mr Jordan,' said young Elsie chirpily. 'Where's Mrs Jordan?'

'She's poorly,' he replied abruptly. 'You young ladies all off home to roast duck now, eh?'

'I can't wait,' said Cassie with a smile. 'I'm hungry.'

Grace Openshaw watched Edward's face as they sat together in the firelight after tea. She sat on the sofa, and Oscar who had drawn the line at the red ribbon she'd tried to fasten round his neck before Edward arrived, had done his best to make up for it. He now lay obligingly beside her, his head against her thigh, looking for all the world like a normal, affectionate family cat.

A gentle smile curved the corners of Edward's lips as he lay back in Mother's fireside chair looking so much at home she could have wept with pleasure.

He patted his stomach. 'That was wonderful, Grace. Delicious hot mince pies smothered in cream – I can't think how long it is since I've been spoiled like that.'

'You deserve a bit of spoiling,' she murmured. 'We all need a bit of that from time to time.'

He turned his head to look at her thoughtfully. 'You've not had much of that, have you, Grace? It's a shame, when you're such a sensitive, caring woman. Your mother was luckier than she realized – or deserved.'

'Thank you, Edward.'

'And it's so cosy here,' he went on, laying his head back and closing his eyes.

She felt a flush of embarrassment. Minerva Street wasn't a patch on his lovely home. 'It's nothing much,' she said, spreading her hands, 'just a modest little house but I've lived here all my life. I was thinking of selling up and moving away – after I retire, that is.'

His eyes still closed, he shook his head. 'I wouldn't plan anything in a hurry if I were you. You've created a lovely, homely feeling here, and anyway, I'd hate to see you go. I feel so content right now I could stay here all day.'

Grace could feel herself glowing and blooming suddenly into life like a Christmas rose. As far as she was concerned he could stay here for ever.

Fanny Jordan stared at her husband with red, reproachful eyes. 'You're surely not off out tonight, love – it's freezing.'

She winced to hear the irritability in his tone. 'I always go for me evening stroll every night, weather or not, you know that. I can't sleep right if I don't.'

117

'But you'll catch your death out there – the frost's as white as snow on them cobblestones. You'd be far better off staying indoors in the warm if you don't want to end up thick with cold like me.'

She sneezed again to prove her point. Harold was already pulling on his muffler. 'I'll not be long,' he said gruffly. 'A man needs his daily constitutional to keep regular.'

She sniffed as she heard the front door bang behind him. Regular, indeed, she thought bitterly. That had more to do with the weekly dose of senna pods she put in his tea than walking around the scruffy streets of Millsbridge. Mother hadn't told her much about what marriage entailed, but the senna pods was one tip Fanny had never forgotten. And Harold had never suspected.

But there was more to it than that. He'd been funny for weeks now. Something was preying on his mind for him to act so secretive. And after thirty years of trustful marriage she had a miserable, sinking feeling that it had something to do with a woman . . .

Cassie sat on the edge of her bed, peeling off her stockings. May stood watching her by the door.

'Come on,' said Cassie, patting the bedspread beside her, 'sit down and talk to me. I can tell summat's up.'

May sat down obediently. 'You're right,' she said quietly, 'there is something. I haven't told a soul – specially Mum. She'd be that upset.'

Cassie shook her head. 'She knows there's summat and all. I've seen the way she's been watching you like a hawk. What is it?'

'Promise you won't tell?'

'Course not. Hey—' Cassie gave her a sharp look. 'You can't be up the creek, can you? Not you?'

May hung her head and nodded silently. Cassie stared, aghast, for a moment, then burst into gales of laughter. 'I don't believe it, not you! Not the pure, innocent little May! How the devil did you manage it?'

Then seeing her sister's miserable face she stopped laughing. 'I'm sorry. I just find it hard to believe. What the hell are you going to do? You'll have to tell Mam for a start.'

'No, I can't. It'd kill her. I've got to handle this on my own.'

'How are you going to do that, for God's sake? It'll be clear to all the world before long. When's it due?'

'Six months, the doctor said. June. Oh Cass, what shall I do?'

Cassie thought for a moment. 'Can't you marry the lad? Who is he?'

'I'm not telling.'

'Why? Won't he have you?'

'I don't want to marry him. That's out of the question.'

'I see. Well, you could get rid of it. Eunice knows a woman down Archer Street—'

'No,' May cut in hastily. 'Not that. I won't have that.'

Cassie sighed. 'Seems to me you can't afford to be so choosy, lass. Either marry him or get rid of it. What else is there?'

May tilted her chin. 'I could go away and have it – no-one need know, not even Mam and Dad.'

'Don't be daft,' said Cassie with a curl of the lip. 'Go where? You'll have no job, no money. Seems to me you either marry the lad or take a chance on the old woman with her knitting needle.'

'What would you do, Cass?'

Cassie shrugged. 'Make sure in the first place that the fellow who bedded me would marry me and keep me comfortable, that's what, but it's no use telling you that now.'

Seeing her sister's stricken face, she laid a hand on May's shoulder. 'I'd tell Mam,' she said quietly. 'She's good at sorting things out.'

'No,' said May firmly, rising from the bed and crossing to look out of the window. 'That's the last thing I want to do.'

Cassie gave a deep sigh and spread her hands. 'Then at

least go and tell the father – he ought to help you – he's got to shoulder his share of the responsibility.'

'I suppose he should,' May murmured.

Cassie came across and put her arm around her shoulders. 'Of course he should. He's had his fun – let him pay for it.'

'Oh my God!' gasped May. 'Look – there's a man looking at us over the back-yard wall!'

Cassie peered down into the darkness. 'Oh him,' she murmured. 'Take no notice. He'll go away now when I draw the curtains.'

May stared at her as she drew the curtains closed. 'I couldn't see his face,' she said hoarsely. 'It was hidden under the shadow of his hat.'

'He's often been there before,' said Cassie demurely. 'He's my admirer, the one I told you about.'

'You know who he is then?'

Cassie cocked her head to one side. 'Want to swap secrets? I'll tell you who my admirer is if you tell me who's the father of your baby. Is it a deal?'

May's lips hardened into a thin smile. 'No deal, Cass. I'll never tell anyone that.'

TWELVE

On Boxing Day afternoon Harold sat stiffly on one of the uncomfortably smart chairs in his sister's dining room. Beatrice had gone upstairs with Fanny to 'freshen up', as they put it, and now just he and Maurice were left at the table.

He stared miserably at the remains of the chocolate cake in the middle of the white damask tablecloth. He didn't want to be here, and if it wasn't for Fanny's determination to stick to tradition he wouldn't be here. The air between him and his sister was just as cool today as it had been ever since Mother died. Nothing had changed.

And there was no reason why it should. They had nothing in common any more. Beatrice would probably hate having to admit to any of her friends that she had a brother living in Millsbridge. It wouldn't do her vanity any good at all. And it certainly didn't help him to feel charitable towards her, seeing how well she lived.

Maurice opened a cigar box and pushed it towards him. Harold shook his head. 'No thanks.'

His brother-in-law selected one, cut off the tip and lit it slowly with a match. After a few puffs he cleared his throat.

'It isn't Beatrice's fault, you know,' he said with deliberation. 'You shouldn't hold it against her.'

'What isn't?' snapped Harold.

'The house – your mother leaving it to her instead of you. Beatrice had nothing to do with it.'

Harold's lips tightened. 'She promised it to me. It was in her will – she told me, many a time and oft.'

'Then she must have changed her mind near the end, but

it wasn't Beatrice's doing. I know you think she brought her influence to bear—'

'What other reason could there be?' snapped Harold. 'For years Mother said it was mine. It was a terrible shock to me.'

'And to her too. She didn't expect it to be left to her.'

Harold turned away, muttering to himself. 'Mother never told me, never a word.'

'She didn't tell Beatrice either. You've got to believe that, Harold.'

'It didn't stop you selling the place. You knew I was counting on that money.'

Maurice blew out a cloud of smoke and shook his head. 'Ah well, we should never count our chickens, should we? Bad business practice, that.'

'There, that wasn't so bad, was it?' said Fanny as they turned out of the gate and headed towards the tram stop. 'Duty done, at any rate.'

'That's the last time,' said Harold curtly. 'I can't abide hypocrisy.'

'Do you mean you or them?'

He clicked his tongue. 'I meant them – giving us tea and cake and all the time they can't stand the sight of us.'

'Oh, I think that's putting it a bit strong, love!'

'Can't you understand?' demanded Harold. 'We give them a pang of conscience every time they clap eyes on us. That's if they've got any conscience, which I doubt.'

Fanny held her tongue, hurrying to keep up with his moody stride. Just as they reached the stop she heard a distant rattle.

'Just timed that nicely,' she said amiably. 'Here's the tram.'

'About bloody time,' he muttered. 'I can't get away from here fast enough.'

Maureen Nagle lay as quiet as a mouse in the big double bed, trying desperately not to move or breathe too loudly. The last thing in the world she wanted was to wake Tim.

He'd been in a filthy mood for the last two days, and all

because he hadn't been able to afford to buy presents for the children.

'What do ye mean, Christmas present?' he'd roared at Dominic. 'Do ye think I'm made of money? Don't I feed ye and clothe ye? A man never has a penny left for himself with the lot of ye.'

So Dominic and the older children had had the sense to mention it no more. Indeed, in a mellower moment, with a jug of porter in his hand, Tim had patted baby Thomas's head and smiled fondly.

'Ah sure now, wouldn't I give my soul to be able to spoil ye all,' he slurred. 'Don't my lovely children mean the world to me? Don't ye know that, Maureen?'

But the moment he caught sight of the blue wool scarf around Dominic's neck the maudlin mood had vanished.

'And where in heaven's name did that come from?' he demanded, catching hold of the end of it and tugging the child to him.

Dominic's eyes widened in fear. 'Mrs Boothroyd give it me.'

'What for?'

'Christmas.'

Maureen had winced to see the way the big hand grabbed hold of the child's ear and twisted it hard. Dominic squealed loudly.

'And what do ye mean by taking charity from the woman, eh?' roared Tim. ' 'Tis an insult, so it is. I'll have no more charity, do ye hear?'

For each of the last three words he'd dealt the child a mighty whack around the head. Dominic had gone missing for the rest of the day, only turning up late tonight just before the fellows carried Tim home from the Fleece. Thank God he'd be going back to work tomorrow.

He lay snoring now beside her, still in his shirt and trousers. As a rule she undressed him and he was always too far gone in the drink to grumble about how she pulled him around, but now she'd grown too fat and awkward to be able to heave his weight about. Just so long as he remained asleep; please God don't let him wake and roll upon me tonight.

If only he'd leave me be. A child every year only made him grow angrier. And these days he couldn't seem to control it. A blow, a kick – these were the only ways he had to give vent to his anger. A father had the right to chastise, but it wasn't just for herself she feared – it was the little ones who couldn't protect themselves or run fast enough. Maureen slid a hand over her bulging stomach in wordless reassurance.

'Never mind, baby, he'll not harm you.' But she was lying, she knew. Little Thomas would never get rid of that scar on his cheek.

A clock struck midnight. Tim groaned and rolled over. She flinched out of reach. If he touched warm flesh he'd react automatically, throw his leg over her, pull her close . . .

Not now, she prayed, not with the baby so near. In a few more weeks there'd be another little mouth, wailing in the night, trying Tim's patience. That was why he'd lashed out at Thomas.

'For Christ's sake, can't a man get a bit of peace in his own house? Keep that brat quiet or by Jesus I swear I'll put a stop to his whining for good, so I will.'

But Thomas was too tiny to understand. That was why he'd wear the purple mark down his cheek into manhood. There were times when Maureen would gladly tear out Tim's eyes to protect her little ones, but what would Father Leahy say when she went to confession?

'Anger is a wicked sin, my child,' he'd told her before. 'It's a form of pride, and pride is a terrible sin.'

'But it's too many babies that cause all the trouble – what can I do?'

'A man has his rights, my dear. You can't deny him.'

'But that means a baby every year, Father, for as long as I can bear them.'

'If that is the will of God, so be it. No matter how trying your husband may be, remember our Lord, and turn the other cheek.'

She'd tried. Sweet Jesus, how she'd tried. But one day Tim would go too far . . .

Fanny lay wide awake. Harold seemed to be fast asleep but her mind was too preoccupied with anxious thoughts to allow sleep to come.

He hadn't gone out for his walk tonight. He'd had his cup of cocoa and gone to bed with barely a word. He'd simply gone down to the privy then put on his nightshirt in front of the fire, then turned his back on her when he got into bed. She couldn't reach him – he clearly didn't want to talk.

Something was troubling him, she was sure of it. He'd never been so bad tempered as he'd been for the last few weeks. It wasn't Beatrice and the house which had made him snap at her all day – he'd known about that long enough. He'd never before been as malicious about his sister as he'd been today.

No, Beatrice had come in for his scorn just as she had herself because something was disturbing Harold badly for him to act so strangely. Still the same frightening suspicion kept creeping back – another woman.

After all, he hadn't touched her for months, hadn't even tried to persuade her the way he used to. She'd had a good look at herself in the mirror tonight before he came up and she'd hated the wrinkles and drooping flesh she saw reflected there, the hair grown grey and sparse. She'd turned away from the unattractive image in distaste. No wonder he felt no desire.

Not that she wanted passion, but his total lack of interest just wasn't Harold. Unless he too was growing old. But it was more than absence of desire that worried her – it was the sneering way he treated her now, as if she was an annoying necessity, as if someone else was far more exciting . . .

Fanny felt desperately lonely and insecure. She nuzzled up to her husband's shoulder, laid a hand on his chest. He growled and pushed the hand away.

Miserably, Fanny turned over to face the wall. Rejection was a bitter pill to swallow.

Cassie still couldn't believe her good luck. As she slid down between the crisp, clean sheets of her little bed in the attic she shared with Maisie, the other kitchen maid, she felt a surge of pleasure.

Clean linen sheets, changed every week without fail, loads of hot water on tap all the time to wash her hair or have a bath – no more tin bath on a Friday night, soaking in the water Elsie had used first. And wonderful meals of the left-over joint from the Chadwicks' own dining table – no more snap tins to make up or trying to eke out a small portion of neck of mutton between five of them.

True, she worked as hard now as ever she did in the box factory, but sore fingers from scrubbing and peeling were infinitely preferable to that horrible, sticky glue in her hair. Nowadays her hair only fell limp from the steam from the kitchen range, but it sprang back into defiant curls the minute it dried out, and it was worth it for the luxury of living in the Chadwicks' house. Here it was always warm, no icy wind under an ill-fitting door, flapping the linoleum.

Cedar Street was behind her now. This was only the start of a new way of life, and she had every intention that it would always be that way from now on.

And it could be. Mrs Chadwick had been waiting for her tonight when she returned to duty.

'I've been thinking, Cassie,' she'd said thoughtfully. 'Since Dora's left so suddenly and according to Glover you've done your work well, I've asked him to train you to serve at table. You'd like to be parlour maid, wouldn't you?'

First step up, thought Cassie. Mrs Henson, the house-keeper, had confided that she too had started out as kitchen maid, and just look where she'd risen to. Not that Cassie had any ambition to be a housekeeper, not at all. What was the fun of running a house like this if you didn't own it? There were other ways to get there. The girls said Mrs

Chadwick had only been a mender in Chadwick's mill before he married her. That proved something. Catch the eye of the right person . . .

So far she had only been aware of Joe, the footman, casting leery eyes on her, and possibly Mr Spivey who delivered the vegetables of a Thursday. But promoted to the dining room, and with the kind of guests the Chadwicks invited to dinner, who knew? There could be a chance of better things. Many a gentleman had been heard of looking at a pretty parlour maid with more than passing interest . . .

'What you chuckling at?' mumbled Maisie's sleepy voice from the far bed.

'Nowt,' murmured Cassie. 'I were just dreaming, that's all.'

Ada unlaced her stays and draped them over the end of the bed, then stood scratching her belly in the dark. It was good to be out of the damn things at last. She wouldn't wear the blessed things at all, but a woman had a duty to keep things from spreading too far.

Maybe she should have a word with May about starting to wear them. She might be only nineteen but she was getting to look a bit heavy round the middle these days. In fact, if it were any other lass but May, a mother might be forgiven for suspecting she'd been up to summat. But not May. Cassie, maybe, but never our May.

She didn't look right these days, though, pale and drawn and only picking like a sparrow at her food. If only she knew what was fretting the lass, for summat clearly was. If only she could share the problem, ease the load off her mind.

'You coming into bed, lass?' Jim's voice sounded weary.

'Aye. Hold your breath.'

She eased herself gently down beside him and lay staring up at the ceiling. Only floorboards separated her from May in the attic above, but the girl's silent reserve was a far tougher barrier to break through.

*　　*　　*

May stood in her chemise, feeling the chill of the linoleum under her bare feet. She held her breath and put her hands about her waist, trying to make her fingertips meet.

Four months now. Her skirt was becoming harder to fasten – how long would it be before it became obvious to the world? With a sigh she let her hands drop. It was no use; she was definitely becoming thicker around the middle. Cassie was right – she wouldn't be able to conceal it much longer.

She sat down on the edge of the bed, watching the flickering shadows cast on the wall by the half-burnt candle. Cassie was right too in saying she'd have to make a decision – but what? If only Cassie was still here to talk to.

She crawled under the cold sheets. The hot brick Mam had put in the bed hours ago was still warm and she curled grateful feet around it.

Think, she told herself firmly. You can't put it off any longer. Three solutions to choose from, Cassie had said. One, see the old woman in Archer Street. That was out of the question. Two, marry the father. That was equally unthinkable. Three, tell Mam and put up with the stigma of having an illegitimate child.

Oh God! That meant not only hurting her but forcing her to put up with other people's wagging tongues, and Mam had always set such store by respectability.

'So long as you've got your good name you've got the most precious thing there is,' she used to say. 'While you've got that, you can hold your head high and feel as good as the King himself.'

What was she going to feel now about a daughter who was the cause of losing that good name? And even if she softened enough to help May through this ordeal, there'd be no wages coming in – Rose's wouldn't have her back, and Cassie contributed less now she was away. May groaned and buried her face in the pillow.

'*At least tell the father. He ought to know . . .*'

Cassie was right. Aaron ought to know. Even if it had only

been a casual interlude as far as he was concerned, he should be made aware of the consequences.

'He's had his fun, now let him pay for it.'

May gave a grim smile. Why not? Her sister was right. There was no reason why Aaron should escape scot-free. She'd find an opportunity to tackle him as soon as she got back to work tomorrow.

THIRTEEN

Mrs Rose was rapturous about her son's engagement.

'What a wonderful start to the new year,' she crowed happily. 'Didn't I always tell you Adele was the right girl for you? You listen to your mother and you'll never go far wrong. Has she named the day?'

'She has,' replied Aaron, crossing his knees and unfolding the newspaper. 'She wants to be a spring bride.'

'Spring,' repeated Mrs Rose. 'That gives us nearly two months. Maybe in that time we can find the right house for you. I think I can persuade your father to buy you something in a good area for your wedding gift.'

Aaron laid the newspaper aside. 'I've been thinking about that,' he said. 'Somewhere near by, perhaps, possibly here in Edgerton.'

His mother threw up her hands. 'Edgerton? We're talking of big money here! You want to rob your father of every penny?'

'Well, maybe Lindley then.'

'Now you're talking. Even we didn't start off in such a good place.' She twisted the jewelled ring on her finger. 'I tell you something, if Adele's father were to make you a handsome gift—'

'Oh, we can hardly ask him to do that.'

'Why not? The man has his pride – Sidney Rabin won't want to be outdone by your father. His daughter's dowry – a fine house in Lindley, or maybe Almondbury . . . Your father would like that.'

Aaron leaned back, smiling as he picked up the newspaper

again. 'Ah well, if you put it like that.'

Esther Rose folded plump hands contentedly. 'I'll talk to him after dinner. You just leave everything to your mother.'

Grace Openshaw disliked intensely having to reprimand May for the erratic seam, but this was the third time in the last few weeks she'd had occasion to rebuke the girl.

'I can't understand it, May,' she said helplessly in the privacy of her little office. 'As a rule you're the one person I can rely on to do things right, without me having to stand over you. It's just not like you to let shoddy work go through. When I think of how Mr Aaron was full of compliments about the work you did up at Thornleigh . . .'

She saw the girl's back stiffen. It wasn't like her to go all defensive the way Mabel would. Something was up for her to behave in this peculiar way, and if she went on, she'd never be made overseer when the time came.

But it was clearly no use just going on at her. Miss Openshaw didn't try to conceal the concern in her voice as she bent to look closely into the girl's drawn face.

'Look, I've seen you – you've not been yourself for weeks now. Is there some sort of trouble at home? I don't want to pry, but if there's something I can do . . .'

'No,' the girl said quietly. 'There isn't, but thank you.'

Miss Openshaw was baffled. She cast around in her mind for some other explanation. 'It isn't the other girls, is it? Only if I find out they've been bothering you—'

'It's nothing like that,' May answered. 'There's nothing anybody else can do. I've just got to sort it out for myself, and I will.'

Miss Openshaw drew herself upright. She'd tried to reach out, but if her efforts were rejected she had no choice but to remain the overseer.

'Well, whatever it is,' she said crisply, 'I hope you'll settle it soon. You've got to concentrate on your work. We don't make do with second-best at Rose's and you'd best remember that.'

'I will,' the girl said grimly. 'I will.'

May sewed furiously, watching the green chintz slide through under the needle, but her thoughts were racing. Second-best, indeed. That's what he thought of her – why else did he conscientiously avoid coming into the workroom nowadays if not to dodge the embarrassment of seeing her?

'Aaaah!'

She couldn't help the scream as excruciating pain shot through her finger. Instinctively her foot slowed the treadle, but it was too late. She stared, mesmerized, at the needle piercing her forefinger, trapping it so that she could not withdraw her hand.

All the other machines whirred to a halt. Miss Openshaw came hurrying over to the bench. 'Get on with your work, girls,' she called out. 'I'll see to it.'

There was little blood but the pain was agonizing. May's head swam but she was aware of Miss Openshaw pressing the flat of one hand over May's and raising the wheel of the machine with the other until the finger came free.

'Come into the office,' said Miss Openshaw. 'I think you could do with a cup of tea.'

May let herself be led from the workroom once more into Miss Openshaw's cubicle. Taking up May's hand the overseer inspected it closely and shook her head.

'Mr Henry's out on business. I'd best call Mr Aaron,' she murmured.

May was still bewildered when Aaron came hurrying in. 'A slight accident,' Miss Openshaw told him. 'She's all right but I thought I'd best report it.'

Aaron hovered by the door. 'Well, if she's all right . . .'

'It needs seeing to with a drop of iodine,' said Miss Openshaw. 'I've got some in the cupboard.'

Aaron nodded. 'Very good. I'm sure it must be painful.'

May found her voice again. 'It's not that bad,' she said quietly. 'I've been pricked by a rose and hurt worse.'

*   *   *

'What did you want to say that for?' demanded Aaron crossly when the overseer bustled away to see to the tea. 'You don't know what she might have made of it.'

May folded her right hand around the bandage, trying to nurse away the pain. 'How do you mean? Make of what?'

He scowled. 'You know very well – suggesting I'd done something, and after the way we've treated you too. That's how gossip starts and I'll thank you to watch your tongue.'

May looked up to meet his gaze. 'Oh? What was I suggesting, do you think?'

He flushed in annoyance. 'That I'd done something to hurt you. The firm's been good to you.'

'This blouse and skirt?' she said calmly. 'A fair exchange for what you did?'

'I did nothing,' he said sharply. 'I entertained you—'

'Entertained?' she cut in. 'Is that what you call it? Taking advantage of a girl—'

'Hush!'

'—and then ignoring her as if it never happened?' May curled her lip. 'I don't find that very entertaining, Mr Aaron.'

The look in his dark eyes was bewildered and angry. He wasn't used to being taken to task. 'Now look here,' he said quietly, 'if you're going to cause trouble—'

She shook her head. 'It's you who's caused trouble, more than you know. Fun like you had has to be paid for.'

His eyes narrowed. 'How do you mean? If you're looking for payment you're no more than a common whore. I didn't think of you like that.'

'Did you think of me as the mother of your child?'

She spoke the words softly, but the effect was devastating. Aaron seemed to go rubbery, his knees melting, and he sank down on Miss Openshaw's chair.

'You're lying,' he mumbled. 'You can't be.'

'If wishes were horses, beggars would ride. I'm four months gone.'

He looked around, fear glistening in his dark eyes. Any

133

minute now the overseer would be back with the tea. 'We can't talk now,' he muttered. 'Come to my office in an hour. We'll discuss it then.'

Grace Openshaw cleared away a patch of frost on the glass to look out of the office window. The sky looked heavy and black. Please God, don't let it snow, not yet. Edward had said he might call round this evening with a new catch for the scullery window, but he mightn't come if he thought he wouldn't be able to do it with snow lying thick in the yard outside.

They'd never arranged to meet again except for walks in the park in the spring, but somehow they seemed to have occasion to call at each other's houses from time to time. Like the time he left his scarf behind on her coat rack. She'd debated whether to pop round with it or wait, and as it turned out he called to collect it on his way home. So he'd stayed for a cup of tea. And he noticed little things, like the window catch . . .

She so looked forward to his visits. Her whole week now centred around the chance that he might call, buying some of his favourite Eccles cakes at Hagenbach's near the tram stop, polishing up the brasses again, grooming Oscar . . .

She turned away from the window abruptly. Stop this, my girl. If it's meant to be, the snow will hold off. In the meantime there's work to be seen to. Now, Mr Aaron wanted to see May upstairs.

Let's hope he's not going to be too hard on her. After all, accidents will happen.

Aaron paced up and down his father's office, tapping his teeth with a pencil. He had to get this business sorted out while Father was out of the way. He'd go crazy if he knew his son had been meddling with one of the staff again.

And not only that, but Adele . . . If this came to light the wedding would be off, which would mean the end of the plan to merge the two empires, the new house would vanish and his whole future would lie in ruins. And all because that mousy little Turnbull girl had got herself pregnant.

There was a tap at the door. Remember, he told himself as he sat down behind Father's big desk, you're the future head of an empire – she's only an uneducated machinist from a back-street slum. Handled firmly, there was no problem.

'Come in.'

She looked composed as she walked in, a thick bandage around her finger. He would not invite her to sit.

'So,' he said, looking at her severely, 'you say you are pregnant.'

'I am pregnant. The doctor confirmed it.'

She was cool. He'd expected tears. 'I see. But you can't know who the father is for sure.'

She drew herself upright. 'What do you take me for? Of course I do. Beyond any doubt. It's you.'

He stood up and walked over to the filing cabinet. She was telling the truth all right; she wasn't the sort to fool around. 'And even if it were me – which I don't admit – what do you expect of me?' he asked quietly, trying to quell the tumult in his guts. He must solve this calmly.

'You could marry me.'

'What?' He spun round, stunned by her impudence. 'I'm engaged already – I'm getting married shortly.' Why did he say that – as if he needed to explain?

'That's all right,' she said calmly. 'I wouldn't marry you anyway.'

'Then what do you want?' He spread his hands helplessly. He wasn't handling this properly at all. He was letting her take control.

'You could acknowledge my child as yours—'

'No! That's out of the question!'

She sat down uninvited and folded her hands in her lap. 'If I married someone else it would still be tough for me. I'll lose my job.'

He nodded. 'No married women, you know that.'

'And if I don't get married, well—'

135

He looked at her face anxiously. 'You wouldn't do anything silly, would you? Like that girl in despatch?'

'Kill myself? Oh no. I don't know what I'd do, but it wouldn't be that. It will be hard-going, a woman with an illegitimate child . . .'

He took a step forward. 'Financially, you mean? Ah now, perhaps something could be arranged – how much were you thinking of ?'

She gave a dry smile. 'How much will you offer?'

Her composure was beginning to irritate him. He was the boss in command, she the employee, yet somehow she was managing to reverse the roles.

'Two shillings a week,' he said firmly, seating himself again at Father's desk. 'I think that's fair.'

Her composure vanished. Her mouth fell open. 'Two shillings?' she repeated. 'To bring up a child for life?'

'It's the best I can do out of my wage.' There he was again, explaining to this chit of a girl. She spread her hands, gazing around her.

'But you have all this – Rose's, the biggest furniture store in the county . . .'

'It's not mine, not yet,' he said brusquely. 'Oh, it will be one day – I have big expectations, but right now I've hardly got two shillings to rub together. It's the best I can do.'

She was still staring wide-eyed. 'You expect me to believe that? Living the way you do?'

'It's true. Father pays me a pittance. He says I live in his house, he pays all the bills, so I don't need much. I'll get an increase when I marry, of course, but right now I've nothing I can call my own – not yet.'

He was aware that he sounded pitiful. She'd got him on a raw nerve. 'I see,' she said quietly. 'Then perhaps I should have a word with the grandfather.'

'What?'

'I'm sure Mr Henry won't want to see his grandchild starve.'

'Oh no!' Aaron leapt to his feet. 'Don't do that! Let me sort it out – I'll get the money from somewhere.'

'Where?'

'A loan from the bank – I'll talk to the manager. I'm sure I can do something. Oh God!'

He sank back into his seat, burying his face in his hands. May brushed down her skirt and stood up.

'Poor Aaron,' she said softly. 'Poor, poor Aaron. Even a child has to recognize his responsibility.'

With that she went out. Aaron remained slumped at the desk, feeling the tremor in his hands. She'd tell Father if he didn't come up with something. Oh God, he couldn't have that!

It was hopeless. The bank would laugh at him if he asked for a loan. He'd tried it once before when that actress in London became too pressing and he'd wanted to settle it discreetly. And just look where that had got him – they'd wanted his father to act as guarantor. If he pawned his gold watch Father would soon notice it was missing, and anyway even that wouldn't raise the kind of money he needed.

He had to forestall the girl. Whether he liked it or not he had to tackle Father himself, man to man, but he had to catch him in the right sort of mood. If Henry Rose was ever in the mood to hear news like this . . .

May went into the workroom and headed for Miss Openshaw's cubicle. The overseer looked up in surprise.

'What is it, May? Fit to go back now, are you?'

May shook her head. 'I'm going home. Mr Aaron told me I could.'

'Oh – I see.'

She was aware of the overseer's mystified expression as she pulled her coat on carefully over the bandaged finger. It had never been known for a girl to be sent home before unless she was critically ill and completely incapable of sitting upright at her machine.

Even though her finger throbbed horribly she felt proud as she walked out of the back door into the cobbled yard. For the first time in her life she'd found the courage to speak out,

137

and she was amazed at her own audacity. Confrontation was something she'd always avoided, especially at work. But courageous or not, she couldn't help wondering what would happen next.

'You did what? You bungling idiot . . . !'

Henry Rose ran the whole gamut of reactions to his son's news, ranging from disbelief and furious disgust to humiliation and heartbreak at the prospect of Sidney Rabin finding out. Esther Rose retired to her room with another of her bad turns, but not before she'd put on a theatrical display of hysterics to show her son how woefully he had treated her.

'No more this meddling with common girls you promised your father, and he goes to great expense to send you to London to save you from yourself!'

'I know, I'm grateful.'

'And this is how you show your gratitude? You can't marry this Gentile – I forbid it! A good Jewish girl or I kill myself!'

'Calm yourself,' muttered Henry. 'There's no question of him marrying her. He's to marry Adele.'

Esther sobbed into her handkerchief. 'How many times must I tell you, you'll catch the nasty woman's disease doing such things – it happened to your uncle Louis—'

Henry tried to intervene. 'That's not the point, my dear—'

'And poor Louis never had sons after that. Only the one daughter he has from before, no more. Now you would rob me of my grandchildren! I cannot believe you would be so cruel, my own son!'

'He'll have sons,' Henry soothed. 'Adele comes from a fertile family. Now please, leave us alone so Aaron and I can discuss what's to be done.'

Cassie was excited. Mr Glover, the butler, had decided that at last she was adept enough to wait, not just on the family but on their dinner guests tonight. If she peeped round the baize door at the top of the servants' stairs she could see them

138

arriving now, shaking the snow off their shoes as they handed their coats and hats to Mr Glover.

'They're all gentlemen,' she reported to Mrs Henson in the kitchen. 'Not a single lady amongst them so far.'

'Of course not,' said the housekeeper, lifting the ladle and sniffing at the lentil soup in the pan. 'It's the master's Conservative Committee. They never have ladies with them.'

'What about Mrs Chadwick then?'

'You'll have to take hers up to her room once you've seen to the men.'

They were a boring-looking lot, thought Cassie as she stood against the wall waiting for the men to finish their soup. While she'd been juggling carefully with the tureen not one of them had smiled or even glanced at her.

Funny how posh folk just sat without moving while you waited on them, she thought as she served the fish, as if they couldn't see you, as if you were a ghost. If it wasn't for Mr Glover's strict training she'd love to mutter, 'Move over a bit, can't you? Let me get this platter past your head.'

It wasn't as exciting as she'd thought, she reflected as she stood against the wall by the sideboard, waiting for them to finish the entrée. Fat men, skinny men, all of them old and either bald or thinning. And they talked about boring things too.

'There's that plot of land near the cemetery – maybe we could acquire that.'

'Too far out – and anyway, Education Committee have their eye on it, I hear.'

During the meat course she was occupied with seeing they all had the vegetables they wanted, a little of this, just a taste of that . . . She'd lost interest in their chatter. But when she came back into the dining room after clearing away the plates Mr Chadwick was talking, and all the others had stopped to listen.

'Silly fellow,' Mr Chadwick was saying, 'overstretched himself, you see. That always leads to temptation.'

Temptation. The word caught Cassie's ear.

'Especially in his position,' Mr Chadwick went on. 'He was Club treasurer at the time – it'd be a couple of years before you were elected.'

'You mean – he helped himself to the funds?' asked the thin man at the end of the table. 'Well I never.'

'Embezzlement, technically. Wanted to buy something he couldn't afford.'

'But surely he didn't expect to get away with it? Didn't you prosecute?'

Mr Chadwick shook his head. 'We let him off lightly. The Committee agreed not to prosecute if he repaid the debt.'

'And did he?'

'It's almost paid off now. He sold his house to repay a large part of it. He's had to struggle for the last couple of years but he's doing all right now, I hear. Taught him a lesson, I think.'

The thin man rubbed his chin. 'Seems to me he was lucky – you dealt kindly with the fellow. The story didn't get out then – I've never heard any mention of it.'

Mr Chadwick flourished his napkin and signalled to Cassie to bring in the pudding. 'We kept mum about it. No-one's any the wiser.'

Cassie set the apricot pudding down and began to serve it into dessert dishes.

'Well,' said the thin man thoughtfully, 'all I can say is, I think you dealt by him very fairly. Harold Jordan should be very grateful to you that he didn't go to prison.'

The ladle slithered from Cassie's fingers and clattered into the apricot pudding.

'May – Mr Henry wants you upstairs in the office right away.'

May could see the puzzled frown on Miss Openshaw's face as she made her way between the benches to the door. This was the summons she'd been expecting. But Mr Henry? Aaron must have decided to tell his father after all.

Mr Henry was alone in the room, standing looking out of

the dusty window over the street. She stood waiting patiently for him to speak.

'Sit down,' he said curtly, indicating a chair in front of his desk, and as she sat he took the leather seat opposite. 'Now,' he said slowly, 'if what my son tells me is true—'

'About the baby? It's true all right.'

He waved an impatient hand and cleared his throat. 'Then we have to find some way to resolve the matter. I think in the circumstances it would be best if you were to leave here before your, um, condition becomes evident to everyone.'

'Where would I go?' she asked warily. 'And what would I live on if I have no wages?'

'I'm coming to that. If you will agree to keep silent about the father, never mention a name ... You haven't told anyone, have you?'

'Not yet.'

He picked up a pen from the tray and toyed with it between his fingers. 'I can arrange somewhere for you to go until after the birth, somewhere out of Hawksmoor where you can rely on discretion. And I think we could agree a sum in settlement, enough for you to tide you over.'

'And what about the child?' she asked coolly. There was no reason why they should get off too lightly.

She saw his mouth twitch. 'If it's not unreasonable . . .'

She smiled. 'Unreasonable? To expect a man to honour his obligations? I don't think so, Mr Rose.'

He slapped the pen down testily. 'Look, I'll give you a lump sum – a generous sum, in total settlement – in return for your guarantee that you'll go away and leave my son in peace.'

'I see.' She sat, hands folded in her lap. Mr Henry took an envelope from the drawer of his desk and handed it to her.

'I think you'll find this is enough to set yourself up,' he muttered. 'You won't starve.'

She glanced inside the envelope and then put it away in her pocket. 'Very well,' she said quietly. 'I accept.'

'Just one more thing,' said Mr Henry. 'Sign this before you go.'

She took the sheet of paper from him. 'What is it?'

'A receipt for the money. I have to keep my books straight.'

She signed it and stood up. He looked at her sternly. 'Now don't come back looking for more. You've undertaken never at any time in the future to speak my son's name in connection with your child – your child, not his.'

'Very well.'

'Especially on the birth certificate. 'It must be *Father unknown*. Understand?'

May nodded. 'I understand.'

'Right then. I'll bid you good day. In a week's time I'll let you know where you can go to have the child.'

As she neared the door he added gruffly, 'I'm sorry to lose you, lass. You've been one of the best workers I've had.'

She glanced back.

'So if you decide to have it adopted, there'll be your old job waiting for you, think on.'

She smiled. 'I don't think so, Mr Rose, do you?'

He shook his head. 'No, happen not. Still, I wish you well.'

That's it, she thought as she walked out of the door. I'm on my own now.

FOURTEEN

On Sunday evening the Misses Bottomley were playing cards on the chenille-covered table.

'You're cheating!' snapped Agnes. 'I saw you pull that king out from the bottom. Beggar My Neighbour indeed! You'd beggar your own sister, you would.'

'Nay I wouldn't,' protested Nellie. 'I'm no cheat.'

'Oh aye? Who was it got that regard ring of me mother's then? The one she promised to me.'

'It were me she promised it to – she told me oft enough! I weren't begging for it.'

'You couldn't get it off her fast enough. She hadn't even been laid out before you was buzzing in there like a sparrow-hawk. Greedy, that's what you are, and nasty with it.'

'Who was it got her pearls then?' asked Nellie sweetly as she played another card. 'You, as I recall.'

'They weren't real, you know that.'

'And that lock of baby hair she wore round her neck.'

'I should think so! You never even knew our Edgar – he died before you was born.'

Nellie snorted. 'There, a queen – pay me out two.'

Agnes played a low card, then a jack. Her face lit up. Nellie laid one card on it and Agnes snatched up the pile.

'I win again,' she said triumphantly.

Her sister glowered. 'You always do. Funny, isn't it, how you never lose? Any road, I let you win.'

Agnes glared and swept all the cards into a pile, neatening the edges. 'Anyhow, we shouldn't be playing cards on a Sunday. It's not right.'

There was the sound of a loud bang through the thin wall. Nellie glanced up. 'Do you think he's starting up again?'

Agnes shrugged. 'Like as not. He'll have just got back from the pub.'

'I don't know,' sighed her sister. 'I'd like to give him a whack round the ears, the way he keeps knocking them kids about. Do him good to have a taste of his own medicine.'

'*Vengeance is mine, saith the Lord*,' quoted Agnes. 'It's not for us to judge.'

Nellie gave a mischievous smile. 'That's not what you said to the coalman. He's not been the same since.'

'That's different! I'd told him umpteen times about minding how he carts the coal down to that shed. There were no need for him to stamp his mucky boots all over my donkey-stoned flags.'

'You didn't have to clout him with the lading can,' remarked Nellie.

Agnes gave her a sly look. 'He hasn't done it since though, has he?'

There came the sound of a thin scream from next door. Nellie nodded towards the wall. 'Hark at that – he's at it again.'

Maureen Nagle cowered against the wall, shielding her head with her hands while Tim raged over her.

'Ye ignorant, stupid besom!' he roared. 'I'll teach ye a lesson ye'll never forget!'

Blows rained down again. Ducking and wriggling, she was dimly aware of Dominic standing in the doorway. Tim spotted him too.

'Get back to bed or I'll take me belt to ye!' he bellowed. The child stood staring, open-mouthed. Maureen felt her heart lurch into her throat as she saw Tim lumber over and deal him a hefty whack. The boy screamed and ran out. Tim turned back to her.

'And don't ye go trying to run after him,' he yelled. 'I want ye here, and I'll have obedience if it kills me. You hear me, woman?'

Another blow thudded round her ear. Maureen slithered down the wall. 'What is it ye want, Tim? What have I done?'

He towered over her as she lay crumpled on the floor. 'Are ye stupid altogether?' he slurred. 'If ye don't know then I'm not telling ye.'

At that moment she felt a searing pain shoot through her back and felt a trickle run down her thigh. Dear God – it wasn't due for another six weeks yet. With difficulty she stumbled to her feet and felt the pain rip through her body again. 'Tim, the baby,' she gasped. 'It's coming.'

She saw the fury in his eyes change slowly as understanding began to seep through his fuddled brain. 'Baby?' he echoed. 'Baby?'

'Go fetch the midwife – down Archer Street,' she muttered, but it was clear he wasn't following. 'A neighbour then,' she whispered, clinging to the chair and arching her back against the pain. 'Mrs Turnbull – she'll know what to do. Only for God's sake, hurry.'

May slapped the flat iron down on the pillow case, thinking how best to break the news to Mam. She was sitting over there by the fire, her feet up on the tuffet. It wasn't going to be easy, whichever way she phrased it.

'Seems funny watching you do that,' said Ada. 'Makes me feel right lazy.'

'You deserve a rest,' replied May. She had to nerve herself up to it, and it would be best while Elsie was out of the way. She laid the flat iron aside.

'What's that?' exclaimed Ada, suddenly jerking upright. May heard it too, echoing footsteps running along the frosty street, and then a loud banging at the front door. Old Mrs Boothroyd stood on the doorstep, her shawl pulled tight about her troubled face.

'Ada, love, I think you'd best get yourself round to the

Nagles' house right away,' she wheezed. 'There's trouble of some sort – Mr Nagle came banging on my door asking for you. Must be drunk again, getting the wrong house, but he said Maureen wants you, urgently.'

Ada snatched her shawl off the hook. 'Is it the baby?' she asked.

'He didn't say – I couldn't make much sense of what he was gabbling, something about her having a tumble, but it sounds like trouble all right.'

'Right,' said Ada. 'You get back indoors out of the cold, and May, you come with me. Don't look so surprised – if that baby's on the way I could need some help.'

May was startled by the scene that met their eyes when she and her mother entered the kitchen. Tim Nagle sprawled over a table littered with breadcrumbs, spilt tea and the remains of a kipper. Maureen crouched against the sideboard, her face contorted in pain. Ada threw her shawl aside and bent over the woman, taking in the bruises marking her thin face, then straightened.

'It's coming all right,' she murmured, then turned to the man at the table. 'Sling your hook, Tim Nagle,' she said sternly. 'You'll be no help to her now. Get yourself off to bed or anywhere out of our road.'

Disbelieving eyes stared at her for a moment out of a beer-sodden face. For a second he seemed about to roar his anger at being given orders by a woman, but then he rose slowly and lumbered away upstairs.

'Pull that kettle over the fire,' snapped Ada, 'and then help me get her comfortable.'

She began pulling off the woman's clothes and clearing a space on the floor. Maureen was whimpering as Ada helped her to lie down. Bewildered, May did as she was told. She knew little about birth but this seemed all wrong.

'Shouldn't it be her in bed?' she asked.

'Not this time,' said Ada. 'There'll be all the kids up there as well as him. Get down here and give us a hand.'

146

May felt alarmed and uneasy. 'Shouldn't we get the midwife? She can handle this better than us.'

'No time,' said Ada tersely. 'By the time you find which pub Bessie Morton's in and sober her up this'll all be over.'

May still felt anxious. 'You've never delivered a baby before, have you?'

'There's a first time for everything,' replied her mother. 'Any road, I've had three of me own so I know what I'm about.'

Maureen let out a hideous scream. Ada bent to her task.

Three hours later the woman was still struggling in labour. Her screams and cries for help completely unnerved May.

'Sweet Jesus, have pity on me!' Maureen sobbed. 'Let me die and take away the pain!'

Her prayers seemed to go unheard, and her suffering tore at May's heart. She looked anxiously at her mother.

'For God's sake, can't we do anything to help her? She can't go on like this!'

Ada shook her head. 'She can. She will. That's what having a baby is – pain and hard labour.'

Oh God! thought May. Is that what I have to look forward to? So much suffering for an unwanted child?

'Hey up, I can see it!' Ada bent down again, working with her fingertips to ease back the skin. Then she sat back, sighing deeply.

'What is it?' whispered May. 'What's up?'

'I think it's a breech,' muttered Ada. 'It's wrong way round. This could take all night.'

Maureen Nagle struggled all night, her piteous cries striking horror into May, but as dawn streaked the horizon a tiny baby girl slid into the world at last. Ada wrapped her in a bit of blanket from the cupboard and handed the bundle to May.

'Here, you mind her. The lass is too worn out to hold her.'

May stared down at the minute face with its incredibly blue eyes. So much pain for such a little result. It didn't seem possible that five minutes ago this little thing didn't exist, and yet now here she was, an individual in her own right.

Maureen's voice was tiny and weak. 'Is she all right?' she whispered. 'Not harmed, is she?'

'Not she,' said Ada comfortingly. 'Not even red like they usually are. White as a lily, she is, and bonny with it.'

'Lily,' repeated Maureen softly. 'That's a beautiful name.'

Fanny came downstairs in her dressing gown to poke up the fire and put the kettle on for Harold's tea. He liked a cup first thing before he had his breakfast.

The sound of running water as she filled the kettle made her wriggle uncomfortably and cross her legs. The privy – frosty as it looked outside in the yard, she must go down there first before she could do anything else.

Pulling her coat on over her dressing gown she set off down the yard. The cobbles struck icy cold through her thin slippers and the metal latch on the privy door almost froze to her fingertips. Pushing the door open, she almost cried out and leapt back in alarm. Something inside on the floor was moving, something alive under a piece of sacking.

And then she saw the thin leg – a child's leg – protruding from a corner. A child, here, in the privy? Whatever was he doing? She pulled the sacking away and saw the grimy, fearful face of the little Irish boy from the Nagles' house.

'What are you doing here, sonny?' she said gently, bending to pull him up. 'Are you locked out?'

He was pulling away from her, cowering down against the brick wall with terror in his eyes, shielding his head with the other arm. Compassion flooded her.

'I'm not going to hurt you, love,' she murmured soothingly. 'Come on indoors with me before you catch your death.'

It wasn't easy to coax him in, but he came at last and stood sullenly on the hearth, looking around him with huge, suspicious eyes. He was shivering violently. Fanny draped a blanket around him, the one Harold kept by his chair to cover his knees when he had his nap.

'How long have you been out there?' she asked. 'You've not been there all night, have you?'

He wasn't even looking at her. His eyes looked dull and vacant, devoid of any expression other than fear, and his face was filthy. Instinctively she reached for a flannel and made to wipe his cheeks, but he backed away.

'Nay, love, you're safe here,' she soothed. 'No-one'll harm you here. Come on, let me clean that muck off your face and then I'll give you a bit of porridge. Yes?'

He was reluctant to let her touch him but at last he yielded, letting her wipe gently over his face and hands. The poor mite was still trembling – he must be perished with the cold if he'd been out there long. She remembered that night in the gutter when she'd seen him scavenging for food.

They didn't deserve children, those feckless Irish folk, and they seemed to have them so easily. There was no justice in the world. All the years she and Harold had yearned for a little one of their own to cherish – they'd even chosen the name Adam for the first – and yet . . .

The kettle was boiling and it took only moments to cook the porridge. She placed a bowl in front of him, sprinkled it with sugar and a drop of milk, then put a spoon in the boy's hand. He stared at it blankly for a moment, then looked up at her.

'To eat your porridge with, love,' she explained, pushing his hand to dip the spoon into the steaming bowl. 'Go on, that'll warm your insides for you.'

After the first mouthful there was no stopping him. He shovelled the porridge into his mouth at an incredible speed, gobbling as though he hadn't eaten in weeks. Fanny watched him with pleasure for some moments before she realized she was still bursting. He wouldn't miss her if she slipped away down to the privy now . . .

In no time she was back and he was scraping the bottom of the bowl to retrieve every last morsel. She poured a little more into the dish before he scraped the bluebells off. When he'd had his fill she'd enjoy getting those ragged clothes off him and giving him a thorough wash-down, especially that greasy, matted black hair. Like washing the windows when they were black with soot, it gave her infinite pleasure to turn something filthy into clean and sparkling wholesomeness. It must be so nice to have a little person to care for . . .

Footsteps came lumbering down the stairs. Fanny looked up in alarm. Absorbed with the child, she'd forgotten Harold.

The door opened and he came in, then stopped suddenly, his jaw sagging as he caught sight of the figure at the table.

'What the devil's going on?' he demanded. 'What's this?'

Fanny came round the table to him. 'He was down the yard, love – in the privy,' she explained, then added in a whisper, 'I think he's been there all night, poor little thing.'

Harold stared. 'It's one of them Nagle kids – we don't want him in here with his fleas – get him out of here!'

'Hush, love.' Fanny looked fearfully at the child. 'He's not that dirty – I've cleaned him up. Just look how he's tucking into that porridge – we can't send him packing yet.'

Harold edged round the table on the furthest side from the boy. 'You heard me – get him out by the time I come back from the privy, you hear?'

He was almost at the back door when Fanny plucked up courage to speak. 'Harold – I've been thinking . . .'

He turned, his hand on the latch. 'What now?'

'Couldn't we keep him? For good, I mean?'

Harold stared. 'What the devil are you on about? Have you gone mad?'

'The Nagles have too many children – you've said so yourself,' Fanny rushed on before her courage ran out. 'We've always wanted one – they won't miss one – and this poor little chap is badly treated as you can see. Just look at them bruises. If we was to adopt him—'

Harold took a step back into the room. 'You have gone crazy,' he muttered. 'You've taken leave of your senses altogether, wanting to take in a flea-bitten runt like him – just look at his face – he's only half there after all the beatings he's had. For God's sake, woman, throw him out and I'll try and put it from my mind that I'm married to a bloody lunatic.'

'But Harold—'

'No more,' he roared, 'or I'll get you into the loony bin this very day!'

Hearing his bellowing tone the boy slithered down under the table and began to howl.

The lamplighter was dowsing the lights when Ada and May finally left the Nagles' house. The cobblestones lay white under a thick coating of frost and Ada slithered as she reached the pavement edge.

'Give us your hand, love,' she murmured. 'I don't want to slip.'

May took hold of her and they walked in silence towards home. She took a deep breath.

'Mam, there's something I have to tell you,' she said quietly, watching the words come out of her mouth in a billow of steam.

'Oh aye?' said her mother. 'Hey up!' She grabbed her daughter's arm. 'I nearly went then. What was you saying?'

'It can wait,' murmured May. 'Let's get a nice hot cup of tea inside us first.'

Fanny got dressed in a hurry. It wouldn't be long before Harold came back into the house and he'd only start on at her again if the boy was still there.

Poor little soul. He put his hand trustingly in hers as they slipped quietly out of the front door, and she loved the feel of the small fingers curled inside her palm. A little body to lavish her love on, to clean and feed and protect . . . Why couldn't Harold understand? Once upon a time he used to understand everything, but not any more.

Dominic, that was his name, she remembered now. Dominic Jordan – the name had a ring about it, the sort of name that could become a bank manager or a schoolmaster like Mr Lucas. That was what Harold had always wanted, and yet now . . .

He was a changed man these days, so brusque and cold she hardly knew him. The man who'd taken Harold's place was hateful, cold and selfish, turning away a pitiful soul like this little fellow trotting along at her side. As she neared the Nagles' door she clasped the little hand tighter, wishing she never had to let it go, and feeling hatred beginning to burn in her thin chest.

No-one answered her knock and she could hear a baby crying. Dominic shrank away but she held on tightly. The green door was unlatched, and she went in.

A grubby little girl of about five sat on the bottom step of the stairs sucking her thumb. She looked up incuriously at the stranger.

'Where's your mam?' asked Fanny.

The child jerked the wet thumb upwards. 'Upstairs.'

'Where's your daddy then?'

'Gone to work.'

She felt the tense little fist relax in hers. 'Come on, love,' she said and, side-stepping the girl, led Dominic upstairs, trying not to feel distaste at the rank smell of unwashed clothes and stale bodies.

'Mrs Nagle!'

She heard a faint voice coming from the front bedroom. Pushing open the door she saw the woman lying in bed, covered in a shabby blanket and a small bundle in her arms. A couple of toddlers roamed about the room, one of them making whining noises, and there was the foetid smell of urine in the air.

'I'm sorry to intrude like this,' Fanny said awkwardly, 'but – I found your little lad sleeping in our privy so I thought I'd best bring him back home.'

The woman gave a weak smile. 'So he's all right, thanks be to God.' She looked down at the tiny bundle. 'I had this little one last night. Lily, God bless her.'

She drew back the corner of the blanket to reveal a tiny face. Fanny couldn't believe the minute, immaculate perfection of the child, and the size of her – she was like a miniature doll.

'Congratulations,' she said, but her voice was husky with tears. One more unwanted Nagle . . . She let go of Dominic's hand and hurried from the room.

Tears were blurring her vision as she hastened along the street. There was no justice in the world, giving that family yet another child they didn't want and couldn't care for while she, who longed for one, was denied.

Harold didn't care any more, not for her anyway. He'd made that clear. He'd blamed her openly lately, and he never used to.

'You're just a barren woman and you'll have to put up with it,' he'd said coldly. How could he be sure it was her fault? Because he couldn't be in the wrong, she thought bitterly. Not now. In the old days in Marchmont Avenue it had been so different.

She'd tried to find excuses for the way he'd changed. Maybe it was guilt or shame at what he'd done. He'd never breathed a word to her until he was found out. He'd been full of contrition then.

'I did it for us, Fanny. Moxon's hearse was a beauty, far better than mine. It was too good a chance to miss.'

'But how on earth did you think we could ever pay for it, love?'

He'd hung his head. 'My mother's house. She were dying. She'd promised it to me.'

So he'd dipped into the Conservative Club funds. He was the treasurer and he'd pay it back before anyone found out.

But it was Beatrice who got the house, Beatrice who sold it and moved up to better things. The disgrace would have been even worse if the Committee had prosecuted Harold, but they'd offered him a way out. A gentlemen's agreement, they called it, so the Party wouldn't have to wash its dirty linen in public.

'I'm sorry but we'll have to sell up, Fanny,' he'd said, so she'd had to lose her lovely Marchmont Avenue home and move down here to Cedar Street. That was when he'd seemed to withdraw more into himself, draw back from her.

Through the veil of tears blinding her eyes Fanny became aware that she was standing at the corner of the street, outside the shop. Deep in misery she'd gone right past her own door. No lights glowed yet inside the dusty window. She blinked around her. No-one was about on the still-dark street.

She stared up at the blank face of stone wall. High above her she could make out the street sign. Cedar Street. Rage and misery flooded her again, and she raised her fist at the peeling sign.

Words burst from her throat, words she never used, words born of frustration and helplessness.

'Damn you, Cedar Street,' she cried. 'You've ruined my life. I hate you!'

Ada poured tea into two cups and handed one to her daughter.

'Well, I reckon that's a good night's work,' she said, rubbing her tired eyes with the back of her hand. 'That poor lass had a dreadful time of it, but she made it in the end. I must say, I'm proud of how you coped. I thought as how you might find it a bit much, not being used to that kind of thing, but you did splendidly.'

'It'll stand me in good stead,' said May quietly, 'when my time comes.'

'Aye, it will, but that'll be a long while yet, I reckon. Now, what was it you was going to tell me?'

May set her cup down and looked her mother in the eye. 'I've been nerving myself up to break this to you, Mam. It's going to be a lot sooner than you think . . .'

FIFTEEN

Ada threaded the string of Elsie's gloves through her coat sleeves, wrapped the scarf round her neck and packed her off to school. She turned to May.

'Now then, we'll have a bit of peace and quiet. Sit down a minute and let's talk.'

May glanced at the mantel clock. 'I haven't time before my tram—'

Ada pointed firmly to the chair. 'There's time for summat important like this. Sit you down a minute.'

May gathered up her skirts and sat. Ada shook her head. 'I can't understand, lass. Why don't you get him to marry you? It's the right thing to do.'

May shook her head. 'He can't. He's marrying somebody else and anyway, I don't want him.'

'Still, we ought to try and make him face up to what he's done, go down and tackle him about it.'

'No. I've taken the money for the baby. That's an end to it.'

Ada rubbed her chin. 'You've thought of other ways out, I take it?'

'The old woman in Archer Street?'

Ada started. 'How do you know about her?'

'Cassie told me. No, I'd rather go away to this place Mr Rose is arranging for me. If I go soon I can avoid all the tongues wagging.'

Ada paced up and down the hearthrug. 'What about the girls at work? Won't they start to wonder where you are?'

May shook her head. 'Mr Rose told them I'm being sent down south on another job for Sir Joseph. Nobody knows but you.'

Ada stopped pacing and looked down at her daughter. 'You could stay here—'

'No! I'd rather go to this home.'

'For fallen women? They won't be your kind, love.'

May gave a wry smile. 'They'll probably be girls who've been duped like me. I'm sorry, Mam.'

'Hush now. What about the baby?'

'What about it?'

'They'll want you to get it adopted, most likely.'

May's gaze met hers. 'I won't do that. I won't bring it home but I'm going to keep it, whatever. I'll manage, I'll find work enough to keep us, somewhere away from here.'

Ada raised shocked hands. 'And me lose both me daughter and me grandchild? Nay, you're not going to rob me like that – he'll be our flesh and blood, think on. You'll bring him back here after he's born, you hear me?'

'But the shame . . . Me dad . . .'

'Never heed about that. I'll tell him when the time's right. In the meantime, you hold your tongue.'

Ada touched her daughter's shoulder. 'We'll work summat out, never you fear. Now you'd best get a move on or you'll miss that tram.'

Cassie wrinkled her nose at the foul smell drifting down from the gasworks as she turned the corner into Fountain Street. Millsbridge looked and smelt dirtier every time she came home these days. She was spoilt now, living in Edgerton's leafy avenues.

It would be the same when she got home, she thought as she bent her head against the biting wind howling through the viaduct. Rag rugs underfoot instead of deep carpets, thick pot cups in place of china. Coarse sheets, boiled mutton . . . They couldn't help being poor, but everything there she'd once accepted as normal now seemed tawdry and objectionable.

Even the smell that met you as you walked in the door. Wet washing and the stink of Dad . . .

She couldn't help feeling a sense of shame that she'd left them all so far behind her now. Mam did her best, but she'd never amount to anything – how could she? And May too – she'd wrecked her chances for ever now, and no mistake.

Lost in thought she swung round the corner into Cedar Street, colliding with a solid, overcoated figure so sharply that she felt the breath driven out of her as her foot slithered from under her on the icy flagstone. She sank into a heap on the cold ground.

'Oh my goodness! I'm dreadfully sorry! Let me help you.'

She blinked up. Mr Jordan's worried face was bending over her, his hand reaching for her arm. For a second she stared up at him, then twisted her lips in a grimace.

'Oh my dear, are you hurt?' he asked anxiously. 'It's all my fault – I should have looked where I was going.'

'No, really,' she said weakly, 'it was my fault. Oh dear,' she added dubiously, 'I think I've twisted my ankle. Would you mind helping me up?'

She held out a gracious hand and let him take it, then rose slowly to her feet and put her foot tentatively to the ground. It didn't hurt at all, but he was holding on tight, his face a picture of distress. She recalled how Mrs Chadwick could come over all faint whenever she wanted, and Mr Chadwick wore just the same expression as Mr Jordan wore now. She was enjoying the moment, the feeling of power.

'I'll be all right in a minute,' she said weakly. 'Please, don't let me keep you.'

'I can't leave you like this,' he said. 'Let me help you. Were you going home?'

She nodded. 'Mrs Chadwick gave me the day off because she wants me to work all this weekend – they've got important guests coming.'

Mr Jordan inclined his head, his hand still firmly cupped under her elbow as she limped along. 'They must think very highly of you.'

She smiled demurely. 'I reckon they do. I don't have to go back until morning.'

She walked slowly and with care, his hand still tight on her elbow and she saw his troubled eyes taking in the marks on the hem of her skirt.

'Such a pretty dress,' he muttered. 'I do hope it will clean up all right.'

She looked down at the marks and waved an airy hand. 'It's pretty enough, but it's only a cast-off, one of Miss Cecily's. One day I'm going to afford to buy nice dresses of my own.'

He smiled. 'I'm sure you will. And I'm sure plenty would be only too glad to buy them for you.'

They'd reached her door. Gently she withdrew her arm and held out a gloved hand. 'Thank you so much for your kindness. I'm perfectly all right now, good day to you.'

For a second she let her fingers rest on his, felt him tremble, and then she turned away. As she put the key in the lock she was conscious of him standing there, his appreciative eyes on her back, and she turned to flash him a smile before she went inside.

Fanny had tears in her eyes as she dusted the sideboard. She was still trying to fight down the unfamiliar bitterness and hate swirling inside her. Such feelings were alien to her nature and she found it hard to reconcile herself to the fact that she was capable of feeling anything so ignoble.

It was all Harold's doing. There was no kindness, no tenderness left in him now. The only words he had for her these days were cruel and completely unwarranted.

'You're barmy, woman,' he'd said contemptuously this morning. 'You live in cloud-cuckoo-land – that's you, you're just plain cuckoo.'

There'd been a cuckoo in her lovely garden in Marchmont Avenue, an unwanted intruder who threw the pretty little thrushes out of their nests. She was his cuckoo in the nest now he'd found somebody else. And there was someone else, she was sure of it. She'd heard him muttering in his sleep.

But no, it wasn't she who was the interloper – it was the woman who occupied his brain night and day, whoever she was.

Not that it would help to know who she was; it wouldn't help her to regain his love. He loathed her now. He couldn't even bear to be near her.

Ten minutes ago he'd put on his hat and hurried out, to see a client, he said, but she knew it was to get away from her. Brushing aside the tears she put down the duster and went to peer round the curtain out of the window. As she looked out over the frost-whitened street she suddenly caught her breath.

He was over there, outside the Turnbulls' house, and he was touching the arm of the young Turnbull girl, the blond one, and they were deep in conversation. Fanny let the lace curtain fall and turned away quickly before he caught sight of her.

The Turnbull girl? Fanny was shaking. She couldn't be more than sixteen or seventeen – Harold was three times older than that. It couldn't be her, surely – could it? But he was touching her, a thing he rarely did . . .

Fanny sank down at the table, plucking at the duster with trembling fingers. Strange things happened with middle-aged men sometimes, she'd heard. Even old men had been known to take young brides. Usually to have children.

Oh God! Was that it? A young woman who would give him the son he'd craved for so long, the one she'd failed to give him?

'Let's face it, woman. You're barren.'

And too old now to hope, she thought miserably. Out of years of habit she rubbed the duster hard over a stubborn fingerprint on the polished table, but she could not rub away the anguish gnawing inside.

To Fanny's relief Harold seemed to be in a happier frame of mind that evening. He actually seemed inclined to chat.

'Nice girl, that lass of Turnbull's,' he said casually as he turned the page of his newspaper. 'Bumped into her in the street this morning and had a few words with her.'

'Oh?' She wouldn't tell him she'd seen him from the window. His mood would turn; he'd accuse her of spying.

'She's in service, you know, up at the Chadwicks' house in Edgerton.'

'Is she now?'

'Got a good head on her, that one, more about her than that mousy sister of hers. She'll do well for herself, she will.'

'I'm sure.' Fanny sat stitching his shirt button on, wondering whether this was yet another dig at her.

'Oh yes,' he went on, not lowering his paper to look at her. 'She's got used to a good way of life up there. Right young lady she is now.'

'Hardly that,' said Fanny tartly. 'She's only a miner's daughter when all's said and done.'

'Maybe, but she's learning all the time. She knows how things are done proper.'

There he goes again, thought Fanny. Another sly gibe at me. I'm like the mousy Turnbull girl.

'I thought as maybe we could ask her over for a cup of tea,' he went on, still with that casual air which didn't deceive her. 'Happen it's time you had a friend or two.'

Fanny felt her cheeks redden. 'After all the time you've been telling me to keep myself to myself? What would I want with a chit of a girl like her?'

Aware of the sharpness in her tone he lowered the newspaper an inch or two and she saw his startled expression over the top. 'Nay, I only thought . . . Oh, suit yourself.' He disappeared again behind the paper and relapsed into silence.

Fanny broke off the cotton and laid the shirt aside. She had a vivid image in her mind of his hand on that girl's arm, the easy familiarity of the way they spoke to each other, as if it had happened many times before . . .

'You sound as if you've got quite a fancy for her,' she said quietly. The newspaper crunched suddenly into his lap.

'What? What the devil are you suggesting?'

'The Turnbull girl. I know.' It startled her how calmly she could say it.

Harold's face turned as purple as a turkey-cock's. His lips moved soundlessly before words came out. 'You're absolutely stark, staring mad!' he breathed. 'You need help.'

She shook her head. 'I know I'm right. I'm sorry, Harold, I really am.'

His mouth was still opening and closing like a goldfish. 'I'll have to have a word with the doctor about you, having delusions like that,' he muttered at last. 'You're heading for Storthes Hall the way you're going on.'

'I'm not mad, Harold. I'm just very sad.'

He leaned forward, shaking his head gravely. 'I mean it, love. Just lately you've not been yourself at all. It would be in your best interest if I had a word with the doctor.'

'Nay, Harold – you wouldn't!'

He shook his head again. 'It's my duty. You're in a bad way, lass, worse than you know.'

Fanny's calmness fled. 'You want me out of the way, that's it, isn't it?'

'What rubbish! I'm only concerned for you.'

'There's nowt wrong with me! It's that girl, isn't it? You want me out of the way so you can—'

'Fanny!' Harold stood up sharply, paused, then turned away. 'Eh lass, there's no two ways about it – you're in a far worse state than you realize. I'll try and make it in me way to see Dr Cavendish in the morning.'

Cassie had decided not to share the juicy titbit of gossip about Mr Jordan with her mother and sister. Somehow she had the feeling that she ought to be able to make use of it, though just how she hadn't yet decided.

And this morning's little encounter with him at the corner of the street had convinced her that he fancied her – there was no doubt of that. She knew that gleam in a man's eyes only too well – didn't Joe and Mr Spivey always look at her like that? But never so far had she seen it in a man as old as Mr Jordan.

She wondered how he would have behaved if he'd known that she recognized him as the fellow who hung around in the back lane at night, watching her window. Daft devil.

Freezing or not, he'd be out there tonight, she was certain, and she smiled to herself. She'd make sure it was late enough for Elsie to be fast asleep, and then she'd give him a show he'd never forget . . .

'Hey,' said Agnes when Nellie came back in from the yard and pulled off her shawl, 'you'll never guess who I saw.'

'When?'

'Just now – while you was down the privy. I saw Mr Jordan walking out with that fair-headed Turnbull lass.'

Nellie's jaw dropped open. 'You never,' she gasped. 'He can't be, he's married,' she gasped.

Agnes clicked her tongue. 'I didn't mean courting her, you daft thing. I meant walking out with her, down the street, holding on to her arm. I wonder does Mrs Jordan know?'

Nellie's pale blue eyes widened further. 'You're not going to tell her, are you?'

Her sister's jaw tightened. 'Of course not. It's none of our business. And you just keep your trap shut and all. It's not for us to gossip.'

'I wouldn't for the world,' agreed Nellie. 'I just wonder what's going on.'

The clock had struck half-past ten. Harold was taking no chances. He would wear his gloves and muffler to go out for his evening stroll tonight. He could be hanging around in the back alley for some time before she went to bed. Please God let her leave the curtains undrawn and the lamp burning again. He felt the old, familiar surge of heat in his guts at the very thought . . .

'You off out?' asked Fanny curtly as he pulled on his coat.

He gave a testy sigh. 'Don't I always?'

162

'I'm off to bed then.'

'Suit yourself.'

She really was impossible these days, he thought irritably as he slammed the door behind him. Moody, unpredictable, illogical – it was completely crazy, wanting to adopt that filthy vagrant child of Nagle's. If the doctor agreed she needed treatment, suggested sending her in to Storthes Hall for a spell, he wouldn't object. He'd just have to manage on his own for a while, that's all . . .

Reaching the end of Cedar Street Harold doubled back along the alley towards the Turnbulls' house. Peering over the back-yard gate he saw lights only in the scullery. She couldn't have gone to bed yet, not so early. It was going to be a cold wait. He chafed his arms with gloved hands, not daring to stamp his feet.

Gradually the cold coming up off the icy cobblestones seemed to eat its way up his legs and he began shivering. It was no use; he had to move or he'd congeal. Three times he walked the length of the alley and back before he saw it – a light glowing in the upstairs room, and his freezing breath stuck in his throat.

Tonight the light was brilliant, as though several lamps or candles were burning, and when the figure finally came into view and stood gazing out into the night, she was illuminated almost as though she were on a music hall stage. She threw aside a scarf or wrap of some kind and he could see clearly the green of her dress as she stood before the window, toying with the buttons at her throat.

Then one by one she began to unfasten them, slowly and with care, and by the time her fingers reached her waist Harold was beside himself with delight. Already he could glimpse the white of her chemise beneath, and when she slid the dress off her white shoulders and bent to step out of it he was in transports of ecstasy. Her skin gleamed like pearl in the lamplight, her hair an amber halo spilling around her throat. She was a goddess, a divine being he longed to touch, to savour, to possess . . .

She was unfastening the string around the neck of her chemise now, loosening it to slide off her shoulders, letting it fall around her waist, and the sight of her small, high breasts sent Harold crazy. In another moment she'd let fall the bloomers, revealing herself like Salome, layer by layer, until he had it all.

'Oh, my lovely Salome,' he breathed into the cold night air of the alley, 'I'd give you John the Baptist's head on a plate – I'd give you anything your little heart desired.'

She bent out of sight, and suddenly the lights went out. Disappointed, Harold waited, but nothing more. For long minutes he stared at the blank square of darkened window, reliving in his head the wonderful spectacle of his Salome, willing her to return.

But she didn't come. He was left alone with his congealed feet and hands, his brain swirling with intoxicating images mingled with vexation. As he reluctantly made his way home the images would not leave his fevered brain, and he knew sleep would not come easily that night.

Cassie lay in bed next to the sleeping Elsie, hugging herself with pleasure. She'd seen him out there before she put on that little show. If he didn't pant for her before, then he certainly should by now.

She'd love to share the joke with somebody, but who would understand? A girl of sixteen encouraging an old man like him – but how could she explain that young men, generally speaking, didn't have money or influence? Not that Mr Jordan was incredibly rich, but those men had said he'd paid off his debt and was doing well again now. Everyone knew Jordan's was a posh undertaker's.

So if he'd taken a fancy to her, if it had been strengthened by what he saw tonight, who was she to object if he chose to offer her gifts? The new dresses she craved might not be so far out of reach.

It would be interesting to see what his next move might be.

*   *   *

Harold made sure to go up to the Infirmary early the next morning. The Earnshaw family had said they wanted him to deal with the cadaver without bringing it to the house. They also wanted it buried in the small churchyard in Lindley where the heavy clay, waterlogged by an underground spring, made for heavy digging, so he'd have to arrange for extra grave- diggers from the nearby churches to come in and help.

As he turned the corner into Portland Street he saw a short, stocky figure ahead of him, and hurried to catch up.

'Good morning, Dr Cavendish,' he said brightly, raising his hat and falling in step beside him.

The doctor smiled. 'Ah, good morning, Jordan. How are you?'

'Flourishing, I'm glad to say.'

'And Mrs Jordan too, I hope?'

Harold's smile fell away. 'Ah well, not so good, I'm afraid.'

'I'm sorry to hear that. What's the trouble?'

Harold shrugged. 'It's hard to say, but I am rather worried about her. She's not herself lately. Acting a bit odd.'

The doctor's eyebrows rose. 'Really? In what way?'

'Well, she has this hankering for a child – at her age too – she's far too old.'

Dr Cavendish nodded. 'A common enough craving in childless women. A thwarted maternal instinct can become obsessive, I'm afraid. Unhealthy.'

'Aye well, I'm afraid it's come to that,' murmured Harold sadly. 'She's even taken to picking up kids off the street.'

The doctor looked up at him sharply. 'You mean stealing them?'

'As good as. She dragged this one in the other day, whether or not, regardless of whose he was. You should have seen the state of him. Verminous, filthy, he was.'

'Dear me,' said the doctor. 'That does sound serious.'

Encouraged, Harold went on. 'And I don't think she knows fact from fantasy either. Found him in the privy, she said. Can you believe that? Nobody's child, so she wants him.'

The doctor shook his head. 'The disturbed mind can deceive itself. I'm so sorry.'

They were climbing the Infirmary steps now. 'Aye,' said Harold mournfully, 'she's disturbed all right. I don't know what to do. She can't go on like this.'

'Treatment might help,' said Dr Cavendish as he headed for his room. 'I could have a look at her, if you wish.'

'Aye, thanks,' said Harold. 'That would help put my mind at rest.'

SIXTEEN

Grace Openshaw was deeply sorry to lose her best seamstress, even if it was only temporarily. Mr Henry said Sir Joseph had specifically asked for her, so really she ought to be pleased for the girl.

It would be more satisfying though if the job was nearer, so that she could support May, sending up the materials she needed, offering advice if need be. Still, the girl was highly capable of working on her own, and the added experience would stand her in good stead when the time came.

So on May's last day at Rose's she drew her to one side. 'I'll be right sorry to see you go, May. You've worked well and done everything that's been asked of you. Work hard, and I'll look forward to you coming back when the job's done.'

If the girl seemed less responsive than usual it was probably due to nervousness, thought Grace. Not surprising, really, since she'd be among strangers for the next few months. Southerners, she'd heard tell, weren't as friendly as northern folk, and May wasn't the outgoing sort who made friends easily. Still, time passed before you knew it and she'd soon be back among her own kind in Rose's workroom.

Jim Turnbull was glad to hear May's light step on the stairs. Apart from Elsie he'd seen no-one since dinner-time, Ada had been that busy with folks calling for their washing. He twisted his head to look round as the bedroom door opened.

'Hello, lass. How are you doing?'

May came across and set down a cup of tea on the dresser beside him. 'Not so bad. And you?'

'Middling. I've been better. What's our Elsie doing?'

May smiled. 'Promise you won't tell? She's sneaked off round to see her pal while Mam's busy. She'll be back for her tea.'

He reached gingerly for the cup, moving slowly so as not to trigger off the pain once more. 'I don't know,' he murmured, 'Cassie's gone, our Elsie's always playing truant, and now you tell me you're going away. The house'll be empty soon at this rate.'

'Nay, Mam's still here, and I'll be back just as soon as this job's over, never fear.'

He set the cup down and looked at her. 'Summat's in the air, I can feel it, but nobody tells me nowt. I know they want to spare me but it's not right. Is it our Cass? Is there summat up with her?'

However sick he might be, he was too sharp, too sensitive to atmosphere, to be easily fooled. May hesitated for only a moment. He mustn't know, not yet . . . 'No, Dad. She's fine, honest. She'll be home again at the weekend, and I'll be back, I promise. Then I'll always be here to care for you.'

Fanny felt desperately, achingly alone. The little house was immaculate, not a speck of dust or an unwashed plate remained to occupy her, to try and drive out the demon thoughts which plagued her.

Looking out of the drizzle-splashed window she could see only wet cobbles under a leaden sky. Nobody was out there. All tucked up warm and cosy indoors, not one of these people knew her, let alone cared about her. All human life was going on around her, only yards away, yet she was cut off from them just as surely as if she'd been cast away on a desert island.

Cast away. Fanny tried hard not to let the tears begin afresh. She must do something – be among people, anybody, just to get away from this abject, self-pitying loneliness.

The corner shop – there must be someone there, if only the shopkeeper. She could spend time choosing slowly what to buy, pass a few precious minutes near the warmth of another human being. Just a packet of salt – Harold couldn't grumble about that surely, even though he'd forbidden her to go in there.

Fanny whipped off her apron and put on her coat and hat.

The shop doorbell clanged as Fanny went in. She was shaking with excitement as the balding man behind the counter glanced up and nodded.

'Afternoon.' He turned to serve his customer who had thrown back her shawl. It was the old lady who seemed to live on her own, next door to the Turnbulls. She had a pudgy, kindly face, and she smiled as Fanny took her place alongside her at the counter.

'Oh, hello. Mrs Jordan, isn't it?'

'That's right,' Fanny replied shyly, feeling her heart flutter in her chest.

The old lady stowed packets of sugar and tea into her basket. 'Haven't had the chance of a word with you before,' she said with a warm smile, 'only your husband. He buried Mr Boothroyd – my husband, that was – nigh on seventeen years ago it was. Right good send-off it were, but I don't expect he'd remember it now.'

'Oh, I don't know,' said Fanny shyly. 'Harold has a very good memory.'

It gave Fanny a glow just to be talking to another human being, a being with a feeling of warmth about her. She moved closer as Mrs Boothroyd nodded.

'Good man, is Mr Jordan,' she said emphatically. 'Kindly man. Nellie was telling me as how he seems to have taken a shine to that lass of Turnbull's.'

Fanny stared at her with a chilly sense of dismay.

'Nice, isn't it,' Mrs Boothroyd went on, 'finding time to spend with the lass when she's no father of her own? Well, not to speak of, him being flat on his back all these years. Mr Jordan must be very fond of the lass.'

'Oh, yes,' said Fanny weakly and watched the old lady shuffle out of the door. Somehow the glow in the little shop seemed to ooze away out into the miserable street along with Mrs Boothroyd.

'Well now, Mrs Jordan, what can I do for you?'

Fanny looked back at the shopkeeper, the rows of shelves laden with bottles and jars behind his head seeming to sway and melt together in a colourful, dizzying dance. She fought hard to find her tongue.

'Salt,' she mumbled, and watched the strings fastening the back of his apron as the shopkeeper reached up for the jar. 'Do you know the Turnbull girls?' she heard herself whisper. He nodded.

'Oh aye. Lovely girls, all of them.'

'What are they called?'

'Well, there's Elsie – bright little thing she is, top of her class in school.'

'And the others?'

He twirled a blue paper into a cone and poured in the salt, then folded the top over. 'There's Cass, but she's not around any more, and then there's May. That'll be tuppence, please.'

May, thought Fanny fiercely as she handed over the coins and took the packet. So now she knew the name of the girl she'd seen with Harold, the one who was the cause of all the trouble.

Jim Turnbull lay uneasily on his side, watching Ada's face as she held the big brown teapot over his cup, refilling it with liquid which glowed amber in the light.

He liked looking at her face and the streaks of grey in her once dark hair. It was a tidy face, not what anybody could call beautiful, but it had a quality all its own, serene and capable and exuding wordless tenderness. When he first met her he'd been attracted by her lively radiance, the eager way she used to run along the street from the factory gate to meet him, her eyes sparkling and her pretty face all aglow with anticipation. Even after they were married and life was hard, that buoyant enthusiasm had never left her – never, that was, until his accident, and after that he'd seen the light in her gradually dim and die.

But however tough life was, she'd never given in, bless her. Nowadays there was a stolid determination in those eyes, a kind of steely strength, as though hardship had driven a rod of iron up through her backbone. Thank God for Ada. He wouldn't trade her indomitable strength for all the beautiful women in the world. Her solidity was her beauty.

She straightened and saw he was watching her. 'You all right, love?' she smiled.

'Grand,' he lied. 'Just help us to turn over before you go.'

She slid strong hands about his shoulders and eased him gently over. He could feel her fingertips rough on his skin, saw the chapped redness of her knuckles and fought back the urge to kiss them as they moved before his face. Love and gratitude surged in him. If it wasn't for him . . .

'Thanks, lass,' he grunted. 'I don't know how you put up with me. There's not many as would. You're a rare 'un and no mistake.'

'Like what your dad used to say – rare as rocking-horse shit,' she laughed. 'Come on now, drink up that tea before it goes cold.'

With a smile she was gone, but the flavour of love lingered on in the sour-smelling little room.

Fanny could not settle to do anything. Mrs Boothroyd's words kept playing over and over in her head.

'Mr Jordan must be very fond of the lass.'

So she'd been right, thinking they seemed familiar when she'd seen them together on the girl's doorstep. And Harold wanted to invite her into the house. Something was going on, and that girl only a child still. It was too disgraceful to think about.

Something had to be done – but what? Try to persuade Harold to see sense? He'd only deny it, say it was all in her head. Talk to the girl then? Fanny shrank from the thought. She had no idea how to communicate with young people.

171

Her mother, then. Mrs Turnbull looked the sensible sort, and Fanny needed an ally. If she knew nothing of what was going on she'd probably be grateful for the warning and see to it that the girl put a stop to this silly business.

There was no time like the present. That damned May wouldn't be there now and the youngest not yet home from school. Fanny put on her coat and hat again and headed for the Turnbulls' house.

Harold Jordan paused outside the gate of the imposing villa he'd just left and pencilled detailed notes into the little pocket notebook he always carried. This job called for extra-special attention seeing that he'd only come by it as a result of Mrs Mayhew's recommendation. A former mayor of Hawksmoor, no less.

He was feeling very pleased with himself. The more high-class jobs like this he obtained the sooner he'd be restored to his former prestige. Debt was no longer the problem; in fact, life was beginning to look distinctly rosy.

He was burning to tell someone of his delight. Fanny – she'd be thrilled. Maybe the good news would help to ease her out of the funny way she'd been behaving lately.

And Cassie should be home for her day off this weekend. Harold's step had a jaunty spring in it as he tucked his notebook back into his pocket and headed downhill towards Millsbridge.

Ada couldn't be certain whether she'd heard a sound at the front door or not. If it was, it was the timid knock of a child. She wiped the flour off her hands and went to answer.

It wasn't a child but a woman, a woman wearing, not a shawl, but a hat and coat and gloves as if it was Sunday. With a start of surprise she recognized the undertaker's shy little wife who never, as a rule, spoke to a soul as she scurried down the street.

'Hello,' said Ada, unable to hide the note of question in her voice. 'What can I do for you?'

The woman gave an embarrassed cough. 'Look, I know you don't know me—'

'I do,' Ada interrupted. 'You're Mr Jordan's wife.'

She nodded. 'That's right. I'd be glad of a word with you, Mrs Turnbull, if it's not too much trouble.'

'No trouble at all,' said Ada, standing back and holding the door wide. 'Come on in.'

The woman hesitated. 'Are you on your own?' she ventured.

'Aye. There's only my husband upstairs in bed. Come and sit down, make yourself comfortable. I'm right glad to see you.'

Mrs Jordan followed her in cautiously, looking around the living room to make certain they were alone before she turned to Ada.

'I know you'll probably think it's an awful cheek but I had to talk to you,' she said nervously, twisting her gloves in her hands, not raising her eyes to meet Ada's.

'Don't you fret,' said Ada soothingly. 'Neighbours should be neighbourly so if there's owt I can do . . . Take a seat, do, and I'll put the kettle on.'

'No,' Mrs Jordan cut in quickly. 'Let me just say what I have to. It's about your lass, do you see? I thought it best to come to you.'

'My lass?' said Ada sharply. Elsie must have been up to some mischief again. It was only a month ago old Agnes and Nellie Bottomley came round complaining about her knocking at the door and running off. 'Our Elsie, do you mean?' she asked.

Mrs Jordan was shaking her head and torturing the gloves into knots.

'Because if so,' Ada went on grimly, 'she'll be home from school in another hour.'

Mrs Jordan seemed near to tears. 'No, not the little girl,' she said in a small voice. 'It's the one who's working – May. She's old enough to know better.'

Ada felt a sudden leap of apprehension. 'Better than what?' she asked quietly. 'What are you trying to say?'

173

The woman looked up, and Ada could see misery written all over her faded face. 'I doubt she's told you,' she murmured, 'so I know it must come as a shock but I don't know any other way to say it.'

'Go on,' said Ada, feeling the chill turning to ice. 'Say what you have to say.'

Mrs Jordan spread thin hands helplessly then sank into the chair. 'I've only just found out meself – oh Lord, I shouldn't have come,' she whispered in a wretched tone. 'I'm only making things worse, and he'll kill me.'

Ada was bewildered. 'Who? What are you on about?'

Mrs Jordan shook her head miserably. 'He'll scold me, tell me I should have held my silly tongue, I know he will. Only I couldn't stand by knowing what she was up to and you not knowing a thing about it. I felt it my duty to tell you, but now I'm not so sure.'

Ice clamped around Ada's stomach. 'Go on,' she said grimly.

Mrs Jordan looked up and Ada could see tears glistening in her pale eyes. 'I think it's been going on for a bit, only now it's gone too far. Oh, don't get me wrong – I'm not blaming May – these things happen even in the nicest families—'

She was weeping now. Ada turned away, the ice in her stomach making her feel nauseous. May – somehow Mrs Jordan had learnt about May's plight, the very thing she'd wanted to keep secret from the world. She stared down at the woman's bent and shaking shoulders.

'But why should it bother you?' she asked wonderingly. 'What business is it of yours?'

Mrs Jordan's red-rimmed eyes fastened on her angrily. 'It concerns me when my husband is besotted with her – a girl less than half his age, when he watches her every move, even wants to invite her into our house!'

Ada stared at her, flabbergasted. 'Your husband? How can he? He doesn't know her – beyond passing her in the street, happen.'

Mrs Jordan's thin lips twisted into an ironic attempt at a smile. 'All the same he worships her, I know that for a fact. And him old enough to be her father too.'

Ada stood by the corner of the table, twisting a fold of the tablecloth between her fingers, trying to take it in. An old man and a young girl? It was unnatural, and the thought sickened her. But not May, surely not? When the girl said Mr Rose had arranged for her to go away she'd wondered if it was Aaron Rose . . .

'I don't see as you can blame my lass for this,' she said gruffly. 'Has your husband done this sort of thing before? Has he been in the habit of going after young girls?'

The woman's head quivered in denial. 'Not as I know of,' she muttered, 'but now I'm not so sure I know anything any more. Can't you stop her – send her away or something? He'll not leave her in peace else. Once she's out of the way happen he'll forget about her and none of this need come out.'

'Then you've no need to worry,' said Ada quietly. 'May's going away very shortly, far away.'

Mrs Jordan pulled a folded handkerchief from her pocket and dabbed at puffy eyes. 'How long for?' she asked.

'For as long as it takes. She'll not be back till it's all over. Nobody else knows but you and me.'

And our Cass, thought Ada, and for a moment suspicion flickered. No-one enjoyed a bit of juicy gossip better than Cassie, but surely she wouldn't let her sister down, not deliberately anyway. But she might have whispered something to another maid in a confidential moment up there at Chadwick's . . . Rumours flew fast around Hawksmoor . . .

Mrs Jordan tucked her handkerchief away and pulled on her gloves, then stood up with a watery smile. 'I feel much better now. You've been very kind, Mrs Turnbull, very understanding, and I'm grateful.'

'Nay,' said Ada as she opened the door. 'There's never a problem too big it can't be ironed out one way or another.'

The woman paused on the doorstep. 'Maybe,' she

murmured, 'only sometimes it's hard to see a way out when you're on your own.'

'You're not on your own now – we're in the same boat and we'll sort it out, never fear.'

'I do hope you're right.'

'I'm sure of it. Your husband'll have no interest in the lass once she comes home bringing the child.'

Ada saw the woman look up sharply, the startled look in her eyes. 'Child?' she echoed. 'What child?'

Ada's eyebrows rose. 'Why, May's, of course.'

She saw the colour drain from Mrs Jordan's cheeks as she turned and almost ran towards home. Ada felt suddenly sick.

The woman hadn't known about the baby at all. Oh my God, how could she have been so stupid?

She had to talk to May, get this sorted out. The girl had never been easy to talk to, to find out what was going on inside that quiet little head of hers. But one minute she seemed to have no interest in men whatsoever, and the next there were two of them in her life. And what was worse, one was married and the other engaged. Maybe May wasn't as naïve as she seemed.

Ada's heart felt like a leaden weight in her chest as she began peeling potatoes for supper. What with Cassie gone, Jim with no will to live, and now this . . . The whole family was starting to fall apart.

May was surprisingly cool but emphatic as she sorted through her clothes that evening.

'Not me, Mam. Mrs Jordan must have got me mixed up with our Cass, that's all I can think.'

Ada stared. 'You mean I got hold of the wrong end of the stick? I was sure it was you she was talking about – she said May.'

'Well, you can take it from me – it must be our Cass because it's not me.'

Ada shook her head and carried on stitching a button onto

176

a navy blouse. 'I never for a moment thought of it being her, what with her being away and all.'

May folded a chemise with care and placed it in her bag. 'She did talk about having an admirer, but she wouldn't say who.'

Ada looked up sharply. 'She never told me.'

May smiled and sat down. 'She wouldn't. She said he hung around the back yard at night – she'd hardly dare tell you that.'

The needle paused as her mother stared. 'Mr Jordan? Well I never! And she let him? No wonder his wife is upset, poor thing.' Ada's lips tightened as she carried on stitching. 'I'll have a few strong words to say to our Cass when she gets home.'

She laid a hand on her daughter's knee. 'And I'm right sorry, love, I don't know what possessed me, believing it was you. And letting out about the baby. Not that I think she's a gossip, but it would have been best if we'd been able to keep it to ourselves. As it is . . .'

May laid a hand over her mother's calloused fingertips. 'It's not that that's bothering me, Mam. If Mrs Jordan thinks our Cass is expecting, she might think it's him.'

Ada pulled away her hand with a groan. 'I've been and gone and done it, haven't I? I'd best go over and sort it out with her right away before there's any more harm done.'

Stabbing the needle back into the pincushion she stood up and reached for the shawl on the back of the door. May shook her head.

'He'll be home by now, most likely – it would be better to see her on her own. Why not wait till tomorrow?'

'You're leaving in the morning – I want to see you safe off.'

'If you go over first thing you can still do that.'

Ada replaced the shawl and sat down with a weary sigh. 'Aye, you're right,' she murmured. 'I'll do it first thing, soon as he's gone to work.'

SEVENTEEN

Fanny sat tense waiting in the gloom for Harold to come home, the lamp still unlit and no supper hot in the range oven. There seemed no point in going through the normal rituals when the world had suddenly turned upside-down.

The girl was pregnant, carrying Harold's child. How long then had his obsession with her been going on? Evidently it must be longer than she had guessed. And then other thoughts rushed into her confused brain . . . All those nights he went out for his constitutional . . . Sometimes for hours in the cold . . . Maybe he'd gone no further than the stable down the bottom of the yard, right under her nose, lying with that chit of a girl . . . Oh Lord, how simple and trusting she had been, never suspecting anything until these last few days!

Try as she might she could not drive from her mind images which kept racing back, images of him and that girl rolling together in the hay in that intimate embrace meant only for married folk, an elderly man and a girl not yet twenty – the monster! And now the girl was carrying his bastard.

'Face it, woman. You're barren.'

Did he know about the baby? Maybe he was glad he was fathering that longed-for child at last. That accounted for the way he treated her these days – he had no further use for her now. She had no place in his life, no place in the world. Fanny buried her face in her hands and wept bitter tears of misery.

There came the sound of a key grating in the lock. Fanny dried her cheeks hurriedly and sat up. Harold's step was light, his manner jaunty as he walked in, laid aside his hat and started to unbutton his coat.

'Well now, I told you that job I did for Mrs Mayhew would stand me in good stead, didn't I?'

Fanny made no move. He laid aside his coat and bent to light the lamp. 'Whatever are you doing sitting in the dark?' he murmured, then went on. 'You know Alderman Clarkson's wife was poorly with that Bright's Disease? Well, she's died, and through Mrs Mayhew's recommendation I'm to bury her. Stroke of good luck that, eh?'

He shook out the match and looked around the room. 'Why, the fire's nearly out,' he said reproachfully. 'It's not like you to let it get that low.'

From force of habit she bent to pick up the coal tongs, then stopped and looked up at him soberly. 'There's something I want to ask you,' she said quietly.

Harold clicked his tongue. 'Haven't you been listening – the Clarkson funeral – I'll be able to make use of that grand coffin I made – you know, the one with the fancy hinged lid I was never able to use when everything fell apart. I knew it would come in handy one day.'

Fanny set the tongs down in the coal bucket. 'What have you been up to with that Turnbull girl?' she said quietly.

She saw the light in his eyes fade and the startled look before he answered. 'What are you on about?' he muttered, but his eyes moved away from hers.

'I want to know,' she went on quietly. 'I want to hear it from your own lips. I've heard, so there's no use lying to me.'

She could see he was shaken. His cheeks were red and his gaze still avoided hers as he sat down to pull off his shoes.

'I want no truck with gossip,' he muttered. 'Here I am trying to tell you my good news—'

'You've touched her, haven't you? Don't deny it.'

He threw the shoes under his chair and took his slippers from the hearth. 'What the devil are you chuntering about?' he snapped, but she could see his fingers tremble as he pulled the slipper over his sock.

'You've lain with her, done things an old man shouldn't

even think of with a child like her. You've been unfaithful to me.'

Harold threw the second slipper down on the rug and glared at her, fury in his eyes. 'How could you say such things? Me, your husband, who's cared for you all these years and never even so much as touched another woman? I thought better of you than that. You ought to be ashamed.'

Fanny sat watching his face, seeing the colour still rouging his cheeks, hearing the bluster in his tone, and recognized guilt. Misery lay heavy round her heart.

'Will you promise me you won't see her again?' she asked.

Harold stood up sharply and turned away. 'I'll promise nothing of the sort!' he shouted. 'You're crazy and I won't listen to another word of this nonsense. Where's my supper?'

He jerked open the door of the range and stared into an empty oven. Fanny watched him sit down again.

'You've got this all wrong,' he growled. 'It's all delusion on your part, you know. I'm not having any more of it. Now where are you going?'

'Out,' said Fanny, reaching for her coat. 'If you won't promise to leave her alone—'

Harold was on his feet. 'Don't be daft, lass – it's freezing out there and you've nowhere to go.'

She tried to wrench her arm free of his restraining hand. 'Don't touch me! Don't ever touch me after you've laid hands on that – that trollop!'

He broke away as if he'd been stung by a wasp, staring at her with disbelief in his eyes. 'Nay, Fanny lass,' he croaked, 'you're out of your head. Come, sit down and calm yourself.'

'You haven't denied it,' she said bitterly. 'I know it's true.'

'Fanny, for God's sake! We'll have a word with Dr Cavendish first thing tomorrow.'

'Oh yes?' she sneered. 'And have me put away? Is that what you want, eh? So you'll be free for your fancy-woman?'

Harold's voice sounded artificial with its exaggerated silk. 'You don't know what you're saying, love. Come on, sit yourself down and we'll have a nice cup of tea.'

'Very well,' she said calmly, hanging up her coat and sitting down on the sofa with an air of resolution. 'But I'm going to sleep down here. I'll never share a bed with you again.'

May lay sleepless in her narrow bed, wondering just what the future held. It had seemed such a sensible solution when Mr Henry suggested it, going away to this Home where nobody knew her, but now it had come to it. This was the last night in her own bed. Tomorrow she'd be leaving home, leaving Mam and Dad to go a hundred miles away to live among strangers, giving birth to a fatherless child, and it still seemed unreal.

Under the sheets she ran her hands down over her stomach. Over four months now and still there was no bulge, nothing to show to prove she was pregnant. She didn't even feel any different. The doctor couldn't have been wrong, could he? The whole thing wasn't just a fantasy, a hideous dream from which she'd wake up any minute?

It was no dream. Her bag lay packed beside the bed and the letter from the Home lay on the dressing table.

'Dear Miss Turnbull, We shall be pleased to receive you on the fourteenth inst. and you will begin work in the laundry the following day . . .'

Mam had given an ironic laugh when she read the letter. 'Laundry, is it? So you'll be following in the family footsteps, seemingly. I'd hoped better than that for you.'

'It's only for a time, Mam. Once the baby's born I'll find a better post. I'll manage.'

'With a child? You've a hope.'

So Mam was still insisting she brought the baby home, but what was the point? The sole reason for going away was to hide from shame, so coming home would only broadcast her situation.

Still, she had nearly five months in which to work

something out. May punched the pillow and tried hard not to think of how lonely Mam was going to feel with only little Elsie, and Dad wasting away upstairs.

She ought to be here, caring for them, bringing in the extra shillings so sorely needed. Instead she was yet another cause for worry to them, and all because she'd let herself fall prey to a handsome young man's charms. It was her own stupid fault, and she'd never forgive herself.

Harold Jordan tossed around irritably in the double bed, unused to the empty space beside him. Fanny's accusing words still burned him. She'd had no right to condemn him for being unfaithful to her, no right at all. He'd never slept with any woman but her, not Cassie nor anyone else. But even as he fumed over the injustice of it, his thoughts could not help roaming. If only he'd had the opportunity to lie with the lovely Salome . . . What he would do to her . . . A thousand times in fantasy his hands had caressed that silken young body . . .

Fanny had caught him off-guard and he hadn't denied her charge. But then, there was no reason why he should. Her words had stung him badly, and trying to punish him by sleeping downstairs as well – this was no way for a good wife to behave. But still, he could have reassured her and set her mind at rest.

She wouldn't like lying alone down there in the parlour and that horsehair sofa would make a hard bed. By morning she'd be more prepared to listen to him. He'd soon convince her that she had nothing to worry about. For tonight he'd leave her be and give her time to cool off.

He rolled over to face her side of the bed. It was odd, not to come up against that cold bottom. He closed his eyes and in his mind he could sense a warm, firm young bottom against his thighs, and once again the heat in his guts roared into flame.

* * *

182

It was getting chilly in the parlour. Fanny shivered and pulled the blanket up close around her neck. Even though she hadn't undressed she still felt cold.

Of course, in the upset she'd forgotten to bank up the fire for the night. It would have gone out by morning. Still, what did it matter now? Nothing seemed to matter any more.

If only she could sleep to escape the misery of the tormenting pictures in her head, but it was difficult in a room growing colder by the minute. Outside in the street she could hear stumbling footsteps on the cobblestones and a man's voice singing drunkenly.

'For all that I found there, I might as well be
Where the mountains of Mourne sweep down to the sea.'

It was that Irishman, the father of the poor little mite in the privy. He had no right to be so merry, drowning his conscience with beer when he caused all the suffering he did. The world was full of misery and injustice. Fanny's eyes filled with tears.

Drink. Some people around here, however poor, seemed to find a deal of comfort in drinking though she'd never been able to understand that herself. She'd been a fervent member of the Band of Hope since she was a child. She could remember still the raddled faces of the men who used to come to the meetings and tell how they'd been led astray by Demon Drink, and how they'd struggled to escape the flames of hell and regain their manhood. She used to lie in bed at night and pray fearfully that the demon never tempted her.

So in all her fifty years she'd never even tasted the stuff, not even a sip of the bottle of sherry Harold used to buy for Christmas. There was still a bottle over there in the cupboard.

Fanny moved stiff limbs to sit upright. Why not have a tiny taste of the stuff? Harold always seemed to enjoy it, and if that Irishman found it an escape from reality . . . Why not? No demon could torment her now any more than she was already suffering.

She filled a small glass and took a sip. It was rather pleasant really, not as sweet as dandelion and burdock but still quite nice, and it made the throat feel warm as it slipped down. Fanny took another sip, and another. The glow was reaching her stomach now. She refilled the glass and sat down again on the sofa.

She couldn't go on sleeping here for ever, but neither could she go upstairs to lie beside Harold again – what was she to do? She could buy a bed for the spare room, but thinking of it filled her with despair. It was no way to live, married and yet not married. Even if she tried to brazen it out, pretend it had never happened, she'd always know what he'd done, and others might suspect. After all, he'd been seen with the girl – Mrs Boothroyd had said someone else had seen them and there were probably others beside. Even if the girl went away, when she came home again with a baby, tongues would wag. Harold's reputation would be ruined . . . Oh, the irony of it! To think they'd weathered the disgrace of that other business only to be brought low by a chit of a girl!

The bottom had fallen out of Fanny's world. Even the glow from the sherry in her stomach did nothing to dispel her wretchedness.

She pulled the blanket close around her shoulders and shivered. No longer his wife, she had no place here. She looked around the room with its heavy furniture and glittering ornaments, the remnants of happier days. Fanny Micklethwaite, as was, had been proud to become Fanny Jordan, but she was no longer his wife, mistress of this house; mistress of nothing in fact. Nothing of her own remained. None of her family still lived; she would scarcely remember their faces if it weren't for a faded sepia photograph or two lying in the sideboard drawer under the neatly wrapped fish knives and forks. No-one wanted or needed her now.

Snatching up the bottle in one hand and her glass in the other, Fanny hurried out of the back door and rushed down the yard towards the stable. She unlatched the door and slipped inside. Dolly whinnied softly in the gloom of the stall as she passed. The sweet smell of the hay brought back forcibly those horrible images of him and that girl. She hurried on through into the workshop, closing the door behind her.

The air smelled heavy with the scent of freshly sawn wood and varnish, banishing the evocative scent of the hay in the stable which summoned up images she'd prefer to obliterate. In the gloom she could make out the workbench where Harold and young Arthur worked, cutting and carving coffins for the clients. There would be candles and lucifers somewhere – yes, there they were. Setting down the glass and bottle Fanny lit a candle, then sat huddled in the blanket as she poured another drink.

On the far bench a big coffin seemed to waver in the flickering candle-light. Its hinged lid was raised and she could see the white gleam of its quilted satin lining. This one was ready for its eternal occupant, a soul never more to be plagued by fear and pain. She could envy such peace, she thought as she downed the last of the glass of sherry.

Out in the night a child's voice wailed. Probably the little Nagle boy, she thought; poor little thing, doomed to a wretched life with no future to look forward to. Death is the only escape from the misery of living.

She set the glass down abruptly. Why not? Death would solve not only her problems but Harold's too. He didn't want her any more. It was the perfect solution. Why hadn't she thought of it before?

But how? What did she have? Poison? She'd always feared pain. She couldn't drink caustic soda and there was nothing else she knew of. She looked around the fuzzy workshop, dimly making out the neat piles of shavings swept into the corner, the bottles of varnish and oil. And then her gaze fell on the wooden box by the bench – the box where Harold kept his tools.

She lifted the polished lid and looked down on the gleaming array, every one shining like new even though Harold had owned them for years. Young Arthur was in danger of instant dismissal if he didn't leave them sharpened and immaculate at the end of each day's work. Poor lad, he worked hard and deserved better than Harold's constant carping. Fanny picked up a spokeshave and examined its smooth clean blade. She drew it across her fingertip, and winced. Although she'd felt nothing, it had drawn blood.

A sudden exhilaration filled her. It would be easy – no pain. Why not? The Jews killed their animals this way, didn't they? And they said it was painless. Life just trickled away gently. Fate had led her to a simple solution to all her woes, so why dawdle? The wrist – that's what Harold told her Mr Roe the solicitor did when his wife left him – both wrists, that should make absolutely certain of it.

Fanny let the blanket fall and rolled back her cuffs carefully, then closing her eyes, she drew the blade swiftly and firmly across her left wrist. She felt a strange sensation, but it was not pain. Opening her eyes again she saw the blood spurting, and alarm filled her. It was gushing fast – cut fingers and knees had never bled like this. But she mustn't stop now – she must make a good job of it. Taking the spokeshave in her left hand and closing her eyes again, she drew the blade once more, this time across the right wrist.

It was surprisingly easy. Fanny wiped the blade and replaced it in the toolbox. Dear me, the blood was splashing everywhere, all over the tools. Oh Lord, Harold would be angry.

Taking up a rag from the bench she started dabbing at the splotches of blood on the metal, but as quickly as she wiped them away they were being replaced by more splotches. Fanny giggled. What was the point in trying to clean them? She was only making things worse. It was all a silly waste of time.

Letting the rag fall she held up one hand, fascinated by the spurt of blood. It was pouring all down her skirt too. Never mind, she thought dreamily, it would all be over soon and such trivial things wouldn't matter any more . . .

Her head was swimming and it was getting colder in the candle-lit room, and she was beginning to feel too tired to worry that her dress felt damp and clammy against her body.

She wanted to lie down now . . . Somewhere comfortable . . . To drift away into sleep.

Sleep. Forget. Block everything out . . . No more images burning in her brain, no more lying, no more the shame of watching Arthur waiting patiently on a pompous hypocrite to pay his wages . . .

She caught the glimmer of white satin wavering in the corner. The Clarkson casket with its fancy hinged lid – fit for a queen, Harold had said. She lifted the lid. Alongside lay the small set of steps he'd made for himself in the early days. With all the dignity she could muster she swayed up them, a royal victim mounting the scaffold to her execution. Holding on to the sides of the coffin she stepped in, then crouched and, lowering herself down onto the satin bed, clumsily arranged her clammy skirt around her.

Despite the cold it was cosy lying here, far cosier than the horsehair sofa. The chill spreading through her body seemed to be giving way to a suffusing warmth and a sensation of peace, like the way she used to feel all those years ago when she and Harold would lie in the spring sunlight of Grimscar Wood, surrounded by a sea of bluebells. She lifted a weak arm, felt the softness of the satin against her fingertips, and smiled as she pulled the lid down over her face. Now she could sleep . . .

EIGHTEEN

Ada eyed her eldest daughter thoughtfully over breakfast. She couldn't say too much with young Elsie all ears as she spooned porridge into her mouth.

'Now are you sure about this, May?' she asked. 'I mean, laundry work is damned hard-going for them who's not used to it.'

'It never stopped you doing it.'

'Needs must when the devil drives. But you was cut out for better things.'

'What's good enough for you—'

'That's not the point,' Ada interrupted. 'Folks always hope for better for their children.'

'I've to do the best I can in the circumstances,' said May. 'I'll be all right, never fear.'

Her mother nodded. 'Aye well, is there owt else you need?'

May shook her head. 'No, Mam. I've got everything, thanks.'

Elsie laid her spoon down. 'I need me shoes cleaned,' she said. 'I trod in some dog-dirt coming home from chapel.'

Ada scowled at her. 'I told you to get them done last night. Go on with you, get yourself a clean hanky to tuck in your knickers – and fetch your dad's pots down while you're at it.'

The child scampered out of the room. Ada spoke without looking at her elder daughter. 'You know, May, you don't have to go . . .'

'I'm getting that train, Mam.' May took something from her pocket and leaned across the table. 'Listen, I want you to have this.'

Her mother looked down at the envelope in her hand. 'What's this?'

'The money Mr Rose gave me. I won't need it at the Home.'

Ada's lip curled. 'The money to buy you off?' she sneered.

'We need it, Mam. Here, you take it.'

Ada hesitated, then took the envelope and shoved it in the pocket of her apron. 'I don't want his conscience money, but I'll take care of it till you and the baby come home. It'll come in handy for you then.'

'It's yours to do with as you choose,' said May. 'Now I'd best get a move on if I'm to catch that train.'

Ada busied herself heaping the porridge dishes, helpless. Words choked in her throat. She ached to tell the girl how much she cared, how she feared for her, how she longed to be at her side to help and comfort her when her time came.

'Aye, well,' she grunted, 'in that case when Elsie comes down you'd best go and say goodbye to your dad. And make it quick – I don't want him upset.'

Harold was still feeling irritable when he came downstairs in the morning. For the first time he could remember Fanny hadn't brought up his hot water and put it on the washstand for him to wash and shave. It was unnatural for a man to come down to breakfast still unshaven.

He looked around the parlour in surprise. Fanny wasn't waiting as usual with the teapot, ready to pour his first cup, and the table was not yet draped in white linen with places set for two. And what was more, no tantalizing aroma of frying bacon drifted from the black-leaded range. They always had bacon and egg for breakfast on Thursday.

Fanny must be still in a mood. With a sigh he crossed the little lobby to the scullery and peered round the door. She wasn't there either. He went back to the parlour and sat down.

It was cold in here. He bent to look at the fire. Dammit, it was a heap of grey ash. The silly woman must have forgotten to bank it up for the night. All that emotional drama had clearly unsettled her. The sooner he put her mind at rest, the better.

She must have gone down to the privy. He needed to go too, but in the meantime he'd try to draw up the fire – there still seemed to be a spark of life in the ashes.

Some kindling and coal lay ready on the hearth but it took a little time to discover where she kept the draw tin. He placed it in front of the fire and waited. Nothing happened. He took a double page from yesterday's *Examiner* and held it carefully over the sheet of tin and within seconds he could hear the roar of the draught in the chimney, heard a crackle as the fire spurted into life. He snatched the newspaper away just as it began to turn brown round the edges.

He glanced up at the clock on the mantelshelf. 'Dammit, woman, what's taking you all this time?' he muttered. 'At this rate Arthur will be here before we've eaten.'

He'd particularly told the lad to come early today to get him started on the Clarkson job before he went round to see Thaddeus about a granite headstone. What a stroke of luck, Mrs Clarkson being a tall woman – he could get that lovely oak casket with best brass fittings off his hands at last. It would be perfect, a grand piece of workmanship like that. Alderman Clarkson was a gentleman who would appreciate its quality.

But time was ticking by and Harold was distinctly uncomfortable. It would be unthinkable if Arthur were to arrive early and find his master still unready and unshaven. Harold's bladder felt as if it would burst if he had to wait a moment longer.

To hell with her, he fumed. He was going down there to bang on the privy door and tell her. He only hoped Arthur wouldn't turn into the yard while he was doing it.

It was nippy out in the half-light of dawn. He could feel the chill striking up through his carpet slippers as he rapped on the peeling brown paint of the privy door.

'Fanny – what's taking you so long?' he whispered urgently. 'You've been ages in there.'

No answer came. 'Fanny?' he repeated.

Still no reply. He tried the latch and the door opened. She wasn't there, only the bare brick walls, the wooden seat and the suspended sheets of newspaper. He stared around the cobbled yard. Where the devil could she be? Still, the needs of the flesh came first.

A minute later Harold came out of the privy and stood frowning. She couldn't have gone far. She wouldn't go round to the neighbours no matter what she might be short of, and it was hardly likely she'd be in the stable. She didn't care much for the sight of his lovely hearse. It only reminded her of things she'd rather forget, she used to say, but whether she meant how he'd come by it or their own mortality, she never explained.

Still, he could check. A man never really knew how a sulky woman might behave and she might be sitting in there talking to Dolly. It was one of her more irritating habits, talking to animals as if they were human. She used to talk to that old ginger cat they used to have in Marchmont Avenue until the wretched beast had the good sense to die.

'Go on, pussy,' she'd say, 'you've had enough fish now. Go and tell Father his tea's ready.'

Father indeed! The silly woman used to coo to it and pamper it as if it were a child. She hadn't done it much with Dolly, just now and again. More often than not these days she walked around mumbling to herself. It wasn't healthy. She definitely needed to be seen by a doctor.

He could hear the horses snuffling in the stalls and in the half light he could make out the dull gleam of the hearse. She evidently wasn't in here. She wouldn't dream of climbing the ladder into the hay-loft as he had done so many times . . .

Thrusting the memory from his mind he crossed to the door of the workshop and pushed it open. At least Arthur would see that his master had been in early.

He hadn't thought to bring the oil-lamp from the house as

he did every morning. Still, there were candles. He groped on the workbench for the candlestick, and clicked his tongue in annoyance as his fingers closed over it. The saucer-shaped base was full of congealed wax. How often had he told the lad never to leave it like that? And the candle was no more than a stump. The idle devil must have worked late and left in too much of a hurry to clean up properly.

Candle-grease and varnish, straw and wood-shavings – all it needed was a candle burnt too low to set the whole damn place alight. He'd give that good-for-nothing what-for when he turned up. A good employer can't be doing with lackadaisical ways.

As he replaced the candlestick on the bench Harold's hand brushed against glass. Bending, he could see by the growing light filtering in through the barred window a bottle and an empty wineglass. It was one of the lead crystal set Beatrice had given them as a wedding gift. That couldn't be Arthur. Fanny must have been down here, but when, and drinking what?

He peered at the label on the bottle. His Christmas sherry? She never touched alcohol. She always reproved him gently whenever he took the odd nip.

'Now then, Harold.'

'It's only one, love, a very small one.'

'That's what the reformed drunks at the Band of Hope used to say. One leads to two, and then three . . .'

He held the bottle up to the light. Only a dreg remained at the bottom. Funny, he'd only had one small nip from it – she couldn't have drunk all that, nearly a whole bottle, not Fanny?

Puzzled, he set the bottle down and as he did so his hand touched something sticky on the surface of the bench, and anger burst in him. Varnish, was it? And it wasn't just on the bench. As he moved Harold could feel the soles of his slippers sticking to the stone floor as though he were walking in treacle.

'Dammit, what the devil's been going on here?' he growled. Here it was, nearly eight o'clock already and he hadn't even shaved, let alone had his breakfast. And Arthur was late.

192

Harold would be late getting round to the stonemason's yard. Wife and apprentice both seemed to be conspiring to make his life even more difficult today.

Funny, the stone floor was tacky underfoot even over here, far from the workbench. It seemed to spread as far as the ledge where the Clarkson casket lay. Ah, maybe it was the sherry – she'd spilt more of it than she'd drunk, not downed the whole bottleful after all.

He touched a finger to the ledge. Yes, the dark, glutinous muck was on here too, and his heart sank. It didn't smell of varnish. Whatever it was, it could have damaged his master-piece of a casket.

He raised the lid slowly, admiring the gleam of quilted white satin under its surface, then his gaze travelled down into the dark recess, and his heart stopped. A ragged symphony of scarlet and white met his eyes, like a barber's pole gone crazy. Saturated in blood, his coffin was ruined, and his wife lay still with her arms folded across her chest and a placid smile on her silly grey face.

Ada stood on the doorstep, her shawl pulled close around her throat, to watch May walk away down the street. She felt proud of the lass, the way she walked off just as calmly as if she were setting off for work as usual, gripping the bag tightly in her hand and without looking back. When she reached the corner she gave one quick wave, and she was gone.

Now for it, up to the Jordans' house. She wouldn't give herself time to brood, to watch for the train bearing May away to cross over the viaduct. The day's work was waiting; the sett pot was steaming and a huge pile of dirty clothes lay waiting to be sorted on the scullery floor. But first she had to explain and apologize.

As she pulled the house door to, behind her, she was already mouthing words to herself, rehearsing what she would say when Mrs Jordan opened the door to her.

'I'm sorry, maybe I misled you last night – about your husband and about the baby.' No, that's not right. *'I'm sorry*

I blurted out a tale like that, but it's nowt to do with Mr Jordan, truly it isn't. Don't let on what a dreadful mistake I made. I only hope as how it's not caused any harm.'

The words were still tripping clumsily over themselves inside her head as Ada knocked at the Jordans' door. There was no sound from inside, no footsteps coming to answer. She waited. Maybe Mrs Jordan, being the shy little person she was, was peering through the curtains first to make certain who it might be.

Ada knocked again, more loudly this time. She must be in – she hardly ever went out. Ada hesitated. Maybe she should go round to the back door. Mrs Jordan could even be out there in the yard, hanging out her washing or something.

But no-one answered at the back door either. As Ada turned to retrace her steps through the arched passageway leading to the street she almost collided with a young man rushing in. She recognized the tousle-haired lad who worked for Mr Jordan.

'I'm late,' he said breathlessly. 'Mr Jordan'll be that mad – I caught the toe of me boot in the tram line and fell over.'

'Eh dear,' said Ada sympathetically. 'I hope you didn't hurt yourself.'

'Nay, I'm fine, but I missed me tram. I've run all the way from Longroyd Bridge but that won't do for Mr Jordan.'

He pointed down the yard to the open stable door. 'Oh heck, he's there before me,' he muttered. 'Now I'm for it.'

Ada glanced towards the stable. Maybe Mrs Jordan was down there with him.

'I'll come with you,' she said to the lad, and at that moment a cry rang out. The youth hesitated.

'Oh Lord, that's him,' he muttered. 'Whatever's up?'

Once more a howl echoed round the yard. Ada grabbed his arm. 'Summat bad,' she grunted. 'Come on.'

Inside in the gloom she could see a couple of stalls where horses stood, and beyond them an open door. As the young man hung back behind her she headed for it, pushing the door wide. On the far side of the dimly lit workshop stood Mr

Jordan, dressed only in a collarless shirt and trousers, and he was grappling with something in a coffin. Sweat was running down his ruddy face, his eyes stared like a madman's, and as he caught sight of Ada he stood away from the coffin and howled again.

'I can't get her out!' he cried. 'She's too heavy!'

Ada stood transfixed. His shirt was spattered with crimson stains and his arms swung helplessly by his side. Over the side of the casket hung a body – a woman's body – and it too was soaked in crimson. Blood. With a sickening feeling in the pit of her stomach Ada recognized Mrs Jordan. Behind her she heard the lad retch. Jordan took a step forward and shook his fist at him.

'Where the devil have you been till now?' he demanded. 'You should have been here twenty minutes ago! You've ruined my day – you and her between you! I'm not having this, do you hear? I've warned you before!'

Arthur's eyes stared out of his head and his voice was only a thin squeak. 'Mrs Jordan,' he whispered, pointing towards the body, 'is she dead?'

Jordan turned back and again seized hold of the body under the armpits. 'I've got to get her out – she's ruining the Clarkson casket,' he moaned. 'Come on, lad, give us a hand.'

In a daze Ada heard the boy gulp, and then suddenly he turned and ran out, his boots clattering away down the cobbled yard.

'Come back here, you lazy good-for-nothing,' roared Jordan. 'Get back here this minute!'

Ada's brain was reeling. Mrs Jordan, covered in blood, lying dead in a coffin? And Mr Jordan splashed with bloodstains, tugging at her body, swearing and shrieking like a maniac? What on earth was going on here? It didn't look like an accident. Had he killed her? And if so, why?

'Fanny, you stupid woman,' he was moaning. Suddenly he stopped and turned to Ada. 'What are you staring at?' he barked. 'Give me a hand, can't you? I've got to get her out of here. Just look what she's done to my casket.'

'She's done?' echoed Ada weakly. 'You mean – she killed herself?'

Suicide! The enormity of it swept over her. Mrs Jordan had killed herself – because of what he'd done? Or because of what Ada had told her? Oh my God! It couldn't be true! Ada's knees turned rubbery under her.

Mr Jordan was still muttering and tugging, pausing to wipe his hands down his trousers and tugging again.

'Oh God, oh Christ!' he moaned. 'I'll never be able to get this mess cleaned up in time. Stupid woman!'

Anger made Ada's wits begin to function. 'That's enough of that,' she snapped. 'Never mind your coffin – is that all you can think about, and your wife lying dead? Let's at least give this woman a bit of dignity.'

Stepping forward she elbowed her way past him and, heedless of the blood, took the woman's head and laid it gently back on the satin pillow, then eased the limbs into a more comfortable position. Jordan stood watching helplessly as she folded the blood-soaked arms over the chest.

'She was going mental,' he muttered. 'And she was drunk. See, the empty bottle's over there.' He pointed to the workbench.

Ada straightened. At that moment a cool voice cut in from the doorway.

'Now then, what's going on here?'

Ada spun round, startled. A large, solid figure in police uniform stood framed in the doorway, and behind him Arthur's white face peered round his shoulder. Jordan's jaw sagged.

The policeman took in the scene slowly, his weather-beaten face showing no sign of emotion. He surveyed Jordan's blood-spattered shirt, then pulled a notebook from his pocket.

He cleared his throat. 'Well now,' he said tersely, 'would somebody like to tell me what the bloody hell's going on?'

Ada threw her bloodstained skirt on the pile of grubby washing waiting on the scullery floor. The smell of soapy steam from the sett pot filtered through into the living room as she slumped by the fire, staring into the glowing coals.

It was all a hideous nightmare, it must be – Mr Jordan covered in blood and out of his head, that poor lifeless thing hanging out over the side of the coffin, drained of blood like a slaughtered sheep. He said it was suicide, but he could have killed his wife himself and was trying to push her into the coffin, not pull her out. But why? The whole hideous scene just didn't make sense.

And if she had killed herself, then who was to blame? Jordan, for deceiving her? Or Ada herself, for misleading the poor woman? Oh God, it didn't bear thinking about!

And the nightmare wasn't over yet. The policeman had made that quite clear.

'*Coroner's job, this,*' he'd said in a tight-lipped voice. '*Because of the unusual circumstances there'll have to be a post-mortem and an inquest. We may need you to give evidence, Mrs Turnbull.*'

Ada sighed and rose wearily. That washing would have to be seen to, whatever was happening. She wouldn't tell Jim, not yet. He'd been unnaturally quiet these last few days. She hadn't liked the look in his eyes when she'd taken him up his morning cup of tea, a look that reminded her of her father towards the end. It was a look of death, and it had made her shiver and turn away.

She picked up the rubbing board and closed her eyes to hold back the tears. The vision of that poor woman dangling out of the coffin swam before her, and she felt angry. What dignity was there in death? It seemed as though Jim had been dying for ever – he'd had to surrender his pride years ago, peeing into a bucket and allowing himself to be handled like a baby. He deserved better, a fine man like him.

She threw aside the rubbing board and rushed upstairs to hug him close. He didn't even open his eyes.

Nellie Bottomley cleared away the breakfast pots while her sister fetched the dolly tub and posser in from the yard.

'I don't know,' muttered Agnes as she slammed the posser into the tub. 'How on earth are we supposed to set about the day's work when we been kept awake half the night by that fellow next door?'

'Drunk again,' agreed Nellie. 'He's not so bad when he's sober. Quite pleasant, in fact.'

'Him?' snorted Agnes. 'He never drew a sober breath in his life. He's a selfish devil – he needs teaching a lesson.'

Nellie sighed. 'Have I to pump up the harmonium then?'

'Aye,' said Nellie. 'He'll not be up yet. We'll give as good as we got – happen that'll learn him.'

Nellie waddled over to the old harmonium in the corner. 'It hasn't done up to now,' she muttered as she pumped the bellows with her foot. 'He takes no heed. He doesn't seem to hear.'

Agnes lifted the lid. 'He'll hear this,' she said grimly. 'Folks have to be prepared to be punished for their sins.'

Nellie wiped her hands on her overall. 'Can I play?' she pleaded. 'Just this once?'

'No,' replied her sister. 'Mother left it to me, not you. You can turn the pages.'

Nellie's face fell, but she gave in with good grace. 'Can we make it something bright and jolly then? Not "Rock of Ages" again.'

Agnes considered while she flexed her fingers. 'Very well then,' she conceded as she turned the pages of the music book. 'This one – and sing as loud as you can.'

From far down the street the sisters' voices could be heard, the shrill one pitched against the rusty contralto of the other.

'Shall we gather at the river . . . ?'

Arthur agreed, reluctantly, to stay and see to the feeding and watering of the horses, but only after the body had been taken away to the mortuary. Harold stumbled back into the house.

He was still in a daze. He'd no idea what time of day it was. He ran a bemused hand over his chin. A shave – yes, he needed a shave. And then he was supposed to go down to see Thaddeus.

The water in the range was still warm from last night. He couldn't find the flowered jug Fanny always used, so he filled a tin lading can and carried it upstairs.

Setting down the jug on the washstand, he stared at the reflection in the shaving mirror, the blue around the chin, the pallid cheeks and staring eyes. It wasn't his face, not Harold Jordan, the best-known high-class undertaker in Hawksmoor. With a scraggy neck protruding from a collarless shirt, two buttons unfastened, it looked like it belonged to one of those shabby vagrants who always tried to beg a tanner off him in St George's Square.

His gaze travelled down the reflection to the crimson that soaked his shirt front. Blood. Her blood. With a moan he reeled away from the mirror and tore the shirt off and flung it on the floor.

Fanny dead. It was inconceivable. Even though he'd seen it with his own eyes, he still couldn't, wouldn't believe it. For over thirty years she'd always been there, by his side. Silly and a bit soft maybe, an easy touch for any hard-luck story, but she was a good wife.

He stared down at the big bed, his pillow all crumpled and awry, the sheets thrown back where he'd stepped out first thing this morning. And then at her side, all neat and tucked in, with her nightdress lying neatly folded on the smooth pillow.

He slumped on the bed and buried his face in his hands. From far away down the street he could hear singing.

> *'Shall we gather at the river,*
> *The beautiful, the beautiful, river?'*

Sobs racked his body. 'Oh Fanny, lass,' he wept, 'I'm so sorry.'

*   *   *

In the house next door to the Misses Bottomley, Tim Nagle was dreaming of his boyhood, cutting peat with his father in a Connemara bog. Down in the village he could hear the women singing. He smiled to himself, farted, then rolled over and slept peacefully on.

NINETEEN

Harold's brain was in turmoil. Half of him was deeply distressed and overcome by guilt over what had happened, while the other half, despite himself, seemed to be standing off and viewing the circumstances through objective, professional eyes. Even if he couldn't bury Fanny until the inquest was over, he had to register the death and notify the Press. He'd make the announcement in the obituary column in few words, carefully chosen.

'*At home, suddenly, Fanny, dear wife of Harold Jordan . . .*'

And Beatrice. She had to be told before she read about it in the *Examiner*.

He found it hard to walk up the garden path and ring the doorbell, and even harder to break the news. At first he could only bring himself to say that Fanny had died suddenly.

His sister and Maurice made all the right moves, showing due shock and concern. Maurice poured him a glass of brandy.

'This morning, you say?' he murmured. 'My dear fellow, what a terrible shock for you.'

Then Beatrice's curiosity got the better of her. 'Mind you,' she said, dabbing at her eyes and then tucking the lace-edged handkerchief away up her sleeve, 'I had no idea she was poorly. You never let us know.'

'She wasn't really,' replied Harold, then added quickly, 'at least, not the way folks think of as poorly, though she hadn't been quite herself of late.'

'Oh?' said Beatrice. 'How do you mean?'

'Well, you know, acting a bit odd. Happen I should have guessed summat was up with her.'

Beatrice nodded sagely. 'I know what you mean. Never quite of this world, was Fanny. What happened then?'

Harold heard his own voice as it came out in a hoarse croak. 'She killed herself. Cut her wrists.'

He heard Maurice gasp as he sat down suddenly. Beatrice sat silent for a moment and Harold could guess what she was thinking. Suicide – the disgrace.

He was right. 'Do many folks know?' she asked.

He shook his head. 'Not yet. The paper will only say she died suddenly, but there's to be an inquest.'

Beatrice fished in her sleeve for the hanky again. 'I always knew there was summat funny about her,' she said quietly. 'I remember warning you when you first said you wanted to marry her. I said them Micklethwaites weren't quite normal.'

Maurice reached over to touch her arm. 'Beatrice, love—'

She turned on him. 'Well I did – he was so besotted he couldn't see – I didn't want my brother marrying one of them, and Mother didn't either. Still, he wouldn't listen.'

Harold hung his head. He could have protested, protected Fanny's name, but it eased his conscience if the world believed she was unbalanced. Even the most loving husband couldn't protect a poor, deluded woman from the capricious fancies in her head.

'It won't be easy for you,' remarked Beatrice, 'but when it's all over you should move away from here. That house must have dreadful memories for you. Start again where folk don't know you.'

She means get rid of me, the embarrassing brother, thought Harold. He shook his head firmly.

'My business is here, where I'm known,' he said curtly. 'I'll not move far.'

His sister sighed and went on remorselessly. 'We all knew the Micklethwaites were a bit weak in the head,' she murmured. 'You deserved better than that, Harold. And now you've no-one, no children to turn to . . .'

She looked up at him sharply. 'I've always wondered about that,' she remarked. 'Was it her? Was she – difficult?'

'Beatrice!' Maurice cut in. 'Really!'

She gave her husband a cool, disdainful stare. 'It's a wife's duty, pleasant or not,' she stated. 'I gave you two sons, didn't I? I did my duty.'

Harold felt he had to step in. 'No,' he said softly. 'It wasn't Fanny's fault. We just weren't blessed, that's all.'

For a moment Beatrice sat silent and he was acutely aware of her eyeing him, reassessing him with a shrewd, calculating stare. He knew what she was thinking and he squirmed: that it was his fault, he wasn't capable of fathering a child.

'Nevertheless,' Beatrice went on, 'if you ever marry again – and you could, you know – you're not that old – then choose carefully. You need a woman with summat about her, strength of character.'

'Like my wife,' said Maurice.

Beatrice inclined her head. 'Exactly. Now ring the bell for Mary to bring up the tea, will you? And seeing as it's a solemn occasion, tell her we'll use the best Royal Worcester today.'

Sudden death was a common enough occurrence in Cedar Street – only last summer one of the Jepson boys from up by the viaduct had fallen in the cut and drowned, only eighteen months after his older brother had been crushed under a brewery dray – but even so, the news of Mrs Jordan's sudden death set tongues alight. Ada stayed indoors in the desperate hope of avoiding the gossip.

But in vain. The first to call was Mrs Tandy. She knocked at the door, still in her pinafore and with a shawl hastily thrown about her shoulders, saying she'd heard the news at the corner shop, who'd got it directly from young Arthur, but she wanted the details confirmed.

'Dead in a coffin, he said she were,' she said breathlessly. 'Hanging out over the side.'

'That's right,' said Ada.

'Absolutely smothered in blood,' Mrs Tandy went on, her eyes gleaming.

'Aye, she were.'

'Well, I'll go to the foot of our stairs! Did she really cut her own wrists then like he said? A quiet little body like her?'

'So it seems,' Ada replied in a flat voice.

Mrs Tandy's eyes rounded. 'Well, who'd have believed it? Why should she do a thing like that? She'd nowt to worry over, surely?'

Ada shrugged. 'Who knows what goes on inside other folk's heads? Very likely we'll never know.'

A little while later Mrs Boothroyd called over the back-yard wall. Ada went out into the pale sunshine.

'Whatever is this I'm told?' called the old lady. 'About the undertaker's wife?'

'It's true, I'm afraid,' said Ada. 'I saw her.'

'Aye, so Mrs Tandy told me. Must have been a dreadful shock for you. I hardly ever set eyes on her meself, but it's still a terrible shame. They say he's gone quite cuckoo, her husband.'

'Well, he's bound to be upset, finding his wife like that. He'll not be able to forget in a hurry. Now I'd best get back inside and see to the mangling.'

Several more neighbours came knocking but Ada didn't answer the door for the rest of the day. Late in the afternoon she heard the tripe man ringing his bell and reached for her purse.

She hadn't had a chance to get down to the market and there was nothing Jim liked better than a nice plate of tripe and onions stewed in milk. The washing still had to be hung and dried, so the tripe would make a quick and nourishing meal, and cheap into the bargain. She hurried out onto the doorstep just as the cart pulled past the door. The tripe man gave her a grin.

'Afternoon, Mrs Turnbull. What's your fancy today, eh?

Nice bit of elder or a slice of thick seam? Or I've a lovely bit of honeycomb.'

She stood by the tail of the cart, looking down on the array of flesh, flaccid and white in the fading light, and suddenly her stomach turned over. Lying there, flabby and lifeless, trapped between the wooden walls of the cart, dead flesh, drained of blood . . . Hurriedly she shoved the coins back into her purse.

'I've changed me mind,' she said abruptly. 'I think we'll have bacon tonight.'

Harold was determined that the Clarkson funeral had to go ahead tomorrow with the very best service he could offer. Arthur was reluctant at first to deal with the coffin, hanging back with big, fearful eyes.

'Do I have to, Mr Jordan? I'd rather not touch it, not after . . .'

'Rubbish,' said Harold sharply. 'I don't have to remind you that the living still have a living to earn. Money doesn't grow on trees, you know.'

The silly lad had understood – he no more wanted to lose his job than Harold did his livelihood. What he did with the stained satin lining when he stripped it out, Harold didn't ask, but the freshly-lined and repolished casket had fitted Mrs Clarkson a treat. Alderman Clarkson was clearly satisfied even if he wasn't able to say much more than a few, choking words.

'Are you sure you still want to do this?' he muttered. 'I mean, after what you've been through?'

Harold nodded gravely. 'We're a professional firm, Alderman Clarkson. You shall have the very best service we can provide.'

So he stood in the dusty road outside the church, the horses' black plumes dipping and waving in the strong breeze, as he watched the pall-bearers, his usual quartet of off-duty firemen, carry the coffin in through the lych-gate. The casket gleamed in the pale sunlight and suddenly he had a momentary vision of a body hanging limp over the side, the grey dress browned with blood.

He leaned against the old oak tree on the pavement edge, a nauseous feeling rising in his throat.

'You all right, Mr Jordan?'

The portly shape of Alderman Clarkson wearing a crêpe armband was peering at him with some concern. Harold shook his head and the vision slowly cleared.

'I'm fine, thanks.'

He removed his hat as he followed the troop of family and mourners into the gloom of the church. You'll have a fine casket too, Fanny, he promised inwardly. I'll see you get one every bit as good as this.

For days the image haunted Ada. Every time she closed her eyes she could see again the lifeless body of Fanny Jordan, and her heart was filled with remorse.

'It's all my fault – I misled the poor soul. If I hadn't misunderstood her, blurted out about May . . . But how was I to know?'

Try as she might, she could find no ease for her conscience. Guilt plagued her day and night. If only there was someone she could talk to, but with May gone and only Jim . . .

That night she stood in the bedroom by candle-light, looking down on her husband's sleeping figure. Her heart was bursting to tell him, but he couldn't take it now. At one time he'd have listened and consoled, advised her what to do, but not any more. Still . . .

'Oh, love,' she whispered softly into the shadows, 'I've done a terrible thing.'

In a low voice she poured out the whole story to her husband as he lay huddled under the thick blanket. The words went unheard, but somehow as Ada loosened her stays she felt slightly easier just for having spoken them aloud.

Mr Henry had spoken far less than the truth when he'd told May that the Home was a refuge where she would work and be cared for until her time came; somehow his words had led her to expect a house where she and the other unfortunate girls in her position would do domestic work, cooking, washing and cleaning, in return for their keep. Mr Henry hadn't said it was in reality a factory where laundry was taken in from the whole surrounding area, an institution run on frugal lines by an order of nuns whose rules were harsh and inflexible. She'd expected routine and discipline, not a pitiless grind akin to a workhouse.

On the day she arrived she was shown into the Mother Superior's office. The black-clad nun had scarcely looked up from the papers on her desk.

'Name?'

'May Turnbull.'

A plump finger ran down a list. 'Ah yes. Number Forty-Two. That will be your name as long as you're with us.'

'My name?'

'That's right. No frills here. You'll find a list of rules pinned up in the dormitory. The rest you'll learn as you go on. Now go with Sister and she'll fit you up with a uniform.'

That night May sat on the edge of her narrow iron bed in the corner of a long, draughty dormitory. At least she had a bed against a wall, she told herself as she peeled off her scratchy grey smock, not stranded in the middle of the long row stretching away down the room.

The other girls were undressing in silence. They looked pale and lifeless as they pulled off their boots and wriggled out of uniform grey smocks. Some of them were heavily pregnant, others barely showing yet, but they all looked completely exhausted, their movements as slow and stiff as those of old women. None of them seemed to have enough energy even to talk to one another.

Some of them seemed almost too old to be having children and others were scarcely more than children themselves. The young girl climbing into the next bed, so heavily pregnant she seemed almost as wide as she was tall, looked no more than twelve.

May smiled at her. 'Hello. What's your name?'

The girl looked surprised. 'Twenty-Seven,' she muttered.

'No – I mean your real name.'

'Oh – Daisy.'

'My name's May. How old are you, Daisy?'

The girl yawned and eased her bulky body down under the blanket. 'Fourteen. Had me birfday three weeks after me dad found out I was up the creek,' she said wearily. 'He wouldn't have me back from Mrs Baldwin's after that.'

'Mrs Baldwin's?' asked May.

Daisy curled her arms behind her head. 'They sent me down Stepney to her when I was a kid. She paid 'em four bob a week for me.'

'Domestic work, was it?'

The girl's lip curled. 'That's what they called it. They knew very well. She had a load of old men lined up waiting for me. She threw me out when this happened.'

May sat aghast. 'Where did you go?'

The girl shrugged. 'Nowhere. Sleeping in doorways and alleys, I was, begging for a bit of bread till this dozy old priest found me and brought me here.'

May spoke softly. 'What will you do when you have to leave, Daisy?'

'Who knows?' the tired voice replied. 'At least I'm getting my food and a bed here.'

She rolled over and settled down to sleep. May reached out to touch the bare stone of the wall beside her bed, damp to the touch, and slithered down under the thin blanket. Daisy was right. Survive for the moment and don't think about tomorrow – that was what she had to do.

The straw mattress was hard and unyielding, and every time she moved it creaked like the midwinter snow underfoot on Lindley Moor. Around her in the darkness she could hear sounds from the other narrow beds, the deep breathing of those girls already asleep punctuated by murmured prayers and occasional sniffles from those still lying awake. Every now and then a thin wail drifted through the stone walls.

'Bloody brats,' snivelled the girl in the bed opposite. 'You'd think they'd put the nursery further away.' Then she buried her head deep in the pillow and May could hear her muffled tears.

Tears weren't far from her own eyes. Hawksmoor and home seemed a million miles away from this dismal, inhospitable place. She'd hate Mam to see how she was living – but then she never would. She couldn't leave Dad and travel this far.

'We're not allowed visitors,' one of the girls had told her. 'Not that anybody wants to come and see me. And we're not allowed to go out neither. We're stuck in here till they throw us out.'

No matter, thought May. Mam would hate it here, the dead faces of the girls, the coldness numbing the spirit as well as the bones. Numbers instead of names – like so many corpses in a mortuary.

If only they were allowed to go out of the Home for a while, to wander out of the big iron gates now the sun was starting to shine again after the winter, and go down into the nearby village – that would help. It was going to be hard to stay shut up for the next few months. It made the place seem even more prison-like.

A muffled whisper came from Daisy's bed. 'You only got that bed 'cos none of us wanted it.'

'Why not?'

'That was Twenty-One's bed. She was all right, she was. Went down to delivery day before yesterday and she never came back.' For a moment there was silence, and then she added, 'The girl who had that bed before her died and all.'

May bit her lip and said nothing. She felt a flicker in her stomach and ran a cold hand down over her belly. Yes, it was the child making its first fluttering movements, she was sure of it, and she was filled with a sudden leap of determination. Nothing was going to happen to this baby. Whatever lay ahead, she'd bear it all.

'Don't you listen to her,' she muttered under the blanket. 'We're going to leave this place together, you and me.'

The first grey streaks of dawn light filtered down through the high, uncurtained windows when the girls were wakened by a shrill bell.

'Another bloody day in Paradise,' grumbled Daisy as she pulled the vast smock over her ungainly body. 'Them bleeding nuns work you from can till can't.'

A nun stood by the door. 'Line up,' she barked. 'And no talking on the way down to Mass.'

May joined the line as they filed silently down the stone steps to a chilly, candle-lit chapel.

'*Agnus Dei, qui tollis peccata mundi . . .*'

She knelt on the bare flagstones, hands clasped, listening to the unintelligible incantations of the white-robed priest standing at the little altar and the thin voices of the Sisters chanting in reply. Beside her she could see Daisy's head nodding, her eyes closed. At last the priest turned to his flock.

'*Ite, missa est . . .*'

Everyone was standing now and turning to leave. May gave Daisy a nudge in the ribs and she almost fell over, then, clambering to her feet, she staggered over to join the others as they filed out of the chapel.

'I could do with God if He took His turn on the scrubbing board,' she mumbled.

Mass over, they ate a frugal breakfast of porridge and weak tea, sitting at long trestle-tables in a cold, bare hall. Only the occasional sound of a tin mug on the wooden table or the clink of a spoon in a bowl broke the heavy silence.

'Aren't we allowed to talk?' asked May.

'Too much bloody effort,' muttered Daisy. 'You'll find out.'

A nun beckoned them and they followed her down to a vast, steam-filled laundry.

'Forty-Two,' she said, tapping May's elbow, 'your job

210

today will be starching and pressing. The others will show you what to do.'

By nightfall May's back and shoulders burned with pain. Not once, except for a brief lunch-break, was any girl allowed to pause or flag in her work or a long, thin cane would swish down on offending hands. May saw a weasel-faced woman gaze in dismay at the blood smearing the back of her hand.

'And mind you don't go getting stains on that shirt, Thirty-One,' the nun hissed in the woman's ear, 'or it's the cupboard for you. We'll have no damaged goods here or you'll find yourself paying for it.'

Sister Anthony seemed to be the one in charge, a sharp-tongued nun who watched their every move. As May stood goffering a lace collar she became aware of the short, plump figure behind her, looking over her shoulder.

'Hmm,' Sister Anthony sniffed. 'You seem to know what you're about, Forty-Two.'

'I was brought up to it,' said May. 'It's my mother's trade.'

'Indeed?' said the Sister. 'Then it seems to me she's a better washerwoman than a mother, letting you fall from grace like this.'

May turned to glare at the nun. 'It's not her fault,' she said coldly. 'She's a fine mother, one of the best, and I'm very proud of her.'

'Proud, are you?' sneered Sister Anthony. 'Just you remember, my girl, that pride is one of the seven deadly sins and must be punished. Bear that in mind when you're crying out in labour.'

The Sister turned abruptly and walked away. May stabbed the iron savagely into the folds of the collar, wishing it was wrapped around Sister Anthony's ugly neck.

Funny, she thought as she finally laid the collar aside, but Miss Openshaw used to wear a collar just like that. Miss Openshaw, who'd been so kind in what seemed now to be a life-time ago.

'*Don't let them bully you, May. Don't let them walk all over you.*'

May smiled to herself as she picked up the matching set of lace cuffs and laid them on the ironing board. Miss Openshaw could teach the nuns a lot about charity.

Thaddeus stood in the doorway of his shed, chafing his hands together to warm them up before getting back to work on the Portland stone. He was about to pick up his chisel again when he saw the black-clad figure of Mr Jordan come striding through under the arch into the yard.

'Morning,' he nodded, noting the black armband on his visitor's sleeve. 'I been expecting you.'

Mr Jordan nodded in reply. 'I know. You've probably heard the news.'

'About your missus? Aye. I'm sorry.'

'Sad business. I just hope I haven't held you up, you needing to know what to carve on that headstone.'

'I've done it. Alderman Clarkson came and told me. It's over in that corner if you want to have a look.'

Mr Jordan turned towards where he pointed, but Thaddeus could tell he saw nothing. The poor fellow was in a bad way.

'If there's owt I can do for you, Mr Jordan,' he said awkwardly, 'you've only to say.'

The other man shook his head slowly. 'Thank you, Thaddeus. I appreciate that, but there's nowt anyone can do right now. After the inquest, happen . . .'

Thaddeus felt a sudden rush of compassion, an affinity with a man he had never been able to warm to before. Hadn't he lost his own Freda and felt bereft ever since? 'Tell you what,' he said curtly, ashamed of his own impetuosity, 'when the time comes, I'll carve her headstone for you – for free. How's that?'

A shadow of a smile touched the corners of Mr Jordan's lips. 'That's very good of you, Thaddeus, and I'll be most honoured to accept.'

*   *   *

Harold felt a tinge of shame that he didn't feel more distressed about Fanny's death. Finding her dead in that coffin had been a terrible shock, but not as appalling as Arthur evidently had found it, but then he'd seen bodies far worse mutilated over his years in the business.

To be truthful, he felt he was only playing the part that was expected of him. The armband and the sorrowful face he wore were more for other people's benefit than his own.

But once the funeral was over . . . It was Beatrice who'd put the idea into his head.

'*If you ever marry again . . . You're not too old, you know . . .*'

He'd never thought of marriage. But she was right, a man needed a wife to care for him and his home, to support him and, if she was young enough, to bear his children.

A secret, furtive excitement grew in him. He knew the very woman. He closed his eyes and a vision of the delectable Cassie Turnbull swam so close he could almost touch it.

But she wouldn't have him, would she? A girl as pretty as Cassie would find it laughable that a man more than thirty years older than herself should even think of courting her.

As he undressed for bed Harold surveyed critically the reflection in the long mirror. It refused to lie even when he breathed in deeply. It showed him a bulky man with thinning grey hair, a body spreading too thick around the middle, belly and backside sagging unpleasantly and the skin hanging loose over what had once been hard muscle. He sighed as he turned away to pull on his nightshirt.

He drew the sheets up around his chin gloomily. It looked like he would have to settle for some scrawny spinster or a well-upholstered widow-woman. No, he couldn't face that.

So if not looks, then what else had he to attract a pretty young girl? Not his trade – even in his schooldays the other kids used to laugh and jeer about Father.

'*Your dad's a scarecrow! Black, weirdy scarecrow!*'

But as Mother used to say, they wouldn't mind earning the kind of money Father did. Harold's shoes and gloves were always of the best leather; he didn't have to wear clogs like the other kids in his class. Like Father used to say, as long as folks died, there was always a good living for the undertaker.

Money – that was it! A girl from a poor family, accustomed to working long hours to earn only a few shillings a week – surely she'd leap at the chance of the comfort he could offer. It would be luxury in her impressionable young eyes.

Yes, money was the answer. Now the debts were cleared and business was looking up again, he could think of extending it, maybe even make an offer to take over old Riley's firm. The old fellow was knocking on a bit and they said he was thinking of retiring. He had no son to follow him – why not try to buy him out?

The idea excited Harold. If he were to absorb his main rival into his own establishment, he'd have the biggest undertaking business in Hawksmoor. Cassie surely couldn't hold out against him then.

That night Harold's dreams were threaded once more with dramatic, sensational adventures, chasing away for the moment the imminent prospect of attending the inquest.

TWENTY

Grace Openshaw had one last peep out of the window. It was no good wishing; Edward wasn't going to call today. Disappointed, she sat down on the sofa and picked up the stocking with a hole in the knee.

It was odd how he'd stopped calling round as often as he used to. For weeks on end he'd seemed to find a reason to drop by almost every day, but just lately it had become only once or twice a week, and for the last ten days she hadn't set eyes on him at all.

As she wove the needle in and out of a neat darn in the lisle stocking she considered. It couldn't be something she'd said or done, could it? She'd never behaved outrageously or said anything controversial. In fact she'd taken great pains to be always as unassuming and ladylike as Mother would have wished.

Maybe that was it – he was becoming bored with her company and looked for a more stimulating companion than a painstaking little spinster who was set in her ways. She sighed deeply and then smiled down at Oscar, who was curled up on the sofa alongside her.

'Looks as though I'm stuck with you, you ugly brute,' she sighed.

The cat looked up curiously as she snipped off the strand of wool and replaced the darning needle in the needlecase. He stood up, arched his back in a tall stretch, then butted his head gently against her hand. She smiled and picked up the hairbrush.

'Well, I suppose you're one gentleman caller I can rely

on,' she murmured. 'Come here, then.'

As Mother's hairbrush glided over the cat's welcoming back she could hear his deep purr of contentment; it was gratifying to hear, but not half so rewarding as Edward's half-closed eyes and throaty murmurs of approval as he savoured her chocolate cake.

'Please God,' she whispered, 'let him call tomorrow . . .'

The earth in the park was soft and sweet-smelling after the night's rain. Harold paused near the gates and breathed in a lungful of fresh air, relishing its sweetness after the malodorous stench of the aniline dye rising from the river in Millsbridge.

Yes, there was definitely a promise of spring in the air. Once today's wretched inquest was over, he could turn his thoughts more positively to the future. The police had made it clear that they were in no doubt that death was due to suicide but even so, the questions put to him were likely to be distressing.

At least it should be a relatively quiet affair; they hadn't considered it necessary to call Arthur or Mrs Turnbull to give evidence. Dr Cavendish would testify if need be that he was about to see Fanny and treat her.

Poor Fanny. As Beatrice said, the Micklethwaites had never been the most stable of people. Maybe he should have recognized the signs years ago. It still troubled him that he hadn't got her to see the doctor earlier; she could have been treated in Storthes Hall . . .

Still, no use crying over spilt milk. What's done is done and can't be undone. Best foot forward now and face the unpleasant task ahead . . .

Harold turned his back on the park, pulled his hat down firmly on his head, and strode purposefully down towards town.

Ada could hear Jack Smedley's boots come clumping down the stairs and she pulled the kettle over on the hob. He'd be wanting a cup of tea before he went home.

'It's no fun going home to an empty house, I can tell you.' He said it every time he called, and once or twice she'd asked him if he'd like to stay on for supper. Jim seemed to be sleeping even more than usual these days and there was only young Elsie for company of an evening . . .

Jack stood hesitantly in the doorway, cap in hand. 'It's all right,' said Ada, 'sit yourself down – the kettle's on.'

He looked big and awkward as he seated himself. 'If you're sure I'm not in the way – I know you've work to do,' he muttered.

'I've time for a cup of tea. Now then, Elsie, shift them books off the table and fetch the ginger biscuits out of the larder.'

Elsie moved the books to the sideboard. 'I can't,' she mumbled. 'There's none left.'

Her mother gave her a sharp look. 'How do you mean? There was this morning – oh never mind, go and see if your dad wants owt.'

The child gone, Jack leaned his elbows on the table. 'Jim's not looking so good, Ada,' he said. 'There's hardly a word out of him.'

'I know,' she replied wearily. 'He's like that, no interest in anything these days.'

She became aware that he was watching her closely. She turned away and busied herself spooning tea into the pot.

'Is there owt else on your mind, lass?' he asked gently. 'You look like you've a load of worry.'

'Who hasn't?' she said sharply. 'Worry's nowt fresh.'

As she bent to pull the kettle forward she felt a touch on her arm.

'Only if I can help – if there's owt I can do, Ada lass, you know I'd do it like a shot.'

She gave him a smile. 'I know, and I'm grateful but really, there's nowt.'

Elsie came in, her face serious as she put her father's empty pint pot on the table. 'Me dad doesn't want no tea but he says his back's bad. I don't have to clean it, do I, now our May's gone?'

'No, love,' Ada reassured her. 'That's my job.'

The child's face cleared. 'Tell you what, I'll borrow Mrs Boothroyd's *Examiner* when she's done with it – he likes me to read out bits to him.'

Jack Smedley reached into his pocket and pulled out a penny. 'Good girl,' he said with a smile, holding out the coin. 'Here, get yourself a penn'orth of humbugs or summat at the corner shop while you're at it.'

Elsie took the penny in disbelieving fingers, then looked up at her mother. Ada smiled.

'Go on then, and don't eat 'em all before your tea.'

Jack swung round in his chair to watch the child skip out, clutching her penny in delight. Then he turned to look up at Ada.

'You can tell me now,' he said gruffly. 'It won't go no further.'

She bent over the table, pouring tea but deliberately not meeting his gaze. 'What makes you think there's owt to tell?'

He shook his head. 'I've known you too long, lass. I can see right through you – you're not like our Brenda was. There's summat.'

She put the teapot down and sighed as she took her seat. Not for the world could she tell him the whole story . . .

'It's Mrs Jordan who died,' she said.

'Aye, a bad business that, but you mustn't dwell on it.'

Ada hesitated. Half the tale would do. 'I'm trying not to, but now Mr Jordan's asked me to clear out her clothes and things once the funeral's over.'

'He's giving 'em to you?'

'I don't want a dead woman's things,' she said sharply, then added more gently, 'I don't like, but he says he can't do it and she'd no relatives. I'm the only neighbour he knows well enough to ask, seemingly. How can I refuse?'

Jack shook his head. 'I don't see how you can, lass. Best get it over and done with.'

* * *

The coroner was clearly in the throes of a distressing head-cold. He looked down from his dais through watery, red-rimmed eyes at the doctor who was giving evidence.

'So death, in your opinion, was due to loss of blood as a result of the severed arteries?' he asked.

'Yes, sir.'

'I see. The post-mortem showed nothing else unusual?'

The doctor hesitated. The coroner raised his eyebrows in question.

'Well,' the doctor said slowly, 'there was some uncommon calcification in the abdominal space, something I personally have never encountered before.'

'Calcification?' repeated the coroner, reaching into a pocket for his handkerchief. 'Do you mean a kidney – or gallstone – or a tumour of some kind?'

The doctor shook his head gravely. 'Not exactly. It appeared to be the calcified remains of some foreign object which had found its way into the abdominal cavity. That must have been many years earlier.'

The coroner blew his nose loudly. 'I see. Have you any idea what this foreign object might have been?'

The doctor looked across the court towards the husband, then looked away and shuffled his notes. 'After discussion with my colleagues who know of similar incidents, I now believe it was the remains of a foetus.'

The coroner leaned forward. 'A foetus – in the abdominal cavity? Surely that is most unusual?'

'Yes, sir, very rare but not unknown. There was a Lydia Scott, in Liverpool fifteen years ago – the case is recorded in medical records. An extra-uterine pregnancy, or an incomplete miscarriage where the aborted foetus then travels back up the Fallopian tube – it can, for a time, feed off the blood vessels in the abdominal wall but inevitably it dies. It cannot then, of course, be discarded.'

The coroner rubbed his nose thoughtfully. 'I see. And this must have occurred some considerable time before death?'

'Possibly twenty or thirty years earlier, judging by the degree of calcification. In lay terms it is known as a stone baby.'

A huge sneeze escaped the coroner before he could reach for his handkerchief. He blinked rheumy eyes and looked down again at his notes. 'But this condition did not in any way contribute to the death of the deceased, I take it?'

'No, sir, not at all. Death was due to loss of blood.'

The coroner dipped his pen in the inkwell. 'Then I think we can safely say that death was due to suicide while the balance of the mind was disturbed. Case closed.'

Maureen Nagle peered anxiously into the wicker laundry basket which once again was doubling as a crib. The baby seemed pale and lifeless. She'd been like this since last night and still she wouldn't suckle. Maureen felt desperately uncomfortable, her breasts as huge and hard as cannon balls. Young Thomas would howl with envy if she unbuttoned her frock and tried to feed the baby again.

But the little one needed to feed. She was perfect, with her fuzz of baby hair as midnight-black as her father's and her deep blue eyes, but she was almost as tiny as the day she was born and that was two months ago now. Tim only growled irritably when she tried to tell him.

'If the child is hungry, she'll feed,' he'd snapped. 'Leave her be.'

Mammy used to say the same about the piglet all those years ago, back home in the green fields of Connemara. But she'd been wrong. The piglet died the day after she said it.

Maureen shivered. The baby didn't seem sick – she had no fever, but she just wouldn't feed and it wasn't natural. All the others clamoured for food day and night – you couldn't fill them.

She heaved young Thomas away from the fire with her foot and opened the door of the food cupboard. Please God she'd find something left to make a supper – Tim had taken the last pennies from her purse last night. On the shelf lay only the bones of yesterday's neck of mutton. Boiled up, they'd make a decent broth – now if she could find Dominic she'd get him to climb over the wall of Armitage House again and pinch a few carrots and swedes to thicken it up. It was no use sending him round the back of Smailes' again to pick up the rotting stuff the old greengrocer left out in the yard; Dominic wouldn't go near the place now the old fellow had got himself that huge dog. The boy couldn't be far away, and Tim would go crazy if his belly wasn't filled before he went down to the Fleece.

But where in heaven's name was Dominic? The last she'd seen of the child he was racing away up the street towards the viaduct. That was three hours ago. Please God the boy hadn't run off again. Tim had given him far worse beatings in the past.

The baby stirred and gave a thin wail. Maureen lifted her gently out of the crib and held her against her swollen breast, feeling the warm wetness of the blanket bundle on her skin. Thomas was too engrossed sucking a lump of coal to notice when she unbuttoned her frock and teased the baby with an erect nipple.

It was no use. The tiny mouth lay open and motionless, the blue eyes staring blankly. Maureen hugged the baby close, squeezing drops of milk onto her lips, willing her to suck. She thought of her mother, forever with a child at her breast. She'd reared only five of them out of nine.

'Come on, Lily,' she urged, then turned her face up to the damp-stained ceiling, murmuring fervent words under her breath. 'Sweet Jesus,' she prayed, 'let her suckle and live.'

Cassie came dashing, breathless, into the living room, dumped her wicker basket on the table then turned, hands on hips, to her mother.

'What's all this I hear about Mrs Jordan?' she demanded. 'Eunice tells me she killed herself – is it right?'

Ada nodded. 'Aye, it's right.'

221

'Cut her wrists, she said, and you was there when they found her.'

'I was,' said Ada grimly, 'and I never want to see owt like that again.'

Cassie stared, wide-eyed, disbelieving. 'Whatever would she want to do a thing like that for?'

Her mother gave her a shrewd look. 'You don't know?'

The girl's mouth hung open. 'Me? How could I? I haven't been home for three weeks. I knew nowt about it till I met Eunice just now in Beech Street.'

Ada sat down. 'You don't think as Mrs Jordan might have heard summat about another woman then? Someone leading her husband astray?'

Cassie's eyes flickered for a moment. 'What you on about, Mam? What other woman?'

Elbows on the table, Ada's hands gripped tightly together. 'I heard you was leading him on. Happen that could have upset Mrs Jordan,' she said quietly.

Cassie's face grew red. 'I did not!' she cried hotly. 'Don't you go trying to blame me – I only ever spoke to him once – no twice, once outside the library and once down the street when I twisted me ankle and he helped me home. That's not leading him on.'

Ada gave her a cold stare. 'Oh? And what about him watching you in the window at night? You knew he was down the yard, didn't you?'

The flush faded from Cassie's face. 'Who told you?'

'Our May, and she wouldn't make up a tale like that. What was you up to?'

Cassie pouted. 'Nowt. And our May's no right to point the finger at me after what she done. I haven't heard you go on about her.'

'That's enough!' snapped Ada. 'It's you we're talking about. I'm not having you teasing folk like Mr Jordan, nor anybody else for that matter, you hear me? Who knows what harm you might have done?'

'Don't talk so daft!' snapped Cassie. 'Do you think I'd

want an old man like him ogling me? What do you take me for?'

Ada felt the anger pound in her head and turned away. Cassie reached into the shopping basket and pulled out eggs and a thick slice of boiled bacon and laid them on the table before her mother.

'Look what I brought you, Mam,' she said quietly.

From the corner of her eye Ada saw her pull out a length of green woollen material. Curious, she turned back.

'Mrs Chadwick says she should never have bought this,' explained Cassie. 'The colour makes her look sickly, she says, so she gave it me. I thought it'd make you a nice winter coat – you've had that old grey one for years.'

Ada was well aware of the conciliation in her tone. She took the material and held it up against her cheek and touched its softness to her lips. 'It's beautiful,' she murmured. 'Must have cost a bob or two.'

'It did – it's from Harris's. I've got a load of Miss Cecily's cast-offs so I'm well set up. It's high time you had summat new to wear and all.'

Ada draped the material over the chair back and grunted. 'I could have a load of stuff if I'd a mind to. Not new, but better than I could ever afford.'

'Oh aye?' said Cassie, seating herself at the table. 'How's that?'

Ada's voice was flat. 'Mr Jordan wants me to take all his wife's stuff. Some of it might fit me, but I haven't the heart to wear them meself. He just wants to get shut of them.'

Cassie cupped her chin in her hands and sat silent for a moment. 'What will you do with 'em?' she asked.

Ada shrugged. 'Give 'em to the totter when he calls round again, happen – or give 'em the Sally Army or the vicar – he'll know folk who could make good use of them.'

Cassie reached to touch her mother's hand. 'I'm sure that'll suit him. Do you want me to go over and ask?'

'That I do not,' replied Ada sharply as she stood up. 'What have I just been telling you? You'll keep well out of Mr

Jordan's way from now on. There's enough gossip about you as it is.'

'Gossip?' Cassie's lip curled. 'Who cares about that?'

'I do – I don't like folk saying my daughter's no better than she ought to be, true or not.'

Cassie rose and came round to put her arms about her mother's shoulders. 'You've got a rotten opinion of me, Mam, thinking me a trollop and I don't deserve it.'

'You're sly,' said her mother. 'You called round at Eunice Fairchild's today – bet you hoped you'd see that brother of hers.'

Cassie snorted. 'Donald?' she said airily. 'I've got better fish to fry than a poorly-paid apprentice. You'll see, I'll turn out best of the bunch yet.'

'Aye,' growled Ada, 'you'll do all right for yourself, I've no doubt of that. I just don't want no prattling about you or our May. If a woman hasn't got her reputation she's got nowt.'

Cassie gave a short laugh. 'You'll have a job protecting our May's name when she gets home with the kid. You can hardly hide that.'

'We'll see,' said Ada grimly. 'I'll think of summat. And in the meantime you keep away from Mr Jordan's, you hear?'

Cassie chuckled and squeezed her mother close. Ada stood stiffly, aware she was being soft-soaped but reluctant to break away. After all this time it was good to feel warm arms about her again.

Harold sat slumped on the park bench, deaf to the sound of the birds twittering in the trees overhead. He was still stunned. He couldn't face going home yet, not after what had just happened.

He'd hurried away out of town as fast as he could to avoid meeting anyone he knew and the park seemed to offer the best chance of solitude. He needed time to reflect for a while, to digest the news. He hadn't understood every word of the medical evidence, but he'd got the gist.

There had been a baby after all. Fanny had been carrying

a dead child all these years, and no-one knew or even guessed. She'd actually conceived that child they'd both longed for – and miscarried without either of them knowing. It was scarcely believable, and yet the doctor was clearly emphatic.

It happened only rarely, he said. It was just Harold's luck that it should happen to him, losing the only child they'd ever managed to create. He cast his mind back over the years. He didn't recall Fanny at any time being sick or having cravings or doing any of the things pregnant women were said to do. In fact she was rarely ill – only once or twice had she complained of a pain in her side which came and went; a grumbling appendix, she'd called it, but it had never stopped her doing the housework or cooking his supper.

But she had once conceived a child, and he'd given it to her. It proved one thing – it wasn't his fault; he was capable of begetting a child. If things had gone right he might now have had a grown son to carry on the business and the family name . . .

With a sigh and a shake of the head he stood up, brushing the dust from the back of his black coat with his gloves. It was Fanny's fault, not managing to carry it to full term, and even when she miscarried, she hadn't made a proper job of it.

Poor old Fanny. She couldn't even get that right.

TWENTY-ONE

Agnes Bottomley leaned her gangling height over the deal table, her arms plunged elbow-deep into a bowl of flour. She glanced over sourly at the fire in the range.

'Don't let that fire go down whatever you do, Nellie,' she said crisply. 'I don't want me lardy cake going all flat and there's still me congress tarts to go in.'

Her sister gave a dreamy smile as she greased the baking tins. She loved the warm, sweet-scented aroma of baking day. It gave the little house a homely glow which it lacked the other six days of the week.

'You heard me,' said Agnes. 'Mend that fire afore it gets too low.'

Nellie rose and waddled across to the big mahogany chest in the corner and pulled out the large bottom drawer. 'I haven't heard that baby shriking a-lately, have you?' she murmured, picking up a shovel.

Agnes growled. 'Happen that slummock of a father has cottoned on and given up drinking so much. Penny saved off his pint'll put some food in that babby's mouth. It'd make a change, I reckon. I caught that little lad of theirs scratting around in our rubbish again yesterday.'

Nellie sighed as she piled lumps of coal carefully on the shovel. 'Poor little mites. I feel right sorry for them.' She scrambled to her feet. 'There's not a lot of coal left,' she remarked gloomily, surveying the shovel. 'It's time we bought another load.'

'You mean you ought to,' snapped Agnes. 'It's your turn. And why the dickens you see fit to keep coal in that drawer I'll never know.'

'It's been lying empty ever since you took Mother's best linen out and took it up to your room. It was handy to put it in here.'

Agnes scowled. 'A drawer's no place for coal, for pity's sake. The very idea! It belongs in the shed down the yard like other folk's. Mother would turn in her grave.'

'Aye,' agreed Nellie sunnily as she carried the coal carefully to the hearth, 'but like you keep saying, things is different now she's gone. We can do as we like.'

'You're going barmy, you are. Men in white suits'll come and take you away. What are folks going to think?'

'They won't know,' said Nellie. 'I won't tell 'em.'

'You dozy ha'porth – every time the coalman comes you ask him to fill up your drawer as well. He's bound to tell folk. Why not leave it down the yard same as we've always done?'

'Not if you say it's my job to mend the fire,' said Nellie as she bent stiff joints to kneel on the hearth. 'I had enough fetching it in, slipping and sliding about on the ice like I don't know what, what with my legs and all. You forget about my legs.'

Agnes glanced down. 'Chance'd be a fine thing,' she grunted. 'I see 'em every day of me life – crooked as a ram's horn, they are. They'd never stop a pig in a passage.'

Nellie looked hurt. 'Can I help it if I had rickets and me legs bowed? And wearing clogs all them years I was at Atkinson's didn't help neither. I'd have given me eye teeth for some proper shoes like you had.'

Agnes lifted her hands and shook off the flour with a sigh. 'That's you all over, our Nellie, never satisfied, always moaning about what you never had. Why can't you be happy with what you got? And be grateful, like me?'

Nellie's mouth opened and closed again. She could point out to her sister that she had good reason to be grateful since she'd plundered Mother's room and grabbed most of her best possessions for herself, fobbing Nellie off with the excuse that as the eldest she had first right. But it would be a waste of time. They'd been arguing the point for the past two years and still they hadn't solved it. They still squabbled over some things. Only last week it was the Paisley shawl Mother had lent Nellie the day before she died.

'She only lent it you,' Agnes argued. 'She didn't give it you.'

'She always said it suited me best 'cos of my dark colouring,' Nellie countered.

'Dark?' Agnes snorted. 'You're as mucky grey as the snow were out in the yard. Any road, she lent it me last Christmas, so there.'

Nellie squatted on the hearth, her fingers black with coal-dust, and looked up at the angular figure pounding the dough on the table. From down here Agnes looked even taller and thinner, like that poplar tree on the road to Meltham which always reminded her of a witch.

'I don't care what you say,' she muttered defiantly, 'that coal's staying in that drawer.'

There was a pause and then Agnes sniffed. 'In that case you'd best order some more,' she said haughtily. 'And it's your turn to pay.'

Mrs Jordan's funeral was a quiet affair. Old Mrs Boothroyd called round to see Ada as soon as the mourners had eaten the funeral tea and left.

'Not many folk there,' she wheezed as she lowered herself into Ada's fireside chair. 'You'd have thought, what with him being a big undertaker and all—'

'He said she had no relatives,' Ada cut in. 'There was his sister and her husband.'

'They looked a well-set-up couple, the pair of them,' remarked Mrs Boothroyd. 'Did you see that nice alpaca coat?' The old lady shook her head. 'I did wonder if we ought to go down the cemetery but I didn't like, not having been invited.'

Ada nodded. 'Best leave him to mourn his own way.'

The old lady accepted the cup of tea Ada held out to her. 'Funny thing that,' she murmured. 'Like I said when that

Nagle baby were born, for every birth there's always a death – have you noticed? Nature's way of balancing things out, I reckon.'

A train rumbled past over the viaduct and Mrs Boothroyd raised her voice. 'I just hope there's no more babies in the street for a while, me being the age I am. I'm in no hurry to meet my Maker, rheumatics or not.'

Ada held her tongue. There'd be another baby soon enough, sooner than the old lady knew. Easter would be here in no time now, and May was due in midsummer. Somehow she was going to have to think of something . . .

The clatter of the train faded away. Ada handed her guest a plate with a slab of gingerbread. The old woman's eyes travelled over her as she took it.

'You're putting a bit of weight on, aren't you?' she murmured.

'I haven't put me stays on,' said Ada, 'that's all.'

'Oh.' Mrs Boothroyd nodded. 'Only I didn't think as you could be in the family way, not with your Jim being like he is.'

Ada felt stung. 'You shouldn't jump to conclusions,' she said crisply. 'He's flat on his face, not his back.'

The old lady looked startled for a moment, then smiled. 'Aye,' she murmured, 'it takes a lot to put 'em off that. I know. Funny how they never seem to lose the urge.'

Until you lose the will to live, thought Ada fiercely. For Jim nothing seemed to matter any more, least of all making love, but she wouldn't dream of letting a neighbour know that.

She cut another slice of gingerbread and thought back. She couldn't remember the last time he'd reached out for her . . .

'Poor Mr Jordan,' Mrs Boothroyd sighed, 'left on his own like that and him so well-set-up and not that old. He'll find hisself a nice widow-woman before long, I dare say.'

Harold brushed his black beaver hat and put it away carefully on the top shelf of the wardrobe. His gaze travelled down to the neat row of dresses and skirts below, the dark greys and browns Fanny always favoured. Why she always chose such mousy colours baffled him. She'd have thrown up her hands in horror at the thought of a rich green like that smart outfit Cassie Turnbull wore.

Still, he mustn't think harshly of her shortcomings, not now. She'd done her best, poor soul, and he'd given her a good send-off. Not the dearest, perhaps, but good, sound quality all the same. After all, Beatrice and Maurice came to pay their last respects so the coffin was a good one even if the brass fittings weren't anywhere near as expensive as Mrs Clarkson's.

It hadn't been a bad do at all. He'd buried her in the Jordan family plot since she'd none of her own. Father had been dead that long now his coffin was well compressed and Mother's had barely begun to rot. Still, there was plenty of room for Fanny and there'd be space enough for him too when his time came.

He closed the wardrobe door and headed downstairs. Once he'd got that wardrobe cleared out there'd be more space for him – he could even squeeze in his thick winter overcoat which, up to now, had had to hang on a hook behind the spare bedroom door. Fanny used to have to brush the dust off it every time he wore it.

He poked up the fire and added more coal, then sat down in the fireside chair. Now she was really gone. Now he was alone. Somehow the fact of seeing the casket being lowered into the grave had put a seal on the finality of it. Thirty years of marriage ended. He looked about the room, the polished sideboard with its thin veil of dust covering her china figurines, the glass dome over the clock, and the ugly pottery dog she treasured because he'd won it for her years ago at the Easter Fair.

That could go out for a start, hideous thing that it was, a revolting caricature of a dog with its grotesque smile. That was the trouble with Fanny; she'd no taste.

The fire was reddening up nicely now. He pulled the kettle over the hob and fetched the bread in from the crock in the scullery. A couple of thick slices, spread liberally with butter – they'd go very nicely with that pair of kippers lying ready in the pantry.

Harold smacked his lips, relishing the taste already. He was vaguely aware of footsteps out in the street but he didn't see Maureen Nagle's white face as she hurried past the window.

Ada stirred the pan of stew over the fire and thought about May. It was hard to tell from her letters how the girl was really feeling. She didn't write very often – the work evidently tired her out but she made no complaint. You could almost hear her voice, the way she wrote, talking about the other girls and in particular the little Daisy she seemed to have taken such a shine to.

But it was what she didn't say that troubled Ada. May had never been one to open up and pour out her feelings, but somehow she seemed to have gone really quiet in her letters. She didn't want to upset her mother by telling how bad things were, that was it. So Ada worried even more.

Her thoughts were interrupted by a sudden frantic knocking at the front door. She knew that kind of knock – it usually meant trouble. She left the pan and hurried to answer.

Maureen Nagle's terrified face peered out of her shawl. ''Tis the baby,' she croaked, pulling aside the shawl to show a tiny face, its eyes closed. 'She's not breathing – I think I've lost her!'

'Come inside,' said Ada. 'Let me have a look.'

She took the bundle from the young mother's arms. Maureen leaned over anxiously as Ada sat to unwrap the baby and touch its forehead, then feel the tiny body under the vest. 'She's got a fever,' she muttered. 'Have you called the doctor?'

Maureen shook her head. 'I've no money for doctors. Oh Jesus, I've never had any of the others so bad before and I didn't know what to do! Can we do anything?'

Ada began peeling off the child's clothes. At that moment Elsie came in and dropped her school bag on the table. 'Miss

Metcalf says—' she began, then broke off on seeing the visitors.

'Not now,' said Ada sharply. 'Go in the scullery and fill the sink with cold water.'

'What for?'

'Never you mind what for. Do it.'

Elsie ran out. Maureen stared, bewildered. 'Cold water?' she echoed. 'What are ye going to do?'

Ada nodded down at the baby. 'She's raging hot – I'm going to cool her down. Happen then she'll start to breathe. Now fill us that lading can with hot water out of the range.'

Maureen seized hold of Ada's arm. 'What are ye doing? I've done me best to keep the child warm—'

'Too warm,' said Ada. 'Now do as I say.'

Maureen's hand fell away, and she turned and picked up the lading can. Ada carried the baby through into the scullery where Elsie stood on a stool by the sink to turn off the tap.

'It's full, Mam.'

'Right. Mrs Nagle, pour that hot water in.'

Maureen did so. Ada stirred the water and tested it with her elbow, then lowered the baby gently in, splashing waves of water over its tiny inert body. Behind her Maureen was whispering tearful prayers.

'Hail Mary, full of grace, the Lord is with thee, blessed art thou amongst women and blessed is the fruit of thy womb . . .'

'What's womb?' asked Elsie.

Maureen prayed on. 'Holy Mary, Mother of God, pray for us sinners . . .'

Elsie peered round her mother. 'Is the baby sick?' she asked. 'Why isn't it moving? It's not dead, is it?'

'Shove off,' said Ada. 'Go and empty out my laundry basket.'

Elsie pulled a face. 'I folded 'em all last night.'

'Tip everything out on the floor. Go on now.'

The child went off. Maureen watched the little body in the sink, still unmoving, and she sobbed on Ada's shoulder. 'Five of them I've had in seven years, but I've never lost one till now. I don't want to lose Lily!'

Ada fancied she saw a movement, a twitch in one of the tiny legs. She kept on bathing and silently praying. She couldn't go on too long – she mustn't lower the baby's temperature too fast. But when was enough?

Suddenly the eyes opened, staring up at her with an indignant look. Maureen cried out and clutched Ada's arm.

'She's breathing! Thanks be to God, she's alive!'

It was true. The little chest was rising and falling rhythmically again. Ada lifted the baby out of the water and folded her in a soft towel. 'Here,' she said gently, offering the bundle to Maureen, 'take her through and hold her a while.'

She watched as the young mother sat by the fire, the child cradled to her breast. The baby's eyes were moving about now, soaking in the scene. Ada took a deep breath. With luck . . .

'What am I to do with this laundry basket?' asked Elsie.

'Make it up into a crib, love, like you do for your dolly. Use them bits of blanket in the cupboard.'

Maureen looked up. 'Can't I take her home and nurse her there?' she asked. 'She's breathing easy now.'

'Best not move her yet,' replied Ada.

Maureen's eyes grew fearful. 'I must be home with the supper ready when Tim gets back or he'll flay me alive.'

'Time enough,' said Ada firmly. 'Try giving her the teat and see if she'll take it.'

Under the folds of the blanket Maureen nuzzled her breast to the baby's face. Elsie, crouched on the floor lining the basket, stood up to watch. Ada took hold of her arm and turned her about.

'Now, what did Miss Metcalf have to say?'

Elsie's face lit up. 'There's going to be an outing to Colwyn Bay at Easter – can I go? Please, Mam, can I?'

' 'Tis no use,' murmured Maureen, 'she won't suckle.'

'Give it time,' said Ada. 'The fever's not gone yet, but she's coming through.'

233

*   *   *

An hour later Maureen took the child home. 'Thanks be to God, and to you,' she murmured at the door. 'I thought I'd lost her, specially after Tim turned up the ace of spades last night.'

Ada snorted. 'Superstitious nonsense! Letting a pack of cards rule your life? How could you think it?'

The younger woman gave a slight shrug. 'Father Leahy says there's more in this life than we can ever understand. I prayed to Saint Anthony, the man for lost causes, and he answered me.'

Ada watched her hurry away down the street, then turned back into the house. So it was a blooming saint who saved little Lily, was it, not the cooling water? Ah well, she was glad she'd been able to help him save the child she'd delivered into the world . . .

'Well?' demanded Elsie, stuffing her doll into the hollow in the basket where the baby had lain. 'You haven't said if I can or not.'

'Can what?'

'Go on the outing to the seaside.'

'How much is it?'

'One-and-six. And I take me own sandwiches.'

Ada deliberated. Money for luxuries was scarce enough in this house but she hated to deprive the child. The other kids would be going – families would scrimp and save to give them their annual treat, so why not Elsie?

After all, there was always the money May had left . . .

'Go on then,' she said crisply, 'tell Miss Metcalf to put your name down. Now then, what about laying the table for me?'

All day the steam had choked May's throat as she pulled the big steam press down on the folded sheets. It was heavy work and when she went to bed her shoulders still burned with pain, but it was better than sluicing down that filthy, tarry deposit off the napkins from the nursery and the soiled

234

bedlinen and bandages sent down from the hospital.

'You can't get toffee-nosed here, cleaning up all that muck,' Tilly, the heavily-swollen girl from Glasgow, had muttered only this morning. 'Like it or not, you have it to do. I'm glad me time's nearly up so I can get out of this hell-hole.'

'May – you awake?'

The small voice came from Daisy's narrow bed. She'd been working alongside her today.

May rolled over. 'Yes, I'm awake. What is it?'

The voice sounded timid, fearful. 'My back's hurting somethink cruel, and I think I've wet the bed. Sister Anthony will kill me.'

May heaved herself out of bed and hurried across to her, feeling the splinters in the rough floorboards catching under her bare foot. 'Don't worry,' she murmured. 'Let me see.'

It was like Mrs Nagle all over again. May straightened and smiled down at the girl. 'I think I'd best call the nuns, Daisy. It looks like you're going to have your baby at last.'

The girl's eyes widened in terror. She clutched hold of May's arm. 'They say you go through the pains of hell,' she whimpered. 'You will stay with me, won't you? Promise you'll stay with me till it's over!'

May withdrew her arm. 'If they'll let me, I will. Now I'd better get Sister Anthony.'

Sister Anthony wouldn't hear of it.

'You can't help – she has to do this on her own. We'll be there if she needs us.'

'She's frightened – she'd like me there. I've helped at a birth before,' May persisted.

Sister Anthony glared at her. 'Maybe you have, but this is our responsibility. Go back to bed.'

'I can help her – when she's in pain. Let me come, please.'

The Sister's eyebrows rose. 'Pain, is it? Pain is the just reward of sin, my girl, now and in the hereafter. She ought to have thought of that before she sinned. Now get on back to bed. Best thing you can do is pray for her.'

235

May watched the squat, black-robed body waddle away along the tiled corridor, one hand firmly steering Daisy towards the delivery room. The white-faced girl cast one last, pleading glance back before the double doors clamped to, shutting her off from view.

May covered her ears, trying not to hear the screams from the delivery room, but by morning they had died away. As she dressed in the regulation smock, she listened in vain for the sound of a baby's cry. It was only after she had lined up with the other girls by the door, ready to go down to Mass, that the news came.

'Such a pity,' said little Sister Francis in her soft Irish brogue. 'Twenty-seven will soon be well again, God willing, but the good Lord saw fit to take the little one home to Himself, so He did. Twenty-Seven should count her blessings.'

'The baby's dead?'

The nun inclined her head. 'Stillborn, I fear. Go ye down to the chapel now and pray forgiveness for his soul.'

May stared. 'Forgiveness – for what? He never lived to commit any sins.'

The little nun turned away. 'All the same his soul is stained with original sin, the sin of Adam. We must all pray for him to be cleansed.'

The line of girls followed her in silence as she led the way downstairs. So Daisy was on her own now, thought May sadly as they trooped in single file into the chapel. Just as the poor girl had always been ever since her parents threw her out, and as she'd still be when she left the Home to face the outside world once more. And these unfeeling nuns thought she should be glad.

Poor little Daisy. But then again, maybe there was some consolation; with no illegitimate child to point out her shame, maybe her parents would take her back, help her find work, give her the chance to start all over again. And maybe in time she'd find a good husband to love and protect her.

May knelt on the stone floor of the chapel, listening to the thin voices of the nuns chanting the litany, and prayed that the same solution would not be granted to her. It might save a lot of finger-pointing and shame to go home alone, but more than anything else in the world she wanted this child now stirring within her to be born alive.

TWENTY-TWO

Ada glanced at the clock. Cassie was late if she was coming home this morning like she'd said.

'Two weeks today, Mam, I'll be back and Mrs Chadwick says I can stay the night too.'

The overalls and other heavily soiled linen which had been soaking overnight were now gently steaming in the sett pot. If she just slipped down quickly to the shops – she'd left the grocery order at Dyson's yesterday so it had only to be collected. If she left the money on the table the rent man would pick it up as usual and sign the book.

Ada sighed. What a dreary life she led, an endless grey round of trying to fit everything in and make ends meet, getting in the food and cooking, washing and ironing and hanging out clothes to dry. Every day had its own pre-ordained routine, the never-ending drudgery from which she couldn't escape. And everything hinged upon those interminable piles of other people's washing. It seemed as though the smell of soap and starch and dolly blue had choked her nostrils since the moment she was born. There must be more to life than just elbow-greasing away the emptiness of her days . . .

Now just you pull yourself together and put aside such selfish thoughts, she told herself sternly. You could be a darn sight worse off, like that poor Mrs Nagle down the street, never knowing whether there'd be enough money left over from the drink to feed her brood. Trapped in that filthy house with that brutal big lout of a husband. No, Ada had a lot to be thankful for.

She put on her hat and picked up her shopping basket. Just a breath of air going down to the shops, that's what she needed, and if Cassie turned up in the meantime she could let herself in and put the kettle on.

'Jim,' she called up the stairs. 'I'm just off down to the shops – I shan't be long.'

Mrs Nagle must have been at the window and seen her passing because she rapped on the glass and came hurrying to the door, her thin face wreathed in a happy smile.

'The baby's suckling again,' she announced in a proud whisper. 'Glory be to God, she's started feeding fine again, and my Tim none the wiser.'

Ada smiled to herself as she turned the corner into Fountain Street, and then a sudden recollection came to her.

'You're putting a bit of weight on, aren't you?'

'No, I left me stays off, that's all.'

'I thought as you couldn't be in the family way.'

If the possibility had crossed old Mrs Boothroyd's mind . . . If Ada looked as if she might be pregnant without her stays . . . After all, she was still young enough . . . Suppose she added to the bulky stomach, just gradually, with bits of blanket, maybe – could she possibly fool everybody and find a way to pass May's baby off as her own?

The wild idea excited her so much that she was completely unaware of the distant figure in lavender hurrying down from the railway station towards Cedar Street.

The front door was unlocked and Cassie let herself in. The smell of wet washing and lye soap spelled home.

'Hello,' she called out. 'I'm back.'

No answering murmur came from upstairs – Dad must be sleeping. She opened the door of the living room. No-one there, only a heap of coins and the rent book on the table. Mam couldn't be far away. Cassie tidied her hair in front of the mirror then lifted the lace curtain to peep out of the window.

Mr Jordan was striding down the street towards home. She

hurried out onto the doorstep just in time to nod a greeting as he passed.

'Morning, Mr Jordan.'

She saw his look of surprise, then a smile of pleasure as he raised his hat. 'Good morning, Miss Turnbull. I must say, you bring a ray of much-needed sunshine to the street.'

She dimpled fetchingly, then suddenly recollected herself. She knew the words to use – Miss Chadwick had read her a letter she'd received about her grandmother's death only last week. 'I was so sorry to hear about your wife,' she said shyly. 'Please accept my condolences.'

He nodded gravely. 'That's very kind of you, my dear. I appreciate it.'

'And if there's owt I can do . . . I mean, like you asked Mam if she'd help you clear stuff—'

His face lost its gloomy look. 'Indeed, I would appreciate help in that respect. It's too distressing—'

'Of course, it must be. I'd be glad to do what I can.'

'You'd come and help your mother sort things out for me? I'd be that glad to get it done.'

'All right,' said Cassie. 'Mam's always busy, she works that hard and she's out just now. I'll come over meself and save her the bother.'

'You will?' he said in surprise. 'When?'

She shrugged. 'No time like the present. It's me day off so I'll come now if you like. Just let me get me jacket.'

Harold could scarcely believe his luck. There she was, his lovely Venus, moving gracefully about his living room, a delectable vision in her lavender gown and the light catching the golden glints in her long hair. With those gentle eyes and elegant hands she was like some wonderful Pre-Raphaelite painting, a goddess who'd be any artist's dream.

She took off her jacket and laid it aside, looking so alive with her glowing young skin and graceful movements. Everything about her was so different from Fanny's stiff awkwardness. He could see the rise of her full young breasts moving provocatively under the lavender wool, not lying flabbily close to her waist like Fanny's.

'Well?' she said gently. 'Where shall I start?'

Suddenly he was aware of the stark contrast between her colourful vitality and the dust and gloom of their surroundings. For the first time his home looked unaccountably dusty and shabby, unfit for such a jewel as Cassie. She deserved a far finer setting.

'There's a heap of stuff upstairs in the wardrobe,' he said gruffly. 'And more in the drawers. I'll bring it down.'

She reached the door before him and laid a delicate finger on the handle. 'Wouldn't it be best for me to go?' she said quietly. 'You just find me summat to pack it all in.'

He stepped back. 'Aye, you're right,' he murmured. 'I'll leave you to it and fetch some sacks from the workshop.'

He couldn't bear to stay and watch her handle the relics, he thought as he trudged down the yard. What on earth would she make of Fanny's dull clothes, the baggy bloomers and hideous vests she always wore? But neither could he bear to stay away down the yard for long.

Having made sure Arthur was well occupied he picked up an armful of sacks and hurried back to the house. She was a jewel, this Cassie. That reminded him, there was that little carved wooden box up on the dressing table where Fanny kept her few treasured bits and pieces, the cameo brooch left her by her mother, the jet necklace she always wore on Sundays.

As he entered the kitchen he could hear her light footsteps upstairs, a voice humming softly. On an impulse, he crept quietly up the narrow staircase and moved cautiously towards the bedroom door. It stood slightly ajar, and through the crack he caught a glimpse of lavender. He had to peep in, just to watch her and soak her in once more, unobserved, while she graced his home.

A neat pile of clothes lay on the bed and Cassie was folding yet another garment. Every move she made had the grace and eloquence of a dancer. He could feast his eyes on her for ever and never have enough. As she bent to lay the blouse with

241

the others he watched the curve of her backside and felt once more a burst of fire in his belly. That night in the back lane he'd seen that lovely figure naked, and his head swam at the memory. He moved back stealthily to the stairs, then coughed.

As he entered the room she straightened and turned to him with a smile. 'Just you leave them sacks with me and go on downstairs again. And think about what you want me to do with them when I've done. I'll be down in a minute.'

He flung the sacks down on the bed and turned to go. On his way out he picked up the little carved box from the dressing table.

Ten minutes later Cassie came down.

'All finished,' she said brightly. 'Three sacks, all tied up and ready. Now then, have you decided? Am I to fetch them away with me, or have I to get the vicar to call? He'll arrange summat, I'm sure.'

Harold tried to ignore the uncomfortable heat in his belly. 'Aye, that's a good idea,' he muttered. 'Fanny would like the idea of some other poor souls benefiting.'

'Right then,' she said, picking up her jacket, 'I'll be off.'

He stood up, barring her way to the door. 'Just a moment,' he said awkwardly, 'I want you to have something – here, have a look.'

He lifted the lid of the little wooden box. He saw her look of surprise, and then she turned her face up to his. 'Oh no,' she whispered. 'I couldn't.'

'Please, choose something. Just a little token of my gratitude, that's all.'

He saw the little white teeth chewing the full lower lip. 'I don't know,' she murmured. 'I hardly like, them being Mrs Jordan's and all.'

'One little thing,' he blurted, 'just to please me.'

He was aware that his voice sounded lame and clumsy, like some gauche schoolboy. 'No, really,' he hurried on, 'she'd no relatives, there's only my sister and she's got more jewels than she knows what to do with. I know Fanny would like you to, I'm sure she would.'

He saw her hesitate for a moment, then dip her delicate fingers into the box and lift out the cameo.

'Then I'll accept this,' she said shyly. 'It'll look lovely pinned on the neck of my Sunday blouse. Thanks ever so much.'

Joy surged in him. He held the jacket by the shoulders while she slid her slender arms into the sleeves. As she turned he caught a glimpse of the white nape of her neck and had an overwhelming urge to kiss it.

'I'd love to give you a real gift, summat much better than trinkets,' he said boldly, 'summat you'd really treasure.'

She was looking up at him, her lovely eyes wide, and he faltered. Had he gone too far? 'I'm sorry,' he blurted, 'I didn't mean to offend—'

'No more you have,' she said quietly. 'I'm very flattered. But I've been here long enough – I'd best get home now before Mam starts to wonder.'

Ada stared at her daughter in amazement.

'You mean to tell me you've been in Mr Jordan's house, on your own? And after me telling you to keep away from him? Now just you listen here—'

'He asked me to go over – I did it to spare you.'

Ada ignored the look of injured innocence. 'Knowing the gossip that'd cause? A young woman on her own in a man's house? If you couldn't wait for me, why couldn't you fetch Mrs Boothroyd to come with you?'

Cassie pouted. 'I never thought. I just did like you do, go and help.'

'Them's thin excuses, and well you know it,' said Ada tartly. 'I'd have gone, eventually.'

'You were taking your time about it. I reckoned it would save you having to, but there's no pleasing some folk, seemingly.'

Ada bit back the words of reproach. Maybe she was judging

the girl too harshly. She laid her hands on Cassie's shoulders, touched a finger to the sulky lip.

'Look, love, I'm not looking to find fault,' she said softly. 'I just want what's best for us all. Folks'll talk about you being in that house— Hello, what's this?'

She broke off and tapped the cameo brooch pinned at her daughter's throat. Cassie's pout retreated into a mischievous smile.

'Mr Jordan gave it me. As a thank-you for helping him.'

Ada stared, feeling the anger rise. 'And you had the bare-faced cheek to take it off him?' she demanded. 'Mrs Jordan's brooch?'

Cassie's face reddened. 'Why not? She's no more use for it and there's nobody else, he told me.'

'It's not right,' protested Ada, 'that's why not! Taking a dead woman's things before she's even cold in her grave! The very idea! Shame on you. It's wicked – you'd no business taking it, and well you know it.'

Cassie rounded on her, eyes flashing. 'He told me I could have owt I wanted,' she snapped. 'I could have had her Whitby jet necklace and earrings, whatever I liked. All I took was this little brooch when I could have had a great deal more if I'd been as wicked as you think!'

Suspicion leapt in Ada. 'What's that supposed to mean?' she demanded. 'What's been going on? Has he been making up to you – is that what you're trying to tell me?'

'Nothing's been going on!' protested Cassie. 'He just said he'd like to give me summat far nicer than trinkets, that's all.'

'Did he now?' Ada muttered through pursed lips. 'Well, I don't like the sound of this. You can just give him that brooch back—'

'I won't! Why should I?'

Ada's mouth opened again just as a loud thudding on the ceiling made both women look up.

'Now look what you've done,' said Cassie. 'You've woken me dad.'

*　　*　　*

'I couldn't help hearing the racket,' murmured Jim from under the sheets. 'What's going off?'

Ada told him. She could see the glisten in his eyes as he growled and buried his head under the bedclothes again.

'It's no good,' he murmured. 'She'll do as she wants, that one. You'll not get our Cass to do your bidding like the others.'

'Happen not,' retorted Ada, 'but it won't be for want of trying.'

'I knew it,' Jim moaned. 'That's what comes of not having a father's hand to guide 'em. They come to no good without.'

'Nonsense,' said Ada stoutly. 'They're well able to take care of themselves, the lot of 'em. Even our Elsie – did you know she beat up a kid in the school yard yesterday for getting at her? Come home with bloody knuckles, she did, and I were that proud of her, thumping a kid much bigger than her.'

She heard Jim's soft chuckle. 'So that were it. I asked her why her hands were sore and she wouldn't tell me. That's the trouble with all you Turnbull women – you never let on.'

Ada smiled to hear the pride in his tone.

'Just like their mother,' his sleepy voice went on. 'Keep their troubles to theirselves, they do, and just get on with it.'

Ada glanced sharply towards the hump in the bed. Was he hinting at something?

Jim yawned. 'How's our May? You said there was a letter.'

She couldn't tell him the truth. So far as he knew May was away working on a job for Rose's. 'She's fine, love. Working hard.'

He grunted and said no more. Did he suspect about May? So far she'd kept it from him, trying to find the right opportunity and the courage to tell him, and so far the moment had never seemed right. Every passing day made it harder, yet every day brought the baby's arrival closer.

'I'd best get back down to Cass,' she murmured. 'She'll bring you up a cup of tea and you can talk to her then.'

He made no answer, but whether he was already asleep or had no words for his daughter she couldn't tell. She closed the door quietly and went back downstairs.

                              *   *   *

'Well?' said Cassie. 'What did he say?'

Ada shrugged weary shoulders. 'Nowt much. He's too sick to take it in. He's almost past caring.'

Cassie sat down and folded her hands. 'Look, Mam,' she said quietly, 'it's no use us shouting at each other. We've got to talk this out and get things straight.'

Ada felt a wry smile trying to curve her lips. As a rule it was Cassie who shouted, she the one who tried to calm the rebellious tears. 'Aye, you're right,' she said.

'You're not to tell me what to do any more.'

Ada bristled but felt the weariness pressing down on her too heavily to argue. 'I'm only trying to stop you making a fool of yourself,' she muttered as she slumped into a chair. 'And I'm your mother, think on.'

'But things is different now,' Cassie countered. 'I don't live here any more. I'm only a visitor.'

Ada started. 'Visitor? Since when?'

'Since I went to live at the Chadwicks' and earn my own keep. That's my home now, not here.'

Ada felt stung. 'Don't talk such rot – this'll always be your home till you're old enough to marry and make your own.'

'Listen here, Mam,' said Cassie patiently, 'I'm not a child any more – I'm a woman in my own right now, old enough to get married, and I'm not beholden to you for anything. I'm a woman grown, and you're not to tell me what to do any more.'

Ada stared, uncomprehending. Before her sat the mischievous, flaxen-haired girl she'd nurtured for almost seventeen years, but this cool, self-possessed young woman who spoke through Cassie's mouth was a stranger.

'Well?' said the girl. 'What's it to be? I'm going to be friends with whoever I like.' She leaned forward. 'Look, I can stay the night, but if you don't want me to I can go home.'

'Home?'

'To the Chadwicks'. I'd like to stay, but we have to understand each other. It's up to you, Mam.'

Ada fidgeted with the folds of her skirt. She knew she couldn't dictate to Cassie ever again, and she didn't want to lose her.

She made one last effort. 'I just don't want to see you making a fool of yourself,' she murmured. 'If folks in the street see you messing about with Mr Jordan they won't want to know you. They'll cut you dead.'

'I can't help that,' Cassie said calmly. 'I'll not have them telling me how to lead my life, any more than you. I've me own way to make, and I'll do it in me own fashion.'

Hadn't she said much the same to her own mother, thought Ada, all those years ago when Jim came courting? And hadn't she clung on relentlessly until her mother gave way? It was a wise old lioness who recognized when the time had come to give way to the young . . .

She crossed to the cupboard in the corner and pulled open the door. 'Better get some aired sheets out for you then,' she said gruffly. 'That bed hasn't been slept in since last time you was home.'

Cassie took the sheets upstairs and made up the bed which had once been May's. It was far more comfortable sleeping in her narrow little bed than trying to settle down in the big one with fidgety little Elsie.

She smoothed down the counterpane and sat on the edge of the bed, recalling the night she'd sat here with May.

'You ought to let the father know, make him face up to his responsibility. I would . . .'

May must be getting near her time now. Funny, but she didn't often think about her sister these days, not since she went away to that Home. Like they said, out of sight, out of mind. Not that she didn't care about her; it was just that so many other things had come into her life since last summer. But she could do something, drop her a letter, maybe, to show she cared . . .

*   *   *

'That you, Elsie?'

Cassie stood up quickly at the sound of the frail voice. 'No, Dad, it's me.'

She edged open the door of his room and slipped in. 'Do you want summat?' she asked. 'Is it your back playing you up again?'

She heard his weary sigh. 'It's hot, lass. Open the window a bit, will you? I'm roasting.'

Cassie stared. 'Are you sure? It's freezing out there.'

'Not in here, it isn't. Come on, it's March, it's spring already. Raise the sash, just a little bit.'

She touched a hand to his forehead. It didn't feel hot. 'It really is cold out, Dad. Spring or not, it's been threatening to snow these last few days. Let me take one of your blankets off instead.'

She saw his tired face, the look of total exhaustion in his eyes. 'Do as I tell you, love, there's a good girl,' he murmured. 'I'm too weary to argue.'

Cassie bit her lip. 'Me mam'll be mad if I open it. She'll shoot me.'

'No need to tell her,' murmured the fragile voice. 'Go on, lass, do it, for me.'

TWENTY-THREE

Grace Openshaw washed up the last plate, wrung out the dishcloth and slapped it down irritably on the draining board. At once she realized her mistake as the plate, balanced against a cup to dry, rolled off the edge. She caught it just in time, more by good luck than good management.

So far today had been one of those blindingly stupid days where nothing had gone right. She'd been all fingers and thumbs from the moment she caught her heel in the hem of her skirt this morning just as Mr Henry came into the workroom. After that she'd broken a fingernail trying to fix the new girl's machine, with the result that it kept snagging on the fine fabric. Then she'd spilt her cup of tea all over her skirt and come home to enjoy a well-earned afternoon off, only to open the back door for Oscar and find him sitting there triumphantly on the step with a huge dead rat in his jaws.

'Oh you beast! Take that thing away this minute!'

But Oscar had refused to part with his trophy. He'd carried it in and sat proudly on the hearth with it until tempted away with a saucer of sardines. It had turned Grace's stomach, forcing herself to pick up that revolting, mutilated rat-corpse with the coal tongs to fling it on the fire.

She'd intended to make good use of her free afternoon, plant a few bulbs in the little patch of earth at the bottom of the yard and then go through all her stockings and darn the ones worth saving. It made more sense to mend them by daylight instead of poring over them at night by gaslight, but her heart wasn't in it. She felt restless and dissatisfied today, and she didn't quite know why.

Maybe it was something to do with the news Mr Henry had announced today – it certainly wasn't unexpected but it had set all the girls twittering and she'd had a job on to get them settled down again. A senseless, silly lot they were these days. All the bright ones seemed to have found reasons to leave.

Like May Turnbull, still off on that long job for Sir Joseph. Now there was a reliable girl. Then the next thought rushed in; reliable in her work maybe, but in all this time the girl had never once contacted her, either with news or asking for help.

Grace had mentioned it once to Mr Aaron when he came into the stock room.

'*Turnbull?*' he'd repeated with a vacant stare, and then waved an airy hand. '*Oh, you've no need to trouble yourself about her, Miss Openshaw. She's perfectly all right where she is.*'

Grace gazed out of the window. Outside, despite the cold, the sun was trying to shine, casting a dull gleam on the grey roofs opposite. She was sorely tempted to leave the chores and go out.

And why not? She deserved a change. For far too long she'd stayed cooped up here waiting for the visitor who, it seemed, was never going to call. He didn't even catch the same tram in the mornings any more. Forget him, Grace told herself firmly. You're going out.

But where could she go? There were no errands to do. A stroll in the park, perhaps? No, the gravel paths and stone arbours held too many memories of Edward.

She could catch a tram into town. Window-shopping only, of course, and maybe have a cup of tea and a fancy cake in that nice little tea-room in King Street. The fact that the tea-room was only a couple of doors away from Harris's store had nothing to do with it.

Oscar brushed against her ankle as he came to sit on the

hearthrug and began curling a licked paw around his complacent smile, washing away the last traces of sardine. Grace withdrew her foot and stood up.

'I'm not spending my afternoon off with a nasty little murderer like you,' she said crisply. 'I'm going out.'

It said Earl Grey tea on the menu and she knew it was what all the ladies drank, but it tasted very different from the Co-op tea they'd always had at home. Grace sipped delicately from a flowered china cup. It was nice to sit near the well-dressed ladies who clearly made a habit of taking afternoon tea here with their friends. She copied carefully the genteel way they sliced the pretty little fancy cakes and conveyed dainty morsels to their lips with a tiny fork.

The plate empty, she pushed it away and half-turned so she could look out of the window. From here she could just see the near half of Harris's double-fronted shop. Somewhere inside that building, she mused, he would be working – on the sales floor, perhaps, overseeing his staff, or in his office?

Where would his office be? Her gaze travelled to the upper level. If he was up on the first or second floor, there was no sign of him at any of the windows. Of course, she reproved herself, he was far too hard-working a man; with such a large and prosperous store to run he'd no time to waste gawping out into the street.

'Will there be anything else, madam?'

The little waitress was looking down at her, notepad at the ready. Grace gathered her bag and gloves. 'No thanks. Just my bill, please.'

So she found herself out again on King Street. As if drawn by a magnet she approached Harris's windows, the one filled with elegantly draped suitings and curtaining, the other with a neat array of gloves and scarves, bags and hat-pins, men's neckwear and socks.

Her eyes lingered on the blue scarf with the fine red stripe running lengthwise. She had no strict need of a new scarf, but she had worn this brown one ever since Mother bought it for her years ago. That blue one in the window would go beautifully with her Sunday-best coat.

She twisted her neck but still couldn't read the price-ticket. The cold was beginning to bite her toes. It couldn't do any harm just to go inside, stroll around casually and maybe ask the price, finger the fine wool fabric for a moment . . .

Heart pounding, she made a complete tour of the sales floor before stopping where the scarves lay piled on the rack behind the counter. Disappointment filled her. Edward was nowhere to be seen.

'Can I help you, madam?'

She made a long process out of it, asking first for the blue and then for more scarves to be laid out on the counter, enquiring the prices, fingering each in turn, humming thoughtfully and then returning to the first scarf and repeating the process.

'Would you excuse me, madam? I'll be back in a moment.'

The young woman assistant hurried away. Grace took the opportunity to gaze across the counters once more, but unless he was hidden behind that high draping of red velvet curtaining, Edward was definitely not on the sales floor. She must have been here a good twenty minutes now. Wouldn't you think, she thought crossly, that the proprietor of such a fine store would stroll around just once every now and again to keep an eye on things?

The young woman reappeared behind the counter with an apologetic smile. 'I'm so sorry. The manager called me away. You are Miss Openshaw, I understand, from Rose's?'

Grace's jaw dropped open for a second before she pulled herself together and closed it. It must look very unladylike. 'Yes,' she said. 'How did you know that?'

The assistant nodded towards a window set high in the far wall. 'Mr Harris saw you from up there in the manager's office. He said to give you ten per cent discount on all your purchases.'

Joy leapt in Grace's thin chest. So he'd been watching her! She swung round to look up at the window, but no-one was there. Slowly the joy faded. If he'd seen her, why hadn't he come down? Was the offer of a discount simply a sop to his conscience? She turned back to the young woman and drew herself upright.

'That's very kind of Mr Harris,' she said quietly, 'but I wouldn't dream of it. I'll take this blue scarf at the marked price, please.'

She paid over the money and watched as the metal canister slid away on the overhead wire towards the cashier. The young assistant wrapped the scarf carefully.

'You'll know the news then,' the young woman said conversationally, tucking in the corners of the tissue, 'you being from Rose's?'

'News?'

'About Mr Aaron getting married. Should be a real grand do, that wedding. Mr Harris has been invited.'

Cassie dipped the pen in the inkwell and scratched more words on the sheet of paper. In a few more minutes she'd have to blow out the candle and settle down to sleep. What else was there she had to tell May?

'I was home yesterday and Mam is fine. Dad wasn't too well again, running a bit of a fever I think because he kept complaining about being hot.'

She chewed the tip of the pen. She'd like to tell May about winning the row with Mam. But it seemed a bit unkind in her circumstances, locked up in that miserable-sounding place.

'Mam and me had a few words about me being friendly with Mr Jordan, but it blew over. I'll still be friends. I shan't tell her I'm going to a concert at the Town Hall with him next week. What the eye doesn't see.

'And the big news is Mr Aaron's getting married to some millionaire's daughter from Leeds, seemingly, and the staff at Rose's are all going to have the day off. I heard about

it from Miss Cecily because the Chadwicks have been
invited to the wedding . . .'

In the half-light of the privy May took the crumpled letter
out of her pocket and peered at the final paragraph.

'Miss Cecily is all excited because she's being fitted for a
new dress specially. There's one good thing out of it – it's
lucky we're the same size and I'll come in for the ones
she's chucking out . . .'

May stuffed the letter angrily into her pocket and marched
back towards the noise and smell of the laundry room. Cassie
had no idea that Aaron had anything to do with the coming
baby, and until this moment May herself had put it from her
mind. So he was to wed a rich man's daughter, was he? Well,
it had always been his plan, and he'd made it clear she wasn't
going to spoil that; she'd been only a pleasant diversion for
a fleeting autumn afternoon.

But I'm worth better than that, she told herself fiercely,
running her hands down over the protruding bulge – me and
the baby he disowned. We'll show him.

Sister Anthony was standing on the raised step where she
always stood to keep her eye on the girls as they worked.
She watched as May took up her place at the steam press.

'You took your time, Forty-Two,' she snapped.

May said nothing, only pulled down the press, letting the
steam hiss out her feelings.

'You'll make up the lost time before you go to supper,'
the nun went on. 'Duty before pleasure.'

Pleasure – that was ironic, thought May as she stared down
at the lump of congealed grey matter on her plate. The
nauseous smell that rose from the suet dumpling was just as
unappealing as its colour, and she hadn't yet summoned up
the courage to taste the stuff.

She broke open the unappetizing grey mound. Towards the middle there was a suspicion of meat – the left-overs of yesterday's glutinous mutton stew, no doubt, padded out with the suet dough to fill all those empty stomachs.

'Looks like they scraped the bottom of the flour bin for this,' muttered the girl next to her. 'Running with weevils by the look of it.'

Across the table Tilly laid down her fork. 'I can't eat this,' she groaned. 'I been feeling sick all day as it is.'

'I thought it was your back what hurt?' said the girl next to her.

'And me belly,' said Tilly. 'If I eat this muck I'll throw up.'

'What's that?' demanded the sharp voice of Sister Anthony as she came to stand behind Tilly's shoulder. 'Are you complaining? Where's your gratitude, girl?'

Tilly growled. 'I was only saying I can't eat this, Sister. I don't feel well.'

'You'll eat it and like it,' said Sister Anthony crisply. 'And if you don't you'll get it for every meal until you do. Now get on with it and give thanks for the Lord's generosity.'

Tilly scowled across at May as she dug her fork into the pudding and raised it to her lips. May saw her eyes close as she stuffed the forkful into her mouth, and her nose wrinkled. Sister Anthony stood close, her hands inside the sleeves of her habit.

'Go on,' she commanded. 'Swallow.'

With a gulp Tilly obeyed, then clasped a hand to her stomach. 'I can't,' she gasped. 'Me belly!'

The nun's face reddened with anger. 'Do as you're told, girl, and stop shamming,' she hissed. 'Eat.'

Again Tilly took a reluctant mouthful, her face contorting as she did so. It was understandable, thought May, for the pudding tasted as awful as it looked. All along the table it was clear that hunger was the only reason driving the girls to overcome the obnoxious taste. Hunger and the malevolent presence of Sister Anthony.

Then suddenly Tilly let out a muffled cry and a spume of

pudding flew from her mouth across the table. She stared for a moment at the mess, then turned and glared at the nun.

'I told you it would make me sick.'

May saw the nun draw her hand out of her sleeve, the short cane swept up in the air and then crashed down on Tilly's shoulders. 'You wicked girl!' she cried. 'You'll scrape that up this minute and eat it! You're not going to waste good food!'

'It's not food,' wailed Tilly. 'It's sick!'

Another blow of the cane landed on the girl's back. May saw her furious, baleful glare before she picked up the spoon and began scraping at the vomit.

'You can't make her eat that.' May found herself on her feet, speaking in a low voice. The Sister glared at her.

'You can mind your own business, Forty-Two,' she snapped, 'unless you'd like a taste of the cane too. Twenty-Four, come with me.'

Tilly was clearly in pain as she stumbled to her feet. May's hand gripped the edge of the table. 'Where are you taking her?' she asked.

The nun's smile was coolly insolent. 'Somewhere she can reflect on her misdeeds for a while. A little solitude is what she needs. Now get on with your supper.'

The girls watched in silence as she prodded the shambling Tilly with her cane towards the door.

'She'll take her to that bloody cupboard,' muttered the girl next to her. 'I been in there once. Horrible it is, chokes you so you can't breathe. Like a bloody coffin, it is.'

'She can't – she's almost due.' May started to step back over the bench. The girl grabbed her arm.

'Leave it – you can't help her. None of us can.'

May sank back on her seat, fuming. The other girls were furtively slipping slices of their own pudding onto Tilly's plate.

'I'll get that bitch in the end,' she muttered savagely. 'I swear I will.'

*   *   *

Cassie had just taken the fancy lace tray-cloth from the drawer and was about to lay up the afternoon tea tray when the kitchen door suddenly swung open and the mistress stood there. Immediately Cook looked alarmed. Mrs Chadwick only ever came down to the nether regions of the house in the morning to give orders for the day; at any other time it was usually to voice a complaint.

'Cook,' she said quietly, 'would you leave us for a moment? I'd like a word alone with Cassie.'

Cook brightened at once. 'Of course, madam. I've plenty I can be getting on with in the scullery.'

She bustled out and the mistress turned to Cassie. 'I'm sorry to bring bad news, my dear,' she said gently, 'but a messenger called just a few minutes ago. It seems your father is very ill and your mother wants you to go straight home.'

'Me dad?' echoed Cassie.

Mrs Chadwick nodded. 'You'd better tell Cook and get off home straight away. I do hope it's not too serious . . .'

Mam was standing on the hearth, a bowl of water in her hand, and old Mrs Boothroyd sat wheezing by the fire. One glance at Mam's face was enough to confirm how grim matters were.

'He's bad, love,' her mother said quietly. 'He's had this terrible fever for a couple of days. I got the doctor out to him last night 'cos he could scarcely breathe. Pneumonia, doctor says it is. Double pneumonia.'

Cassie sank into a chair. Dad had always been ill in bed, for almost as long as she could remember, but the thought of him dying . . . It was unthinkable.

'He'll be all right, won't he?' she whispered. 'Folks can get better from pneumonia, can't they?'

'Not lying flat and choking like he is,' said Mrs Boothroyd. 'We can't prop him up on pillows with his back. Drowning in his own spittle, he is. I've seen it before. Best send for your May, I reckon, before it's too late.'

'No,' said Mam. 'It's no use doing that.'

'Why not?' countered the old lady. 'She'd want to be at her father's bedside at the end.'

'Too late,' said Mam. 'She's too far away. I must get back upstairs now.'

Cassie got to her feet. 'No, you give me that bowl and sit down. I'll go up to him.'

Her mother gave her a smile as she held out the bowl. 'Just bathe his head with cold water like I've been doing, but don't expect too much, lass. There's nowt we can do. It's only a matter of time now, I fear.'

Cassie could hear the rasp and splutter of his breathing as she climbed the stairs, and felt sick. This time it was not the stench of his back which nauseated her, but a sweeping sense of guilt.

She'd been the one who opened that damned window the other day, despite the fact she knew it was far too cold. Mam must have found it open – she'd know who'd done it. Oh God, if only she hadn't listened to Dad's pleading!

She pushed open the bedroom door and went in. Fevered eyes stared at her from his hollow face half-hidden by the blanket.

'Help me, lass,' he croaked. 'I can't breathe – I'm choking.'

He began to cough, a harsh, racking cough which brought thick yellow ooze sliding from his mouth. She stared down at him helplessly. He didn't look like Dad, this corpse-like creature with death already in his eyes. She didn't recognize him; it wasn't the father who used to toss them playfully into the air when they were small, who used to come in from work singing as he poured sweeties into their laps. He wasn't even the man who'd lain here all these years moaning in pain with his back.

The coughing paused for a second and piteous eyes stared up at her. The words were hardly more than a rattle in his throat.

'For God's sake, help me – help me to die!'

*   *   *

By morning it was all over. As the first grey streaks of dawn marbled the sky over Hawksmoor's grey roofs, Jim Turnbull, his throat clattering, struggled noisily out of this world.

Daughter clung to mother wordlessly. Death was horrifyingly new to Cassie, overwhelming in its pain and finality. The world would never be quite the same again without Dad. That might be a stranger lying in the bed, but even so, there should be some dignity in death. She had no words to express the bewilderment she felt, the devastating sense of grief and loss – only tears.

'*Open the window for me, lass, just a little bit . . .*'

Guilt engulfed her. But for her he might still be alive. She would have to carry the guilty secret to her grave, and she couldn't bear it. She sobbed into her mother's neck.

'It's my fault, Mam. I opened that window.'

She felt Mam's arms tighten around her. 'Aye, love. And I left it open. It's what he wanted.'

Mam's tears ran silent and warm down Cassie's neck. Cassie held her mother close. 'Don't worry, Mam, I'll take care of you,' she muttered.

'Aye, I know.' The words were lost in Cassie's long hair.

'We'd best let our May know – I'll see to it.'

Her mother stood back and wiped away the tears. 'Don't make her feel she has to come – it's up to her. Go on down now and tell Mrs Boothroyd. Tell her I'd be glad if she'd come and help me lay him out.'

At the door Cassie hesitated and looked back. She didn't like leaving Mam alone in this chill air of death. Her mother raised a hand in dismissal.

'Go on, now. Leave me alone with him, just for a minute.'

TWENTY-FOUR

'Forty-Two, you're lagging behind again! And what's that in your hand?'

Sister Anthony's sharp voice behind her startled May back into reality. 'It's a letter from home, Sister,' she said quietly. 'My father's died. He's being buried on Thursday.'

The nun looked up at her shrewdly. 'I'm sorry to hear that. We'll pray for his soul and that his suffering is over – he must have suffered a great deal already from your disgrace.'

May fought hard to control her voice. 'He'd been ill a long time, Sister. For years, in fact.'

The squat nun's eyes narrowed. 'And I don't suppose your shameful behaviour made him feel any better,' she said maliciously. 'Now get along downstairs with the others before I take the cane to you.'

'You just try,' muttered May as she stuffed the letter into her pocket and turned to go. 'You just try.'

'What's that?' demanded Sister Anthony, hurrying after her. 'Do I hear insolence? You know what happens to those who are insolent. Where's your respect, girl?'

'Kept for those who deserve it,' snapped May. 'How much respect do you show to us?'

The nun stared, open-mouthed, for a second, then drew herself up to her full height, folding her arms inside the sleeves of her habit. 'I can hardly believe what I'm hearing, Forty-Two,' she said tartly. 'You, one of the better sort, or so we believed, harbouring such sinful thoughts. I never thought we would have to punish you with the cupboard.'

'Like you did to Tilly?' blurted May, all control deserting

her. 'Locking her in that dreadful place for a whole night while she was in labour? She suffered agony, and you just left her there alone, screaming!'

'Twenty-Four refused to eat up her dinner,' the little nun said righteously. 'She knew the punishment.'

'You shouldn't have done that to her when you knew she was in labour! Sisters of Mercy, indeed! You're cruel, heartless bigots, the lot of you!'

The nun's face grew pale and as she withdrew her hand from her sleeve May saw the stubby cane with the splayed end as it rose and fell, whacking hard across her shoulder. 'That's enough!' hissed Sister Anthony. 'Mother Superior will have something to say to you. You're coming with me to her office this minute.'

May could feel a stinging pain in her upper arm where the cane had lifted away a shred of flesh, and anger seethed in her. 'Gladly,' she retorted. 'I've got one or two things to say to her.'

Mother Superior stood listening, calmly aloof by the window, while Sister Anthony catalogued her complaints.

'. . . Forty-Two was extremely insolent, Mother. She challenged our rules and defied our authority. And what is worse, she shows no repentance. She seems to feel she should be excused on account of her father's death, but I feel she should do penance, Mother, and be given time in the cupboard to reflect on her sins.'

The little nun folded her hands and stood back with a complacent smile. May stood silent, holding a hand over the painful weal on her arm and fuming inwardly. Mother Superior's cool grey eyes turned on her. 'Is this true?' she asked.

May jutted her chin. 'I challenged the rules, yes, because they're cruel and heartless.'

'And you defied Sister's authority?'

'And why not? You treat people here like animals, not human beings.'

261

She heard Sister Anthony's incredulous gasp. With a nod Mother Superior dismissed her, and then turned again to May.

'Human beings?' she repeated. 'These are humans who have sinned, may I remind you, and need to be brought back to the path of righteousness.'

'Sinned?' snapped May. 'And who the devil hasn't?'

The nun's face expressed pain at the unholy word and she made the sign of the cross. May rushed on.

'What makes you think you're so much better than us?'

Mother Superior gave a patient sigh. 'I'm not here to argue with you, Forty-Two, but we are dedicated to God's work. We have not succumbed to sins of the flesh.'

'Because you haven't had the chance! For heaven's sake, where's your Christian principles? Where's your charity? You show no love or even affection for the girls in your charge, and you won't even allow them to be friendly with each other.'

'That sort of thing can lead to mischief, that's why.'

'Rubbish – we all need affection. You won't even let us know what happens to the girls after they go down to the delivery room – we never see them again.'

'In your best interests – they'd scare the others with their tales. By sending them to a separate lying-in ward we're just trying to protect you.'

'Or yourselves,' May flashed. 'How many babies are born dead like poor Daisy's? Maybe if you hadn't worked her so hard—'

'It was God's will,' Mother Superior cut in quietly, 'and who are we to question His ways? Maybe it was a blessing, since Twenty-Seven herself didn't live for much longer.'

May caught her breath. 'Daisy – died?'

'Of childbed fever, a week after the birth.'

Dad, and now Daisy. So the poor girl never left the Home, the day she'd dreaded. May swallowed down the lump in her throat. Somewhere out there in the grounds there'd be just another unmarked grave where Daisy and her baby lay, in peace at last . . .

Mother Superior was eyeing her thoughtfully. 'Childbirth

is fraught with danger, so you see why we don't tell you everything. We know what we are doing, both for the glory of God and to spare you, so you see why it would be best not to question our actions. Accept, suffer whatever pain is coming to you, and offer it up in atonement for your wrongdoing, and there may yet be a place for you in heaven.'

May stared. 'I never heard such rubbish in all my life,' she muttered. 'I'll make life the way I want it.'

Mother Superior sighed and walked back to look out of the window. 'You make things very difficult, Forty-Two.'

'May. My name is May, not Forty-Two. We're not lots in an auction.'

'As I say, you make things very difficult. If any other girl were to behave like you I would have no hesitation in throwing her out of this sanctuary, but in your case – well, maybe I could be charitable. I'm indebted to Mr Rose—'

'For the money he paid you?' sneered May.

The nun ignored her. '—so I think in this case I can be lenient. You will not, of course, be able to attend your father's funeral since you cannot leave here until your baby is born.'

The girl glared at her. 'You can keep your charity,' she muttered. 'I'm not staying in this hypocritical hell-hole! You're not going to lay your evil hands on my baby!'

Mother Superior snatched up a small handbell from the desk. 'I fear Sister Anthony was right,' she murmured. 'You need to be taught the virtue of Christian humility.'

She rang the bell loudly. Sister Anthony reappeared in the doorway. 'Take Forty-Two down to the cupboard, Sister,' said Mother Superior. 'And don't let her out until I tell you.'

The infamous cupboard stood at the end of the long stone-floored corridor leading to the cellars. A huge, old-fashioned armoire, it looked like some monstrous sentinel on duty at the palace gates, taller and broader than a coffin but just as funereal and awe-inspiring with its heavy carved black doors.

The far-away sound of voices singing in the chapel drifted

along the corridor as Sister Anthony stopped in front of the cupboard and jerked open the big oak doors.

'Quick, inside,' she snapped. 'I'm late for chapel.'

She stood aside to leave room for May to pass. Instead May thrust her weight against her, propelling the nun's squat body forward so that she stumbled headlong into the dark recesses of the cupboard. She caught a glimpse of her startled eyes before she slammed the doors and turned the key in the lock.

From inside she could hear the Sister's protesting cries. 'Let me out, you wicked girl! Open the door this minute!'

'You just sit there, you two-faced little prig,' muttered May. 'It'll do you good.'

There was a thunderous knocking on the panels of the door. 'For God's sake, let me out!' a piteous voice wailed. 'Don't leave me in here – I'll suffocate!'

'No you won't, more's the pity,' said May grimly. 'Anyway, suffering is good for the soul – you told me that. Offer it up, Sister, offer it up.'

As she hurried back up to the dormitory May's first instinct was to change out of the hated smock into her own clothes, snatch her belongings, and sneak unobtrusively out of the building while everyone was still in the chapel.

But why should she? Her mind was made up. She wasn't going to let anyone stop her now. No-one could force her to stay here. She'd no money, no plans, but one thing was certain; she was going to shake off the misery of this place once and for all. Wherever her baby was born, it would be in a better place than this.

There wasn't much to collect. All the girls' clothes were kept in bundles in the little stock room at the far end of the dormitory. It was never locked; as soon as any girl went into labour they took both her and her bundle to the delivery room so that she never set foot in here again. May found hers quickly. A brown paper tag was tied to it with a piece of string. Number Forty-Two. With a snort of disgust she tore off the tag and watched it flutter to the floor.

It was no use. The clothes she'd come in were far too small now to encompass the six-month bulge. She pulled on her coat over the detested smock, but try as she might she could get only one button to fasten. It would have to do.

Wrapping a scarf about her neck she carried the bundle of possessions proudly down the stairs and out of the front door. She slammed it loudly behind her, cutting off the wretched sound of plaintive voices in the chapel.

'*Dominus, non sum dignus . . .*' She never wanted to hear that sound again.

The unaccustomed March air outside blew cool on her cheek, and she drew in deep lungfuls, feeling it refreshing and revitalizing her jaded spirit. As she marched down the drive towards the gates a sudden exhilaration flooded through her. She'd escaped from the tyranny and hypocrisy of the nuns; she was free!

But free to go where? Out in the lane she hesitated. Down to the left lay the village and the railway station. She had no money for a rail ticket home – Mother Superior took whatever bit of cash the girls had when they arrived and kept it locked up in her office.

If she asked for help in the village she might be recognized as an inmate of the Home and taken back. She needed to get further away from danger – but where?

Take the road to the right, towards open country, and just keep on walking . . .

Mrs Chadwick had generously given permission for Cassie to take the whole week off until the funeral was over, three days of which were to be taken out of her annual holiday. In the meantime Cassie had done all she could to relieve Mam, writing to May and to Uncle Eddie in Leicester and Auntie Fran in Ipswich, though no-one expected them to travel so far to attend the funeral.

She'd bought special black-edged notepaper and envelopes for the letters. It was the least she could do.

'You'd no need to go to all that expense,' Mam had protested. 'Plain ones would have done.'

'I wanted to,' Cass had replied. 'I wanted to do it for Dad.'

How could she explain that it was the only way she could think of to ease her conscience? He deserved the best send-off she could muster, and she knew Mam felt the same. They'd paid a penny a week for the funeral insurance for what seemed like ages now, but that wasn't going to pay for everything. Mam had been to see Mr Jordan about the burial but she refused to discuss the cost.

'Give me some idea, Mam – ten pounds? Twelve? Fifteen?'

'None of your business, lady. That's my problem.'

'I could chip in – I've a shilling or two saved.'

'That you won't. I'll sort it out, don't you fret.'

Sort it out. So she hadn't the money to pay or she'd have told her.

Right, thought Cass, I need to see Mr Jordan myself, to tell him I can't go to the concert now. There must be something I can do. Let's see if he really does have a soft spot for me and, failing that, there are one or two things I've learned about him that I'm sure he wouldn't want other folk to know . . .

'I'm sorry I can't go to that do in the Town Hall, Mr Jordan, but I'm sure you understand . . .'

Harold sat entranced, gazing at the mournful beauty sitting on his sofa and felt sorely tempted to put a consoling arm around her slim young shoulders. 'Of course, my dear,' he murmured, 'I didn't expect you would, in view of what's happened.'

Tragic eyes looked up at him from a pale face. 'My mother has so much worry on her mind and my sister won't be able to get back from down south to help . . .'

'I know, I know. It's a very trying time for you. If there's anything I can do – I'd be only too glad to repay some of the kindness you showed to me.'

He saw the beautiful young breasts rise and fall in a deep sigh. 'You're very kind,' she said sadly, 'but the help Mam needs isn't the sort folk hereabouts are able to give. They're hard put to it as it is to make ends meet.'

Of course, he understood her now. Money was the problem. He cleared his throat and spoke cautiously. 'I know it's not always easy – I've experienced that difficulty myself in the past – but if I can help – I mean, the cost of your father's funeral—'

She gave him a wan smile. 'You're very generous, Mr Jordan, but my mother is a proud woman. Maybe if you were to let us pay it off little by little, a bit every week – I'd give you my wages every pay day—'

'No, no,' he cut in sharply. 'I wouldn't dream of it. I couldn't take a penny from you.'

He broke off. She was looking up at him, a hint of a smile beginning to curve those lovely lips. Now why had he said that? He hadn't intended to offer a free funeral, only to be lenient about the payment, maybe do it only at cost. Still, now he'd committed himself . . . 'I said I wanted to make you a gift,' he muttered hoarsely, 'but I meant it to be more than this.'

She stood up and held out a slender hand. 'You've been kindness itself,' she said softly. 'I'll not forget that. Mam won't want to but I'll find a way to persuade her to agree. But I can't accept any more from you.'

He took the little gloved hand in his. 'Maybe soon, when you are feeling more yourself again . . .'

She inclined her head, her eyes huge and lustrous. He'd seen grief many times before, but he'd never seen it render a woman so beautiful, and he felt his chest swell with tenderness for her.

'Give it time, Mr Jordan,' she murmured. 'My father was a fine man and first I want to see him go to his grave with all the dignity he deserves. No skimping, I want the very best for him.'

Harold clutched the little hand close to his swelling chest. 'And that you shall have, my dear, I promise you. Nothing but the very best.'

On the doorstep she turned. 'Mam will be so relieved, thanks to you. It will take such a weight off her mind, knowing there's no big bill to come.'

'None,' he said proudly. 'It will be my privilege.'

TWENTY-FIVE

May was exhausted. She couldn't have walked more than three or four miles but after being cooped up for so long in the Home she was no longer used to fresh air and walking up hills. Not that these were real hills, not like those around Hawksmoor. Back home in the old days she had climbed the one-in-five Birchencliffe hill and thought nothing of it, but now . . . With this uncomfortable bulge leading the way, the heavy bag didn't make things any easier.

But it was essential to put as many miles between herself and the Home as she could before nightfall. And then she'd have to find somewhere to sleep. Yorkshire seemed such a long way off. She couldn't possibly walk all that way, especially not with Dad's funeral being on Thursday.

And what was more, she was beginning to think it had been a mistake to take this road. In all this time she'd seen no sign of life beyond an occasional cottage and heard only the distant rattle of a train. As she paused, breathless, at the brow of the hill she could see nothing ahead of her, only the road still snaking away into the far green of yet more fields.

But now there was another sound, the far-away clopping of a horse's hooves. She set the bag down close to the hedge and turned to look back. The sound grew louder, and she shielded her eyes against the sun. Yes, it was an open cart drawn by a grey horse coming towards her. She waited until it came close, then waved to the young man on the driving seat. He grinned and reined the horse in.

'Hallo,' he said in a voice as cheery as the gaudy red and white neckerchief knotted at his throat. 'You're a long way from town. Want a lift?'

'I'd be that grateful.'

'Climb up here by me then.'

Behind him huge piles of carrots and potatoes, turnips and cabbages leaned colourfully against each other. May settled herself down thankfully beside him, cradling her bag on her knees.

He jerked his head towards the vegetables. 'Taking 'em to Holney market,' he explained. 'Where are you heading?'

She took her cue. 'Looking for somewhere to stay in Holney. Do you know anywhere reasonable?'

She could see him eyeing her up, her condition and the bag perched on her lap. It was evident from her question and her appearance that she hadn't much money.

'After a new job?' he asked.

'Perhaps.'

He slapped the reins on the grey's smooth back and thought for a moment. 'There's old Mrs Fairweather,' he murmured. 'I know she lets out rooms from time to time and she's very clean.'

For a moment May hesitated. She had no means of paying for a room, but she had to find somewhere before nightfall. She couldn't afford to be picked up in the street by the police and risk being sent back. 'Could you direct me there?' she asked.

He gave a cheery smile. 'Better than that. We'll pass right by her door so I can drop you off.'

He not only pulled up and helped her to climb down, but also walked with her up to Mrs Fairweather's front door with its shining brass knocker. The door opened and a vast figure in a print apron filled the doorway.

'Well, if it isn't Will Napier!' she exclaimed in delight. 'I haven't set eyes on you for many a long week.'

Will smiled and indicated May. 'Meet a friend of mine,

Mrs Fairweather. She's looking for a room for the night. Can you help her?'

The old lady's gaze travelled over May. 'Well, I haven't a bed aired at the moment,' she said dubiously, then seeing May's crestfallen look she added, 'but I reckon I could get the blankets out and air them by the fire. Or better still, in the oven now the meat's done. Come on in, lad, and bring your friend with you.'

'May. My name's May Turnbull.'

The old lady stood aside. 'Come inside and welcome, May. The kettle's all about boiling.'

May stepped in. Will pulled off his cap and followed. In the neat little parlour with its glowing fire and savoury scent of meat and onions she turned to the old lady.

'Mrs Fairweather, I've got to come clean with you,' she said quietly. 'I haven't any money – not with me, that is – but I've plenty at home. If you could just give me a bed for the night, I promise I'll pay you back.'

Will said nothing, just twisted his cap round in his hands. The old lady looked puzzled. 'And where's home?' she asked.

'Yorkshire. I want to get home in time for my father's funeral.'

'Yorkshire?' Mrs Fairweather repeated. She couldn't have sounded more startled if May had said she was on her way home to Turkey. 'Oh, I don't know,' she murmured. 'How are you going to get back there?'

'I don't know yet,' May replied. 'But when I do I'll make certain to send the money on.'

Mrs Fairweather shook her head slowly. May pulled back her coat and dug into the pocket of her smock.

'Here,' she said, pulling out a crumpled sheet of paper. 'I'm not lying to you about the funeral. Here's my sister's letter.'

Mrs Fairweather's pudgy hand closed over hers. 'It's all right, love, put it away. Now let's see – you'll need money for the train, you in your condition and all. Where's your husband?'

May saw her eyes shift to her left hand, to the finger with

271

no ring. 'I haven't got a husband,' she said in a low voice. 'He's dead.'

She hadn't intended to say that – how did the words slip out? Still, as far as she was concerned, the father of her child was as good as dead.

At once the old lady's eyes filled with concern. 'Oh, you poor love,' she said gently. 'It's terrible being on your own. I lost my Albert fifteen years ago and I still miss him. Of course you shall have a bed for the night. Sit ye down, both of you, and I'll make that tea.'

Her big body swayed out into the scullery. As May seated herself on the horsehair sofa Will tossed his cap in a chair and went out after the old lady. May could hear voices murmuring.

'Threatening to rain . . . in the family way . . . can't see her stranded outside for the night . . .'

A low voice answered, so low she could catch only a word or two. 'If there's any problem . . . settle up . . . I'll see you're all right.'

Another minute passed before the two of them returned. Mrs Fairweather was smiling broadly. 'You've no more need to worry, my love,' she said, touching May's shoulder as she passed to lay the teapot on the table. 'Will and me has it all settled.'

Will nodded. 'Aye,' he said gruffly. 'A couple of shillings should see you right for the train ticket.'

May stood up, tears pricking her eyes. 'I've no right to ask anything of you,' she said in a choked voice, 'but I've really no choice. My dad—'

'No choice at all,' Will muttered. 'I never heard about my mam being dead until it was too late. I'll get you to the station for the first train in the morning.'

It was no use. May's shoulders were shaking with the effort to hold back the tears. The old lady came forward and folded her plump arms around her.

'There now, you've no need to fret any more. You'll get back in time, have no fear.'

May smiled through her tears. 'Saying thank you isn't enough. I'll never forget you for this, and the minute I get back I'll see you get the money, I promise.'

'No hurry, you see to yourself first,' said Mrs Fairweather. 'It can wait till after you've settled down.'

'No,' said May. 'I've always paid my way. It'll be the first thing I'll do. Mrs Fairweather, I can't thank you enough.'

'Nay,' said the old lady, 'it's him you should thank. He's promised to pay every penny if you fail. Now come on, you look all in. Let's have that cup of tea.'

May turned to look at Will. He busied himself pulling out a chair from under the table and sitting down, knees spread wide.

The old lady chuckled. 'He's a good lad, is Will Napier. He'll make some woman a fine husband one day.'

'They'll have a job on,' growled Will. 'I'll take some catching.'

Grace could feel the feverish excitement buzzing around the room. Silly girls, they were as giddy and unsettled as if it was them getting married tomorrow, not Mr Aaron. Still, Mr Henry had given the whole of the staff, workroom and shop, the day off in celebration. He was full of it, proud as Punch that his son was marrying the Rabin girl. He was still beaming when he came into the workroom once more, carrying a sheaf of papers.

'It's going to be a grand do in Leeds tomorrow,' he said in tones of great satisfaction. 'I'm fair looking forward to it.'

'I'm sure it's going to be a wonderful day,' Grace agreed, 'and we all wish Mr Aaron the very best. Now, about me leaving—'

Mr Henry wasn't listening. 'I persuaded Mr Aaron's little lady to arrange it for a Thursday,' he preened, 'since there's never a lot going off in the shop on a Thursday. Worst takings of the week, Thursdays are.'

'Yes, sir,' said Grace. 'Now, like I say, about me leaving . . .'

273

He laid the sheaf of papers down. 'Look, I know good head seamstresses are hard to find, Miss Openshaw, but if you're set on retiring we have to find somebody to replace you.'

Retirement. Grace shuddered at the word. Not so long ago she'd been looking forward so much to having time of her own, to do the things she wanted, but not any more. Not since Edward had dropped out of her life, leaving only a vacuum. Now the word retirement had an ominous ring about it, like the church bell tolling at a funeral.

'You don't have to go,' Mr Henry murmured. 'I'd be more than delighted if you'd stay on.'

'Well,' Grace replied tentatively, 'we've always said as May Turnbull was shaping up well to the job. Now that her father's died—'

Mr Henry bristled. 'You can forget about her,' he snorted. 'She's gone.'

'Gone?' exclaimed Grace. 'You mean she's not coming back?'

But Mr Henry was clearly not disposed to discuss the matter. 'So if you'd like to reconsider,' he said tersely, 'let me know.'

And with that he snatched up his papers and hurried out of the workroom.

Now come on, snap out of it, Grace told herself firmly that evening as she put Oscar's supper down in front of him. There's others far worse off than you, like the Turnbulls, for instance. What on earth had happened to May to make her quit her job like that? Surely Mr Henry hadn't dismissed her. And now her father had died too, poor girl.

Then a thought came to her. A day off tomorrow and nothing particular to do – it would be a nice mark of respect if she were to go to the funeral – it said in the *Examiner* that it was to be held at St Thomas's at three. Maybe she might catch sight of May, find the chance to talk to her even. She'd like to know how she was, and anyway, it would help to pass the day.

Pass the day – what a pessimistic way to think. Time was, not so very long ago when she'd have welcomed the prospect of a free day to herself. Maybe she should think seriously about taking up Mr Henry's offer and stay on at Rose's. After all, work would fill her days, as it had done for thirty years and more.

Grace's musings were interrupted by a knock at the door, just as she was putting down Oscar's saucer of milk. Now who could that be on a Wednesday evening?

She lifted the lace curtain and peered out of the window. These days you could never be too careful . . . A tall figure in a greatcoat and wearing a well-brushed hat – Edward! With a little cry of delight she hurried to unlatch the door.

He took off his hat as he came in, looking taller and thinner than she remembered, but his smile still had that grave look of amusement.

'Have I offended you, Grace?' he asked.

His directness flustered her. 'Whatever makes you say that?'

'The other day in the shop – why didn't you take advantage of the discount I offered? I'd have come down to see to you myself only I was tied up with the manager from the Yorkshire Penny Bank.'

So that was it. But it didn't explain why he hadn't called. She indicated a chair and watched him as he sat down. His straightforward question deserved no less from her.

'I haven't seen you in ages,' she said. Her tone was quiet, stiff even, but it belied the agitation inside.

He shook his head sadly, not meeting her gaze. 'You've every right to scold me,' he admitted. 'I've been very ungracious. The truth is, I stayed away from you because I felt I was growing too fond of you. Too dependent on you, perhaps. I didn't want you to feel obliged in any way.'

Too fond! The words rang in Grace's ears, and she felt herself growing dizzy. 'Obliged?' she repeated dully. 'Obliged?'

'To respond to my feelings,' Edward explained. 'You must have become aware of how I felt about you.'

She could hear Oscar guzzling the milk noisily. 'No,' she murmured, 'I was not.'

'So much so,' Edward went on quietly, 'that I was in danger of proposing to you. I know that would have been a mistake and I didn't want to upset you, knowing how you value your freedom, how you're looking forward to your retirement . . .'

'No, no,' Grace cut in, taking a step towards him. 'You've got it all wrong. In fact, I'm thinking of delaying my retirement. Mr Henry is very anxious for me to stay on.'

Edward bowed his head. 'I'm sure he is. He's a shrewd man, is Henry. I've got a lot of time for him even if I can't stand his son. But tell me, has my neglectful behaviour influenced you in your decision? Is that why you're going to continue working?'

Grace gave him a demure smile. 'I haven't said I will carry on yet. I said I'm thinking about it, but yes, I've missed seeing you very much.'

Edward smiled, that slow, grave smile that warmed her heart. 'Perhaps then, if you don't think too harshly of me, we could have a cup of tea and we'll talk about it. If you can find it in your heart to forgive me?'

In the grey light of dawn May stood dressed and ready, waiting for Will to arrive. Her landlady surveyed her critically.

'Have you no black to wear? I mean, going to the funeral—'

May looked down at the regulation smock, the coat barely stretching to fasten across it. 'I fear not. This is all I have that'll fit me.'

Mrs Fairweather shook her head. 'I think we can do better than that,' she murmured. 'I've a good black coat and dress upstairs that'll go nowhere near me since I put on a bit of weight. Come with me.'

Both the dress and the ample coat fitted comfortably over the bulge, almost too comfortably, but several safety pins later

Mrs Fairweather's deft fingers had made sure that the slack was well and truly gathered in. Then the landlady delved into the depths of her wardrobe and produced a black hat.

'I haven't had occasion to wear this since my Albert passed away,' she said wistfully as she turned it round to brush the brim. 'See, it's still got the veiling on. That'll finish you off a treat.'

'I'll see you get everything back,' May promised. The old lady shook her head. 'No need to bother, love – I'll never fit into them clothes again, but you can hang on to the hat. I paid good money for that, I did.'

May packed her old coat into her bag but it was a pleasure to discard the hated smock at last. Mrs Fairweather took it gladly.

'I've been needing a new apron,' she said. 'Cut down, it'll do me a treat. It's a bit of good stuff, is that.'

By the time Will knocked at the door May had been transformed. As she emerged from the house he pulled off his cap.

'By heck, you look grand,' he said admiringly, then, taking her hand, he made a mock bow. 'My lady, your carriage is waiting.'

Before May climbed up on the cart she turned. 'Mrs Fairweather, I can't thank you enough—'

The old lady smiled from the doorstep. 'Go on with you,' she called. 'You just make sure you catch that train.'

It was still quiet in the little town. The shopkeepers had not yet taken down their shutters and only the sound of the grey's hooves clattering over the cobblestones broke the eerie hush of dawn.

'You all right for money?' Will muttered as the railway station came in sight.

'Yes thanks – I've got two shillings for the rail fare. That should be more than enough.'

He reined in the horse, then came round to help her climb down. For a moment he stood, holding her gently by the elbows. By the light of the gas-lamp over the station entrance she could see his earnest face.

'When's the little one due?' he asked with a touch of awkwardness.

'Nearly three months yet – early June,' she answered.

He bit his lip. 'May, listen,' he said urgently, 'I live at Chardley Farm. If ever you need help you'll find me there.'

She smiled. His hands felt tight on her arms. 'And if ever you find yourself up in Hawksmoor, I'm at seven, Cedar Street. Oh listen – is that my train pulling in? I'll have to hurry.'

He let go of her arms and dug deep into his pocket. As she turned away he grabbed hold of her hand. 'You might have need of this,' he grunted. 'Good luck, May Turnbull.'

He leapt up again onto the driving seat and slapped the reins against the horses' back. May stared down at the coin gleaming in her hand.

A florin. A whole two shillings, almost as much as she'd earned in a week when she started work at Rose's.

TWENTY-SIX

Nellie Bottomley squatted on the hearth, brush and shovel in hand as she cleared the ashes out from under the fire. She felt very virtuous that for once she'd risen before her sister, an event which hadn't been known to happen for years.

She looked up as Agnes came in, still in her flannel nightgown and with her thin grey hair not yet pinned up in the usual neat coils but streaming wispily about her neck.

'What happened to you this morning then?' Nellie crowed. 'As a rule you're out of bed and down the stairs before the lamp-lighter's finished knocking up. I'd have thought you'd have been up extra early today, it being Mr Turnbull's funeral.'

Agnes slumped into a chair without a word. Nellie searched her face. It wasn't like her not to flash back with some stinging retort. 'What's up?' she asked. 'You look like you seen a ghost or summat.'

Agnes ran a weary hand across her forehead. 'I don't feel too good this morning. I didn't get a wink of sleep last night.'

Nellie glanced at the wall. 'It wasn't him next door again, was it? I never heard nowt.'

Agnes gave a slow shake of the head. 'It wasn't him. I just had this tight feeling in me chest and it wouldn't go.'

Her sister flicked the last crumb of ash into the shovel and pursed her lips. 'I said not to eat them pickles,' she said self-righteously, climbing with difficulty to her feet. 'You know they don't agree with you but you wouldn't be told.' She was quite enjoying this – it made a nice change.

'I know,' admitted Agnes, 'but I don't feel well at all. I

279

think I'll go back to bed, just for a while. Happen it'll go away in a bit.'

Nellie stared up at her sister in shocked amazement as she shambled wearily out of the room, and then she looked around her with an uneasy feeling. What was she to do now, with no Agnes to boss her about? By now she'd have given orders to make the porridge or put the washing on to boil. What was to happen to their routine if she stayed in bed for any length of time?

But she wouldn't, Nellie reassured herself as she pulled the kettle over the hob. Agnes hated staying in bed. She always said folk died in bed. She'd be down again before you could say Jack Robinson. Yes, of course she would; not for all the tea in China would she miss going to Mr Turnbull's funeral.

The moment May stepped out of the railway station into Hawksmoor's busy St George's Square she knew she was home. The smoky atmosphere, the noise of clattering vehicles and clogs on cobbled streets, the bustle, the sensation of suppressed energy in the air hit her forcibly after the quiet of the countryside.

Drawing the crêpe veiling on Mrs Fairweather's hat down over her face she set off along the Manchester Road. St Thomas's Church lay only a mile or so out of town and there was over an hour yet to go before the service was due to start. With luck she could settle herself in a secluded corner at the back of the church before anyone else arrived. With luck no-one would recognize her in the street either. No-one would connect a heavily veiled and thick-bodied woman with May Turnbull and after all it was a long time since anyone round here had laid eyes on her.

Ada could hardly see through the mist of tears as Cassie led her into a pew near the front of the church. Elsie clung to her hand in silence, still too bewildered by what had happened to take it all in. If only May had been able to come, the family circle would have been complete.

The thought saddened Ada. The lass would be heartbroken, not being able to bid her father goodbye. So close they'd been, those two, closer somehow than he'd ever been with the others.

The organ had stopped playing. The minister climbed into the pulpit and began droning words she couldn't take in. Elsie was sniffling. Cassie had her head bowed close to her chest, her eyes closed. In the centre aisle lay Jim's coffin. Ada fixed her eyes on it, willing her silent, loving thoughts through the wood to reach him.

'We're here together again, love, just like that day all them years ago when we got married. What a day that was! That's when we were both working at Crowther's, and we ran down here in our dinner-break, remember? And remember how the heavens opened and the rain came down in torrents? I'd borrowed me mother's best hat – she'd have killed me if I'd got it wet. I had to wrap it up in me scarf while we ran back to work. We did laugh, you and me. We laughed a lot together, didn't we, Jim?'

The lump in Ada's throat began to grow larger. He hadn't had occasion to laugh much in the last few years. It wasn't right. A man didn't deserve to lose his dignity the way Jim had.

The minister was saying something about resurrection of the flesh and the eternal life to come. Please God if You resurrect Jim, be merciful and let him come back the way he used to be, whole and strong and healthy, not the way he was at the end. He couldn't bear to suffer that all over again. He'd been a fine man; no woman could want for better . . .

Cassie sat slumped, feeling guilt wash over her while the minister spoke words about love and respect for the deceased. Over so many years she'd given him little thought at all, that figure in the bed upstairs. He'd been like a piece of the furniture, undemanding but not contributing anything to her life. In fact she'd resented him, the all-pervasive stink of him which had meant she never used to bring Eunice home from school because of it. Downstairs the house always reeked of wet washing, but as you climbed only halfway up the stairs you came across the smell, hanging like a sickly sweet cloud waiting to engulf you.

That was why she'd always hated having to see to him, having to clean up that hideous, festering mess on his back. She'd have done anything to dump the job on May who didn't seem to mind, and it had been a secret relief to escape to the Chadwicks' house where everything smelled clean and perfumed and expensive.

And now he was gone; too late to tell him that she really did care. And it wasn't only that troubling her. No-one could know how bad she felt about opening that window. She hadn't known it would kill him. He'd used her at the end, made her his unwitting accomplice. She'd tried to tell Mam.

Cassie stole a sidelong glance at her mother's face, pale and drawn and lips tightly compressed. She was a good 'un, was Mam.

'*If you hadn't done it, love, I would have.*'

That was her all over. She might be quick to attack when her daughters gave offence, like that time Cassie stole a shilling from her rent tin, but she was equally quick to defend and draw off their pain.

Cassie slid her fingers silently into her mother's lap and gripped hold of her hand.

Grace Openshaw slipped, as quietly as her creaking shoes would allow, into the gloom of the church and took a seat hurriedly in the nearest pew, next to a heavily veiled woman in black. She glanced around nervously, embarrassed that she'd had to sneak in when the service had already begun. She could have sworn it said three-thirty in the *Examiner*.

There were quite a lot of people here, considering it was a working day. She craned her neck. Three people sat in the front pew near the coffin, a middle-aged woman, a young fair-haired one and a little girl. They must be May's family, but there was no sign of May.

282

Pity, thought Grace. She wasn't the sort to miss her own father's funeral. But then, what sort of girl was she, just disappearing from Rose's like that with no explanation? Evidently not as solid and reliable as she'd thought. She'd always been a reserved girl, so who knew what went on in her head?

Still, she was sorry to lose sight of her. Of all the seamstresses who'd come and gone over the years, May Turnbull had been the one closest to her heart. She'd almost come to think of her as the daughter she'd never had. Ah well . . .

She glanced across at her neighbour. The woman's face was completely obscured by the crêpe veil but there was something familiar about the way she sat, hands clasped in her lap and head bowed in an attitude of composed resignation. Grace started. It was for all the world the way May Turnbull used to sit at her workbench.

Don't be silly, she told herself, it can't be. Just because you were thinking of the girl – if she were here she'd be sitting down at the front of the church with her family. And in any case, this one's in the family way.

So that settled it. Girls under her supervision had been known to get into trouble, but May Turnbull was definitely not that sort. Unlike the others, she didn't even have a sweetheart so far as Grace knew. Then Mother's words came echoing in her head.

'No, Grace, you're not going down to the Band of Hope meeting. There's too many lads go there, and although you've been brought up right, wherever there's lads the most unlikely girls have got theirselves into trouble.'

Grace sneaked another look at the woman's gloveless hands lying in her lap. Even in the gloom of the church she could see there was no gleam of a wedding ring on that third finger.

The minister's eloquence was lost on Grace as she gave herself up to wild speculation. If it was May . . . If she was pregnant and unmarried, it would explain a great deal. Maybe her family had disowned her and that was why she wasn't sitting with them. And it would explain Mr Henry's scornful words.

'You can forget her. She's gone.'

He always sacked the careless ones who got themselves into trouble, without notice and without pay. But then another thought crossed Grace's mind – how would he get to know about her condition if she was working so far away on that job for Sir Joseph?

That job for which she never seemed to need either advice or materials. Suspicion flickered in Grace's mind. From the corner of her eye she caught sight of a movement. The woman was reaching into a pocket, pulling out a handkerchief, lifting the veil to dab her eyes. For a fleeting second Grace could see her profile, young and fresh-skinned, and she caught her breath.

There was no mistaking May Turnbull . . .

Love, anger and frustration choked in May's throat. He should never have died so young, so broken, only half his life used up. There was no God, no justice, when a man was robbed of the good and useful life he could have enjoyed.

Jack Smedley was down there near the front, with Charlie Andrews and a couple more of his pit-mates, looking all stiff and unnatural in his best suit and clean starched shirt. Big and hard-muscled, he had probably thirty years ahead of him to look forward to, thought May. If the pit didn't get him as well. It wasn't fair what had happened to Dad . . .

But broken or not, he was loved and respected. It was good to see so many of the neighbours here. Even old Mrs Boothroyd had made the effort to drag her rheumaticky old bones down to the church, and that bow-legged little Miss Bottomley, the one folks said wasn't quite all there.

She couldn't see Mam and Cass without craning her neck round the head of the man in front, but she'd seen them come in with little Elsie and it had been hard not to run to them on the spot, to hug them close in wordless grief. Only the tone of Cassie's letter had stopped her. It had told her of the funeral but somehow, without actually forbidding her, its tone had implied that they did not expect her to come.

Maybe Mam had had a change of heart since the days she'd wanted May to brazen it out. Maybe she felt that the sudden appearance of a heavily pregnant daughter was too much to explain away. Whatever the reason, thought May, she had to tread cautiously before showing up at the house. If she could manage a private word alone with Cassie . . .

If she leaned slightly to the left she could just see Dad's coffin in the aisle, bare but for one spray of yellow flowers. It hurt to think of him lying there, face-up, on his poor back. Soon they'd put him down in the earth where he'd rot away, just as his flesh had been rotting for years.

Resurrection indeed! Anger filled her. The body may die, Dad, but your gentle spirit can never die. It was too fine a spirit to disappear without trace. It will linger somewhere, I know, waiting to return. Some day it will come back to warm the world in some lucky child still unborn.

The mourners left the church to follow the family and the minister outside for the interment. May hung back in the shadowy corner of the pew until they'd all gone, all but the woman beside her.

The woman turned to face her and reached out to touch her hand. 'I'm so sorry, May,' she murmured, 'truly I am.'

Miss Openshaw! May stared in amazement, powerless to find words. The other woman smiled.

'You've no need to say anything, May,' she whispered. 'I think I can guess. Don't let me detain you now, but I just want you to know, you've got a friend if ever you need one. I live at fifty-one, Minerva Street. Call on me, any time.'

May felt the quick, light pressure on her hand before Miss Openshaw turned and hurried away, the squeak of her shoes echoing down the length of the church as she made for the door.

For a moment May sat stunned. So her veil had not fooled at least one person who knew her. How, then, was she to intercept Cassie without anyone else knowing? If she joined the circle of mourners at the graveside someone else might also penetrate her disguise. Maybe it would be wisest to wait in the church until they'd all left the cemetery before she emerged into the open.

Grace hurried out of the churchyard. She had no intention of joining the group clustered around the open grave. It was too painful to see the misery etched on the faces of the bereaved, having to watch their loved one being lowered into the ground.

But out in the bustling street she hesitated. That poor girl in there had been alone, isolated from her family. It wouldn't do any harm to hang on a bit longer and see what she did when she came out. If she needed help . . .

Through the iron railings she saw the minister fling a handful of earth down into the grave, and then the two women from the front pew did likewise. The little girl clung tightly to the older woman's hand, sobbing quietly. Then they all turned away and came slowly, the women arm in arm, towards the gate. It was over.

As they came closer she could see the wretched, hollow look on the mother's face and felt a rush of compassion for her. Without thinking she stepped forward and spoke shyly.

'Excuse me – you don't know me – my name's Grace Openshaw,' she found herself babbling. 'Your daughter May used to work with me at Rose's – she told me once how ill her father was. I just wanted to offer my condolences, that's all.'

She broke off suddenly, appalled by her own temerity. The mother gave a wan smile. 'That's very kind of you, I'm sure. Our May wasn't able to come, I'm afraid.'

A stocky man in black took hold of the younger woman's arm and ushered the family away. The other mourners were filtering out of the gate and melting away into the crowd. Grace stood by the railings, watching, but still May had not come out.

And then she spotted her, a dark figure hovering in the

286

shadows of the church porch. Grace waved a hand, and then watched as the girl came down the path towards her.

May smiled as she came near. 'I'm sorry,' she said, 'I was taken by surprise in there just now. I didn't mean to be rude.'

'No more you were, love.'

'And thank you for being so kind – offering to help, I mean.'

'And I meant it, every word. You don't have to explain anything.'

The girl glanced down. 'No, I suppose it's pretty obvious,' she said wryly, 'only I didn't want to embarrass my family while folks were about so I kept away.'

Grace cocked her head. 'Are you planning to leave again now, then? Without talking to them?'

May sighed. 'I want to talk to them, but I can't yet. There'll be folk back at the house now. I'll go down after dark when they've gone and nobody'll see me.'

Grace took her arm. 'It's a long time till nightfall. Come back home with me and we'll have tea before you go – you've no other plans, have you?'

'None,' said May, 'and I'd be glad to come with you.'

After tea May sat on the sofa with Oscar's black head nuzzled against her thigh. She watched Miss Openshaw scooping up cake crumbs from the tablecloth with a small brush and crumb tray.

'You've guessed what happened, haven't you?' she murmured.

Miss Openshaw flashed an embarrassed smile. 'Well, I did start putting two and two together when I saw you today, you vanishing like that without a word, Mr Henry giving me some cock-and-bull story about a long job for Sir Joseph and no-one ever asking for materials – I wondered what he was covering up, and now it starts to make sense. I'm just sorry it happened.'

May fixed her with a direct look. 'You mean you've guessed who the father is?'

Miss Openshaw put the crumb tray away in the sideboard drawer and snapped it shut. 'It's none of my business, my dear, but I couldn't help thinking how you was on your own for so long up at Thornleigh Hall. I could hazard a guess, but like I say, it's none of my business. I just want you to know you've a home here if you need it, for as long as you need it. There'll be no questions, I promise you.'

May stared at her in wonder. Who'd have thought it, Miss Openshaw, the martinet who ruled over the girls at Rose's with an inflexible rod, becoming the supporter and ally of a girl who'd fallen from grace, as the nuns would have it? She showed no sign of shock, though she'd clearly guessed it was Aaron.

'No-one knows who the father is but Mam and me,' May said quietly, 'not even my sister. I'd like it to remain our secret.'

Miss Openshaw shook her head vigorously, as though blowing the fact out of her memory. 'It's forgotten already and you can stay here as long as you want,' she repeated. 'Until the baby is born, if you like. It would be nice to have a baby born in this house.'

The swelling in May's throat made it hard for her to speak. She smiled, then touched the older woman's hand. 'You're very kind. Look, now it's getting dark I'll go and talk to Mam and see how things are.'

Harold Jordan was feeling rather pleased with himself as he unhitched Dolly from the hearse and led her back into her stall. It had been a good funeral as working-folk funerals went, not too many wreaths but plenty of mourners to admire his handiwork. The widow had seemed pleased when he took the three of them back to the house.

'Thank you, Mr Jordan,' she'd murmured quietly as he stood in her little parlour drinking a cup of tea. 'My Jim would have been that pleased . . .'

He didn't always accept invitations to go back to the house for the funeral tea but this was different. He hadn't wanted to lose sight of Cassie so soon after he'd touched her, helping her up the steps. The flesh of her arm had felt so firm and at the same time so soft he'd wanted to pull back the sleeve and kiss it. And what was more, he was curious to see her in her own setting. She'd looked up at him from under those long, silky lashes while she offered him yet another of those damned ham sandwiches. If only he had a penny for every one of the wretched things he'd been forced to eat over the years. But this one was good, juicy meat between nutty brown slices. There was no doubt about it, whoever made it had a wonderful hand with bread.

'I baked it myself this morning,' Cassie had admitted, and he gazed at her in awe. This was a woman who had everything.

He had good reason to congratulate himself, he thought as he watched Dolly contentedly munching hay. It had been a very shrewd move on his part, offering to do this job for free. Although she hadn't said a word about it, Cassie knew she was indebted to him now, and that was going to stand him in very good stead . . .

TWENTY-SEVEN

'*Roasta patata*,' cried the dark-eyed little Italian as he tossed a potato, too hot to handle, into a paper twirl for the youngster holding out his penny.

May could feel the heat of the charcoal burner as she passed the sparkling-eyed old man. Winter and summer alike old Joseppy stood there in Fountain Street, never seeming to grow any older. When the weather turned warm he'd swap the charcoal burner for his cart packed with crushed ice and tantalize the children with his delicious ice-cream.

The ground began to shake underfoot as a train rumbled over the viaduct. As May turned the corner into Cedar Street the lamplighter touched light to the last lamp. Under its yellow glow hung a hazy mist, heavy with the sulphurous odour of the gasworks and the sooty smell of trains. Between the lamp posts lay dark pools of shadow and silence. May felt like a ghost come back to haunt the scene of her childhood, the carefree time when she'd known nothing of sin and guilt.

She trod carefully past the lighted windows till she reached number seven. Some of the mourners might still be there. Behind the drawn curtains a light glowed but she could hear no sound of voices. She tapped at the door and stood back.

Cassie's black-clad figure appeared in the doorway. She peered out into the dark street, and her mouth opened wide. 'May!' she exclaimed. 'What you doing here? Come on in.'

'Is there anyone else here?' May whispered.

'There's only Mam and me. Come on. Mam – look who's here.'

She threw her arm around May's shoulders and guided

290

her into the living room. Mam was already on her feet and, seeing May, she flung her arms around her, a sob dying in her throat. For a moment all three women clung silently together.

At last Ada stood away and wiped the back of her hand over her eyes. 'You look a bit thin in the face, love,' she remarked as she helped May off with her coat. 'Still, it's good to see you. And this.' With a smile she patted the swell of May's stomach. Cassie was gazing at it in awe.

'He's grown fast, my nephew,' she murmured. 'I'd no idea you'd be so big already.'

'I've been gone over two months,' said May as she sat down on the sofa. Cassie settled herself next to her.

'I'll have to start getting used to being called auntie. Auntie Cass – doesn't it sound funny?'

'Not half so funny as me being called Grandma at my tender age,' chuckled her mother. 'I don't know whether I should forgive you for that.'

'Why not?' retorted Cass. 'You did the same – made your mother a grandma before she was forty. Serves you right.'

They were doing it on purpose, thought May, making it easy for her. She turned to face her mother.

'I didn't know whether you wanted me at the funeral today,' she said quietly. Mam looked startled.

'Why the devil shouldn't I? You're our daughter. I'd have loved you to be there but we didn't know whether you'd be allowed out.'

'I ran away. I was in the church this afternoon.'

She saw them both staring, their mouths open. 'Ran away from the Home?' gasped Cass. 'How did you manage to get back here?'

'I was lucky – I found friends who helped me.'

'You were there, in the church?' Mam was still staring at her. 'I didn't see you.'

'No. I sat at the back. Folk would have seen the way I am.'

Mam's face flushed angrily. 'So what? It's not right, you having to skulk round at your own father's funeral like

291

you was a thief or summat. You'd no need to spare us – you'd every right to be there.'

May shook her head. 'It wasn't just to spare you – or me. It was for the baby's sake. It's not fair for him to be labelled a bastard when he's done nothing wrong.'

'I agree,' said Cassie. 'It's not the little one's fault. Dad would have said the same.'

'Aye, he would and all,' agreed Mam. 'He couldn't abide to see anyone hurt.'

May could see the tender look which stole over her face as she gazed into the fire.

'He was a lovely man, your dad. Remember the time he saved you from a walloping, Cassie, when you pinched my treacle tart off the scullery table? It was my fault, he said, for leaving temptation in your way.'

Cassie chuckled. 'He never told you I gave him a slice of it.'

'You bribed him,' smiled May. 'I remember. Soft as putty, he was. Remember the time Teacher had us growing a bean in a jar of sawdust? Mine wouldn't sprout any more than an inch or two. I was that upset, so he tied a six-inch runner bean on, and I thought I'd grown it all by myself.'

Mam was wiping her eyes, laughing. 'Aye, he couldn't bear to see you disappointed. He loved to see folk happy.'

Silence fell over the trio for a few moments. May took a deep breath. 'Mam, I saw Miss Openshaw at the church today.'

'Oh heck,' said Cass. 'Did she recognize you?'

'It didn't do any harm as it happens. Listen, I've no intention of going back to that rotten Home. You've no idea how awful it was.'

'I guessed as much,' said Mam. 'From what you didn't say. So what do you plan to do?'

May told them about Miss Openshaw's offer. 'It's very kind of her, and it makes good sense,' she argued. 'It would solve a lot of problems.'

'I don't see the point. You've got a home here,' said Mam.

'Newsome is far enough away from Millsbridge. If I have the baby up there, no-one here need ever know.'

'They'll know soon enough when you bring it home,' countered Cassie. 'You can't hide it then.'

'I know,' said May. 'I'll have to find a job away somewhere.'

'I've got an idea about that baby,' murmured Ada. 'It came to me the other week – it's a bit daft—'

Cassie leaned forward eagerly. 'What is?'

Ada got to her feet, brushing down the ample folds of her skirt over her fleshy stomach. 'Well, look at me, the size of me,' she said. 'I could be having one this minute for all anybody knows. Why can't we say it's mine? I'm not too old.'

Both girls stared at her, stupefied. Cassie found her voice first. 'But me dad—' she faltered.

Her mother rounded on her. 'What do you know about your dad? He loved kids.'

'But his back—'

Mam gave her a stern look. 'There's ways and means, you know. Other folk wouldn't find it that strange. Why, not so long back Mrs Boothroyd asked me if I was expecting, so there.'

May was turning the idea over in her head. Wild it might be, but not beyond the realms of possibility. But she could already anticipate complications. 'If I had the baby up at Newsome—' she began.

'We could smuggle it back here while you're still lying in,' Mam cut in.

'And pretend you'd just had it,' breathed Cassie. 'We could fool everyone. It'd mean you having to pad yourself out a bit more, Mam.'

'I've plenty of cushions and bits of blanket. Anyway, it can't be that long now. Eight weeks or so.'

'I hardly think you'll need the cushions,' laughed Cassie, 'but you'd have to pretend to go into labour so the neighbours could hear. It'd be a great lark.'

Ada's face broke into a smile. May looked up.

'I wonder – do you think we could get away with it? Could it possibly work?'

'We'll make it work,' said Cassie firmly. 'Just wait till Elsie finds out she's going to have a little brother – or sister. I won't be Aunt Cassie after all.'

'And I won't be Grandma,' smiled Ada. 'That settles it.'

'I'll have to go,' said May, rising awkwardly to her feet. 'Listen, those people who helped me, they lent me some money. I want to get it back to them – have you got mine handy?'

She saw her mother's eyes, the tiny trace of hesitation before she stood up. 'Of course I have. I'll get it for you.'

'What is it?' asked May. 'There's summat.'

Mam bit her lip. 'I need to borrow a bit of it – the funeral . . .'

May squeezed her arm. 'That's all right, I only want a few pounds. You can use what you need.'

'Forget it,' Cassie cut in sharply. 'That's all settled. Mr Jordan and me has it all sorted out, don't worry.'

Mam frowned. 'How do you mean, sorted out? I asked him to send me the bill – twelve pounds four shillings, he said it would be.'

'It's settled, Mam. Now forget it,' repeated Cassie.

Mam scowled and went upstairs. Cassie turned to her sister, holding out her coat. 'Did anybody see you come?'

'No,' said May as she slid her arms into the sleeves, 'I made sure of that. And no-one will see me leave again either – I'll go the back way.'

Mam came back with five sovereigns in her hand. 'Will that be enough, love?' she asked.

'Plenty,' said May, and kissed her cheek. 'I'll think about this baby and we'll talk again soon.'

As she slipped out of the back door into the darkness of the yard to make her way down the alley to the tram, May could hear Mam's voice behind her in the scullery.

'Now just you come here, lady,' she was saying sternly. 'Never you mind slipping off upstairs – you've got some explaining to do. What's all this about you and Mr Jordan and my bill . . . ?'

Grace Openshaw was on tenterhooks. No sooner had May left than Edward called in to see her and it had got her all in a fluster. She tried hard to hide her agitation, but her fingers kept fumbling with the playing cards as she dealt them out for the last round of Beggar My Neighbour.

What if May came back while he was still here? How was she to explain away a very pregnant young woman arriving so late at night, coming to stay in her house?

'Your turn,' said Edward.

Absently she paid two for his queen. A young woman without a wedding ring at that. She could make up a story about a relative, perhaps . . .

'I win,' said Edward triumphantly. 'That's three to you, two to me.'

It was growing late now – past ten o'clock so it didn't look like she'd be coming back after all. Edward began gathering up the cards.

'Time's getting on, Grace. I'd better be on my way,' he said gently as he replaced the cards in the box. She felt a rush of disappointment mingled with relief.

'The weather's getting nice again now,' she remarked as he picked up his gloves. 'We could start walking in the park again.'

'On Sunday? I look forward to it.'

They were in the little lobby, his hands enfolding hers, when the knock came at the door. Grace leapt as though she'd been scalded. Edward frowned.

'Whoever can that be, at this time of night? You'd best let me answer.'

He'd opened the front door before she could protest. May Turnbull stood on the step, a startled look in her eyes. Edward was clearly taking in her condition.

Grace pulled her scattered wits together. 'Why, it's my niece!' she exclaimed in feigned surprise. 'Come on in, May, love. Mr Harris is just leaving.' She turned to Edward. 'This is May,' she explained. 'She and I are very close, specially since she lost her husband.'

She saw his puzzled expression vanish, replaced by a sudden look of concern. 'Oh my dear, I'm so sorry,' he murmured, 'but I'm very pleased to meet you. Look, I'll get along now and leave you to talk to your aunt. Good night.'

With a smile he shook hands with May and left. Grace closed the door behind him and leaned against it, smiling at May apologetically. 'I'm sorry, love, it was the first thing I could think of. I hope you don't mind.'

'No,' the girl replied. 'I just hope I wasn't interrupting – you don't mind me coming back like this?'

'I'm delighted, truly I am. It's going to be nice having company again. All I've got is Oscar, and you can have too much of a good thing.'

After she'd settled her guest in the spare room Grace looked at her reflection in the bedroom mirror, and was delighted with what she saw.

Where was the sagging face, the jaded woman dreading the years ahead? She was gone, and instead there was a woman with a sparkle in her eyes and a look of eager anticipation. That face, aglow with enthusiasm, was ten years younger than the one reflected there a week ago.

And she knew the reason. First there'd been Edward. He'd brought new hope into her life, made her feel like a woman again, made her feel wanted. Now there was May, and May needed her. No-one else had since Mother died, and it had left a strange hole in her life. It was a wonderful, powerful feeling, to be both needed and wanted.

And to be entrusted with a secret. She and May were conspirators; she was privileged to take part in a clandestine plan to help the girl, and the thought thrilled her. She didn't even feel guilty about telling Edward that fib – she'd been quite quick-witted about that, she prided herself – but she'd have to sustain it now.

She pulled on her nightgown and bounced into bed. She'd never felt so excited since those far-off days when she used to elude Mother's jealous eyes to keep a rendezvous with handsome young Thaddeus – in their secret place in a corner of the graveyard, round the back of the church.

Grace curled her toes around the stone hot-water bottle. She'd come alive again. There was so much to look forward to now, more lovely walks in the park with Edward, having May here for company, having the bustle and flurry of a birth . . . For a second she felt a flicker of apprehension.

A midwife. They'd have to engage a good one for May. And set about gathering the little one's layette. Gowns, bibs, nappies . . .

As she drifted into happy sleep Grace was already preparing the list for Edward's consideration. In view of the circumstances he might feel disposed to offer May a 10 per cent discount as well.

Nellie Bottomley felt deeply troubled. Here it was, bedtime, and Agnes had not shown any sign of wanting to get out of bed all day.

She'd done her best to rouse her, up and down those stairs till her legs ached, telling her what the milkman said and who she'd seen calling at the Turnbulls' house. But Agnes wasn't having any.

'Shove off,' she'd kept muttering. 'Leave me in peace.'

It had been hard to give a shape to the day without her giving orders the way she usually did. And when Jordan's big hearse pulled up at the Turnbulls' Nellie had raced up the stairs.

'The funeral's starting – you can't miss that, Agnes – come on!'

Surely she'd want at least to watch it from the window, see who came and what they were wearing.

'Well, have I to go on me own then?' Nellie asked

dubiously. 'At least then I can tell you all about it?'

Agnes had simply buried her face in the pillow and groaned. It had been a hard decision to make on her own, but in the end Nellie had waddled off as fast as her legs would carry her down to St Thomas's.

'Guess who was there?' she'd said coaxingly on her return to the gaunt figure in the bed. 'There was that Jack Smedley – you know, the fellow whose wife left him and took the kids.'

No response.

'Mrs Turnbull looks fatter than ever these days, but her Cassie's growing into a lovely girl. Do you know, though – I never saw the other daughter, May. Funny she wasn't there. I wonder if summat's up?'

Agnes ventured no explanation. Nellie played her last card.

'I tell you who else was there, though – Charlie Andrews. Remember him? Worked down the pit like Mr Turnbull, used to let us have a bit of coal cheap now and again?'

No answer. Nellie grew irritated. 'You must know who I mean,' she added sharply, 'you had quite a fancy for him once, as I recall. Not that it did you any good – he never took a blind bit of notice.'

This time a grunt came from the bed, nothing more. Nellie gave up. If that didn't goad her sister into life, nothing would. Ah well, she thought as she made her lonely bedtime cup of tea, maybe in the morning she'd be back downstairs again, bossing and criticizing and making life difficult, and then everything would be back to normal again.

TWENTY-EIGHT

By next morning Nellie was worried out of her mind. Agnes hadn't got up out of bed again today, nor had she eaten anything and here it was teatime already. However many times Nellie clambered upstairs to have a look at her, she didn't speak and she never seemed even to have moved.

She hadn't used the chamber pot either, and that was worrying. With her funny waterworks she had to use it several times a night as a rule. She seemed to want to sleep all the time and it was more than Nellie dared do to touch her or try to wake her. Agnes would be sure to shout and call her names.

The quiet which lay over the house was unnatural and disturbing. Nellie felt agitated and desperately lost. What was she supposed to do today? Without Agnes to prompt, it was hard to think. If only she could remember their routine. Come to think of it, what day of the week was it? It felt like a Saturday, but she couldn't be sure unless the rent man called, then she'd know.

By the time dusk fell Agnes still hadn't moved, and the rent man hadn't called so it couldn't be Saturday after all. What if it was Sunday, and she'd missed going to chapel? Oh dear, that would never do! And if it was Sunday, then it would be Monday tomorrow – oh Lord, should she get the sett pot ready for the day's washing? She'd have to ask Agnes.

Her sister lay unmoving, still on her side the way she'd been lying ever since yesterday. Nellie leaned over her, candle in hand.

'Aggie? You awake?' she whispered.

Agnes made no move.

'Aggie?' There was alarm in Nellie's tone. 'Aggie!'

Nellie bent lower, holding the candle to one side to peer at her sister's face. She looked a funny colour, not pretty and pink like the big china doll Mother would only allow them to play with on Sundays. Half an hour only, she used to say sternly, and Agnes always kept it clasped tightly to her bony chest for twenty-five minutes. Agnes didn't look pretty – she looked sort of blue-grey.

'Aggie – are you all right? Have I to fetch the doctor for you? Come on, tell me what to do.'

Still no response. Nellie laid a finger to her sister's face. It felt cold as ice, like the big china doll.

Agnes wasn't going to wake up, not yet. With a sigh Nellie shambled back down the stairs. It really was most aggravating, upsetting their routine like this. Just typical of Agnes. For all Nellie knew, she could be doing it on purpose, pretending to be asleep because she was sulking about something. Or she could be just trying to get attention. Well, two could play at that game.

Even so, it was lonely down here with no-one to talk to. The street outside seemed unusually quiet, and there was no noise from the Nagles next door. Heavens, maybe it was Sunday and they were all at church!

Nellie flicked the dust off Mother's old harmonium and lifted the lid. If anything was going to shift Agnes it would be hearing the harmonium play. Nellie settled herself down and began pumping up the bellows with her feet, which was never easy with her short legs. Then she flexed her fingers and began to play. She threw back her head and sang.

'All things bright and beautiful . . .'

If it wakened Agnes, so much the better.

Henry Rose was already feeling irritable as he sat at the breakfast table. Esther had apologized for the fact that she'd forgotten to order more of the marrow and ginger jam he always spread on his toast for breakfast, but apologies weren't enough to soothe away his annoyance.

'I'm in no frame of mind to go to work without my ginger jam,' he grumbled. 'It starts me day off all wrong. You know how I like my routine.'

'Haven't I said, I'm sorry? Think about how well the wedding went off yesterday – such a splendid affair for everyone to see. That should put you in a good humour.'

Henry wasn't to be pacified. 'As if I shan't have enough on, coping with Aaron's work as well as me own while he's away.'

Esther sighed and waved a teaspoon towards the pile of letters alongside his plate. 'You haven't opened the post yet.'

He growled as he slit open the first, then she saw the letter start to shiver in his hand as his face grew visibly redder.

'Of all the damn nerve!' he exploded as he tossed the letter aside. 'Would you credit it?'

Esther spread her toast thickly with marmalade. 'What is it?' she asked mildly. She wasn't really interested; it would be sure to be something boring like the bill for that Spanish marble he'd ordered for the parlour fireplace. Only last night he'd said he thought the stonemason might try and diddle him.

'That girl I sent to the Sisters of Mercy,' Henry raged. 'Mother Superior says she's run off. There's gratitude for you, after all I did for that girl!'

Esther frowned. 'Girl? What girl?'

Henry waved an impatient hand. 'You know – the one from my workroom – the one Aaron messed around with – got her into trouble, stupid boy. I thought we'd heard the last of her.'

Esther laid her knife down and wiped sticky fingers on her napkin. She remembered her now, but it seemed a long time ago. 'I thought you paid her off, didn't you?' she murmured.

'I did indeed,' said Henry emphatically, 'and paid those nuns to keep her there till it was all over. Fat lot of appreciation she shows, being kept and cared for, all for free, and then she clears off like that!'

'I wonder where she's gone,' Esther mused, pouring another cup of tea.

'What the devil should we care? She's on her own now. Just so long as she doesn't show up here again.'

'Didn't you make her promise not to bother us any more?'

Esther saw her husband look up, his eyes anxious. 'She wouldn't do that – come back here, would she? We can't have her pestering Aaron when he gets back off his honeymoon. Adele would never understand his little peccadillo.'

Esther's cup clattered into the saucer. Adele's father wouldn't understand either. Sidney Rabin would go berserk if his daughter's married bliss was wrecked by a girl turning up with a baby she claimed was Aaron's. But he wouldn't call off the wedding agreement about combining his business with Henry's – would he? If the thought hadn't yet occurred to Henry, she wasn't going to blight his day yet further by bringing it to his attention.

She looked dubiously at her husband. 'She took the cash, didn't she? Let's hope she's a reliable girl and keeps her word.'

Henry grunted. 'She used to be but now – who knows?'

Esther refilled her husband's cup. 'There's no need to mention any of this to Aaron when he gets back. It would only upset the boy and he's had enough excitement lately.'

'Aye, you're right,' growled Henry. 'Best let sleeping dogs lie.'

It was an unusually warm day for spring. Mrs Boothroyd struggled to carry one of her rush-bottomed chairs outside the front door, then sank down on it gratefully. It would do her creaky old bones a world of good to soak up the sun's warmth for a while.

She screwed up her eyes and gazed around the street to see what there was to be seen. It was no use; everything looked just as hazy as it did through Albert's spectacles. She could see her own front doorstep though, and it looked like it could do with a bit of donkey-stoning to match up to Ada Turnbull's next door. Still, she wasn't expecting visitors so what did it matter?

Was that a door she could hear creaking behind her? She

craned her stiff neck round. Ada stood on her front doorstep, shaking out a duster.

'Afternoon,' she said, and the duster fluttered from her hand. Mrs Boothroyd watched her stoop to pick it up. Goodness, she could hardly get down. She was that fat round the middle these days and she always used to be such a shapely woman.

'You're putting a lot of weight on, aren't you?' she grunted. 'You're nearly as stout as me. Left your stays off again, have you?'

She could swear the younger woman dimpled like she was embarrassed. 'Not exactly,' she smiled. 'It's just nature taking over, I'm afraid. I can't do nowt about it.'

Nature? What was she on about? Judging by that smile Ada Turnbull was keeping summat up her sleeve. A blond head appeared behind her – Cassie.

'Come on in, Mam,' the girl said severely. 'You know you have to rest, you in your condition and all. Come on now.'

Condition? Mrs Boothroyd's ears pricked up. Ada – in the family way – and her husband dead? Surely not – she'd denied it not so long back, hadn't she?

Ada was still on the step, smiling down at her, the great fat stomach so close she could almost touch it. She couldn't resist the temptation. 'Am I right? Are you expecting?'

Ada's hand flew to her mouth. 'You've guessed! Oh dear, I hadn't meant anyone to know yet – I might have known nobody fools you.'

Mrs Boothroyd straightened her aching back and smiled a toothless smile. 'Ah – I guessed some while back. I know the signs, I do. I should do, all the years I've lived.'

Ada bent and touched her shoulder, the one she'd been rubbing with wintergreen only this morning. 'You're too quick by half, you are,' Ada whispered into her ear. 'I should have known I couldn't pull the wool over your eyes. But do me a favour, Mrs Boothroyd – don't tell the neighbours, not just yet.'

303

Fascinated by the bulge, Mrs Boothroyd swallowed hard then looked up. 'When's it due then? It can't be far off, judging by the looks of it.'

Ada stood away, smiling broadly. 'Right again. Only a few weeks now.'

Mrs Boothroyd shook her head sadly. 'And your poor husband never lived to see his little one – such a shame. Makes you wonder, doesn't it? Sometimes it seems like there's no justice.'

Cassie could scarcely suppress her giggles until her mother had closed the door. The minute she came back into the living room Cassie flung her arms around her ample body, shrieking with laughter. Ada too was smiling.

'That's done it – she's in no doubt now!'

'Aye,' Ada chuckled, 'and I swore her to secrecy so it'll be all round the street by bedtime.'

She pulled a small cushion out from inside the waistband of her skirt. 'By heck,' she said, tossing it onto the sofa, 'it's getting a bit hot for this game. Thank God it's not for much longer.'

Cassie prodded the remaining padding with a mischievous grin. 'I reckon if you add any more of them cushions you'll be giving birth to a bolster. Now then, can I give you a hand with owt before I have to go?'

Her mother surveyed the piles of clothes waiting to be ironed. 'Do you know,' she said reflectively, 'I'd give owt to be shut of this damn washing for ever. I'd give me eye teeth to do summat else for a living.'

'Like what?' Cassie asked.

Ada thought for a moment. 'Cooking. I love cooking, specially if there's no shortage of stuff to cook.'

'That's a bit daft, seeing as there's only you and Elsie here to cook for now.'

'I don't mean for two – I mean proper cooking, gallons of soup and stew and dumplings. I could feed an army, I could, and love every minute of it.'

Cassie pulled a face. 'Not my idea of fun. Still, why don't you, if that's what you want.'

Ada snorted. 'It takes money, and that doesn't grow on trees. Which reminds me – I'm still not happy about that bill of Mr Jordan's. Why should he want to do us a favour like that?'

'I've already told you – as a thank-you, for all the help you gave him when he found his Fanny dead like that.'

'Aye well, that's as may be,' rumbled Ada, 'but I don't like it. I don't like being beholden to anybody, least of all to him.'

Cassie wasn't going to ask why – it was dangerous ground. 'He's not such a bad sort, Mam,' she said soothingly. 'He's very kind.'

'Aye, and there's a reason for it. I'm not daft, you know. He's still got a fancy for you, I reckon, and you've not got to encourage it.'

'If it means you saving twelve pounds I'd have thought you could accept with good grace,' said Cassie. 'I just hope he doesn't get to hear how downright churlish you sound. Any road, I'd best be off now if I'm to meet our May before I get back to work.'

The two girls strolled side by side around the ornamental lake in the park, the path ahead of them dappled with sunlight filtering through the trees. On the far side of the lake May could see the arches of the stone bridge reflected in the scarcely rippling water. She stole a sidelong glance at her sister. What reflection would they see from the other side? A green-clad figure, slender and delicate as a reed, and another, black and swollen like an overripe plum. With every day that passed it grew harder to fasten Mrs Fairweather's voluminous black coat.

'You getting on all right with Miss Openshaw?' asked Cassie. 'It must be funny, living with your old boss.'

'She's very kind,' said May. 'I'm very lucky. And what have you been doing? What's all this about Mr Jordan?'

Cassie gave her an impish smile. 'He's taking me to the

Hippodrome next week. I've always wanted to go there. Promise you won't tell Mam?'

May could remember the ten-year-old's fit of jealousy when her best friend Eunice was taken to the theatre's opening. She'd crowed ever since about seeing Vesta Tilley.

'Only I know Mam would say it's early days yet to be gallivanting off like that,' Cassie went on. 'What would the neighbours think, she'd say. So I shan't tell her. What the eye doesn't see . . .'

'You're leading him on,' said May. 'Are you sure you know what you're doing?'

Cassie pouted. 'Why not? He likes it and so do I. He can give me things nobody else can.'

May smiled. She felt heavy and hot and needed to sit down. 'You know what Dad used to say when we kept asking for things – when you're young you want everything in the shop window . . .'

'And it's only when you get older that you know what's what. Yes, I remember. I'm older now, but I still want everything in the shop window. And I'm going to get it.'

May stopped and turned to face her. 'And you think Mr Jordan is the way to get it?'

Cassie's lip came out. 'Why not? It's a damn sight quicker way than working for donkey's years.'

'Mam won't have it, you know that.'

'She'll have to lump it then. She came round when she heard about the mess you got yourself in.'

They sauntered over the grass to a bench. Cassie looked quizzically at her sister. 'You never did tell me who the father was,' she murmured.

'And I'm not going to now,' May replied quietly. 'He's out of my life, forgotten.'

'Yes, Mam told me you got shut of him.'

May gave a dry laugh. 'That was kind of her – it was him who got shut of me, paid me off, or at least his dad did.'

'Mmm,' mused Cassie. 'Why don't you ask him for more?'

May gave a firm shake of the head. 'No, that's the end of it. I promised.'

Cassie's lip curled. 'All I can say is, I wouldn't let a man off that lightly if I'd got a hold over him. You're dead soft, you are. That's always been your trouble.'

Her sister smiled. 'Your hold over Mr Jordan might not last – he might soon tire of a girl less than half his age, then what?'

Cassie folded her arms complacently. 'I know things about Mr Jordan he doesn't know I know. And he wouldn't want anyone else to get to know them. I'll be all right.'

'Cassie! That's blackmail!'

Cassie shrugged. 'So long as I get everything in the shop window . . . Hey, what about that fellow who lent you the money to get home – have you heard any more from him? He sounded nice.'

'Will – yes, he wrote to me after I paid him back.'

'What did he say? Are you going to see him again?'

May spread her hands. 'I doubt it. Holney must be a hundred miles or more from here.'

The sun was dipping behind the trees. From down in the smoky town the sound of the parish church clock could be heard striking the hour. Cassie leapt up. 'Heavens, I must run! I've the dinner table to lay up, the napkins to fold – oh Lord, I'll never make it!'

May rose stiffly, conscious of her ungainly bulk. She smiled wryly. 'Just look at me,' she murmured. 'I look a right duck compared to you.'

Cassie squeezed her arm. 'Ah well, with any luck some of us ugly ducklings will turn into swans. Goodbye, love, and good luck.'

TWENTY-NINE

Grace Openshaw threaded her way between the clattering sewing machines to the door. If the girls were to get the Hopkinson order finished today they would need some more of that pink lace frilling. She'd have to leave them unsupervised for a moment to go up to the stock room for it.

She unlocked the door of the dusty room, but after searching every shelf the frilling still hadn't come to light. Grace frowned. She clearly recalled ordering it from Mr Aaron a week or more ago. In his excitement over the wedding he must have forgotten to deal with it. Now what was she to do?

Mr Henry's portly figure walked past the door and on seeing it open he turned and came back. Grace busied herself, rooting once more through the shelves.

'Everything all right?' he asked.

Grace straightened. 'The Hopkinson lace – it doesn't seem to be here,' she told him.

He scowled as he came to join her. 'It must be,' he muttered. 'You ordered it, didn't you?'

'From Mr Aaron, sir, like I always do.'

Mr Henry opened every box and turned it inside-out then, sighing, he gave up. 'Aaron,' he muttered. 'So much for the new stock-ordering system he was so mad about. Mrs Hopkinson will blow a gasket if I have to tell her the order is delayed.'

'What else can we do?' asked Grace. 'There's not an inch in the place – not pink, anyway. Do you think she might settle for another colour?'

'Why the devil should she?' Mr Henry snapped. 'She comes

308

to us because we pride ourselves on being reliable.' He turned and headed for the door, still muttering. 'Just wait till that young whipper-snapper gets back,' he growled. 'You've no idea the bother he's caused me.'

He went off, mumbling crossly in an undertone. Grace watched him go. In all these years, since she first came to work for him in the little shop he started with down by the Beast Market when he was still slim round the middle, he'd never changed. Tetchy even then, he was downright bad-tempered now.

She smiled grimly to herself as she closed and locked the stockroom door. She knew a great deal more about Mr Aaron than Mr Henry guessed, and it afforded her malicious pleasure that the jaunty young upstart was going to get it in the neck the minute he arrived home from his honeymoon.

Grace was still humming happily to herself as she left the shop that evening. It was a pleasure these days to head for Minerva Street; no more cold, empty house with a hungry cat eyeing her accusingly but May waiting, the kettle already boiling, to welcome her home.

She stood waiting in New Street for the electric tram, watching the passers-by heading for home or for a night out. Then she caught sight of the pretty young woman in green on the far side of the road, on the arm of a stocky man. She knew that face from somewhere – yes, at the funeral – it was May's sister, and the man was the one she took to be the undertaker, the one who'd been so helpful that day.

He was gazing down at her affectionately, she looking up at him with a happy smile. They passed on by and were lost to sight in the crowd.

Grace speculated. He was quite a lot older than May's sister but they were clearly on close terms; perhaps he was a relative – an uncle, maybe. She'd ask May about him when she got home . . .

*   *   *

Cassie leaned excitedly over the balustrade, peering down at the crowds pushing their way into the theatre. She was exhilarated by the smell of the plush upholstery, the babble of conversation and the atmosphere of enthusiastic anticipation. She was conscious too of Mr Jordan's eyes watching her every move.

'I'm so looking forward to this,' she breathed. 'I've never been to the theatre before.'

He stared. 'Not even as a child – to the pantomime?'

She shook her head, aware that her blond curls shimmered in the lamplight. 'There was never money to spare for luxuries like that. Every penny counted.'

His shoulder moved closer to hers. 'I'd like to give you luxuries, Cassie,' he murmured. 'Everything you've ever dreamt of.'

She could see musicians with their instruments filing into the pit below. 'It must be lovely to have lots of money,' she sighed, staying close to the rough fabric of his shoulder. 'Like the Chadwicks. Miss Cecily is still raving on about that wedding she went to, and the gorgeous gown the bride was wearing. She swears she'll have one like it one day, all embroidered with seed pearls, it was. Just imagine, being able to have a dress like that.'

'And why not?' he whispered. 'It would do justice to your beauty.'

She gave a soft chuckle. 'If wishes were horses . . .'

'Do you want to be married, Cassie? I mean, you're so young.'

The musicians began tuning up. Cassie shrugged. 'If Mr Right came along, why shouldn't I? I don't want to spend my life in Cedar Street like Mam.'

She heard him take a slow, deep breath. 'Cassie . . .'

She turned her face up to his. 'Yes, Mr Jordan?'

The lines around his mouth settled into a smile. 'Please call me Harold – we've known each other long enough to be friends, haven't we?'

She smiled and bowed her head, her fingers toying

idly with her gloves on the balustrade.

'Listen,' he said gravely, 'I've been through a bad time—'

'Well, of course,' she interrupted. 'I know all about Mrs Jordan.'

He laid a hand gently over hers. 'No, no, apart from that. Financially, I mean, but that's all over. Things are going very well for me again now.'

She let her hand lie where it was, feeling the heat of his palm. 'I'm very glad to hear it – Harold.'

The hand tightened a little more. 'In fact, the business has picked up so well I'm thinking of expanding. I went to see the manager at the Yorkshire Penny Bank this afternoon.' He glanced around him. 'This is all in confidence, you understand.'

'Of course,' replied Cassie. 'Who would I tell anyway?'

He leaned closer, his mouth almost against her ear in order to be heard above the tuneless racket from the orchestra pit. 'Having seen my books, he's agreed to lend me a thousand to expand.' He straightened, thrusting out his chest with pride. 'In fact he was willing to advance me twice as much. I can go ahead with new premises, including a Chapel of Rest . . .'

Cassie pulled a face. 'I don't know how you can bear to live where there's dead bodies – I know I couldn't.'

He patted the hand. 'Of course not,' he smiled. 'I shan't do that – I'm going to buy another house, away from the business.'

She stared at him. 'Move away from Cedar Street?'

'I shall keep the house and workshop, of course – put a manager in, probably, but I'd like to live up Marsh or Edgerton way.'

Edgerton – where the Chadwicks lived! Cassie looked up at his weathered face with a dazzling smile. Edgerton. Maybe after playing the old trout so carefully these last few months she was going to land herself a salmon . . .

'So I think a little celebration is in order,' Harold went on contentedly. 'After the show perhaps you'd let me take you to the George for supper and we'll have a bottle of French wine and drink a toast to our future.'

Wine, like the Chadwicks drank, in the George Hotel? Cassie's cup of happiness ran over. 'Oh yes,' she breathed. 'I'd love to.'

The orchestra struck up a lively tune, the lights dimmed and the curtain began to rise; Harold's face brushed against her ear as they settled back.

'So you see, any fancy frock you wanted – it's not beyond your reach – I'd make sure of that.'

Grace smiled up gratefully to May as she laid a plate on the table in front of her.

'Oh May, you spoil me, you really do! How did you know I was going to make toad-in-the-hole tonight?'

May slithered her bulky body under the table with difficulty as she sat down. 'You asked me this morning if I liked it. I found sausages in the pantry – it wasn't hard to guess. Now what were you saying about seeing my sister?'

'In New Street, while I was waiting for the tram,' mumbled Grace around a mouthful of sausage. 'Looked very smart, she did, with the man who was so nice at the funeral. I thought he might be an uncle of yours or something?'

May paused before putting the fork to her mouth. 'At the funeral?' she repeated. 'Ah, you mean Mr Jordan.'

'Jordan, is it? I was right then about him being an undertaker.'

May was gazing absently at Oscar who sat waiting, eyeing the sausage still speared on her fork. 'So she's still going on with it,' May murmured. 'I do hope she doesn't come unstuck.'

Nellie Bottomley could hear the banging at the front door but she wasn't going to take any notice. If Agnes could just lie up there and take no responsibility at all, then so could she. It was probably only the rag-and-bone man anyway, and they had no jam jars for him this week.

Now tea was over she'd get on with washing the pots. That was a lovely bit of haddock she'd found on the pantry slab. Agnes wouldn't deign to touch the piece she'd taken up to her and it would have gone to waste if she hadn't eaten it herself.

Now somebody was banging at the back door. Whatever could all the fuss be about? For two pins she'd lift the curtain and peep out, but somebody might spot her and then she'd be forced to answer the door. Not she, not if Agnes wasn't going to budge.

She took up the sheet of newspaper which had come wrapped round the fish and peered at it closely. It looked like a page out of the *Examiner*. If she got Mother's pince-nez out of the drawer maybe she could read a bit of news. She ignored the rapping at the window. It gave her pleasure to fondle the forbidden silver-stemmed spectacles between her horny hands. Agnes would shriek with fury if she saw her, but Agnes wasn't here to berate her.

Studying it closely, she'd just made out the first few words of the headline when a voice startled her out of the chair. A man stood in the living room doorway, and with relief she recognized Mr Marsden, the coalman.

Nellie gave a shy smile. 'I don't think we need any coal this week, Mr Marsden – see, we've still got a drawerful.'

She waddled over to pull out the drawer to confirm it. Mr Marsden took no notice.

'Are you all right?' he asked, wiping a sooty hand across a black-streaked brow. 'I kept knocking but no-one answered.'

She stared at him, bewildered.

'Folks have been worrying about you,' he went on, 'not seeing hide nor hair of you nor your sister for days.' He glanced around. 'Where is she?'

Nellie felt embarrassed to tell him. 'She's upstairs,' she said shyly. 'I think happen she's in a huff with me about summat – she's not speaking to me.'

'Not speaking?' He sounded wary. 'How long's that been going on?'

That flustered her. 'I don't know. What day is it today?'

'It's Thursday,' he said gently. 'Can you call her down – I'd like to see her.'

'Oh no,' Nellie said quickly, agitation spurting in her. 'She wouldn't like being called. She's mad enough at me as it is, though I can't for the life of me remember what it is I've done wrong.' Agitation gave way to resentment, and Nellie gabbled on. 'She's just paying me out, she is, lying there like that and pretending she hasn't heard. She never misses a thing, doesn't Agnes.'

Mr Marsden twisted his cap in his hands. 'Hasn't she been down, or talked to you at all then?'

'No, she hasn't,' Nellie replied petulantly, 'and she won't touch the food I take up to her neither.'

Mr Marsden moved towards the foot of the stairs. 'Look,' he said gruffly, 'I'd like to see her. Is it all right if I go up to her? Happen she'd like a visitor.'

That flustered Nellie even more. A gentleman in Agnes's bedroom, and her with her hair all down and uncombed? 'Oh, I don't know,' she said hesitantly, then cast a dubious look at his filthy boots. 'It's not proper,' she murmured.

But he was already halfway up, his boots clattering on the wooden treads. Nellie felt helpless. Agnes would go crazy if he left coal footmarks on her bedroom lino.

She picked up the newspaper again and smoothed out the crackled bits where the wet fish had dried on. After a couple of minutes Mr Marsden came back down. He stood in the doorway, clutching his cap between grimy hands.

'Nellie, love,' he said awkwardly, 'I'm afraid it's bad news.'

'It's all bad news,' she said, holding out the newspaper to him. 'Have you seen the *Examiner* – about them shop workers wanting a sixty-hour week? Fat lot of chance they've got – they'll never get that.'

Ignoring the newspaper, he took a step closer. 'No, love – it's your Agnes. She isn't going to wake up again, I'm afraid. She's gone, Nellie, and judging by the looks of her, she's been gone for some time.'

314

'They'll never get it,' repeated Nellie firmly, 'never in a month of Sundays.'

Harold Jordan stood in the shadows by the huge stone gate post marking the entrance to the Chadwicks' drive. The night air was soft and warm and Cassie's little hand lay tightly clasped in his, sending a shiver of delight up his spine. In this dim light she looked like an ethereal nymph, a vaporous spirit which would dissolve all too soon out of his grasp.

'Will you let me take you out again, Cassie?' he said eagerly.

He could hear her smile. 'Of course I will.'

'Often? I'd like to.' He couldn't help the urgency in his tone – in a moment she'd be gone.

There was a chuckle in her voice. 'I don't see why not. Specially if you treat me like a queen, like you did tonight.'

He raised the little hand to his lips. He could smell the scent of violets on her fingers – the violet cachous she'd asked him to buy for her. 'Just give me the chance,' he murmured. 'When?'

She took the hand away. 'Soon – I'll see you in Cedar Street next time I've a day off and tell you then.'

She turned her cheek up to him. For a dizzying moment he touched his lips to the sweet softness of her skin, and then she turned and hurried away up into the darkness of the driveway. For a while he stood staring into the blackness of the rhododendrons bordering the drive, striving to catch one last glimpse of his lovely Venus, but she was gone.

Reluctantly he turned away at last. His lips could still feel the softness of her cheek, and she'd agreed to let him take her out again! There was a bounce in his step to match the jubilation surging in him. He felt like a young man courting his first sweetheart, bursting with eager life and love.

He didn't want to catch the tram home, to sit staring at all those jaded, world-weary faces who knew nothing of the joy he felt. He wanted to be alone, to hug his happiness to himself.

He'd walk down Gledholt and through Paddock, savouring his precious thoughts.

She liked him, he felt sure, despite the difference in their ages. Like they always said, older men had experience to offer, not the clumsy fumblings of an inept youth. Well, maybe he didn't have that much experience after all, but if he played his cards right, who knew . . . ? In fancy he could see her now, mistress in his new house, presiding at his table, undressing for bed, holding out her lovely arms to him . . .

But it was far too soon, both for him and for her. He'd have to play this one cautiously, just as he would if he was to take over old Riley's business. The old rules were the best. Softly, softly, catchee monkey . . .

THIRTY

Ada stood in the sunlit window, watching Elsie hand over the blue-striped quart jug to the milkman. She hadn't wanted to go out herself; this game of padding was getting too hot and uncomfortable in this weather.

The milkman filled the jug to the very brim, then handed it back to Elsie. Ada knew his old familiar joke – 'Sup afore spill,' he'd say, just for the pleasure of watching the child have to slurp a mouthful before she could carry it indoors, a tell-tale moustache of froth frilling her upper lip.

'Why doesn't the milkman never use them lading cans he has for measuring?' Elsie asked as she put the jug down carefully on the table. 'He's got two of them clipped on the edge of his churn.'

'Nay, lass,' said Ada, shaking out the pile of wet washing, the first of the day, 'don't ask me. Now you'd best get off to school before you're late.'

She hadn't been gone five minutes before old Mrs Boothroyd's rag-curlered head appeared over the yard wall. Elbows stretched out flat along the coping stone, she rested her chin on the backs of her hands. 'Morning,' she called. 'Have you heard what happened with them Bottomleys?'

Ada took a peg out of her mouth and ducked under the billowing sheets. 'No,' she said. 'Only that Agnes was found dead in bed, that's all.'

'Heart, they said,' Mrs Boothroyd told her. 'Often happens to them with a quick temper, have you noticed?'

'I didn't know she had a quick temper – I hardly knew her at all,' said Ada.

317

'Well, happen I do her a disservice saying that, but she and her sister was always squabbling, that I do know. And she was a woman you couldn't befriend – Lord knows, I tried and better tried, but she wasn't having any. Just snapped at you and went inside.'

Ada shook her head. 'Even so, poor Nellie's going to be lost without her. I wonder what'll happen to her.'

Mrs Boothroyd's scanty eyebrows rose. 'That's what I'm telling you – they've taken her off to Storthes Hall, seemingly. The house is empty.'

'Oh dear! Poor Nellie.'

'Well, she always was a bit soft in the head, was Nellie, though harmless enough. Now they say she's gone completely doolally. She can't manage on her own and there's no-one to see to her, so they've had to carry her off to the loony-bin. She'll be all right there.'

There came the sound of loud knocking. Mrs Boothroyd straightened up. 'Hey – is that your front door or mine? I'd best go see.' And the curlered head vanished from view.

Jack Smedley stood on the doorstep, his cap between his hands and an awkward smile on his face. He had a nice face, thought Ada, not good-looking but there was gentle good humour in his blue eyes and laughter lines corrugating the corners.

'What you doing here so early?' she asked, standing back to let him enter. He wiped his boots energetically on the doormat.

'I'm sorry I've not been round in all these weeks,' he said shyly, 'only I thought as you wouldn't want anybody butting in for a bit. I thought as now maybe I could be a bit of help.'

'Why aren't you at work? It's only Tuesday.'

He shrugged big shoulders. 'I've been off sick for a few days – bit of bother with me chest but it's all right now. I'm going back tomorrow.'

He followed her into the living room. She saw his gaze travel down her body, then rise again to scrutinize her eyes. 'You having Jim's child?' he asked. 'I didn't know.'

'Nobody did,' said Ada stoutly. 'It's my business.'

'Did he know?'

She looked away. 'No. Good job and all, as it turned out. Could you manage a cup of tea, then I'll have to get on?'

'Can I help?' he asked eagerly, taking a step towards her.

She chuckled. 'Not unless you fancy putting a load of sheets through the mangle. The first lot'll be dry in no time then I can get this lot out.'

He threw his cap aside on the chair. 'You shouldn't be mangling,' he scolded, 'not the way you are.'

'Happen not, but I've a living to earn same as always. Sit you down and have that cup of tea.'

As he sipped she looked at his face, thin and drawn.

'Have you heard owt from your Brenda?' she asked. He never mentioned his wife these days.

He nodded. 'A while back. She wrote and told me she was off to Wales with the kids and her fancy man. She said not to come looking for her because she won't be coming back.'

'I see. Are you eating proper?'

'Oh aye, I manage well enough.'

'Doing your own cooking, are you?'

He smiled. 'Surprising what you can do when you have to.'

'What do you cook?'

A shrug, another smile. 'Bacon, eggs – owt I can do in a frying pan over the fire.'

'Vegetables?'

'Don't reckon much to 'em meself.'

'Nay, you can't go on like that,' Ada protested. 'You come round and have a bit of supper with us tonight.'

Elsie watched, fascinated, as he devoured the plate of sausage and mash. He finished at last and pushed the plate away, smacking his lips in relish.

'That were fair grand, Ada, lass. Thanks.'

She smiled as she swept the empty plates away and put the apple pie in the middle of the table. She felt good; it was a long time since she'd cooked a meal for someone who appreciated it so much. Jim hadn't eaten a proper meal for years.

'Give over picking your nose, our Elsie,' she snapped. 'Stop it this minute.'

The child pulled a face. 'I'm only trying to get that button out. You want me to get it out, don't you?'

'Not at the supper table, I don't. Any road, I told you I found it under the sideboard so it can't be up your nose.'

'That must have been another one just like it. Mine's still here.' Elsie rammed her finger up her nostril again. Ada looked at Jack with a sigh.

'She's got nothing of the sort, Jack,' she told him. 'It's all in her head.'

'That's what I mean,' wailed Elsie. 'It's still stuck in my head!'

'What button's that?' he asked.

'Off me dad's shirt.'

He put his spoon down and pushed back his chair 'Come here, let's have a look,' he said. Elsie jumped down and ran round the table to him. He removed her finger and peered up her nostril.

'It's been there for years,' Elsie said defiantly, 'and I know it's still there 'cos I can hear it whistle through the holes.'

'Can you now? That's very clever,' said Jack solemnly. 'Can the other kids do that?'

Her lower lip jutted. 'Don't know, but I don't want to do it.'

He looked across at Ada. 'Pass us that skewer on the side, will you? I'll soon sort this out.'

Startled, Ada stared at him. 'Skewer? What for?'

He tipped her a quick wink. 'Don't you worry, I know a sure-fire way to deal with buttons.'

Ada watched as Elsie's distrustful look melted gradually into trust and she leaned back her head beneath his hand. She saw him tickle the skewer gently just inside the child's nose for a moment, then sit back.

'There, that's done it,' he said with an air of satisfaction. 'It's gone.'

Elsie's finger scuttled up her nose and poked around. 'Are you sure?' she said dubiously. 'Where's it gone?'

'Down into your tummy,' he said triumphantly. 'It'll not bother you any more – you won't see that button again.'

Elsie gave him a mischievous smile. 'I could do, 'cos when I go to—'

'That's enough of that, young lady,' snapped Ada. 'If you've finished your pudding you get yourself ready for bed. Me and Mr Smedley want to talk.'

He smiled. 'Come on now, Ada, Mr Smedley's a bit formal, isn't it? Let her call me Uncle Jack – I'm as good as an uncle to her – I've known her long enough, ever since she were born.'

'Aye,' admitted Ada. 'All right then. Now off to bed with you, love. Uncle Jack and me has things to talk about.'

Jack leaned back in the armchair, stretching his feet out towards the fire. 'Come on then, lass, what's on your mind?' he asked genially.

Ada eased her aching back and put her feet up on the leather pouffe. She nodded towards the row of garments hung up to air along the brass rail under the mantelshelf. 'It's this lot,' she said. 'I'm sick to the back teeth of it. I'd be glad if I never saw other folk's washing for the rest of me life. I want to pack it all in and do summat else.'

'Oh? Like what? Go back mending in the mill like you used to?'

'No. I've a fancy to open a dining room.' She saw his startled look and hurried on. 'Nowt special, mind, just soup and stew and the like for working folk. It'd be far better than greasy pasties out of their snap tins. Trouble is, I'd need money to rent some premises and furniture, not to mention the food. I'd need help and all, and that means wages.'

She'd meant to state it quietly, as a fact, but she could hear the enthusiasm beginning to bubble in her voice. Jack was watching her soberly.

'How long have you been thinking about this?' he asked.

'Ages, since before Jim died. And listen, I think I know the very spot.' She leaned forward eagerly. 'There's that big place under the viaduct – you know, where Henderson had his haulage business. He's moved out to a bigger place. It couldn't be handier for me and for all the mills. Folk could easy nip out in their dinner-break. They'd be glad of summat warm in their bellies, specially in the winter, and there's nowhere else.'

Jack was eyeing her speculatively. 'You've thought this out, haven't you?' he murmured. 'Only how would you raise enough cash for it? I couldn't scrape together more than a few pounds, nowhere near enough.'

Ada snorted. 'I'm not asking you for owt, only advice. What do you think?'

He shook his head. 'There's the baby – when's it due?'

'In a few weeks, but that's no problem. I've done it oft enough before, working with a little one to see to.'

For a moment only the tick of the mantel clock disturbed the stillness of the room. Then Jack leaned forward and laid his hand on the arm of her chair.

'Listen, love,' he said quietly, 'I've been thinking. There's no need for you to go out to work if you let me help. No, hear me out,' he said, waving his hand as she made to protest. 'Look, there's me living on me own, and you doing the same. Two gas bills, two rents, two everything – what sense is there in that?'

'Jack Smedley! You're not suggesting what I think you're suggesting?'

'Why not?' he said equably. 'Not right away, perhaps, but you might consider it. I can earn enough for the two of us – and for little Elsie and the baby. You'd want for nothing, neither of you, and I'd be that proud.'

'No!' She stood up abruptly and began snatching the clothes off the rail, folding and piling them with undue energy. Jack watched her thoughtfully.

'Have I offended you, Ada?' he asked at last. 'I didn't mean to – I just want to take care of you and the little ones. Like Jim would have done.'

'It's a barmy idea,' Ada objected. 'Anyway, I'm older than you. I'm nearing forty, you know.'

'No-one would ever guess, and it's nobbut a year or two difference. Makes no odds to me. Think about it, Ada, no need to rush.'

'It's not right,' she growled. 'I mean, setting up with my husband's best friend—'

'If you mean because I'm still married – she won't be back, you know, never. I could come to live here, as your lodger.'

He got up to go, then stood in the little lobby, cap in hand. 'Like I said, love,' he murmured, 'take your time. Only there's nothing would give me greater pleasure than to take care of you. Good night.'

She could hear his boots clattering away down the cobbled street as she sank back into the armchair with a sigh. He was a good man, Jack Smedley, kindly and gentle, a real family man who'd been robbed of his own family. It was obvious he had a fondness for little Elsie, and the child's face lit up whenever he came to call, bringing her sweets and bits of toys. She could do far worse than settle down with Jack, but . . .

No, I'm free now and I've got to manage on me own, she thought fiercely. Me and May and Cass – we've all got to sort us own lives out. What was it Jim once said about Turnbull women? Tough, he said they were. Nothing got them down for long. They knew where they were going, and they didn't need the sort of help Jack Smedley was offering.

Harold Jordan was feeling very pleased with himself as he walked home. Old man Riley had seemed more than interested in his offer although, in his wary business man's way, he hadn't exactly leapt at it straight off. He'd give the matter some thought, he said, which meant he'd make sure there was no better bid in the offing before he committed himself.

And nobody else in Hawksmoor was likely to do that, Harold congratulated himself. It was too generous an offer for even the best bargain-driver to refuse. Overnight his business would become an empire, and not even the delectable Cassie could fail to be impressed.

And not only that, but the night he'd walked home after seeing her back to the Chadwicks' place he'd found the very house he'd been looking for. He was so lost in thought he'd almost passed the *For Sale* sign half-obscured in the hedge before he recognized it. It was Lucas's house, the schoolmaster who'd been widowed last year. The poor fellow had said he'd like to get away. Judging by its appearance he must have gone some time ago for it looked every bit as neglected now as it had then.

Harold's hopes soared. The original price might not have been within his means but in its present run-down state, with luck and a bit of careful bartering, he could snap up a bargain here. And in Thornhill Road, no less, so close to Edgerton it could well have an Edgerton postal address.

Already he was visualizing living there, with Cassie at his side. Heaven lay within his grasp if he persevered and kept his patience . . .

'Evening, Mr Jordan.'

The voice startled him out of his reverie. An old man doffed his cap, and under the arc of yellow light from the lamp he recognized old Thaddeus.

'You'll not forget yon headstone I promised I'd carve for your wife, will you, Mr Jordan?' the old man said. 'You just let me know the words and I'll get started.'

'*In Loving Memory* . . .' An image of grey granite leapt into Harold's head. Somehow as he turned the corner into Cedar Street the bounce had gone out of his step.

THIRTY-ONE

Grace Openshaw couldn't believe her ears. Life was growing more exciting by the minute.

'Pass the baby off as your mother's when it arrives?' she echoed breathlessly. 'Oh May, how on earth are you going to manage that? I thought we were just going to keep it a secret?'

'It's Mam's idea,' said May, 'to save the baby from being a bastard all his life. She's a rare one, my mother.'

Grace fingered the one hair that grew from her chin, turning the thought over. 'He'll grow up thinking his grandma is his mother, though, not you. Have you thought about that?'

'He'll be a lucky child to have my mam as his mother. He couldn't want a better.'

'But what about you? How are you going to feel, him not knowing you're his proper mother?'

May gave a tight little smile. 'I'll have to get used to it. I'll be his big sister who spoils him rotten.'

'Well,' said Grace, shaking her head, 'who'd have believed it? There's more to you than I thought. Still waters, as they say . . .'

'Yes,' agreed May. 'I've surprised even myself.'

Grace bent to stroke Oscar's freshly groomed back. 'It's a wonderful idea if you can get away with it, but how on earth do you reckon to carry it off?'

'That's what we need to discuss, Mam and Cassie and me. It's risky me going down to Cedar Street, even at night, so will it be all right if I ask them to come round here?'

'By all means,' Grace replied eagerly. 'I'd like to meet them properly.' She gave herself a little squeeze. 'Oh, how exciting!

325

A real conspiracy! I'll have to make sure Edward doesn't call round that night.' She drew herself upright. 'This is women's business.'

Already her mind was whirling ahead, planning what she'd need to do before the big night. She'd have potted meat sandwiches and caraway seed cake ready in case they were peckish. And the house – she glanced around the room. There'd be Mother's brasses to polish up till they gleamed like new, and the cushion covers could do with taking off and washing.

And Oscar. She looked down at the coil of black fur resting against her ankle, and wondered. He didn't exactly enhance the place. If she brought home a nice bit of red ribbon from work, could she possibly persuade him to give up struggling long enough for her to tie it securely around his scraggy neck?

It wasn't easy trying to explain to Edward.

'I'm sorry,' Grace said shyly, 'but I'm afraid I've got other plans for Thursday. Could we make it Friday evening instead?'

He smiled. 'Of course, if you prefer.'

'Oh, it isn't that I prefer – it's just that – oh dear, I don't know how to explain . . .'

'There's no need,' he interrupted, covering her hand with his. 'Between friends explanations are unnecessary.'

She looked up at him with a smile. 'You're so kind, Edward, and I don't want to shut you out. It's not really my business, you see. It's May's.'

'I understand.'

'I can't tell you the whole story. I promised.'

'Enough said, my dear. A promise is a promise.'

Grace looked up at him shamefaced. 'Only I told you a fib, and I feel bad about that. She's not really my niece at all, just a good friend.'

'I know.'

She stared at him in surprise. 'You knew? How?'

Again that gentle smile she was getting to know so well. 'It's hard to have a niece if you have no brothers or sisters. I'm afraid you're not cunning enough to be a good liar, Grace.'

'But you didn't say anything?'

He shrugged. 'Why should I? I knew you'd have good reason for it.'

Grace flushed with pleasure. 'She'll be having her baby soon,' she murmured. 'Maybe here.'

'Really? In that case, would you like me to arrange for a good midwife to attend her?'

'Oh Edward! You're so kind, but I don't think so. She's not yet settled her plans.'

He squeezed her hands between his. 'May's a delightful girl, and she obviously means a lot to you. If there's anything I can do, just call on me. I'll be glad to do all I can to help.'

The planned meeting was arranged for Thursday evening because Cassie had time off from work. Grace felt as exhilarated as a child as she sat in her living room with the three other women. Two of them had so much difficulty in tucking their bulk under the table that they didn't seem to notice her best china cups or the plate of lovingly made gingerbread men she'd set before them. The younger sister did though; she nibbled a leg thoughtfully.

'How long have we got before it's due?' Cassie asked.

May smoothed a hand over her stomach. 'They told me the beginning of next month.'

'That's why I'm wearing so many cushions,' said Ada.

'You're welcome to have the baby here,' said Grace. 'I'd like that.'

'Well, I reckon we need alternative plans,' said Ada, 'depending on when it arrives and whether or not May is here alone.'

'That's possible,' Grace admitted, 'if I'm at work.'

'It could be at night, when Miss Openshaw is here,' said Cassie, brushing a crumb from her skirt.

Ada pulled her chair a little closer. 'But on the other hand it might not, so there has to be other arrangements.'

'I'd like you to be here, Mam,' May said quietly. 'I saw how you coped with Mrs Nagle.'

Her mother nodded. 'So let's plan just what we can do. If you have it at Cedar Street then we have to smuggle you in first.'

'There's Elsie,' Cassie pointed out. 'What about her?'

Her mother nodded. 'We'll have to get her out of the way. She's too nosey by half, that one.'

'Where is she now?'

'Playing Newmarket for halfpennies with Mrs Boothroyd.'

'Hey – what about her?' said Cassie. 'The old lady?'

'I can't ask her to help. She might cotton on.'

Grace cut in eagerly. 'Maybe I can help—'

'Hold on a minute,' said May. 'Let's work this out step by step, so we all know exactly what we're going to do . . .'

By the time her guests left, Grace felt she could burst with excitement. She waved away May's offer to help her clear up and insisted that she go and have a lie down.

Empty china cups rattled in her fingers as she carried them through to the kitchen. Secret plans, with alternatives to remember – it was almost as thrilling as being a Government spy.

Grace's stomach rumbled. With all the to-do preparing for the meeting she'd completely forgotten to have supper. She nibbled the leg off a gingerbread man, then put the rest of them away in the biscuit jar. They were really rather good. Edward would like these.

As she prepared for bed Grace's stomach was still in a flutter. If ever Mr Henry came to hear of what his overseer was up to, he'd have an apoplectic fit.

At the tram stop in Cowlersley Ada turned to her daughter. 'It's early yet – you going straight back to the Chadwicks'?' she asked.

Cassie gave a mischievous smile. 'No, I'm going into town.'

'Are you? What's going off there?'

'You won't like it if I tell you.'

'Like what?'

'What I'm going to do. I'm meeting Mr Jordan.'

'Oh, love!'

'I know,' said Cassie as the tram came lumbering along the road, 'I told you you wouldn't like it. Still, it's my life and I know what I'm doing.'

Ada shook her head. 'I hope you do, lass, I really do.'

She watched her daughter climb aboard the tram, then turned and headed downhill towards Millsbridge. Despite its gaunt greyness and the stark lines of the gasometer, the village looked almost pretty. Mellow evening light lay over the slate roofs and the tall arches of the viaduct. The mills lay silent, no whirring machines clattering as she passed, and as she crossed the iron bridge the stinking steam of dye which usually rose from the river had evaporated for the day. Only brown water curdled under the bridge, its ripples creamed at the edges. Few people were about, and a pleasant evening hush lay over the place. She'd just about get home before dusk swirled gently down from Nab End tower up there on the hill and settled over the village.

The moment she swung round the corner into Cedar Street she spotted the tall figure emerging from the entry, a young man, broad-shouldered and with a spotted kerchief about his neck and with a canvas bag in his hand. He wasn't a local fellow. What was he doing round the back?

He stopped outside number seven and banged the knocker loudly. Ada hurried towards him. Hearing her footstep he turned and smiled.

'Who are you wanting?' she demanded, eyeing him over. He looked respectable enough with his bright, clear eyes.

'A lady called May Turnbull,' he answered, pulling off his cap. 'Do you know her?'

He didn't talk like folks around here. 'Who wants to know?'

He didn't seem surprised by her guarded reply. 'My name's Will Napier,' he said, dropping his bag on the pavement. 'I met her a while back, only I can't get any answer here.'

'You wouldn't. There's nobody in.'

Ada took out her key and pushed past him to unlock the door. Napier. Somehow the name seemed to ring a bell. 'Napier,' she muttered, then suddenly she turned back to him. 'Hey, are you the fellow as lent her some money?'

He grinned. 'She paid me back, every penny.'

'She would. She's like that.' Ada held the door wide. 'Come on in, lad, and welcome.'

She surveyed the young man as he sat in the fireside chair nursing a mug of tea between large hands. They were capable-looking hands, weather-beaten and calloused from hard work.

'What you doing up here then?' she asked. 'You're a long way from home.'

He shrugged. 'There wasn't enough work for me down there,' he said quietly. 'I thought I'd go north in search of a job, Newcastle, the shipyards perhaps. Since I was passing this way I thought I'd just call and see how May was getting on.'

'She's all right.'

'She hasn't had the baby, has she?'

'Not yet. Any time now.' Ada watched his face. There was honesty in those grave blue eyes. 'How much did she tell you?' she asked.

He drained off the last of the tea. 'Not a great deal,' he said, setting the mug down on the table, 'only that she wanted to get home. Can't say as I blame her if she was locked away in that nuns' place. Rumour has it a lot of girls have had a bad time there.'

Ada eyed him sharply. 'She never said she was there, did she?'

He shrugged. 'I just guessed she was, the way she looked. I'm glad she got home safe. Did she make it in time for the funeral?'

Ada set her cup down carefully. 'It's thanks to you she did, lad, you and that landlady. Only she's not living here just at present – she's staying with friends for a while.'

He reached for his cap. 'Well, just tell her I was asking for her.'

Ada rose as he uncurled his height and stood up. 'If ever there's owt we can do for you – you're welcome to stay the night here if you like.'

He shook his head firmly. 'Thanks, but I've got fixed up.'

'Some supper, then – stay and have a bite to eat.'

'Thanks, but I'd best be on me way.' He held out his hand. It felt hard and strong. 'I'm sorry about your husband.'

'Thanks, lad. If ever you're round this way again,' said Ada, 'I'm sure our May'd be right glad to see you.'

'Thanks very much, Mrs Turnbull. Wish her all the best from me.'

She stood in the doorway watching him stride jauntily away down the street into the dusk. He was a good-looking fellow and a good man into the bargain, that Will Napier – she could feel it in her bones, sturdy and reliable like Jim. He too used to wear that amiable smile and walk with that proud, rakish air.

She smiled to herself, her hand patting her ample stomach. Heavens – the padding! He must have noticed – he'd be thinking both mother and daughter were pregnant at once!

The thought amused her. She was turning to go back into the house when a sudden sound came to her ears, a scuffle and a wail. A small body came hurtling out of the Nagles' front door and went flying away down the street, howling and clutching his ear.

Poor little Dominic. With that drunken bully of a father the miserable little devil was always in the wars. Which reminded her – it was high time she fetched Elsie back home from next door before she robbed Mrs Boothroyd blind.

A sleepy-eyed Elsie growled as her mother pulled a clean nightdress over her head.

'I was winning threepence-ha'penny just before you came,' she grumbled. 'Now I've only got a ha'penny.'

'Be grateful for small mercies,' Ada soothed. 'You're a ha'penny better off than you were.'

'What with me Saturday threepence to come and all, and the penny you promised me for taking that bag of washing up Whiteley Street—'

'You've had that and spent it already,' Ada reminded her.

'Have I? Are you sure?'

'Positive,' replied her mother. 'Monday. Whip and top, wasn't it?'

Elsie's face fell. 'Oh yes – I forgot.'

'Where is it now – I haven't seen you playing with it?'

'I gave it to dozy old Coppernob.'

'Whatever for?'

'Swapped it for a pile of them comics you don't like me reading. She wanted my top 'cos of the pattern I drew on it.'

'Her down Archer Street? The one who used to push you around?' asked Ada. 'Well, you do surprise me.'

Elsie rammed small fists into her eye sockets. 'She let the other kids have a read of her comics but not me. So I made her give me the whole lot for me top. It didn't spin right anyway.'

Ada smiled. So there was yet another good bargain-driver in the family. 'Listen, love,' she said cautiously, drawing the little body as close to her as the padding would allow, 'how would you feel about going off on a little holiday, stay with a friend of mine – on your own, just for a few days?'

The child looked up at her. 'Holiday? While school's still on, do you mean?'

'Very likely. You'll get on well with Miss Openshaw – she's a real nice lady.'

'What'll the 'Tendance Officer say?'

'Never you bother, I'll square it with him. Would you like that?'

Elsie gave a wide yawn. 'All right then.' She patted her mother's jutting stomach. 'It'll keep me out of the way while you have our new baby, won't it?'

*   *   *

On Sunday evening May sat on the sofa with the cat while Grace saw Edward out. She could hear a deal of whispering in the little lobby before Grace came back, a contented smile wreathing her lips.

'He's asked me to go to the Theatre Royal with him tomorrow night,' she said happily. 'Will you be all right if I do?'

'Of course I will,' said May. 'You go and enjoy yourself.'

Grace looked dubious. 'Are you sure? Only if I go straight after work you'll be on your own for a long time . . .'

May scratched Oscar's head. 'We'll be fine, won't we, puss?' she murmured. 'You've no need to worry – it's a few weeks yet to the beginning of the month.'

Grace brightened. 'I would like to see that play – I've heard such good reports on it, and I know Edward's keen. So if I took me best hat to work with me in the morning . . .'

'You do that,' said May. 'And don't forget some of that lovely scent to dab behind your ears.'

Henry Rose felt apprehensive as he watched his wife take off her hat before the dressing table mirror. On the way home from the newly-weds he'd sensed the tension in the air, and the way she yanked the hatpin out and stabbed it viciously into the pincushion threatened that at any moment her pent-up words would burst forth. He couldn't for the life of him think what he might have done.

He hung up his overcoat in the wardrobe and turned to sidle quickly out of the room, but he was too late.

'There's trouble in the air,' Esther muttered to the mirror. 'Something is wrong with the boy, I know it.'

So that was it. Henry breathed a sigh of relief. She was just fretting about her son again.

'He's fine, Esther, a picture of health,' he soothed. 'A new house, a pretty bride – what more could he want? You worry too much.'

She whirled round on him. 'What kind of mother am I if I don't worry? Three months he is married and such a look he

333

wears, like an old man already. You too should worry.'

Henry's eyebrows rose. 'Me? Why? He does his work well enough.'

'Maybe it is the work which troubles him,' muttered Esther. 'Maybe you expect too much.'

'No, no – he does what he always did, no more.'

'Then it must be his marriage,' his wife said darkly. 'With only a mother like hers to advise her, maybe Adele does not know what is expected of her. We should do something.'

'My dear! We cannot interfere in such things!'

Esther ignored him. 'Maybe Aaron is too enthusiastic, but something is wrong for the boy to wear such a look. Twenty-four years old, and to look as old as you! Talk to him, Henry, find out what it is. If it's that silly, dim-witted girl—'

'I thought you liked Adele?'

Esther shrugged. 'As a mother for my grandchildren, she will be fine. I just don't want her bringing that look to my boy's face. Dear Aaron, he is so patient. Your grandson should be on the way by now. You must help him, Henry. Find occasion to talk to him in private, man to man.'

Henry sighed. He knew when he was beaten. He couldn't wriggle out of it or she'd never let him rest in peace.

'Very well, my dear. I'll see, if the opportunity arises.'

She came across and patted him on the shoulder. 'You will make the opportunity. Very soon. Our grandson cannot be left to chance.'

May awoke in the morning to the sound of a cup clinking in a saucer. Grace was standing over her as she struggled to sit up.

'I've brought you a cup of tea, love,' said Grace, 'and then I'm off to catch the tram. Now are you sure you'll be all right till I get back tonight?'

May rubbed her eyes and took the cup of tea. 'I'll be fine, honestly. I'll wait up for you – I want to hear how the play went.'

'Well, if you're sure . . .'

May heard the front door slam behind her. She sipped the hot tea thoughtfully, planning what to do with the day. As she reached over to place the cup on the bedside table she felt her stomach tighten with a cramp-like feeling. It must have been those sardines – they'd never really agreed with her.

After a moment the cramp eased away. May rolled over in the comforting, downy depths of the mattress. Before long Oscar would push open the bedroom door and come in yowling for his breakfast. There was time enough to have another forty winks before he leapt on the bed and began kneading her thighs . . .

THIRTY-TWO

May caught her breath as the spasm of cramp seized her, and she gripped hold of the door handle. All day these fits of cramp had been going on, getting stronger and lasting longer each time. At first she'd taken little notice; the baby wasn't expected for three weeks yet and the nuns used to tell the girls that their muscles might tighten up from time to time in practice for the day.

But now it was more than that; it was not only the spasms which were acutely uncomfortable but also the dull ache low in her back.

It couldn't be starting, could it? And yet it felt like the sensations the girls at the Home used to describe. Sometimes they worked on for hours, stopping every now and again to gasp and pull faces, until at last they were led away by the nuns.

And then there was that trickle of water this afternoon. What was it Daisy had said about wetting the bed just before Sister Anthony dragged her away? May paced up and down the little living room, wishing Grace was here. If something was about to happen she needed to get down to Cedar Street as soon as darkness fell . . .

The audience, laughing and chattering, spilled out of the Theatre Royal into the lamplit street. Edward drew Grace's arm through his as they headed up the road towards the tram.

'A pretty good show, eh?' he remarked.

'It was lovely, Edward,' Grace replied happily. 'I can't think when I've enjoyed myself so much.'

He smiled down at her, squeezing her arm against his side. 'I'm glad. Just think, we'll be able to do things like this more often now you're retiring.'

Retiring. She'd almost forgotten. Mr Henry's jaw had sagged when she told him this morning of her decision.

'*Well, if you're certain,*' he'd rumbled moodily, '*but I felt sure as you'd stay on yet a while.*'

'*No, Mr Henry. My mind's made up. There's other things I fancy having a go at.*'

'*Well, all I can say is, I hope you know what you're doing.*'

If only he knew . . . Any day now his grandchild would be born, ostensibly a washerwoman's child, and she, Grace Openshaw, was colluding in the deception!

Edward cut in on her thoughts. 'You'll have a lot of time on your hands soon. Have you any idea what you're going to do to fill it?'

She smiled. 'For a start I'm going to have May's little sister to stay. The only thing is,' she added dubiously, 'I don't know much about children. Maybe you could help me entertain her if you like. What do small children enjoy doing?'

'Well now,' he replied thoughtfully, 'if my son's two little boys are anything to go by, they like to have stories read to them, show them how to make something, take them down to feed the ducks on the lake – I can give you a list as long as my arm. And it would give me great pleasure if you would let me accompany you on some of your outings.'

She snuggled up close to the warmth of his arm as the tram drew up. It was going to be fun having a child in the house, especially if Edward was going to be around to help.

Another spasm of pain clamped fiercely around May's guts. She bent over a chair, arching her back and closing her eyes tight against the onslaught. The cramp seemed to be springing from the small of her back and encircling her completely, crashing over her as relentlessly as stormy sea-waves on a rocky shore. This must be it. The baby was on the way, and she was filled with a terrible feeling of inevitability.

She couldn't wait any longer for Grace. If she didn't go now, she might not reach Cedar Street in time. It was dark outside now, safe enough to go. She scribbled a quick note, then reached for her coat, locked the door and hurried away down the street. She must get as far as she could before the next spasm attacked her, then hide in the shadows until it passed over . . .

Grace frowned as they neared her house and Edward unlatched the garden gate.

'There's no light burning,' she said. 'May said she'd wait up for me.'

She took the door key from her bag. 'She's probably gone to bed,' said Edward. 'She's bound to tire easily these days.'

But May wasn't in her room. Grace came hurrying breathlessly down the stairs.

'Something's happened, Edward, I know it! Oh Lord, I shouldn't have left her alone for so long!'

Edward picked up the sheet of paper on the table and glanced at the handwriting. 'There's a note for you,' he said.

Grace scanned it quickly, and her fingers flew to her lips. 'It's started,' she said weakly, 'and I wasn't here – I was supposed to go with her! Oh dear, what shall I do now?'

'Go where?' Edward asked.

'To her mother's, in Cedar Street. Oh Edward, I've got to go down there, straight away.'

'The last tram will have gone by now. Can't it wait till morning?'

'I've messed up all the plans – I was supposed to bring little Elsie back here!'

'I could go for you.'

Grace bit her lip. 'I was supposed to get word to her sister too. Don't you think I ought to go myself, like I promised?'

Edward picked up his hat. 'Not at this time of night,' he said, turning for the door. 'I'll let them know you'll go down first thing in the morning. Leave it to me – I'll see to everything.'

*　　*　　*

Ada looked up, startled by the tap at the window, then hurried to open the door. As soon as she saw the white-faced girl leaning against the door-frame, she took charge.

'Has it started?'

May stepped in wearily. 'It can't be long – it's getting bad.'

Ada took her arm. 'Upstairs, love, get into my bed,' she said crisply, 'then I can have a look at you.'

May lay exhausted in the big bed, gasping for breath after the latest spurt of pain. She was aware of her mother bending over her, of fingers probing gently.

'It's early days yet,' Ada pronounced as she straightened. 'You've a bit of sweating ahead still afore it comes.' She pulled the covers back over her. 'Where's Miss Openshaw? I thought she was to come with you?'

May shook her head. 'She's out for the evening.'

Ada sniffed. 'Good job Elsie's fast asleep in bed then. Now who's going to fetch Cassie?'

'Grace will come – I left a note.' The tightening feeling was coming on again. May braced herself. Ada saw the look on her face and bent over her.

'Ah well, one thing at a time,' she murmured. 'First let's get you sorted out.'

It was coming on harder. May gritted her teeth, waiting for the crescendo. It broke over her, ebbed and flowed like a tidal wave, then gradually receded once more.

'You reckon it could be here by morning?' she muttered.

Ada cocked her head. 'First baby, not very likely, but who knows?'

'Mrs Nagle started at night and had her Lily by morning.'

'That's as may be, seeing as she's had some practice, dropping one every year. But I shouldn't bank on it being that quick for you.'

There was another spasm brewing up. May could feel her guts contorting once more and she screwed up her face.

'Easy now, love,' she heard her mother murmur. 'Just breathe easy and try to let it all wash over you.'

May could say nothing. It seemed she was plunged into an interminable black tunnel of pain where no other sensation existed . . .

Throughout the night the pains kept sweeping back to engulf her, swamping her in torment, wiping out time and space, but in the brief interval between bouts she was aware of her mother's gentle hands and soothing water helping to ease the agony, and in those moments she thanked God she was here, safe at home, and not with the nuns.

All those poor girls who'd passed through their hands, girls suffering nightmare pain like this and receiving no comforting words, only harsh reminders of their disgrace.

'Pain is the just reward for sin – you wouldn't have to endure this now if you hadn't yielded to temptation. Carnal knowledge is evil . . .'

From below she was vaguely aware of a knock at the front door. Ada cast her a wary look. 'I'll go see who it is,' she said quietly. 'Try not to make a sound.' At the door she turned. 'It could be Miss Openshaw.'

There were voices downstairs for a few moments, and then the sound of the door closing again. Ada came in carrying a wicker basket which she set down on the floor just as the next pain started. May grabbed hold of the bedrail, willing herself to have the strength to see it through. She could feel Ada's hand stroking her forehead.

'Easy, love, easy,' she murmured. 'You're doing just grand.'

But it didn't feel grand. It felt hideously, grindingly slow and laborious. May felt like a trapped animal, struggling to fight its way out of the agony of the gintrap, prepared even to lose a leg in order to escape.

But there was no escape from the inexorable. The only consolation lay in knowing that, God willing, at the end of all this she would hold in her arms the baby she'd dreamt of and for whom she had such plans.

340

Come on, baby, for God's sake, come on!

During a brief, lucid moment she was aware of Mam sitting on the edge of the bed and telling her about Mr Harris calling.

'He said he'll get a message to our Cass, and Miss Openshaw will come for Elsie in the morning. So let's just hope that little madam doesn't twig what's going on,' she said with a wry smile. 'Once she's gone – hey up, is that another pain coming on . . . ?'

May opened her eyes. She was drenched in sweat. It must be morning now for there was sunlight outside the window. Her mother came into the room carrying an armful of blanket pieces.

'It's all right,' she said, laying them in the wicker basket, 'Miss Openshaw and her friend have been and fetched Elsie away. Little love, she was that excited she never noticed anything out of the ordinary.'

'What about Cassie?' May asked weakly.

'He's gone for her – that Mr Harris. He knows to say only that she's wanted urgently at home. They've said all along that they'd let her go when the time came. She should be here directly.'

May rolled her head from side to side. 'I'm dead-beat. If only I could have a breather, just for five minutes.'

Ada shook her head. 'That's not the way it goes, I'm afraid. Just hang on – it'll all be worth it in the end, you'll see.'

'Mam, I'm home! Are you upstairs?'

Ada heard the front door bang and Cassie's call but she had her hands full. May was struggling, grunting as she heaved, and although Ada could see the baby's head straining to emerge, it was getting nowhere. She heard the sound of footsteps pounding up the stairs and then the door burst open and Cassie stood there.

Ada seized May's shoulder. 'Come on, love, push!' she encouraged. 'It's nearly here.'

'I can't push any harder,' May gasped. 'Cass – get out of here.'

Ada turned to look at the girl, transfixed in the doorway, her eyes huge. 'Fetch me a bowl of hot water from the range,' she said sharply. 'And a jug of cold water too. Hurry!'

Cassie vanished. May lay panting, beads of sweat running down her face. 'The next push,' she muttered. 'I'll have it on the next push if it kills me.'

'Good girl.' Ada saw the grimace returning to her face. 'Right, lass, here we go.'

Every muscle was straining and heaving to the limit and May's body felt as if it was ripping apart. Sensation had gone beyond the border of pain now and felt more like a kind of religious ecstasy, as if she was on the verge of another twilight world.

'Stop, for God's sake! Stop pushing!'

Dimly she was aware of her mother's voice, as if through a mountain mist, but to stop now was impossible. A hand was shaking her arm.

'Stop it, I tell you! The cord's around his neck!'

What cord? Whose neck? It made no sense. All that mattered was to obey what her body dictated. It was as relentless, as inevitable as death . . .

There was a huge, convulsive torrent of sensation, a terrible cry, and then pain seemed to slide away like an ebbing tide from the seashore. Then there was silence, and peace.

Something warm and wet touched her face. 'Look, May,' Mam's voice came out of the fog, 'look, you've a little daughter, and she's perfect.'

May took the little body and held it close, marvelling at the tiny hands and puckered face. 'Is it really mine?' she murmured.

'Yes, love, she's yours, and she's beautiful.'

May stared down at the tiny bundle and a surge of tenderness flooded through her.

'You're an ugly little thing,' she smiled, 'and you're mine, all mine.'

*　　*　　*

May and the baby were sleeping peacefully. Ada rinsed off the soiled draw sheets and put them to soak. Cassie sat by the fire, looking pale and thoughtful.

'I don't never want to have babies,' she muttered. 'Not after seeing our May like that, I don't.'

Ada felt she had to reassure the girl. 'Having a baby's always a messy business,' she said briskly, 'but it's not half so bad as it looks. Any road, it'll be a while yet before your turn.'

'Not me,' growled Cassie. 'I'd sooner adopt one.'

'You'd never get one as bonny as that little love up there. I wonder what our May'll call her?'

For a moment Cassie sat silent, then suddenly she leaned forward, elbows on knees. 'Listen, Mam, there's summat I have to tell you.'

Ada looked up. 'Oh aye? Summat I won't like, by the sound of it.'

'Very likely. I met Mr Jordan as I was coming home.'

'Oh – him again.'

'He's doing very well these days – he told me he's bought out Riley's business and he's buying a new house up Marsh.'

'Good for him. What of it?'

'He's going to find a manager who'll live here in Cedar Street and mind the yard, and he'll need someone to keep house for him in his new place.'

'Oh aye?'

'So he's offered me the job – to be his housekeeper.'

'His what?' exclaimed Ada. 'Now look here—'

'In fact he's asked me to marry him,' Cassie went on smoothly, 'but he reckons it's a bit soon yet, so I'm to move in as housekeeper for the time being. He's showed me the new house – it's lovely.'

'Cassie! You can't! It's far too soon – he's far too old for you!'

Cassie shrugged. 'What of it? It's a lot easier than working and he'll give me anything I want. I'll be able to help you, and I'll be a rich widow when he's gone.'

'Help me?' echoed Ada. 'Do you honestly think I'd take a penny piece that comes that way?' she said indignantly. 'You can forget that, and you can forget about marrying him. You're still too young, think on, only sixteen—'

'Nearly seventeen.'

'—and what makes you think I'd give my permission for you to get wed?'

'You will, because otherwise you know I'll run off. I'm going to marry him, whether or not.'

'For your own selfish reasons. You don't love him.'

'Happen not, but I like him well enough. He knows how to treat a lady. And he won't want babies.'

For a long moment Ada glared at her daughter, but by her rigid posture and the cool look in her eyes she knew she was defeated. What could she do? Argue with her and risk alienating her for ever, or give in to a suggestion she found repugnant?

'The neighbours'll be shocked,' she muttered. 'A girl your age, and him.'

Cassie pouted. 'I don't care. I won't be living in Cedar Street any more. Any road, why worry about them if you can put up with May's baby?'

'My baby,' corrected Ada. 'I gave birth to a daughter today, think on. So happen we'd best get ourselves organized so I look like the new mother before the neighbours start calling.'

'What time is it?' asked Cassie, half-rising from the chair.

'Going on six – why?'

That familiar mischievous smile again. 'I told Harold I'd let him know summat by teatime. I'll just pop over and give him the good news.'

Father Leahy stood amid a heap of crawling children. Husband and wife eyed one another distrustfully from opposite sides of the untidy room, an unsavoury steam rising from the wet nappies draped round the fire.

'So why does she always have those bruises on her cheek,

Timothy?' Father Leahy asked the husband. 'Have you been beating her?'

Tim glared at Maureen. 'She'd no right telling you that, Father,' he growled. 'That's our business.'

The priest shook his head. 'She didn't have to tell me. I see them every time she comes to church. What is it, Timothy? Why do you do that? Is it when you've been drinking again?'

The husband lowered his head. 'There's only the drink between me and insanity, Father,' he muttered. 'Down the filthy pit all day for a few paltry shillings then back to a filthy house at night. She's no wife to me.'

The priest shook his head gravely. 'She does her best, I'm sure. She cooks and washes for you, rears your children – what more should she do?'

'She doesn't know her duty.'

'And what is that, Timothy?'

Tim looked down at the floor, kicking sullenly at a child's wooden box. 'I can't tell you,' he muttered.

'Why not?' the priest persisted. 'You'd tell me in the confessional.'

'That's different. Nobody else knows. I can't say them words with kids here. I can only say she's not a proper wife.'

'Ah,' said the priest, 'so it's marital duties, is it? Your conjugal rights? Well, we've talked of this before, haven't we? I thought I'd made it plain to you that if you couldn't accept God's will about having more babies, then you'd no choice but to practise abstinence. Maureen is agreeable to that, I take it?'

'Yes, Father,' Maureen said quickly. 'I am.'

Tim's heavy features turned red. 'But why the devil should I – abstain?' he barked. 'Surely a man has a right to some comfort when he's worked his guts out all day! Why would he take a wife if not to comfort him?'

'To be sure,' the priest murmured appeasingly, spreading his hands as though in blessing, 'but there's no need to beat her like this.' He pointed to the weals on Maureen's face.

She cradled the baby closer to her breast. 'It's not that I

don't want to,' she said miserably. 'We've five already and I just don't want another one yet a while. We can't afford it.'

Father Leahy touched Tim lightly on the shoulder. 'My son, abstinence is the only answer if you cannot accept God's will. Leave her be, and no more beating. 'Tis a sin.'

'No, Father,' Tim muttered in a surly tone.

'And I'd like to see you come to Mass more often. You didn't come to make your Easter duties.'

'No, Father.'

'You wouldn't have missed back home in Connemara. I want to see you at confession next Saturday and Holy Communion on Sunday.'

'Yes, Father.'

Father Leahy took up his hat, satisfied. 'Well now, I'll leave you to your supper in peace. God bless you both.'

The minute the door had closed behind him, Tim turned on his wife and dealt her a furious whack across her cheek. 'What the devil do you mean, bringing him here?' he demanded.

Maureen cringed back against the wall, covering her face and peering at him fearfully between her fingers. 'I never did, I swear! Never a word passed my lips!'

Tim grabbed his jacket from the back of the door. 'I'm off down to the Fleece,' he growled, 'and when I get back I'll teach you a lesson you'll never forget, God help me if I don't!'

Tim Nagle's burly figure hurried past the door as Cassie stepped out into the sun-warmed, dusty street. As she headed towards Jordan's house she caught sight of Maureen Nagle squatting, hunched, on her doorstep, a limp baby in her lap.

Small Nagles stood grouped behind her in the doorway, unmoving and bleak-eyed as they watched their father receding into the distance. As Cassie drew close she could see the reddening patch on the woman's cheek and the forlorn, defeated expression in her eyes.

'You all right, Mrs Nagle?' she asked softly.

Tim Nagle's burly frame disappeared around the corner into

Fountain Street. The miserable, scrawny little statues behind Maureen came to life and began nudging her.

'Mammy, I'm hungry . . .'

The woman looked up at Cassie. There was blood on her lip and her eyes were hollow, as though they were looking down the vista of dreary years ahead, all filled with pain and misery.

'I'm as right as I'll ever be,' she muttered, then stumbled to her feet and led her brood indoors.

Cassie was filled with anger as she rapped the knocker on Harold Jordan's door. I'm more determined than ever now that I'm going to marry him, she swore. She'd seen women like Maureen Nagle before, all those jaded, worn-out wrecks up at the box factory. Nothing on earth's ever going to turn me into an empty, broken shell, she vowed. I'm damn well not going to finish up like that poor cow.

THIRTY-THREE

There was a loud knocking at the front door. Cassie peeped out of the window.

'It's Mrs Boothroyd – quick, into bed, Mam, before I let her in.'

Ada rushed upstairs and into the front bedroom. May, who was sitting up in bed, eating her breakfast off a tray, watched as her mother snatched up the baby in the wicker basket and raced out. In Elsie's room Ada tore off her blouse and pulled on a bedjacket, then leapt into bed.

Downstairs she could hear Mrs Boothroyd's shrill voice. 'By heck but it's hot – the sun's cracking the flagstones out here. Is your mam in?'

'She's in bed,' Cassie replied. 'With the new baby.'

'Baby?' echoed the old lady. 'You mean it's come? Well, I'll go to the foot of our stairs! I'd no idea! Are they all right, both of 'em?'

'They're fine. Would you like to see them?'

'If your mam's feeling up to it. What have you got – a new brother or a sister?'

Ada could hear the old lady's slow, trundling steps up the stairs as Cassie opened the door and came in. She tipped her mother a wink. 'A little sister,' she said with a broad smile as she held the door wide, 'and she's lovely.'

'Ada, love,' wheezed the old lady as she advanced upon the bed, 'eeh, lass, I'd no idea you was in labour. I heard someone crying out last night, sure enough, but I thought as how it was them Nagles fighting again.'

Cassie cut in. 'I'll just go see to things,' she said. Ada saw

348

her quick jerk of the head in the direction of the front bedroom. 'But don't you go tiring yourself, Mam. You've had a rough time.'

Mrs Boothroyd shook her head. 'Don't worry, I'll not stay long. I'll just have a quick look at the little one.'

Cassie left, closing the door behind her. Mrs Boothroyd bent her stiff old body with difficulty to peer into the basket. 'Eeh, but she's bonny,' she murmured, screwing up her eyes. 'Do you know, I fancy she has a look of your husband about her. It's her eyes, I reckon. It's like your Jim had come back and was looking at you.'

'Ah well, she is half Turnbull,' said Ada.

The old lady intruded a gnarled finger into a tiny fist. 'I'm glad Cassie's here to take care of you while you're lying in. Does your May know yet?'

'Cassie'll see she gets to hear.'

Mrs Boothroyd let go of the baby's hand and sank, wheezing noisily, into the bedside chair. She fanned her face with the corner of her flowered apron.

'You chose a good time, any road,' she remarked. 'You'll feel a lot cooler and comfier now you've shed that load.'

Ada smiled. 'Yes,' she agreed, 'I couldn't wait to get rid of that lump, I can tell you.'

The old lady nodded contentedly, then suddenly her face creased into a worried frown. 'Hang on,' she said, 'who delivered the baby for you? It surely wasn't Bessie Morton 'cos I heard this morning she was rolling drunk last night, making a terrible racket.'

'No, it wasn't Bessie. What was she up to?'

'Sitting on somebody's doorstep in Crow Lane she was, according to Mrs Tandy, singing her heart out when Constable Drake found her. She told him she was celebrating 'cos she'd just delivered twins in Dowker Street, but there's been no twins born as I've heard tell of. I reckon she was just seeing double again.'

'Very likely,' smiled Ada, and to her relief the door opened and Cassie came in.

'Time you had a sleep now, Mam,' she said, tucking the sheets tight around her mother. 'Mrs Boothroyd can come and see you again soon.'

The old lady rose obediently. 'I'll be off then, love,' she said to Ada, 'and I'm right pleased about your precious little gift.' She waddled towards the door. 'And just you mind out when it comes to your turn,' she admonished Cassie with a wink, 'or you could wind up with a dozen precious gifts like what my sister did. I had more sense.'

'Good for you,' said Cassie. 'And I will and all.'

Over the next few days Ada spent a great deal of time in bed as more neighbours dropped by to offer their congratulations. Mrs Tandy almost caught her out but Cassie managed to keep her in the kitchen, folding sheets, until Ada was back at her post.

Many callers wanted only to leave a small gift. 'Mrs Jepson left you this redcurrant jelly,' Cassie announced, holding up a jar at the bedroom door. 'She said not to worry about the bit of mould on the top – she must have put the wax lid on before it was properly cold. They've gone through several jars already and come to no harm, she said – just scrape it off.'

'I'll do no such thing,' retorted Ada, 'but it was a kindly thought. Did you tell her to pass the word round as I won't be doing any more washing for a while?'

'I did. I said as you might not be doing it any more.'

'Nay, I've had plenty of time to think, lying here. I've little choice if we're to eat. I'll have to start again once May's up and about.'

Cassie smiled knowingly. 'We'll see about that. You talked about setting up a dining room, didn't you?'

'Idle pipe dreams. I can't afford it.'

'Happen not. I've had a word with Harold about—'

'Cassie! I told you, I won't take a penny piece—'

'—about that place under the viaduct. He's going to make some enquiries about the lease. No harm in that.'

Ada frowned. 'Happen not, but how I earn my living, that's

private. You shouldn't be talking my business with him.'

'Mam, there won't be any business if you don't start the ball rolling. That's all I'm doing, finding out. The rest's up to you.'

'Aye well, no harm in that, I reckon. I never want to see that damned washing again, but I've got to earn somehow.'

'Then it'll have to be the dining room or back to mending in the mill.'

Ada shook her head fiercely. 'I'm blowed if I'll ever go back into that barracks,' she growled. 'I've better things to do with my time.'

'That's right,' agreed Cassie, 'like making dreams come true. We can make it happen if you really want it to.'

Ada surveyed her thoughtfully. The girl was a trier, even if she didn't always approve of her methods.

She swung her legs out of bed. 'We'll see about that,' she said. 'Now I'd best go down and make a start on the supper. You take the baby back to May – it's time for her feed.'

Cassie took a quick step forward. 'Now you be careful Mam, we don't want you—'

Her hand was on Ada's arm, her eyes full of concern. For a second the two women stared at one another and then Cassie burst into a fit of the giggles and the two of them sank back on the bed.

'See, you've got me believing it now,' chuckled Cassie.

Edward's garden looked wonderful in the summer afternoon. A gentle breeze was stirring the flowers and a heady scent of sun-warmed violets and lily of the valley filled the air. Grace watched as Elsie pranced around, following Edward as he moved between the flower-beds, cutting a bloom here and there and handing it to her.

She laid the flowers down on the grass and stepped onto the low wall bordering the rosebed, picking her way along it with care.

'We haven't got a garden like you and Aunt Grace at our house,' she told him, 'with lots of grass and flowers. We've got a back yard though, with a coal shed and a privy me mam scrubs out every Saturday.' She jumped off the wall and added proudly, 'I'm in charge of stringing the paper.'

'And I'm sure you do a thorough job of it,' said Grace, anxious to close the subject. 'Now, which flowers do you think your mother would like when we go to see her?'

'Them,' said Elsie, pointing to the roses, 'only they scratch.'

Edward smiled at Grace over the child's head. 'I think we can do something about that,' he said.

'I wonder if she's fetched our new baby yet,' said Elsie.

Grace felt the colour flood her cheeks. 'I'm sure she'll let you know as soon as she does so you can go home and see it.'

'Well now, what shall we do this afternoon?' Edward asked the child. 'How would you like to go to Dewsbury and play with a couple of little boys I know? They're very nice boys.'

Grace could hear the touch of pride in his tone as he spoke of his grandsons. Elsie shrugged non-committal shoulders.

'All right,' she agreed. 'Lads are better to play with than lasses. They don't fight over whose turn it is to hold the skipping rope.'

'Then that's settled,' said Edward. 'All we need to decide now is what colour roses your mother would like best.'

'Pink,' Elsie answered promptly. 'Pink for a girl.'

Grace smiled. 'How do you know it will be a girl baby?' she asked.

Elsie shrugged. 'It'll have to be. I want a baby sister and anyway, you haven't got any blue roses.'

May was sitting by the window looking down into the street when Ada came into the bedroom.

'Nay, lass, you shouldn't be out of bed yet!' she admonished her. 'You're supposed to be ten days lying in before you get up.'

'I'm as right as rain now,' May protested. 'I've had enough of bed this last week. I want to get back into the world again now.'

Ada considered. 'Well all right, if you stay up here for a couple more days, out of sight . . .'

May caught hold of her arm. 'Mam, that lease – Cassie's found out the rent. With that money I've got we could manage to start.'

Ada stared. 'You've been talking, you and her! Plotting behind me back!'

May smiled. 'Talking out the possibilities, that's all. Why don't we all get together and try and work out what you'll need, see how much it would come to . . .'

Ada sat on the edge of the bed. 'Too much, that's for sure,' she said tartly. She held up a hand and began counting off on her fingers. 'For a start there'd be a range to cook on, tables and chairs, crockery, cutlery, saucepans, tea-towels, not taking into account the food . . .'

'Hold on,' May interrupted. 'You'd better fetch paper and pencil so we can list it all down.'

It was the arrival of Jack Smedley which threw Ada into a spin. Racing back into Elsie's bed yet again, she felt an absolute fraud. It was all very well conning the neighbours but Jack, with his open, honest nature and obvious concern, was another matter.

He peered into the cradle at the little one, then came to sit by the bed. 'You've done a good job there, lass,' he said quietly. 'And I'm that relieved you're all right. They say a woman's never closer to death than when she's in childbirth. I can't tell you how worried I was.' He leaned across and smiled as he patted her hand. 'But I should have known you'd pull it off all right.'

Ada held her tongue. If there was anyone in the world she'd like to confess the truth to it was Jack, but she couldn't split on May. Complete secrecy was the whole purpose of the exercise.

His hand still lay on hers as they sat in silence for a moment, then Jack cleared his throat. 'I meant what I said that time,' he muttered, 'you know, about taking care of you and the girls. I'd be that proud.'

Ada drew her hand away quickly. 'No,' she said abruptly, then immediately felt contrite. 'I didn't mean that nastily, love,' she hurried on, 'only that I'm not ready for owt like that – I want us to stand us own, me and the girls. I have this wild idea—'

'That dining room you told me about?'

'If I could see me way to get the money together—' Ada waved a dismissive hand. 'Oh, it's probably a crazy notion but I'd love to have a go and the girls are keen – they'd back me up.'

Jack leaned forward eagerly. 'I will and all, lass. Owt I can do, I will.'

'You've your time filled, down the pit.'

'There's me day off, and when I'm on nights I have all day free. I'd be glad of summat to occupy me.'

Ada gave him a grateful smile. 'Aye well, it's nobbut a pipe dream as yet. I shall be getting up tomorrow and then we'll see.'

Grace Openshaw felt inordinately happy. Going out on excursions with Edward, taking little Elsie for a day at Hope Bank pleasure grounds and to Dewsbury to visit Edward's son and his family, watching the little one's expressions of wonder and delight – it was a whole new world of closeness which she'd never known before.

This was what it would be like if she'd married and had a family of her own, she thought wistfully; this was what Mother had robbed her of. But for her, Thaddeus might well have been the man walking at her side, taking her to visit their own grandchildren.

But it no longer mattered. She was happier in Edward's company than she'd ever been, and they were taking a very excited little girl home to see her new baby sister.

Edward was carrying a huge bunch of roses. Elsie was skipping along, holding on tightly to his free hand as they walked down the steep hill into Millsbridge.

'I wonder what we'll call our baby?' the child said eagerly. 'It's got to be a nice name – I hate mine.'

'Goodness me!' said Grace. 'Why?'

'There's too many blooming Elsies in our school, that's why. Why couldn't I have summat nice and posh?'

Edward smiled. 'Like what?' he asked.

The child shrugged. 'Dimity's nice – that's in my story book. And Rapunzel – she has ever such long hair. I want long hair like Cassie when I grow up.'

'Rapunzel Turnbull,' said Edward thoughtfully. 'How does it sound?'

Elsie gazed up at him in awe. 'Oh, it's beautiful,' she sighed, then turned to Grace with a proud smile. 'I'll tell Mam she can give it to our new baby.'

It was late that night before Elsie could be persuaded to put her nightgown on ready for bed. Cassie and May sat on the sofa, the baby lying between them, and it was difficult to prise Elsie away from marvelling at the tiny, perfect fingernails and huge violet eyes.

May's arm lay along the back of the sofa. She twined her fingers in Cassie's long hair. 'Are you going back to work again now?' she asked.

'Aye, tomorrow. I can't give me notice and start me housekeeping job until Harold's found a new manager for the yard.'

'That shouldn't take much doing. There's plenty looking for work.'

'Master craftsmen don't grow on trees. Soon as Harold finds him, he'll be off to the new house.'

'Look,' cried Elsie, pointing to the baby, 'she's blowing bubbles!'

'Never mind that,' said Ada. 'Come here and let me wash your face.'

Elsie submitted and closed her eyes. 'She smells funny, though,' she said between sweeps of the soapy flannel across her mouth 'Why's that?'

'She needs a wash too and she'll have it directly. Now dry yourself.'

Elsie tickled the baby's nose with a corner of the towel. 'I wish me dad could have seen her. He'd have liked her.'

Ada nodded. 'Aye well, he were taken away from us but we were given the baby to love instead. We should be grateful for small mercies. What you doing to your eyes?'

Elsie was running the towel carefully from the bridge of her nose out to her cheeks, her eyes screwed tightly shut. 'I'm flattening me eyebrows out,' she said. 'Aunt Grace says ladies always do that when they're wet so they won't stick out all spiky. What are we going to call our new baby, then, if you can't spell Rapunzel?'

Ada looked across at the two older girls. 'I can't decide. What do you think?'

'Theodora,' said Cassie.

'Ugh, that's ugly!' cried Elsie. 'We're not having that.'

Ada looked directly at May. 'What do you think, love?'

May spoke softly. 'I've been thinking,' she murmured. 'The Nagles have a Lily. Why don't we have a Rose? It's a lovely name.'

For a moment Ada stared, and then understanding dawned. May stood up and crossed to the window, and as she passed Ada caught sight of the smile about her lips.

Elsie clambered onto the sofa and stroked the baby's forehead. 'Rose – that's nice. Can we call her that, Mam?'

Ada looked at the trio on the sofa, Cassie and Elsie crooning over the baby. She bent and took the baby's tiny fist in hers.

'Rose it is,' she pronounced softly, 'a rose between two thorns.'

Henry Rose led the way into the George Hotel and sat watching his son as he ordered the drinks. He would be an uncommonly good-looking fellow but for that scowl which never seemed to leave his face these days. Esther was right – something was wrong with the lad and he was under orders to try and find out what it was.

He took a sip of wine and shuddered. It was far too dry for his taste. It was yet more proof that Aaron had something weighing on his mind that he hadn't even asked his father what he wanted to drink. The lad was staring moodily into his glass, clearly unwilling to chat, but Esther would never forgive him if he missed this opportunity. There was no other way but to come straight out with it. Henry took a deep breath.

'Look, lad, I don't want to pry into your business, but your mother keeps on at me. She's sure there's something bothering you.'

Aaron didn't look up. 'Is she? Is that why you asked me here?'

'It's only a mother's natural concern – she's worried about you.'

His son gave a moody shrug. 'She's no need to be. I'm fine.'

Henry took another sip, grimaced, and tried again. 'To be honest, I'm a bit concerned and all. You're not your usual self these days, haven't been for a while. Look, lad, if there's owt you want to tell me . . .'

'There isn't. I can handle things.'

He wasn't going to be deterred that easily. Henry tried again. 'I know there are some things a young man, newly-wed, may need to learn from someone more experienced in these matters . . .'

God help him for the lie! He'd never been able to rouse Esther since the day she'd given birth to Aaron. Duty was done, she said, so there was no need to endure all that business any longer.

Aaron wasn't reacting to the prompt. He was swirling the wine around in his glass and staring at it dully. Henry searched around in his mind and hazarded another guess.

'It's not money, is it?'

The boy snorted. 'No more than usual. Now stop fretting. I'm fine, never been better in my life.'

Henry changed tack. 'It's not Adele, is it?' he said

357

tentatively. 'She's not poorly, is she?' Now that could be it, he thought. She could even be pregnant!

Aaron looked up sharply, his glass halfway to his lips. 'What makes you say that?' he demanded. 'Has someone been talking?'

Henry was flustered. 'No – why? Is summat up?'

'Nothing that concerns anybody else,' Aaron snapped back. 'Now are we having another drink or are we going home?'

Henry sighed and forced himself to down the rest of his drink. It was no more bitter than the scolding he'd get from Esther when he got home.

THIRTY-FOUR

'Them roses of Mr Harris's have lasted well,' remarked Ada as she scooped the fallen petals from the window-sill. 'Over two weeks now. Shame to chuck 'em out but they're pretty well past it.'

May held the baby to her breast and said nothing. For her the thick, cloying scent of them would forever remind her of that sultry evening in the rose garden at Thornleigh Hall, with Aaron's whispered, persuasive words of passion. What a fool she'd been in those days, so blindly infatuated that she'd let him lead her by the nose. Could it really be less than a year ago? So much had happened since then it seemed a lifetime away. It was as though those stark months in the Home had almost wiped from her memory the life she'd led before.

The baby let go of her nipple and burped. May became aware that her mother was talking to her.

'What do you think then? Time we made that trip into town, isn't it? Our Elsie'll be breaking up from school this week – she'll be under our feet all day.'

'I suppose so,' agreed May.

'No time like the present. Let me change Rosie while you get ready.'

The heat of the summer afternoon lay heavy over the smoky town as May and Ada walked through Hawksmoor. Ada was carrying baby Rose in her arms because May's breasts were still stinging from feeding her.

At last they reached the office with its brass plate gleaming in the sunlight. *Registrar of Births, Deaths and Marriages.* Ada turned to her daughter.

'Well, have you made your mind up?' she asked. 'Is she my fourth daughter or not?'

May shook her head. 'Only as far as the rest of the world is concerned. We can't go in here and tell a lie. I want it down on paper that she's mine.'

'Tell the truth and shame the devil. Right.'

Inside the cool, dark office a cadaverous-faced man with wisps of grey hair sprouting in clumps around his ears stood behind a long mahogany counter. He opened a large book, dipped his pen in the glass inkwell and took down the details.

'Child's full Christian names?'

'Rose. Just Rose.'

He wrote laboriously in neat copperplate writing. 'Rose. Female. Mother's name?'

May took a deep breath. 'May Turnbull.'

'Address? . . . Occupation?'

'Seamstress.'

'Father's name?'

May was aware of her mother's quick, questioning look. 'Do I have to give that?' she asked quietly. 'We're not married. I'd rather not.'

The thin-faced gentleman gave her a frosty look and shrugged. 'It's up to you. If he does not want to acknowledge paternity—'

'He doesn't. Can we leave it blank?'

The gentleman blotted the page, took up a ruler and laid it across the book. 'In such cases we put a line through the space for his name, address and occupation. There, that's done. Legally now, your child has no father.'

May took the certificate and turned to her mother with a smile. 'Good,' she said quietly. 'Now she's a real person with her own document. No-one else need ever know what's on this piece of paper.'

*   *   *

'Well, now we've got that over,' said Ada as they emerged into the street, 'I'll go down Shambles Lane for a piece of meat for supper. It'll probably be me last chance to be out on me own.'

'In that case,' said May, 'I'll go and look round the shops.'

Her mother gave her a shrewd glance. 'You don't have to go looking for work, not yet, I told you. It's early days still.'

May shook her head. 'One of us has to earn, Mam. If you're not going to open the dining room—'

'Who said I'm not?' retorted Ada. 'I'm looking into it.'

May's lips parted in surprise. 'Are you? Doing what?'

Her mother gave an embarrassed half-smile. 'As a matter of fact I'm on me way to the bank. See if they'll lend me a bit of brass.'

May gave her arm a warm squeeze. 'It's worth a try. Want me to come with you?'

'No,' said Ada shortly, handing over the baby. 'I want to do this on me own.'

May walked purposefully down to King Street. If Mam was now seriously thinking of opening the dining room then she'd need some idea of the cost of materials. Mr Harris was the man to talk to. What he couldn't supply he'd be sure to know of others who could.

Hitching the baby up closer, she turned into the shop and looked around. He wasn't in sight; he must be in the office. She smiled at the young woman behind the counter.

'Is Mr Harris in today? I'd be most grateful if I could have a word with him.'

A moment later quick, light footsteps came hurrying, and Grace Openshaw's delighted face smiled up at her. 'I was up in the office with Edward. Oh, my dear! How nice to see you out and about again! How's our little Rose?'

She peeled back the corner of the wrap to peer at the baby. 'Oh, she's lovelier than ever,' she enthused. 'Let me hold her for a minute. Edward will be down directly.'

He appeared a few moments later and shook May warmly by the hand. 'And what can I do for you, my dear?' he asked.

The baby began to whimper. Grace looked around at the other customers. 'Look,' she said to May, 'I'll take care of Rose upstairs while you two talk business.'

May came straight to the point. Fishing in her pocket for the list, she held it out. 'These are the things we'd need if the plan for the dining room takes off,' she explained. 'It's not definite yet, but it just might.'

Mr Harris inspected the list. 'I could supply some of the linen for you, at a discount of course, but as to the furniture and hardware . . .'

'You must know most of the traders in Hawksmoor,' May urged, 'and the wholesalers. What I need to know is where we can get the stuff at the best possible price. Just in case.'

Mr Harris nodded. 'I can sound around for you. Leave it with me,' he said, tucking the piece of paper into his pocket, 'and I'll let you know when I come up with anything.'

May held out her hand. 'That's all I ask and I'm very grateful to you. Can I go up and fetch Rose?'

'By all means.'

Together they turned towards the staircase. At that moment a portly figure came in at the entrance and, spotting Harris, hurried towards him. With a sudden lurch in her stomach May recognized Henry Rose.

'Ah, Harris,' he beamed, 'I wanted a word with you – about this sixty hours a week maximum for shop workers.'

He didn't seem to have noticed May. She stood there, uncertain what to do.

'Yes?' said Harris. 'What of it? I've been doing that for some time. As well as a half-day off.'

Rose's face fell. 'Can't we get round it? Give 'em two weeks' paid leave or summat?'

'Not if it becomes law, as seems likely. You'll just have to put the best face on it.'

Rose turned to May as if about to appeal for sympathy. Instead a puzzled frown crept onto his pudgy face.

'Oh, excuse me,' he murmured, 'but haven't we met? I seem to recall your face.'

Harris smiled. 'Miss Turnbull used to work in your shop at one time.'

The frown faded and May could see recollection dawn in his eyes. 'Ah yes – the workroom,' he murmured, and then she saw his gaze flick over her body. 'You are well, I hope?' he asked.

'Very well, thank you.'

He waited. She saw the look of relief when she said no more, and his expression softened.

'Have you managed to find a new position, Miss Turnbull?'

'No.'

'If you'll excuse me,' Harris cut in, 'I've business to see to upstairs. Good day to you both.'

May saw a flicker in Mr Rose's shrewd eyes and then he cleared his throat. 'Look, my dear, there's no need to worry about that – er, that little misunderstanding we had . . .'

'Misunderstanding?' May echoed loudly. Mr Rose glanced around nervously.

'Whatever you like to call it,' he said abruptly. 'The point is, I might be in a position to help you. If you wanted to come back to us, you might like to apply for Miss Openshaw's job – she retired recently, you know.'

May met his gaze levelly, but said nothing. Encouraged, he went on. 'We have two businesses to run now, since my son was married, and he spends most of his time in the Leeds warehouse. So it's very important to find the right calibre of person to be overseer at our place, someone who's not afraid of responsibility.'

'Of course,' May agreed.

'And since we already know the quality of your work,' he went on, searching her eyes to gauge her reaction, 'and that we are fully able to rely on your loyalty and discretion . . .'

May cocked her head to one side. 'Yes?'

He spread plump hands. 'Like I said, we'd be willing to

consider you for the post. More money than you were getting before, of course. I take it you're interested?'

May smiled. 'In laying my head on the block once more? No thank you, Mr Rose, I've no intention of doing anything that silly ever again. Those days are over.'

He stared at her, disbelieving. 'Look, I'm willing to let bygones be bygones – I'm offering you a plum job – loads of girls your age would give their eye teeth for it!'

'Then let them have it – give it to some other gullible fool. I've had all I want from you.'

She turned away and swept up the staircase to collect her daughter. By the time she came down again there was no sign of Henry Rose.

Cassie was only too eager to take the baby from her when she arrived home. Mam was peeling potatoes into a mixing bowl on the table.

May sank into a chair. 'How did you get on at the bank, Mam?'

She saw her mother's lips tighten. Cassie answered for her. 'They turned her down flat. They said she'd never get a loan from anybody without some sort of security to back it up.'

May unbuttoned her blouse in silence. Maybe she'd been too hasty turning down Mr Henry's offer. But then, she could never have gone back to that place.

'But I'm not so sure,' Cassie went on as she handed the baby over and watched it clamp onto May's breast. 'I'll ask Harold if there's other ways of borrowing the money. We're not beaten yet.'

'No, we're not,' agreed May. 'And I've enough for a few months' rent—'

Ada threw the last peeled potato into the bowl. 'I'm going to pay me own way,' she said quietly. 'Every last penny.'

'Right,' agreed Cassie. 'Even if it's a loan you'll have to repay it. I'll have to pick the right time to see what Harold says. He's a bit put out at the moment about the new carpenter he's taken on. He doesn't think he's shaping up right to be left in charge of the yard after all.'

'I can't be doing with it,' Harold said testily. 'He's going to have to go.'

Cassie smiled sweetly. 'He can't be that bad. He came with a very good reference, didn't he?'

'Aye, and he's a good-enough worker with the wood,' Harold conceded. 'It's his manner I can't stand. Surly, he is, both with me and me customers, and he treats that poor horse like an animal. Never a pat on the nose or an extra handful of oats when he tucks her up for the night. She's been used to that for years.'

Cassie inspected her nails. 'So what do you think you'll do?'

'Sack him,' replied Harold. 'But not till I find somebody else.'

'Good. That's settled. Now what about what I was asking you?'

He bent over her anxiously. 'I'm sorry, my dear. What were you asking me? Anything you want—'

'About a loan. For my mother and her dining room.'

'Ah, yes.' Harold drew back and rubbed his chin. 'On a proper business basis, you say? Regular weekly repayments?'

'Of course. Starting the week after it opens.'

'With interest?'

'Same as she'd have paid the bank.'

He couldn't help smiling as he reached forward and tenderly touched her cheek. 'You're a proper little business woman, Cassie Turnbull,' he said admiringly. 'You've got a good brain in that pretty little head of yours. No competitors, it's a good commercial proposition. You've convinced me, my love. I'll make out a cheque.'

'Cash please, Harold. Folk like us don't know what to do with cheques.'

He smiled indulgently. 'Whatever you say, my love.'

* * *

Cassie came in and hung up her jacket on the back of the door just as May held out a piece of paper to her mother.

'Grace brought this note from Mr Harris,' May told her. 'It's not as bad as I expected. He's obviously gone out of his way to get good prices.'

Ada looked down at the list of figures. 'It's still a sight more than what we've got between us,' she said slowly.

'It's all right, Mam,' Cassie said proudly. 'Harold's sorted it out. You can have the loan whenever you're ready.'

Ada fixed her with a searching look, then planted her hands on her hips. 'You're a poor liar, Cassie Turnbull,' she said sternly. 'It's his money, isn't it? I've told you before, I won't take a penny off him.'

'No, Mam, you've got it all wrong—'

'What's it matter where it's from?' May cut in quietly. 'The fact is, you've got it within your reach now to start up.'

Ada shook her head. 'He's only trying to buy our Cass with it, I know.'

Cassie jumped up and put her arms around her mother. 'He doesn't need to – I want to be with him. Look, you'll hand over a weekly repayment, with interest, same as if it was to the bank. No favours, all perfectly businesslike. Now don't be stubborn – you'll ruin your chances.'

'She's right,' said May. 'A chance like this is once in a lifetime.'

'What if we don't make enough to pay him off?' murmured Ada.

'We'll damn well have to make sure we do. Once we pitch into this we'll have to give it all we've got.'

Ada gave a thin smile. 'You're talking like we're going ahead with it.'

May met her gaze. 'Well, aren't we?'

'I don't know . . .'

There was a sudden heavy knock on the door. Cassie looked up, startled. 'Whoever can that be at this time? Oh Lord, I ought to be gone by now.'

She grabbed her jacket from the hook and slid one arm

inside as she went to open the door. A tall, good-looking young man stood on the step, a bag at his feet.

'Hello,' he said with a smile. 'I'm looking for May. My name's Will Napier.'

From inside Cassie heard her mother's cry of surprise. 'Will!' she exclaimed, hurrying to the door, 'Will Napier, come in, lad. You're in luck this time – she's here.'

Cassie followed as he pulled off his cap and went into the living room. She saw May rise to greet him, the flush of pleasure on her face matched by the glow on his. He was gorgeous, and he clearly had a soft spot for May.

'What you doing here, lad?' Mam asked him, indicating a chair. 'I thought you was up in Newcastle?'

He shrugged broad shoulders and sat down. 'It wasn't as easy to find work as I hoped. There's trouble brewing up there for the stevedores and they reckon there could be a strike before long. It was pretty obvious there was nothing doing for me.'

He smiled, white teeth flashing in the lamplight as he leaned forward. 'How are you, May?'

She blushed. 'I'm fine. So is my little daughter. We called her Rose.'

'I'd like to see her.'

'You will, but she's asleep in bed right now.'

Mam started talking again and Cassie saw the way Will's eyes lingered on May while he listened. Was there something between these two, she wondered? Something May had never told her? She'd always been a cagey one, keeping secrets like nobody else ever did.

And then a sudden thought flashed into her brain. Could he be Rose's father? Was that why he had come? May had only said he'd helped her get home, not whether she'd known him earlier. If he was, then May had ensnared a man worth capturing. But why hadn't she married him? He was beautiful.

Mam was telling him about the dining room. 'We've found the ideal place if we do it, under the viaduct, only about a

367

hundred yards from here, where a haulier used to keep his horses and wagons. It's in a bit of a mess – mucky old stalls that'd have to come out. There'd be a heck of a lot of work to do to get it right.'

'Maybe I could have a look at it for you,' said Will. 'In the morning, perhaps.'

Mam looked surprised. 'But weren't you on your way somewhere? Back home or summat?'

'I'd no plans except to see that May was well. My time's my own.'

Cassie saw May's lips part and her eyes gleam. Mam looked at Will doubtfully.

'Are you sure?' she said warily.

'Like I said, I've nothing else to do. I can spare a week or two.'

Ada looked across at May. May gave her a broad smile. 'Why not? Maybe everything's coming together, as though fate meant it to be.'

'Happen so,' growled Ada, 'but I'd rather make me own decisions, never mind fate.'

'Well, I'd best make a move,' said Will, rising to his feet.

'Me too,' said Cassie. She sidled round behind him as he moved towards the door, close enough to catch the scent of his skin, warm and dark and masculine. It would be a crying shame to let him vanish from Hawksmoor too soon . . .

Ada rose and held out a hand, catching hold of Will's sleeve. 'Where do you think you're going at this time of night?' she demanded. 'You stay here and have a good wash-down, then you can sleep on the settee tonight.' She turned to Cassie. 'Isn't it time you were off, love?'

Cassie caught the young man's eye and gave a rueful smile. She'd been hoping to have him all to herself, at least as far as the tram stop.

The air in the vaulted stable smelt sour and dank. Ada cast a glance around the bare stone walls and up at the high, arched ceiling, and despite the heat of the day she shivered.

'It fair stinks of horse-dung in here,' she muttered. 'Was I mad thinking I could do owt with this?'

Will walked up and down the flagstoned floor between the stalls, kicking at the blackened bundles of decaying straw. 'Oh, I don't know,' he murmured. 'It's niffy all right but it's got possibilities.'

'All them stalls would have to come out for a start.'

'Not all, necessarily. You could leave every other one where it is, turn them into eating areas. And the end one, by the back wall, that could be your cooking area.'

Ada sniffed. 'I wouldn't fancy any food cooked in this mouldy old hole. It'd need scrubbing from top to bottom, plenty of bleach, and then a good coat of paint.'

Will ran his hand along the top of one of the stalls. 'It's good wood, this,' he remarked, 'and it's amazing how old wood will come up if it's planed and treated right.'

Ada stared. 'Make summat from it, do you mean?'

'Aye, table tops with the wood we take out. And them stone troughs there,' he pointed to the long wall, 'would come in handy for bases.'

Ada came forward eagerly. 'Could you do that? It'd save me a bob or two if I didn't have all them tables to buy.'

He smiled. 'I'm used to knocking things up. If you can borrow some tools and provide the nails and paint, I can do the rest.'

He spoke with an air of quiet confidence she found appealing, but she was still uneasy. 'You do realize what you're taking on?' she murmured. 'Even if the girls and me do all the scrubbing—'

He grinned. 'I'm not daft. I know.'

Ada bit her lip. 'I couldn't afford to pay much.'

'No pay,' he replied quickly, and waved towards a stall. 'I can sleep here while I work, and a good hot dinner at night – that'd see me right. How's that suit you? I can soon have the place ship-shape.'

Ada thought it over. 'All the mills and shops will be shutting down week after next for Wakes Week,' she murmured, 'and folk'll be away on holiday. Reckon it could be ready to open for when they get back?'

'Oh aye,' said Will, 'if we get cracking straight away.'

Ada turned and headed outside, away from the foetid stench of the stable, into the street, heavy with the odour from the gasworks. 'Right,' she said purposefully, 'I'll go straight round to the railway office and sign up for that lease before anybody else beats me to it.'

THIRTY-FIVE

For over a week now they'd been hard at work on the stables. The muck and filth which had accumulated and decayed ever since last winter had been shifted, trundled out in heavy barrow-loads, then the whole place scrubbed and bleached till Will was able to make a start on the rebuilding.

Ada could feel her eagerness deepening into excitement. May too seemed to be full of energy and enthusiasm, though Ada was careful to see to it that she only did the lighter jobs.

'We can't have you overstraining yourself, lass,' she warned, 'otherwise your milk'll dry up and that'll never do.'

Baby Rose seemed content enough, lying propped in her crib on the floor, sucking her fingers and watching every move with big violet eyes.

Ada threw the scrubbing brush back into the pail of water and stood, hands on hips. 'Them big doors where they used to bring the carts in,' she said thoughtfully, pointing to the high double-door entrance, 'they could come in handy. We could just use the little door when it comes cold in the winter and we can keep them big ones open wide when the weather's hot like it is now.'

Will stopped hammering and straightened. 'Aye,' he agreed, 'and if we could get hold of a bit more wood you could even have a bench or two for folk to sit outside if the weather's right.'

'That'd be a sight better than eating your snap sitting on a mill-yard wall,' May grunted as she wheeled the empty barrow back in.

Ada nodded. 'Aye well, first things first. Let's hope we get enough backsides in here for a start.'

It was worth looking into though, she thought. Somebody must know of some demolition work going on where she might be able to come by a bit more wood. It needn't cost much – she could bargain with the best of them. She was beginning to feel like a child at Christmas, full of bubbling anticipation.

As the hammer thudded, Ada's thoughts raced. Today Millsbridge had virtually emptied out, half the residents having scraped their pennies together to get away to the sea-side for Wakes Week. Next Monday, however, the millhands would all be back at their looms, the shop assistants at their counters, and the clerks at their desks. If this blazing weather continued she'd need to offer cold snacks as well as hot meals. One way or another she had to entice the customers in or the whole venture would collapse round her ears.

The small door through one of the double doors opened and a girl's figure stood silhouetted in the shaft of blinding sunlight. Will's hammer fell silent. Ada shielded her eyes against the glare.

'Cassie!' exclaimed May, moving forward to meet her. 'What are you doing here?'

Ada frowned. 'What's up?' she asked. 'I wasn't expecting you.'

'Nowt's up. Why should it be?'

'Then either pick up that broom and give us a hand or shove off. We've no time to waste.'

The girl came forward, May's arm about her shoulders as she cast a smile at Will. Then she disentangled herself and bent to coo to the baby. She looked uncommonly pretty with the sun burnishing the tumble of long bright hair.

'The Chadwicks have gone off to Scarborough for a couple of days,' she explained. 'So I thought I'd have another look in to see how you was getting on.'

May lifted the baby from the crib. Ada saw Cassie's eyes fasten on Will as he bent over his work, and she guessed why

372

the girl had come. May handed the baby to Cassie.

'Here, you can nurse her for a bit. I've got to nip down to the cobbler's.'

Ada carried on sweeping wood-shavings into a pile in the corner. Cassie swung the baby up and down gently, cooing to her as she sidled over to stand beside Will. For a time he continued working while she watched him closely.

'You're very good at this,' she remarked after a while, then gave him a smile. 'Anybody would think you'd done it before, chopping up a stable and turning it into a dining room.'

He paused to look down at her and grinned. 'I've done all sorts of things in my time but I like wood. I'm really at home with a good bit of oak.'

He wiped the back of his hand across his mouth and turned to Ada. 'I think I'll have a bit of a break now, Mrs Turnbull,' he said. 'I need a drink to slake me thirst, I've that much sawdust in me throat.'

Ada propped her broom against the wall. 'I've some home-made ginger beer back at the house – I'll fetch you some,' she offered.

'No, it's all right,' said Cassie, laying the baby back in the crib. 'You just carry on – I'll see to it.'

As she watched Cassie step through the small door and then Will duck to follow, Ada shook her head. It was no good. Cassie seemed to thrive on teasing. Once a flirt, always a flirt. She wasn't ready to get wed, not yet by a long chalk. If she went ahead with her plan, that Harold Jordan didn't know what he was letting himself in for.

Harold was happy. His world was complete. Business was flourishing and the delectable Cassie, who could have had her pick of at least a dozen men in Hawksmoor, had agreed to marry him.

There was a bounce in his step as he turned the corner into Cedar Street and his head was buzzing with plans. He'd have himself measured for a new suit – no, two, dammit, why not? Best Hawksmoor worsted, with a pin-stripe, maybe. He'd always fancied himself in pin-stripe but restricted himself to plain black and dark clerical grey for the job.

And he'd arrange to take Cassie up to the new house again to discuss the décor before the painters moved in. Judging by her taste in clothes she'd have a good eye for these things.

Then suddenly the breath caught in his throat. There she was ahead of him, as though thinking of her had somehow conjured her up! She hadn't said she'd be off work today. Involuntarily he hastened his step, and then he became aware of the young man at her side. Harold couldn't see his face but he didn't look familiar.

He slowed his steps and watched. Cassie was looking up at the fellow's face and laughing. As they reached her door she took out a key and unlocked it, and the young man followed her indoors.

A sudden spurt of jealousy leapt in him. Don't be ridiculous, he told himself, he's probably only a tradesman. Even so, he couldn't resist following in their footsteps and as he reached the open door he could hear Cassie's tinkling laugh.

Through the doorway he could see her bending over the table, pouring something from a jug into a glass. The young fellow sat waiting. Cassie looked up and spotted him.

'Harold! Come on in and meet Will,' she said brightly. 'Will – this is Mr Jordan, a neighbour of ours.' She smiled up at Harold. 'Will's doing some work on the stables for Mam. Would you like a drink of ginger beer?'

'No thanks,' he answered gruffly. He couldn't explain, even to himself, why it hurt to see the two of them at the table. They looked right together, of similar age, both full of the glow of youth.

Will tossed back the last of the drink and stood up. 'Nice to meet you, Mr Jordan,' he said cheerily. 'Thanks, Cassie. I'd best be getting back now.' And then he was gone.

Harold stood uncomfortably by the door, uncertain what to say. 'Good-looking lad, isn't he?' he murmured at last.

Cassie shrugged. 'Not bad. He's doing a great job down there for Mam – you'll have to go and see what he's done.'

He tried hard to sound casual. 'Where did you come across him? He doesn't belong around here, does he?'

'He's a friend of May's – she met him down south somewhere. Which reminds me – May wants me to take care of the baby for a while so I'd best go back and relieve Mam.'

So he was the older girl's young man. Relief surged through him. As he turned to go Cassie laid a hand on his sleeve.

'You didn't think he was with me, did you?' she asked softly. 'Surely not?'

'No,' he replied quickly, too quickly. 'Of course not.'

'Only you should know by now,' she murmured softly, 'young men don't interest me. I'd much rather have a mature man. They have so much more to offer. Now,' she added, inching her fingers up his arm, 'how do you fancy walking me back up the road?'

Aaron Rose stood looking out of the window over the sunlit lawns. Adele could sense that he was in a sullen mood yet again today, and she ventured to speak in a timid, tentative voice.

'Had a good day, dear?' A silly question, she reproved herself the moment she'd spoken. His stiff back and jutting lip showed all too clearly that the day had not gone well at all.

'Bloody awful,' he muttered without turning. Adele blundered on.

'Is it your father again? Is that it?'

Aaron turned to her, his face thunderously dark. 'Isn't it always? I get blamed for everything,' he growled. 'According to him I can't do anything right.'

Adele moved closer. 'Oh, that's not true, and you know it,' she said soothingly. 'It's just a mood he's in.'

Aaron scowled. 'What would you know about it? According to him I'm only half a man. He wants to know when he can expect a grandchild. There's a laugh.'

Adele's fingers flew to her lips. 'Did you tell him?'

Aaron snorted. 'How could I? He's enough trouble right

now with the business without being told his son's wife is barren.'

Adele winced at the venom in the last word. 'I'm sorry,' she murmured. 'Does it matter so much to you?'

'Matter?' He snorted and turned away. Adele hurried after him.

'You said it was me you wanted – didn't you mean it? You never said I was only here to give you children.'

The pathetic tone in her voice clearly irritated him. He brushed her hand away. 'Every man wants a child of his own,' he snapped. 'Why the devil didn't you tell me before we got married? It's the deceit that hurts.'

Adele could feel the tears beginning to prick her eyes. 'I wasn't to know till the doctor said, and we were engaged by then. It wasn't my fault, and anyway I thought it was me that you wanted.'

Aaron wasn't listening. 'Every time I see Mother she keeps asking if you're in the family way yet. I can't go on like this, knowing they're watching and waiting. They've no idea . . .'

He whirled round to face her. 'And that's another thing – your parents knew about this before the wedding – they cheated us. They took damn good care my father didn't find out before they signed the marriage contract.'

Adele felt deeply hurt. She couldn't help the tear trickling down her cheek. 'You only stood to gain from it,' she said miserably. 'You got Father's business along with me.'

Aaron planted his hands on his hips and glared. 'And who are we to hand it on to if there are no little Roses, may I ask?'

'Couldn't we adopt a baby?' Adele offered timidly.

'That's not the same,' he growled. 'It wouldn't be our flesh and blood. They'd never accept it.'

Adele was growing desperate. 'Couldn't we pretend it was ours then?'

He threw up an impatient hand. 'For God's sake stop talking rubbish,' he muttered, and then groaned. 'Why the devil did I have to get saddled with you?'

Adele brushed away the tears and stood her ground. 'Are you going to punish me for the rest of our days?' she asked quietly, trying hard to hide the catch in her voice.

'Don't you think you deserve it?' he replied coldly.

She saw his hand drop angrily on the doorlatch, then he wrested the french windows open and strode out into the garden. She heard his footsteps crunch quickly away down the gravel path.

She sat miserably on the sofa, twisting between her fingers the thick gold wedding band, the symbol of the start of all her wretchedness.

'*You'd best have a word with the doctor about you having the curse so often,*' Mother had advised as she pored over the growing guest list. '*There might be something he can prescribe. You don't want to be saddled with that on your honeymoon.*'

But Adele had not been prepared for the doctor's verdict. His words had knocked the stuffing out of her, words so technical she hadn't been able to follow them, but his gist was clear enough.

'*Constitutional abnormality . . . conception is impossible . . . nothing that can be done . . . have to resign yourself, I'm afraid . . .*'

She'd sat afterwards in the restaurant of the big department store, waiting for Mother, and feeling as if her whole world had collapsed. Strange how one could walk into a surgery full of confidence and hope, and come out again deflated and totally demoralized. There had been a momentary feeling of relief that she'd never have to undergo the horrific pain of childbirth which Mother had described so often and so graphically, but it had soon given way to an overwhelming sense of failure.

Even as she sat toying with the slice of gingerbread cake it was hard to take in. In years to come she'd never be able to sit sipping tea and talking animatedly with her daughter like that well-dressed woman at the corner table.

Like Mother. She'd wanted so much to be her mother's

daughter, capable of taking control in every situation, only with a little more style perhaps. Mother couldn't help her humble origins, of course, but in spite of the family's hard-earned wealth, every once in a while they did force their way through the thin veneer of gentility. '*Muck come up,*' Adele had heard one of the carters describe her as he loaded a set of Queen Anne chairs into the wagon, and she'd vowed the staff would never see her that way. After all, she spoke nicely, moved well after all those deportment lessons, and her parents indulged her lovingly, just as her new bridegroom would do – she'd felt every inch a lady, in complete control of her life. Until that visit to the surgery . . .

Mother was late meeting her in the restaurant. It was Father who arrived first to take them home, and he sat listening, chewing the tip of his thumbnail as she'd poured the news out to him.

'*What'll I do, Father?*' she'd wailed. '*How can I break it to Aaron?*'

Father had taken her hand. '*I know it must be a big shock, love, but I'd hold my tongue if I were you. There's no doubt the boy loves you and that's all he's bothered about, I'm sure. I'd tell no-one.*'

'*There's Mother—*'

'*I wouldn't even tell her. You've come this far, the wedding's all fixed – it'd only spoil things. Anyway, your mother's revelling in it, getting everything organized. The reception's all booked – I'd just keep this between you and me – it'll not go any further.*'

'*But what's going to happen when Aaron finds out? He's bound to, sooner or later.*'

Father's hand had been warm over hers. '*One step at a time. There's always ways and means – as a last resort, there's always adoption. You just get on with it. It's not the end of the world.*'

Adele sighed. She'd been wrong to listen to Father's advice, just because it suited her. She should never have deceived Aaron. Now he knew about it, she'd lost her position of control for ever. Now she was the culprit who had to sue for peace and forgiveness, and it was a losing battle . . .

A breeze fanned the back of her neck as the french windows opened once more and Aaron strode in. He flung himself down in the far chair and snatched up the newspaper.

'I'm sorry,' Adele murmured. 'I was wrong—'

'My God, you were,' he cut in sharply.

'—to think you loved me,' she went on. 'But if there's anything I can do to put things right – anything at all . . .'

Aaron turned and gave her a weary, defeated look. 'You could tell my father yourself. Oh, God help us when he finds out . . .'

Ada stretched her arms above her head and yawned.

'I don't know about you, lass, but I'm ready for me bed,' she said sleepily. 'I'm whacked.'

'Me too,' said May. 'But it's well worth it. The place is coming on a real treat.'

'Aye,' agreed Ada. 'Even Mr Jordan said it looked fair grand. I wonder he didn't think of taking over them stables for himself. Any road, he was having a word or two with Will so I reckon he told him it was a good bit of work and all.'

'He did – Will told me.' May smiled as she busied herself folding napkins. 'In fact he asked Will if he had any more work on hand after this job. If not, he said he'd be willing to give him a trial at his place.'

'Did he now?' Ada mulled over this piece of information for a moment. 'Cassie said Mr Jordan was looking for a new foreman to take over the yard. The lad could end up with his own house if he suits. He could be a neighbour of ours.'

'Ah well,' said May with a quiet, contented sigh, 'it remains to be seen.'

After supper Harold went down to the workshop to do his routine check that all had been left as it should be. As he crossed the cobbled yard he could hear a man's voice bellowing up the street. That tipsy Irishman again, he grumbled to himself, on his way to the Fleece, no doubt. In an hour or two he'd be staggering back, probably singing and swearing raucously. It would be good to get away from this seedy street at last to the more salubrious Thornhill Road.

In the workshop the warmth of the day still lingered under the low ceiling, scented with the sweet, clean familiarity of wood-shavings, and he found it comforting. Though the light through the little window was dimming fast he was in no hurry.

He sat on the bench, gazing around him in the dusky twilight. They'd left the place tidy enough, Arthur and Jessop, the new man. Pity the two of them didn't hit it off together, and it wasn't that Jessop's standards were too exacting for the lad. Arthur was willing enough, and capable, but like Harold himself, he couldn't abide the new manager's grudging, grouchy ways. Harold had tried speaking to him about it.

'It'd help if you put a smile on your face now and again,' he'd pointed out.

'Oh aye?' Jessop had growled, eyebrows arched. 'I thought as this were a funeral parlour, not the palace of varieties. Death's nowt to smile about. You won't catch me having a laugh about that.'

'Happen not,' Harold retorted, 'but clients need a bit of a smile – not too much, mind you, just enough to make 'em feel welcome.'

That was the trouble, he thought. Folk didn't recognize the skill of being a good undertaker, the judgement needed to keep a balance between the sombre expression of the mute pall-bearer and the cheerful good will of the man willing to ease the burden of death in any way he could.

Jessop wasn't interested in the niceties. He'd simply snorted and carried on planing. The casket was finished now, lying over there on the bench, gleaming dully in the twilight. He was a fair-enough craftsman but his manner wouldn't do for the biggest and best undertaker's in Hawksmoor. He'd have to go, whether or not, just as soon as the right man could be found to replace him.

Harold eased his weight off the bench and moved across to where the casket lay. The wood felt smooth and warm to the touch, like living flesh, like Cassie's vibrant young body. He felt a shiver of pleasure at the thought. His little Cassie, who'd promised to become his wife.

His wife. For a moment Harold stood stock-still, shocked into a memory he'd tried so hard to forget. It was here he'd stood that night, tugging at Fanny's flaccid old flesh, trying to pull her from the coffin where she'd bled her life away. Poor Fanny, poor foolish, desperate Fanny.

And what had driven her to such despair? A lump formed in his throat. Silly and irritating she might have been, but she didn't deserve that. Maybe he could have done something – if he'd treated her differently, more kindly, with more under-standing – she might still be here. If he'd gone to look for her that night instead of leaving her alone – he might have reached her in time to save her . . .

But then a shameful thought occurred – if he had, he wouldn't have this rosy future ahead of him with his beautiful Cassie. Oh Fanny, I didn't want you to die, but because you're dead and I'm free, a whole new future beckons . . . Even so . . .

A sob rattled in his throat. Tears were blinding his eyes. He let go of the coffin and groped in his pocket for his handkerchief, then sank on his knees on the cool stone floor.

'I'm sorry, Fanny,' he sobbed, 'I'm right sorry. You weren't a bad wife – I could have behaved better. I tret you real bad. Oh love, I'm so sorry.'

For a long time he knelt there, overcome by grief and guilt. By the time the tears had sobbed themselves out darkness had fallen and the workshop was shrouded in gloom. Harold rose stiffly and blew his nose hard, then locked up and walked slowly back up the shadowed yard to the house. It was odd, he thought, but somehow he felt strangely calm and cleansed.

He was totally unaware of the small boy squatting, huddled, in the shadows behind the rubbish bin, clutching his throbbing cheek and holding his breath in terror.

THIRTY-SIX

July continued in a blaze of glorious weather. May and Ada held their breath as the dining room opened and they waited for customers to arrive. At first it was only a trickle of curious shoppers who must have relayed the news to their menfolk for the next day brought a steady stream of millworkers, most of them gagging for a drink in the heat.

'There's more sitting outside drinking than in here eating,' remarked Ada, wiping a hand across her forehead. 'Never mind, it's brass they're spending and that's what counts.'

May laid a tray down on the counter and wiped away the spills. 'Jack Smedley's one of them out there,' she said. 'He says he didn't want to poke his nose in but if there's owt you want doing . . .'

'Aye,' said Ada, 'there is. Tell him he can go and get his handcart and fetch me some more dandelion and burdock ready for morning.'

August blazed even more blisteringly hot than July. Ada sat at the kitchen table after supper, the door to the street wide open to catch a cooling breeze, while she totted up the week's takings. May was ticking off the bills and Elsie stood, finger in mouth and one foot twisted round the other calf, watching in amazement as her mother heaped piles of coins in neat rows. She'd never seen such wealth in her life.

She took the finger out of her mouth. 'Bet the King doesn't have that much money,' she said, waving a sticky forefinger towards the table. 'Is he as rich as us?'

Her mother shook her head and carried on counting.

'Can I come and work with you and May?' Elsie went on. 'All of us together?'

May smiled. 'Not yet, love. When you're old enough to leave school, happen.'

Elsie pulled a face. 'No point me going back to school for all the good it does me,' she grumbled. 'Any road, I make dumplings as good as yours – Mam said so. Can I be the dumpling-maker?'

Ada made a note of the final figure. 'Dumplings are for winter, love. Now get me that canvas bag out of the scullery to put this lot in, there's a good girl.'

As the child scampered out May passed a sheet of paper across to her mother. 'There's just this vegetable bill to pay – the rest's seen to,' she said.

Ada wiped the sweat off her forehead and laid the paper alongside her final figure and compared the two. 'By heck,' she murmured wonderingly, 'we've made ends meet again.'

May smiled. 'There you are, even though you kept worrying about food going off in the heat.'

'It did and all – more than I bargained for.'

'We had to allow for some loss. We're still making a small profit.'

'It's going great,' said Ada. 'If we keep on pulling them in at this rate we'll be able to start paying Mr Jordan off. To think we had hardly anybody in the first week.'

'Word's getting around,' said May. 'At least we're paying our way and a bit over. It'll get better week by week, you'll see.'

'Course it will, specially when winter comes on,' replied her mother. 'We'll make us fortunes yet, you and me.'

'And Cassie too,' added May, fingering a pile of coins. 'If she's to marry Mr Jordan she'll be well-set-up.'

Ada's smile fell away. 'Aye,' she muttered. 'I just hope it doesn't all end in tears.'

May shook her head. 'I doubt it. Cassie always knows what she's doing.'

'Does she? Is he fit to have a wife after what happened to Mrs Jordan?'

Elsie came back and laid the bag on the table. May began scooping up handfuls of coins and shoving them inside. 'Like I said,' she murmured, 'Cassie's not daft. And once she's set her mind on something—'

'She'll have it, whether or not. I know,' sighed Ada. 'Ah well, we'll just have to let her stew in her own juice.'

Elsie laid a hand on her mother's arm. 'I could do that – I could stew juice for you—'

'Off to bed with you, young lady,' said Ada as she twisted the top of the bag and knotted it tightly. 'Will Napier'll be here any minute for his bath. Off you go, and mind you don't wake the baby.'

May brought the zinc bath in from the yard and placed it ready before the fire. When Will turned up she took her time about ladling the hot water out of the range while he took off his neckerchief and began unbuttoning his jacket.

'I look forward to Saturday night,' he said with a grin. 'Having me bath – it reminds me of home when I was little and my mother used to set about me with the scrubbing brush.'

She smiled. 'If you move into Mr Jordan's house you'll be able to have a bath as often as you like.'

He sat down to pull off his boots. 'Chance'd be a fine thing. Let's hope.'

May left him to it and went to sit in the scullery with Ada. She could hear the splash of water as he stepped in, then his voice as he started to sing. It was nice having a man in the house again, singing cheerfully like Dad used to in the old days before his accident. Will seemed at home here. She hoped he'd get that job permanently with Mr Jordan, but she was in no hurry for him to stop coming round.

'Did you pull the kettle over the hob?' her mother asked.

'Yes.'

'He'll want a cup of tea once he's dry and dressed. Your dad always did.'

* * *

Will drank the tea, put down the cup and then turned to May.

'That was grand, thanks. Fancy a walk down by the cut? It's a lovely night for a stroll.'

May glanced quickly at her mother, and then nodded. 'Yes, I'd like that – it'll be a bit cooler now.'

'Take your time,' said Ada. 'It's Sunday tomorrow – you can have a lie-in in the morning.'

They'd just left the house when Jack Smedley tapped at the open door. He pulled off his cap and smiled apologetically.

'I was on me way home – I thought as how I'd just look in and see you was all right for the morning,' he explained. 'Is there owt you want?'

'It's Sunday – I'm not opening tomorrow.'

Ada looked him up and down, taking in the streaks of coal-dust on his face and the grimy state of his clothes. He saw her look and flushed.

'I'm sorry – I've just come off shift,' he muttered. 'I shouldn't have called.'

Ada stood back, jerking her head in the direction of the living room. 'Come on in,' she said gruffly. 'There's a bath full of water still hot by the fire. Get them filthy things off and get in.'

For a moment he stared, then smiled and wiped his boots hard on the mat. 'I will and gladly,' he said eagerly. 'I shan't have any hot water at home.'

He came in and tossed his cap on a chair. 'There's nowt like having your back scrubbed for you – it fair makes you feel coddled,' he said.

Poor man, thought Ada. He hadn't been pampered since his Brenda left. 'And what makes you think you're going to have it scrubbed tonight?' she growled. 'I offered you a bath, that's all.'

He glanced back at her, his grubby face wreathed in a mischievous grin. 'A man can hope, can't he?'

'Go on with you,' she grunted. 'Get in while it's still hot.'

She turned to go, but in the doorway she paused. 'Just give us a shout when you're ready.'

It was not yet seven in the morning but already Ada could feel the warmth of the sun on her back as she pegged out the baby's nappies before setting off for work. Old Mrs Boothroyd's head suddenly appeared over the yard wall.

'Not much to hang out these days,' she remarked. 'Not like the old days, eh?'

'No, thank God,' replied Ada. 'I can't think why I didn't pack it in sooner.'

'Business doing all right, is it?' wheezed the old lady. 'They say the strike's spreading – railway men and carters, it is now.'

'So I heard, but it hasn't affected us yet. I just wish they were drinking less and eating more.'

The curlered head nodded. 'It's only while this weather lasts. Folk say how good it is at your place, and cheap too,' she murmured. 'Only don't you work too hard. You don't want to go knocking yourself up, love. It takes a while to get over having a baby, specially at your age.'

Ada smiled. 'Not to worry, Mrs Boothroyd. May takes her share of the work. She's a good 'un, is our May.'

'Aye, she is,' agreed the old lady. 'Shall we be hearing wedding bells afore long?'

Ada looked up sharply. 'How do you mean?'

'I see that young man of hers is still around. Handsome young fellow, he is.'

'Will, do you mean?' asked Ada. 'Oh, he's not her young man, he's just a friend.'

'Oh dear, I've put me foot in it. Only you could have fooled me. They seem to get on right well, him and May. I heard they was out walking together.'

'Very likely.'

'Late at night, down the towpath – holding hands, they were.'

Ada smiled to herself and clipped the last peg into place.

386

'That's it,' she said. 'Now I'm off to work, and judging by the feel of it we're in for another scorcher.'

That evening May walked again with Will along the towpath. After another day cooped up in the sweltering heat of the dining room it was refreshing to feel the cool breeze against her cheek and watch the slow ripple of the water. And it was pleasant to have Will's easy company all to herself.

'How's your baby?' he asked. 'Cut a tooth yet?'

She looked up at him archly. 'Whose baby?'

He laughed. 'Your mother's – your little sister Rosie.'

'She's fine.'

They sauntered on a little further, past the gasworks and on towards the open fields. 'Your trial's all about up,' May remarked. 'Will Mr Jordan keep you on, do you think?'

He glanced down and in the dim light she could make out his grin. 'Would you like me to stay on, May?'

She felt the blush rise to her cheek. 'Don't be silly, of course I would. We all would.'

Will stopped and turned to her. 'I'm glad. He told me today I could move into the house as soon as he's gone. You see before you the new foreman of Jordan's yard.'

She looked up, genuine pleasure flooding through her. 'Oh Will, I'm so glad. And Mam will be tickled pink.'

Will smiled. 'He's not daft, you know, your Mr Jordan. It's not an easy time for me to take over, not with this strike spreading. When it comes time to go down to the timber yard for more wood, it'll be me that has to take the cart. There's bound to be pickets, and it's not Mr Jordan who's going to have to face them. Things are getting bad.'

May nodded thoughtfully. 'I heard some of the customers talking – you can tell they're worried. They're afraid the mills will run out of wool and they might be put on short time.'

'The papers say there was a riot in Liverpool,' said Will gloomily. 'Troops were called out. It's going to get worse before it gets better.' He moved closer and took her hand.

'Still, don't let's dwell on that,' he murmured. 'We've got good news to celebrate, haven't we?'

She gazed up at him, aware of his face close to her own, his calloused hand firm and strong on hers. 'Yes,' she whispered. 'You've got a good steady job and a new house. Let's go home and tell Mam – I think she might find something stronger than ginger beer to drink a toast.'

'I've got a better idea,' murmured Will, and he bent his head to touch his lips to hers.

'As if I haven't got enough on my plate as it is,' snapped Henry Rose. 'What with goods not being delivered and having to let some of my best customers down – it can't go on like this.'

Aaron said nothing. There was nothing he could say. Father was right. If things went on this way the business would be in trouble.

'So I'm sick to the back teeth of your mother pestering me every day and all. I can't get out of the house fast enough. Is there owt I can tell her?'

'No, Father.'

Henry sighed. 'We'd be suspecting there was summat wrong with you but we know there can't be – not after that other business last year.'

Aaron's bottom lip jutted. Father was never going to let him forget that one stupid slip with a girl of no account.

Henry darted him a sudden look of suspicion. 'Hey – you haven't caught what your mother calls the nasty woman's disease, have you?'

Pained, Aaron sighed. It was time he put a stop to this ritual embarrassing interrogation. 'No, Father,' he said quietly. 'It's not me, it's Adele – she's barren.'

There, it was out. His father stared at him blankly for a moment before words stuttered to his lips. 'Barren? You mean she'll never have children?'

'No, Father. It's unfortunate, but there it is.'

'Unfortunate? It's a bloody tragedy! How long have you known?'

Aaron shrugged. 'A little while.'

'But are you sure it's right? Couldn't it be a mistake?'

'While we were engaged she had a bit of what she called women's problems and went to see her doctor. He told her she'd never be able to conceive. She had an abnormality of some kind.'

Henry stared, open-mouthed. 'You mean she knew before she married you?'

Aaron turned away with an irritable snort. 'What's it matter now? The point is, there will be no grandchild so you can both stop going on about it.'

Henry's face turned purple. 'What's it matter?' he raged. 'It matters because if Sidney Rabin knew, he cheated me! I've been made a right fool of! A fat lot of good it is getting the business together if I've no heir to leave it to!'

'You've got me.'

'And who'll inherit after you? Her sister's kids, that's who! Naomi's already engaged, isn't she? I planned this wedding so my grandchild would inherit the lot! My God!'

'Adele and I have talked about adopting,' Aaron said tentatively.

His father waved a dismissive hand. 'That's not the same,' he wailed. 'It wouldn't be our flesh and blood.'

He leaned on the desk and buried his face in his hands. Aaron could hear him almost sobbing into his fingertips. 'The old bastard,' he moaned. 'Palming his barren daughter off on us – I bet Sidney Rabin was laughing up his sleeve when we shook hands on the deal.'

Aaron touched his shoulder. 'You'll have to put a good face on it.' He turned to look out of the window. 'I wouldn't tell Mother yet either,' he added. 'Like you said, we've enough on our plate right now.'

Henry looked up and scowled. 'It's going to take some getting used to, this not having a grandchild to take over the business – such as it is. And don't think I'm going to break

389

it to your mother; not me – she'll go hysterical. I'll leave that to you.'

Later in the day Henry strode into Aaron's office, the scowl now vanished from his ruddy face and instead a bright look of hope. 'Listen,' he said eagerly, 'that girl in our workroom – the one you messed about with . . .'

'Oh, not that again,' Aaron sighed.

'No, listen,' Henry went on breathlessly, 'I saw her the other week – in Harris's shop. She's not pregnant any more. I wonder . . .'

'Really, Father,' Aaron said irritably, 'I thought you'd put that out of your head. It was all done and finished with last year.'

'I wonder was it a boy?' his father mused. 'A son, a little Rose . . . Just think.'

Aaron stared for a moment, following his father's drift, then shook his head. 'She might have got rid of it for all we know. It makes no odds anyway. Adele would go up the wall if she knew about that.'

'I don't know,' said Henry slowly, 'not if you make her see sense. If you're thinking of adopting anyway – what could be better? That child is your flesh and blood no matter who the mother.'

Aaron rubbed his chin. Maybe Father had a point. If Adele was made to realize – the inheritance would go to the first-born . . .

'What was that girl called?' Henry asked. 'Turner, was it? No, Turnbull, that's it. Where does she live?'

Aaron grew irritated. 'How the devil should I know? She could have moved anyway. You paid her good money to get out of our lives, remember.'

Henry turned away, unflustered. 'We'll find her, wherever she is. Even if her address isn't in our records, Harris will probably know.'

'And then what?'

Henry shrugged. 'If she's still got the child, make her an

offer no girl of her sort could possibly refuse. Let's just hope she hasn't already got rid of it.'

Cassie was brimming over with excitement the next time she came home. She could hardly wait to get inside before she burst out with the news.

'I've given me notice,' she announced proudly. 'I'm leaving Chadwicks next week and moving into Thornhill Road with Harold.'

'Already?' said Ada in surprise. 'Is it finished then?'

'It looks wonderful – you'll have to come up and see it, you and May, just as soon as I've got the furniture arranged to my liking.'

May smiled. 'So we'll be seeing you shifting it out across the road, will we? That'll have all the neighbours out in the street.'

'Not all of it,' Cassie replied. 'Harold's only taking some of the best stuff from here. He's taking me down to Rose's to have a look at what they've got. That way he can leave enough for Will to move in.'

'Very thoughtful of him,' murmured Ada.

'Well, I told him I'd rather have new. I don't want all his Fanny's stuff around me.'

May sat, chin cupped in hands, listening. 'How long do you think you're going to get away with this housekeeper story, talking like that?' she asked.

Cassie did a pirouette on the hearthrug. 'I won't have to for long,' she said happily. 'Harold's decided he'll end up in Storthes Hall if he has to wait a year for me. So I've agreed to marry him at Christmas.'

THIRTY-SEVEN

Cassie's announcement weighed heavily on Ada's mind. If it was what the girl wanted, all well and good, but if only she could make sure Harold Jordan would treat her right . . . She'd have to have a private word with him.

The opportunity came sooner than she thought. It was Friday evening and trade had been slack all week in the dining room now that many of the millhands were being laid off. May had already taken the baby home for her evening feed and Ada had long since finished clearing up. Only a couple of drinkers sat outside in the yard, and one of them was Jack Smedley who seemed reluctant ever to leave the place. Ada decided she might as well shut down early.

She locked the doors and headed for home. At every street corner cloth-capped men seemed to be lounging against lamp posts and walls, a restless, hungry look in their eyes. Poor devils. This damn strike was hitting everybody one way or another.

A rather well-dressed man just ahead of her was about to turn into Cedar Street and she recognized him as Harold Jordan. She hurried to catch up.

'Mr Jordan, I'd like a word with you.'

He looked startled as he doffed his hat. 'Good evening, Mrs Turnbull,' he murmured, slowing his step to match hers. 'What can I do for you?'

'It's what you can do for our Cass,' she replied. 'Look, I know I'm beholden to you but I've got to speak me mind.'

'Do, by all means,' he replied politely. 'After all, I'm soon to be family.'

'That's what I'm on about, you and my Cass. You know I was against this from the start, you being so much older than her.'

'Well, yes,' he admitted, 'the whole arrangement must seem somewhat irregular, but—'

'Irregular?' retorted Ada. 'It's downright immoral, a man and a girl sharing the same house.'

'Oh my dear lady, I do assure you it will be perfectly proper – I have a great deal of respect for Cassie – I intend to behave as a gentleman should.'

Ada sniffed. 'It's not only that that bothers me – I saw the way you used to treat your wife. Don't you forget, I was there at the end. I saw you without your shine on.'

'I know you did,' he muttered. 'And I still feel ashamed of meself.'

'But whatever I think, Cassie's set her heart on it. There's nowt I can do to stop the pair of you. She seems to think the world of you so I reckon I'll have to go along with it—'

His anxious expression gave way to a broad smile. 'That's very good of you, Mrs Turnbull. I can't tell you how relieved—'

'—but only if you make sure you treat our Cassie right,' Ada went on firmly, pulling up as she reached her front door. 'Don't you ever dare treat her the way you tret your Fanny, or you'll have me to answer to. Good night, Mr Jordan.'

As Ada swept into the house she felt at least she'd done what she could for Cassie; the rest was up to her.

'The takings are right down again this week, lass. We're going to have to think of summat.'

May surveyed her mother's worried face with concern. 'I don't know what else we can do, I'm sure. We've got the best deal we can from the wholesalers and cut right back on perishable stuff – what else is there?'

Ada's lips set in a hard line. 'I know one thing – I don't want to close down. We've still got to be there when this strike's over.'

May nodded. 'Times are tough all right, all them folk out of work, not enough money coming in for a decent meal. That's what they need.' She chewed her lip for a moment. 'That's a thought – how about us just providing a good nourishing meal on the cheap? Turn the place into a kind of soup kitchen for a while?'

Ada stared. 'We can't run a charity, May. We can't afford it.'

'We can't even afford to pay the rent if we go on like this. Look, we know about making good cheap broth. We could buy bones and scrag-ends, use them to build up a good stock pot, plenty of vegetables – we can sell it for coppers and they'll know they're getting a decent meal inside them.'

Ada considered. 'If we could sell enough . . .'

'We can talk to all the wholesalers and local butchers, starting with Mr Brierley. I'm sure they'll help us if they want our custom when all this is over.'

'And we'd still keep our customers when they get back to work . . .'

'There'd be no shortage of takers, I'm sure. It's the only way, Mam. We've got to try.'

Ada nodded. 'You're right. Shall I go and see Mr Brierley, or will you?'

May stood up. 'I will – I'll go now.'

Ada smiled. 'Aye, lass, you do. I thought I was good at haggling but you've got me beat into a cocked hat. Go on then, leave the little 'un with me.'

Mrs Boothroyd thought it was a great idea.

'But have you got enough big pans, Ada lass?' she asked. 'I can let you have a lend of my brass preserving pan if you want it – I never get round to using it these days – and I know Mrs Tandy's got one and all.'

May tackled Mrs Tandy. She straightened up from donkey-stoning her front doorstep, a worried frown on her face.

'Well,' she said dubiously, 'so long as you let me have it

back in time for the plum season – Mr Tandy can't abide a scone without a bit of my home-made plum jam.'

Reassured, she handed it over, its brass gleaming like the Crown Jewels. 'It was me mother's, and me grandma's before her,' she confided proudly. 'Polished every week that was, without fail. She was a very particular woman, me mother. Folk used to say she were that house-proud that when she'd finished the range she'd go out and blacklead the tram lines and all. Only she didn't, of course.'

'I'll see you get it back safe,' May promised.

The big brass pan stood on Ada's kitchen table alongside Mrs Boothroyd's. Elsie fingered the gleaming brass.

'Are they cold-runs?' she asked.

'Are they what?' said Ada absently.

'Cold-runs, like what witches have. Mrs Boothroyd looks like a witch sometimes.'

'Pearl barley,' said her mother. 'Remind me to tell May to put a sack on the order list. It's famous stuff for purifying the blood and it'll thicken up our broth nicely.'

Henry Rose did his best to make his question sound casual. He didn't want to point out its importance by tackling Harris in his shop, but he knew the draper was in the habit of looking in at the Conservative Club on half-closing day.

So Henry had been hanging around in the Club, a glass of wine on the table in front of him, for the best part of an hour before he saw his quarry come into the room.

A couple of the other fellows nodded to Harris and he joined them at the bar. Henry strolled across, glass in hand. A few polite words, and then he plunged in.

'Oh, by the way, Harris,' he said nonchalantly, 'you know that girl who was in your shop the day I called to see you? The one who used to work at my place?'

'May Turnbull, do you mean?'

'That's the one. I wonder if you know where I could find her.'

Harris raised his eyebrows. 'Find her? Whatever for?'

Henry waved an airy hand. 'I could do with her back at my place. It's damned hard finding a good overseer. Do you happen to know where I could get hold of her?'

Harris took a sip of his drink before answering. 'I doubt if she'll be interested in going back to your place,' he said cautiously. 'Not now she's opened a business of her own.'

Henry's jaw started to drop in surprise before he managed to control it. 'Her own business?' he repeated. 'At a time like this? What sort of business?'

Harris laid his glass down. 'A nice little dining room. Under the arches it is, and from what I hear it seems to be thriving despite everything . . .'

'Under the arches?'

Harris turned back to his drink. 'Down under the viaduct in Millsbridge. Nothing much to look at, but she seems to be making a go of it all right, her and her mother. So I reckon you're going to have to look elsewhere for your overseer.'

Maureen Nagle made sure none of the children was watching when she peeled back a flap of the torn brown wallpaper and took out a sixpence. She'd learnt this trick of hiding money from Tim a long time ago. So long as there was a penny piece in her purse, sure as Fate he would take it from her and go off down the pub. The hanging wallpaper was one place he'd never think to look.

It was a sin, she knew, deceiving him like this, and she'd confessed it to Father Leahy more than once. But a woman had to have some way to be sure of paying the rent man, otherwise she and the children would end up out on the street. There were a few more coins lurking behind there along with the bed bugs. She'd take just one, to fill the children's bellies . . .

'What you doing, Mam?'

She turned away from the wall, startled. Dominic stood waiting.

'Saying me prayers, sweetheart. Go on now, find the others

396

and tell them we're going down the road for a bowl of soup. Hurry now.'

Henry's footsteps carried him down Lowergate faster than he wanted to go, but the slope was steeper than he remembered. He hadn't been into Millsbridge for a long time now, but the sulphurous smell of the gasworks brought it all back.

He could see below him the rows of grey terraced houses, clustered together so closely there was scarcely room between them to breathe, just like the yard in Leeds where he'd grown up. Thank God he'd prospered well enough to escape from such a scruffy, miserable way of life.

He was sweating profusely by the time he reached the bend where the road swung round under the viaduct and into the village's main street. He didn't need to search for the dining room; under the viaduct a pair of big green-painted doors were thrown wide, and from inside drifted a tasty, appetizing aroma. The long queue of people straggling down into the cobbled street told it all. Bankhouse and Stonefield mills might be closed, and the tanyard too, but the girl was clearly not short of customers.

They were easing their way slowly into the building. He could hear the clink as folk leaned forward to drop money into a tin bowl held out by a youngster, a pretty little fair-headed lass with a red ribbon in her hair. Canny people like Hawksmoor folk didn't part with hard-earned cash that easily unless they were getting good value.

Hang on, wasn't that her now – the one carrying a baby in a crib? Henry shielded his eyes against the sun. Yes – it was her, and she was pushing past the queue to disappear into the gloom inside. Dammit, if only he'd seen which way she'd come from.

For twenty minutes or so he hung around, trying to feign interest in the variety of clogs on display in the cobbler's window. She didn't reappear, nor did the queue diminish. As soon as bodies emerged from the place to sit with bowl and spoon on one of the benches outside, more giggling girls and cloth-capped men arrived to join the line. Men, women, children – she seemed to have captured them all. The girl was clearly doing well, dammit.

A faded-looking woman carrying a baby and with a tribe of unkempt children milling around her heels crossed the road to join the queue. With a sigh Henry turned away. He might well have to shell out more than he'd intended to get what he wanted. But at least he knew now she still had the child.

He'd struggled halfway up Lowergate's steep incline once more, sweat trickling down inside his collar, before he realized he still didn't know what sex the baby was.

Ada paused for a moment, ladle in hand and ran a finger round the neck of her blouse. May could see the sweat beading her forehead.

'I'll take over for a bit, Mam. You have a sit-down.'

Her mother shook her head. 'It needs two pairs of hands here. We could do with taking somebody else on.'

She looked up and caught sight of Elsie, staggering under the weight of the tin bowl. 'Is that getting heavy, love? Bring it here and you have a rest. Oh, hello, Mrs Nagle. How's little Lily?'

Elsie plonked the bowl down on the counter beside the steaming pan and ran off out into the yard. Ada ladled out one bowl of broth after another and handed them over to the eager-faced little Nagles. Maureen hunched the baby under one arm and reached into her pocket.

Ada waved aside her outstretched hand. 'You put that back in your purse, love,' she muttered. 'Have this on me.'

The look of surprised delight on the woman's bloodless face was thanks enough. As Ada looked up she caught sight of May's smile and turned away in embarrassed silence.

Will was clearly as excited as a child with a new kite as he showed May around his new home. To her it looked dusty and neglected, but Mr Jordan had at least seen to it that Will had all he needed. There was even a small china cabinet in the corner of the living room, with one solitary cup sitting on the middle shelf.

'Isn't it great?' Will enthused, bouncing up and down on the sofa in delight. 'After roughing it for so long this is Paradise.'

'You can have a bath on your own hearth now,' May remarked. 'And cook your own meals.'

He grinned. 'I think I'll get by on your broth for the time being. Come and have a look upstairs – I've a thumping big bed all to meself.'

Once in the bedroom he flung himself on the patchwork counterpane and did another bounce. 'See? And just look at the size of that wardrobe!'

He flung wide the double doors of the huge oak press. May smiled to see the one lonely jacket hanging on the rail. Will turned to the washstand and trickled water from the jug down his fingers into the bowl.

'Course,' he said quietly, 'Mr Jordan's been here on his own a long time. What this place really needs is a woman's touch.'

May shrugged and smiled. 'Happen you should get yourself a housekeeper then – it seems to be the fashion in your firm.'

He laughed and closed the wardrobe door. May led the way downstairs.

'I've got something else to show you,' Will said, taking her arm at the foot of the stairs. 'Close your eyes.'

She did so, feeling his arm round her waist as he guided her into the scullery. He pressed a small square object into her hand. 'Right, open your eyes now,' he said.

She stared down at the small block of wood, polished smooth as marble. 'What's this?' she asked, mystified.

'The first brick for Rosie,' he said proudly. 'I'm going to carve a whole set of them and a little truck with wheels to pull 'em along in. With luck it'll be ready by the time she's walking.'

She felt a rush of warmth. 'Oh Will, that's kind.' She looked up at him, holding the brick close. 'This means a lot to me,

Will,' she said candidly. 'You know how I feel about her.'

'Aye, I know. Not surprising, after all you been through. It can't have been easy, denying she's yours.'

Encouraged, May went on, pouring out words she'd never thought to hear herself speak aloud. 'That's been the worst part of it. You know, Will, when I see her floating in the bath water, looking up at me with her big trusting eyes – I don't know, I feel as if my heart's turning over inside me. She's everything in the world to me. I'd love to be able to walk down the street and tell everybody she's mine.'

Will's hand covered hers, so tightly she could feel the brick pressing into her palm. 'I know, lass,' he said gruffly. 'I know.'

For a moment they stood, unspeaking, then he broke away, pulling at her hand. 'Hey, come on – I've still to show you me workshop.'

He opened the back door and stepped out into the yard. May tried to lighten the mood as she followed.

'You getting the hang of this coffin-making business yet?'

She heard his chuckle. 'I'm just about keeping half a yard ahead of Mr Jordan. I'm learning though, and he seems happy enough. By the way, I've been thinking – you needing meat, I could get a rabbit or two and maybe some pheasant if you like. No questions asked.'

'Poaching, you mean?'

He glanced back over his shoulder and grinned. 'Oh well, if you want to be pernickety about it . . .'

She could hear his chuckle as he opened the stable door and led the way inside. May could hear a snuffling sound and could make out the shadowy shape of Mr Jordan's old mare in her stall.

'Well now, Dolly old girl,' Will said softly, slapping the mare's rump. 'Enjoying your supper are you, lass?' May saw him stiffen, and heard his breath catch. 'Hello, who's that?' he demanded. 'What you doing there?'

And then she saw it, the huddled figure half-lying in the straw, eyes huge and fearful. As she bent closer she recognized him.

'Dominic! What is it, love? What's up?'

From behind her a light flared as Will put a match to the oil-lamp. By its glow she could see the child's face more clearly, the ugly weals on his cheek and the blood oozing from his lip.

'What happened, love?' she asked gently, reaching to touch him. The boy shrank back and began to whimper. She looked round at Will.

'It's that drunken bully of a father again, I reckon,' she muttered. 'He's no damn right to keep doing this. Those poor kids, and their mother . . . Come here, love, I won't hurt you.'

Dominic winced as she touched him, clutching his arms around his skinny body. Over his head she could see Will's face in the lamplight, white and tense and his eyes afire with anger.

'I'm worried, Will,' she murmured. 'It could be worse than we think.'

'Take him home and tend to him,' Will muttered. 'I've things to see to.'

THIRTY-EIGHT

Grace Openshaw arrived just as Ada was carrying the baby up to bed.

'The little love,' she cooed, touching a finger to the baby's cheek. 'I swear she grows bonnier every day. Is May at home?'

'She'll not be long,' said Ada. 'Go on in and sit you down.'

Once the baby was settled Grace sat chatting on Ada's sofa. 'So we hoped, Edward and me, as you'd let us borrow little Elsie now and again,' she said eagerly, 'like a kind of adopted niece. We've quite missed her bright little ways and it would be nice to take her on a seaside excursion. We thought maybe Bridlington . . .'

'I'm sure she'd love that,' said Ada. 'She's at a loss what to do with herself, school holidays being so long.'

'And since I was coming here anyway with this letter,' Grace went on, taking an envelope from her handbag, 'it seemed as good a time as any to ask.'

'Letter?' repeated Ada. 'Who from?'

'Mr Rose sent it for your May. He gave it to Edward because he didn't know the address, seemingly.' Grace's eyes grew mischievous. 'I wonder what it could be about.' Seeing Ada made no comment she hazarded a guess. 'It could be he's offering her my old job.'

'I doubt it,' said Ada. 'She's already turned it down.'

Grace's face fell. 'Well, what then . . . ?'

'Whatever it is,' said Ada firmly, 'he'll be up to no good. I wouldn't trust that man as far as I could throw him. Ah, that sounds like our May now.'

The door opened and May came in, gently pushing in front

of her the diminutive figure of Dominic who clearly didn't want to come in. He pressed back against her thighs, whimpering. Ada caught sight of the swollen purple bruises, the cut under his eye and the blood on his lip and she started to her feet.

'Good God, whatever's happened? Come here, love.'

She drew the child to her. At first he struggled to get free, tears running down his grimy cheeks, but gradually he gave in. May opened the cupboard and took out bottles.

'Now then, let's clean you up a little bit,' she said softly. 'Don't worry, nobody's going to hurt you here.'

Gently she wiped the blood and tears from his face while he cowered between Ada's knees. Ada stroked the child's matted hair while she delicately peeled away his clothes, revealing the lacerated cuts and weals on his thin body. Grace watched, open-mouthed and silent.

'Was it your daddy, love?' Ada murmured. 'Did he do this?'

Dominic snivelled and nodded. 'He took his belt off to me.'

Ada swore under her breath as her fingers probed his ribs. 'Looks like you got the buckle end and all. Still, no bones broken, I think.'

May dabbed witch hazel to the bruises, then took the cap off the iodine bottle. 'I'm afraid this'll sting a bit, love, but it'll make you better. Close your eyes.'

The boy looked down at the pad in her hand then turned his head away. Not once did he cry out. Ada ruffled his hair and smiled.

'You're a brave lad, Dominic. You shall have a sweetie in a minute.'

Grace found her voice at last, small and breathless. 'I can't believe it – his own father did this to him? What kind of man is that?'

There was a sudden commotion outside in the street, a door banging and voices raised in angry shouts. May turned her head to listen for a moment, then rose to her feet. 'A cowardly bully,' she replied calmly. 'And I rather think he's about to get what's coming to him.'

'Seemingly,' said Ada, 'and we'd best keep our noses out. Where's them humbugs?'

Will stumbled blindly out of the yard and down the street, feeling he could burst with the black, murderous hate raging inside him. He hadn't felt so blinded with hatred since that day years ago when the village lads caught poor Tabby, the farm cat back in Holney, and tortured the wretched animal till it screamed in agony. He'd been ready to thrash those lads within an inch of their lives, but a man who could do that to his own child . . . Reason had deserted him. Will was ready to tear the bastard limb from limb.

He'd be down at the Fleece now as he was every night, no doubt smashed out of his brain with drink, but father or not, drunk or not, he had no right to beat a helpless child like that.

Will crashed into the Fleece and looked around. Faces turned to stare and glasses paused, halfway to lips. The Irishman was not amongst them.

'Anyone seen Nagle?' he demanded.

'Why, he left not five minutes ago,' said the landlord.

Will rushed out into the night once more. If the fellow reached home still out of his feeble brain with the drink, his wife and the other children might be in danger . . .

He raced along Cedar Street. Even before he reached the house he could hear the racket. Someone was banging loudly on a door.

'Let me in, ye whore!' a deep voice bellowed. 'Let me in my own house this minute!'

It was Nagle all right. Evidently his wife, terrified, had locked the door against him. The blood was singing in Will's ears as he ran towards him, itching to get his hands on that drunken bastard's throat.

'I want you!' he yelled as the hazy shape of the Irishman came into view. The figure stopped thundering on the door and tottered round to stare at him.

'You talking to me?' he barked. 'Who in devil's name are ye?'

'Now then, what's all this about?'

In his furious haste Will hadn't been aware of curtains twitching, nor had he seen the burly figure of the police constable making his steady progress from the far end of the street. He lurched to a halt and his outstretched hands fell to his sides.

'This – this madman,' he rasped, 'he all but killed his little boy. His wife's in there now with her kids, scared out of her wits.'

The pale, wide-eyed oval of Maureen's face was peering out of the window. She drew back and let the lace curtain fall.

'Is that right?' the constable asked. Nagle shook his head.

'Ah now, sergeant,' he drawled amiably, ' 'tis no crime for a man to punish his own boy now, is it? Where would we be if we let our children run wild?'

'He beat the child up – he could have broken his neck,' snapped Will. 'He needs teaching a lesson.'

Nagle swayed on his feet, then swung his fists up in a pugilistic stance. 'And who's to teach me then? You, or our fine police officer here, is it? I'll take ye both on, that I will.'

'Take it easy, sir,' said the constable. 'No need for that.'

Nagle swung round to face him, still with fists raised. 'You want a fight, eh? I'll give ye a fight, so I will. Champion of Connemara I'd have been if I'd stayed. Come on then, boyo, up with 'em.'

The constable took out his notebook. 'I'm going to have to charge you, drunk and disorderly. Your name, sir?'

'Oh, so you won't fight, eh?' jeered Nagle. 'Ye big jessie, and ye in a uniform and all. Well, ye don't catch a Connemara man that easy.'

Nagle's thick fist swung round and up, catching the police officer on the chin so hard his helmet flew off. The force of the blow sent the constable hurtling into the gutter. Nagle stumbled over to him and raised his heavy boot. Will watched, mesmerized, as it crashed into the policeman's ribs and the fellow rolled over, groaning. Nagle's foot rose again. The policeman curled into a ball and cradled his head against the next blow.

Without thinking Will leapt forward, seized hold of Nagle by the throat with one hand and swung a vicious blow to his nose with the other. For a second he was aware of Nagle's startled expression and the pulped remains of his bloody nose before he fell. Will stood astride the burly figure, itching for him to rise so he could smash his ugly face again, but the bulky shape lay still.

The constable scrambled to his feet and retrieved his helmet from the gutter. He nodded to Will. 'Thanks,' he said, tenderly feeling his ribs, then he looked down at Nagle. 'Get up,' he snapped. 'You're coming with me.'

Nagle didn't move. The constable bent to turn him over. Blood was oozing from his battered nose and his eyes were wide and staring. As the constable slipped a hand inside his shirt the door opened and Maureen appeared, her face white and anxious.

'Is he out for the count?' she asked timidly. 'Thanks be to God. He'll be more peaceful when he's slept it off.'

The constable looked up at Will. 'He won't be sleeping this off,' he muttered. 'I think he's dead.'

Will stared, disbelieving. 'Oh my God!' he moaned. 'I've killed him!'

The constable gave him a sharp look. 'Now don't let's go jumping to no conclusions. Looks to me like he smashed his head on the kerb when he fell – must have broke his skull, wouldn't you say?'

Will was still shaking when he asked May to come out on the doorstep.

'Dead?' she echoed. 'I can't believe it.'

'Nor me,' muttered Will. 'One minute he was roaring like a bull, the next he was just lying there, dead.'

May felt the leap in her chest. 'And you hit him? What's going to happen now, Will? Do you have to go to the police station?'

He shook his head. 'Not tonight. Constable Drake's going to say how Nagle attacked him and a passer-by came to his aid. The deceased fell in the struggle and struck his head, is how he put it. Mrs Nagle said she would testify to that – mind you, the poor girl doesn't know if she's coming or going.'

'I bet she doesn't,' said May. 'I'd better go down to her.'

Will sighed. 'We'll have to break it to that poor kid in there. I just killed his father.'

May touched his cheek. 'No you didn't – it wasn't intentional anyway.'

Will took hold of the fingers on his face. 'I thumped the drunken bastard so hard I've robbed the family of their breadwinner,' he murmured. 'How the devil is that poor woman going to manage now?'

'One thing at a time,' said May, drawing him indoors. 'We have to tell Dominic first.'

'There's been an accident, love. Your daddy's gone and he won't be coming back.'

The child looked up at her, his lips swollen and suspicion in his dark eyes. 'Gone where?' he asked. 'Down the pub?'

'No, love. He's gone right away. He won't be coming home again, not ever.'

The battered little face stared at her blankly for a moment, open-mouthed and one eye half-closed above the cut, then he turned to Ada for confirmation. She nodded and stroked his hair.

'Not coming home?' he whispered. 'Not never?'

'No, love, not never.'

A glimmer of light in his eyes began to grow and swell until a smile reached his lips. 'Is my mammy at home?' he asked. 'I want to be with Mammy.'

He broke away from Ada and hurried towards the door, cuts and pains forgotten for the moment. May took hold of his hand.

'Come on then, I'll take you.'

A huge beam of delight covered the ravaged little face as

he waited for her to open the door. Before she could step outside he broke away and scurried, limping and stumbling, up the street towards home.

Grace had gone home by the time May came back and Ada told her about the letter. May picked up the envelope and turned it over.

'Now what could Mr Rose be wanting with me?' she murmured as she slit it open. Ada waited in silence while she read. At last she laid the sheet of paper down.

'Well?' said Ada. 'What's he want? Whatever it is, it'll be trouble.'

'He wants to see me,' May said calmly. 'He says he has a business proposition to put to me.'

'Business?' echoed Ada. 'What's he up to?'

May picked up the letter again. 'He says it could be greatly to my advantage. I wonder?'

Ada snorted. 'To his advantage, more like, or he wouldn't have taken the trouble to get in touch. The cheek of it, after the way he treated you, paying you off to get rid of you. Aye, there's summat fishy there,' she growled.

May looked thoughtful. 'Yes, he's a clever man, a shrewd man . . .' She refolded the letter and laid it down. 'I'm going to meet him,' she said quietly. 'Like you say, he's up to something and I want to know what it is.'

'No harm in finding out,' agreed her mother. 'But he's a business man, cunning as a barrowload of monkeys. I'm coming with you.'

May patted her shoulder. 'Thanks, but I'm not one of the girls in his workroom now, Mam – I'm in business too. So I'll go, I'll listen to his proposition, but this is something I have to handle on my own.'

It was long past midnight and despite the sultry clamminess of the night Maureen Nagle lay shivering in the big double bed.

He wasn't coming back, not tonight or ever. It was hard to

believe. She ought to be grieving, wailing and lamenting like the women did at home in Connemara at a wake, but the tears wouldn't come. The only emotion she could feel was immense relief.

There'd be no more cruel words, no more blows, no more having to watch the children being knocked about, and no more brutal, painful pinning down under the blanket while he strained and groaned, his beer-laden breath choking in her nostrils.

He'd been in a fearful foul temper tonight before he went out and once more it had been poor Dominic, God help him, who'd suffered. The boy had ducked and fled before Tim's fury gave out, and he'd gone off to the pub vowing she'd know the full measure of his wrath on his return. She'd taken as much as she could stand of his twisted ideas of justice; for the first time ever she'd shown defiance, locking the door on him like that, knowing she'd have to pay for it later. Him thundering on the door like a maddened bull had scared the living daylights out of her, and the kids had gone scuttling under the bed in terror. But for that young man of May Turnbull's . . .

It wasn't his fault, what happened. She'd seen it all from behind the curtain. It was Tim and his drink-fuddled raging – he'd brought it on himself, going for the policeman like that, and she'd testify if need be. Old Mrs Nagle had always said her son's quick temper would be the ruination of him.

Even so, the bed felt strange and empty without his big, snoring body lying stretched out beside her. She'd have to let both the families know, not that any of them could afford to come over for the funeral. Maybe Kitty Nolan could make it. She wasn't all that far away in Manchester.

It was beginning to sink in. She was a widow now, with five hungry mouths to feed as well as her own. How in God's name was she to manage without Tim's money coming in?

Money. Just how much did she have? How long could she make it last? She swung her legs out of bed, catching her toe in that hole in the blanket she'd never got round to patching.

As she tiptoed, barefoot, across the linoleum she heard baby Lily sigh in her sleep. No sound came from the other room where the four eldest lay. She must remember to lift Dominic out onto the jerry soon before he wet the bed again. He usually did after he'd taken a beating.

As she turned to go down the stairs she could hear Thomas snoring. It was his adenoids, Mrs Boothroyd had said, whatever that might mean. Please God it wasn't serious like Deirdre Callaghan's thyroids.

The old tin teapot lay on the hearth and by the weight of it there was still quite a bit of tea inside. Strong and thick and black, the way he liked it – a hot drink was just what she needed now to calm the rioting thoughts whirling in her head. She raked over the embers till they glowed. There was no more coal and only enough kindling for the morning. Paper then . . .

A bed bug scuttled across the far wall and darted behind a hanging ribbon of dirty brown wallpaper. Maureen set down the teapot and taking hold of a corner of one sheet of the paper she tore it lengthways from the wall, then seized hold of another and wrenched it free. Pennies and startled bugs tumbled together to the floor.

A great surge of pent-up emotion swept through her as she ripped away in a frenzy. There was real honest-to-God pleasure and satisfaction in the destruction. He was never coming home again to put the fear of God in them all. Never again would she need to hide those secret pennies away. There was no need to hide anything any more.

THIRTY-NINE

The tide was coming in fast. Elsie was reluctant to leave the beach but at last Grace managed to persuade her it was time to empty the sand out of her shoes and the pockets of her smock.

'We'll take a walk along the front,' she promised, 'and buy you some candy floss.'

Elsie looked mystified. 'What's candy floss?'

Edward smiled. 'It's all pink and fluffy and sweet, on a stick – you'll like it.'

For a time they strolled in the heat. Edward took off his hat and fanned his face with it. Elsie let go of Grace's hand and climbed onto the railings, pointing out towards the horizon.

'I can see Ireland,' she announced proudly.

Grace shielded her eyes against the sun. 'I don't think so, love,' she murmured. 'Not from Bridlington.'

'Yes I can,' argued the child. 'It's all green like Mrs Nagle told me. It's over the water, she said, across the sea, so it must be Ireland.'

Edward touched her arm. 'If you like we'll take you to Fleetwood one day and then you can really see Ireland. Out there it's probably Holland.'

The child gazed up at him in awe. 'Holland?' she repeated reverently. 'Dutch people – with windmills?'

'That's right.'

Elsie climbed down and took hold of Grace's hand. 'Just wait till I tell Coppernob I've seen Holland,' she said proudly. 'She'll say I'm telling fibs again, but I don't care. I've seen Holland.'

She hadn't, Grace thought to herself. It was all wishful thinking – she hadn't seen anywhere. If Grace remembered correctly from her schooldays it was more likely Denmark or even Norway over there, far too far away to be visible. Edward's knowledge of geography seemed about as good as Elsie's.

The child scampered off along the front ahead of them, overtaking a young couple walking hand in hand and gazing deep into one another's eyes. For them no-one else in the world existed.

Grace smiled and nudged Edward, whose hand cupped her elbow. 'Just look,' she whispered. 'Isn't that nice?'

He cocked his head. 'Did you ever look like that, I wonder?'

She coloured, remembering. She could still recall Thaddeus's hands, calloused from working on the stone, sometimes nicked with cuts. They'd been strong hands, protective hands, and she'd yearned . . . 'Once, a long time ago,' she answered quietly, 'but it wasn't meant to be.'

'That blessed mother of yours again?' Edward ventured. 'She's got a lot to answer for. I can just imagine you with children like Elsie. You'd have loved that.'

Grace said nothing, watching the child's lithe little body dancing happily ahead. If only . . . Edward cut in on her thoughts.

'To think,' he murmured, 'that thirty years ago we were both living in Hawksmoor only three or four miles apart, and neither of us knew the other existed. Just think how different life might have turned out if we'd met then.'

'No,' Grace said hastily. 'It doesn't do to dwell on what-might-have-been. I've wasted enough years doing that.'

'I'm not complaining, you understand,' Edward went on. 'I was lucky. I had a good wife and two fine children, but what about you? It's interesting to speculate—'

Grace could hear the sharp tone in her voice. 'Mother was right – marriage isn't everything – you have to get on with what you've got and make the best of it. No use whining.'

Edward looked down at her, his eyes dark and serious. 'It's

412

not too late, Grace – oh, too late for children, maybe, but we can always borrow little Elsie. We can pretend she's ours.'

Grace felt the blush burning her cheeks, but before she could reply Edward went on smoothly. 'We could take her to Fleetwood next week and show her Ireland. The three of us, like a real family of our own. What do you say?'

For a moment she hesitated. He squeezed her arm tightly against his side. 'Say yes, Grace,' he urged. 'Please.'

Elsie came running back and tugged eagerly at Grace's skirt. 'I've found the candy-floss stall, Aunt Grace,' she said excitedly. 'Can I have some now, please, can I?'

Grace was looking up at Edward as she nodded. 'Yes,' she said shyly. 'Oh, yes.'

The dining room was heaving with customers. Ada laid down the soup ladle for a moment and mopped her brow with a corner of her apron.

'By heck,' she muttered, 'I'm fair roasting. I wish I was at the seaside with our Elsie. Who'd have thought we'd get this many folk every day when the strike's not over yet?'

May pulled another pan of soup along the counter. 'And they say they'll still keep coming even when it is, so we can't grumble. Then we'll really start to go.'

Ada took up the ladle again and began serving. 'We could do with a bit more help as it is, never mind if we get any more – no two ways about it.'

May gave a mischievous smile. 'You could always ask Mr Smedley to give us a hand – he's always around. Never takes his eyes off you.'

The flush of heat on Ada's cheeks hid the blush which leapt unbidden. 'Less of your lip,' she rebuked her daughter. 'He's a very kind man. I don't know what we'd have done without him.'

Harold Jordan sat at his ease in his new living room, the afternoon *Examiner* on his lap. In a moment Cassie would bring him tea. All was right in his world. He brushed away

413

the bluebottle which had the temerity to try to land on his scalp.

The door opened and Cassie came in. She had no tea in her hand, only a frown marring the creamy skin of her forehead.

'There's Will Napier outside,' she said. 'He's been waiting for ages at the back door. Have I to bring him in?'

'No,' said Harold. 'Not yet.'

Cassie's frown deepened. 'What am I to do with him then?'

'Leave him there. It won't do him any harm.'

'How long for? He's walked all the way up from Cedar Street for his pay.'

Harold sighed. 'He can wait till I'm ready. I always keep my employees waiting.'

Cassie came to stand in front of him. 'Whatever for?' she demanded. 'It doesn't make sense.'

He smiled benignly. 'You don't know about these things, my dear. That way they learn respect.'

'Do they heck!' she snapped, sweeping the newspaper up off his lap. 'You get out there and pay him now.'

Harold stood in the shade of the rhododendron bush while he handed the pay packet to his foreman.

'But listen here, Will Napier,' he growled, 'I've no quarrel with your work but we can't have the manager of the most prestigious undertaker in Hawksmoor brawling in the street with the likes of that dreadful Nagle fellow. It just isn't good enough.'

'I wasn't brawling, Mr Jordan,' Will countered quietly as he pocketed the coins. 'He attacked the policeman – what else could I do?'

'You all but killed him – at any rate, he died. Admittedly, we didn't bury him but you'll have folks saying we're trying to make more customers for ourselves. I won't have it, do you hear?'

Will nodded. 'I think I can safely say it won't happen again, Mr Jordan. At least it's not very likely.'

Harold was unaware of the upstairs window opening and Cassie's fair head leaning out to listen. 'Not very likely?' he blustered. 'I should think not indeed! How on earth is Jordan's to hold its head high if the foreman lets himself be dragged in on a drunken squabble like that? More self-respect, Napier, that's what you need.'

From high above, Cassie's voice floated down. 'Harold! Get in here, I want you.'

Harold's face turned pink. 'Ah, I'd better go in now,' he said awkwardly. 'I think my housekeeper would like a word with me.'

Mrs Boothroyd was waiting for Ada when she arrived home from the dining room. She tapped at the window as Ada passed and then came out onto the step, leaning against the door-frame and breathing heavily.

'Got a parcel for you,' she wheezed. 'Well, it's for your May really. Lady called Miss Openshaw brought it while you was out. Hang on a minute.'

She turned and waddled indoors, reappearing a moment later with a parcel swathed in brown paper. 'I wasn't nosing,' she said as she handed it over, 'but I couldn't help seeing what's inside. Nice skirt and jacket, that. Lovely bit of stuff – must be best worsted, that.'

'Aye, it is,' said Ada.

'Going somewhere, is she?'

'I don't ask,' replied Ada. 'Happen it's for Cassie's wedding. It's not that far off now.'

Mrs Boothroyd gave a knowing smile. 'Aye, and who knows? You could be losing both your lasses before long. I've seen your May with that young man again.'

'Aye, well, I wouldn't set too much store by that if I was you. Our May has a mind of her own,' said Ada.

The old lady shook her head. 'Even so, she'll make a fine wife for somebody. I've seen her out in the yard with your little Rosie – she's wonderful with that baby, like a real mother to her, she is.'

Ada smiled as she turned to go. 'She is that,' she murmured. 'You never said a truer word.'

May came in soon after with the baby in her arms. Ada pointed to the parcel on the table.

'Grace has done your outfit, love,' she told her. 'Give Rosie to me and try it on.'

'Later,' said May, putting Rosie into her mother's lap. 'Listen, you know you said we needed more help – well, what about Mrs Nagle? She could do with the money.'

Ada stared. 'Maureen? How can she, with all those kids?'

May planted one fist on the table. 'She's got her sister-in-law, that pretty dark-haired woman who was at the funeral. Maybe something could be arranged.'

Ada recalled seeing her that sweltering day the hearse carried Tim Nagle away to the Catholic church, Cedar Street's usual bustle stilled as the neighbours stood bare-headed and in silence at the kerbside to watch the little cortège go by. Maureen had been leaning heavily on the other young woman's arm.

'But she's from Manchester, isn't she?' Ada queried. 'She'll no doubt be off home to her own family before long.'

'That's just it,' said May. 'She has no family, seemingly. Her husband left her a couple of years ago and she's no children.'

Ada stared. 'How do you know all this? I've heard nowt.'

'Mrs Tandy. She makes it her business to know everything. Kitty Nolan's been working in a cotton mill since he ran away and now she's been laid off. And since she seems in no hurry to go back home, it might be worth while having a word with Mrs Nagle, don't you think?'

Ada sat precariously on the rickety spindle-backed chair in Maureen Nagle's living room. Judging by the creaking noise whenever she moved and the way the legs jutted at a strange angle, it felt as though it might collapse under her at any moment.

But despite its shabbiness, the house felt different. On the far wall only a few strips of wallpaper remained; a damp patch stood out darkly on the plaster yet somehow the place seemed more wholesome than it had done. There was a smell of carbolic in the air – they must have been cleaning it up, Maureen and that sister-in-law of hers.

Kitty seemed a nice, cheerful young woman. She was upstairs now putting the little ones to bed. Across the hearth Maureen detached baby Lily from her breast and buttoned her blouse.

'So I was wondering,' Ada said, 'if you might be able between you to arrange something. If you could give us a hand it would suit me very well.'

Maureen wiped a dribble of milk from the baby's chin. 'I'd be delighted,' she murmured. 'I've been fretting how to make ends meet.'

'It wouldn't be a lot of money,' said Ada. 'Not straight off anyway.'

'No, of course not. Kitty and me was only talking this morning. She's going to stay here with me for a while. We've always got on well together. She'll help me with the little ones and there'll be only the one rent to pay.'

Only one rent . . . Memory flicked in Ada's brain. Those were the very words Jack Smedley had said to her months ago. He was a good man, always kind, and, as May had said, always there . . .

'I'd love to work at your place,' Maureen's voice cut in on her thoughts. 'Kitty will be delighted to mind the children for me. We could share the work, her and me, turn and turn about.'

'That's a great idea,' said Ada. 'I can't tell you what a relief it will be to May and me, having an extra pair of hands.'

'And a blessing to me too,' said Maureen fervently. 'One minute everything is so black and then before ye know where ye are, 'tis all coming right again.'

She held the baby high in the air and laughed up at her. 'You hear that, Lily? Your mammy is going to earn a living for herself and the lot of ye. Isn't that wonderful news?'

417

The baby burped in agreement. Maureen lowered the child and turned back to Ada. 'Will I call and see ye at the dining room tomorrow then?'

'You can't start too soon for me,' said Ada, rising to go.

From above came the sound of a voice singing softly, a haunting Irish lullaby. Maureen's haggard face softened into a gentle smile. She jerked her head towards the stairs.

'She'd always a sweet voice, that Kitty Nolan,' she murmured. 'I remember it well, since long before I met and married her brother. 'Tis great to hear singing in the house again.'

As Ada opened the door to go out she caught the sound of a child's chuckle upstairs. Aye, she thought, there was indeed a feeling of peace and gentle joy in the place. After all the years of tears and misery, the house deserved to sing again . . .

FORTY

Ada brushed down her daughter's skirt and stood back admiringly.

'You look fair grand, May love, a real toff,' she murmured. 'Grace has done you proud.'

May adjusted her hat and surveyed her reflection in the mirror. 'I would have run it up meself. Grace said I could borrow her Singer treadle, but she was itching to get her hands on the cloth because I got it from Mr Harris. I'm quite proud of the blouse I made; I'll do another one in time for Cass's wedding.'

'Aye,' said Ada, 'then you can get rid of that old skirt and blouse you've had on your back this twelvemonth or more. I'm sick of the sight of them.'

Me too, thought May. I'll be glad to get shut of them, the outfit Rose's bought for me when I went to work up at Thornleigh Hall . . . 'Yes,' she said quietly. 'Chuck 'em out.'

'Nay,' said Ada, 'that I'll not. I'll give 'em a wash and offer 'em to Maureen Nagle. She's about your size and I reckon she might be glad of 'em.'

It felt like stepping back in time as May climbed down off the tram and walked along Hawksmoor's busy main street towards the shop. So many mornings she'd hurried along this road to work in the old days, and if it hadn't been for what happened last summer she might have been doing it for the next forty years.

As she turned the corner of the side-street towards Rose's, from force of habit she found herself heading for the back

419

entrance before she recollected herself. She was no mere chit of a girl now, an employee fearful of the boss's wrath; she was a grown woman with a child and a business of her own and Mr Rose was going to be left in no doubt of the fact. This was why Grace had made her the skirt with its matching long jacket, and the new hat finished the outfit off beautifully. She could walk tall, show Mr Rose she was doing well. She wasn't going to let him think that she'd landed on the rubbish heap after he had thrown her out.

Whatever Henry Rose had to say to her, she was going to meet him on equal terms.

She smoothed back the leather of her kid-gloved hands, the gloves like Miss Openshaw's she'd yearned for in the old days, then holding her head high, she walked proudly up the steps and in through the wide double doors of Rose's front entrance.

Promptly at two o'clock there was a light tap at the office door. Henry Rose straightened his tie before answering. 'Come in.'

His secretary entered. 'Miss Turnbull to see you, sir.'

'Very well. Show her in.'

This was to be the most important meeting of his life, he thought as he watched the girl come in, but she mustn't realize it. She looked very smart; he'd been correct in thinking she was doing all right. He must appear casual.

'Ah yes,' he murmured, rubbing his chin. 'I sent for you, didn't I?'

'You asked to see me,' she replied calmly, 'if I could spare the time.'

Her coolness startled him but he wouldn't show it. He waved her towards the chair on the far side of his desk. 'Sit down, Miss Turnbull. You're well, I hope?'

She seated herself and inclined her head. 'I am very well – now.'

'Good, good,' he said warmly. 'Well now, I won't beat about the bush. As you know, I am a man who takes his responsibilities seriously, very seriously. I don't think you would disagree with that.'

She didn't answer but she was listening quietly, her head cocked politely to one side. Encouraged, he went on. 'No, of course not. You will recollect that I was concerned to see to it that you had no cause to grumble over that little affair last year. I made sure you were catered for in a good home—'

'Home?' she repeated. 'More like hell on earth, it was. Sisters of Mercy, indeed!'

He felt stung. 'May I remind you,' he said sharply, 'that girls in your position do not expect to live in the lap of luxury.' Calm down, he told himself, stay calm. 'However, that is not what I wanted to discuss. The point is—'

'Some of those poor girls never came out alive,' she cut in quietly. 'And those who did often had to leave their babies behind. The nuns used to sell them off to childless couples.'

'But not yours,' Henry cut in eagerly. 'You still have your baby, I believe?'

The girl nodded. 'Of course.'

'A son, was it?'

'A daughter.'

Henry stifled a momentary pang of disappointment. The child was still of his blood. 'My granddaughter,' he murmured.

'No,' the girl said quietly. 'She's nothing to do with you, remember? She's mine.'

This wasn't going right at all. Henry sought to re-establish the upper hand. 'Look,' he said gently, leaning across the desk, 'forget what was said in the heat of the moment when we were upset. We won't renege on our obligations. What we're prepared to do is this.'

'We?'

'Aaron and me. He thinks very fondly of his child, you know, even if he doesn't know her yet.' Henry watched the girl's face closely. It remained impassive and it was hard to judge how she was reacting, but at least she wasn't protesting. He plunged on.

'Aaron and his new wife – did you know he was married?

Lovely girl, Adele, lovely girl – well, they're prepared to bring the little one up as their own and one day she might inherit the whole business. I think you can see the huge advantage that would give your daughter. You can hardly argue with that.'

Henry paused, but the girl still sat erect, her hands folded in her lap.

'She'll lack for nothing,' he went on. 'I do realize, of course, that you should have some kind of redress for the loss of her company and I'm fully prepared to make it worth your while.'

Sharp eyes challenged his. 'You want me to sell my child?' she asked.

He waved impatient hands. 'It's not like that – I simply want what's best for my grandchild, can't you see that? My granddaughter can be given a good start in life – it's been weighing on my mind, my responsibility to her.'

'Am I to presume your son and his wife can't have children of their own?'

'No, no, not at all! What on earth makes you think that? But your child would be the first, and she'd inherit.'

'And where would I fit in this little scheme?' the girl asked quietly. 'After all, she's my daughter.'

'I like to think of her as our daughter too, our flesh and blood.'

'You want me to give her up, let you take care of her?'

She was beginning to get the message. He could afford to be generous. 'Of course it won't be easy for you, my dear,' he murmured, 'but I'm sure something can be arranged. Regular progress reports, photographs, that sort of thing. You won't lose track of her entirely. You'll be kept fully informed, I guarantee.'

She was starting to pull on her gloves. Henry tried another tack. 'Look, they tell me you have a little business,' he said urgently. 'I'm sure a bit of extra capital wouldn't go amiss . . .'

'I don't need your money.'

'It's what's best for her! Surely as her mother you can see

422

that! I can give her the very best.' He lowered his voice to a wheedling tone. 'A very healthy figure indeed I'm talking about – you could be very comfortably off. Just listen to my proposition.'

She put on her gloves, finger by finger, then flicked a speck of dust from her skirt and stood up. 'Like I said, I don't want your money, Mr Rose,' she said calmly. 'I told you once before, I've had all I want from you.'

'Never mind you,' Henry pointed out. 'It's the child we must think of. She's the important one.'

The girl gave him a cold stare. 'And you want me to sell her across the counter like she was a length of cloth.'

Anger prickled him. 'Don't you ever say that to anybody!' he snapped. 'The only stipulation I make in return for the money is that you never, ever say you're the mother of this child.'

For several seconds her gaze held his, and then she took a deep breath. 'I tell you what I will do, Mr Rose—'

'Yes?' He leaned forward eagerly. At least she was prepared to barter . . .

'I promise I'll never, ever say Aaron is the father of my child. I promised you that once before, and I never break a promise.'

Dammit, she was being very obtuse. 'Listen,' said Henry, 'it's hard for a woman alone in business. You can do with all the help you can get. We can do so much to help you and her.'

The girl gave a cool, confident smile. 'By the time I've finished I'm going to have a business to be proud of and make sure my daughter never wants for anything.'

'It's tougher than you think,' said Henry, 'a woman getting by on her own. You're going to regret this.'

He could see the light of amusement in her eyes. 'Watch me, Mr Rose,' she murmured. 'You just watch me. Now I think I've heard all I want to hear.'

She turned towards the door. Panic seized him and he hurried round the desk to bar her way. 'You can't do this to me,' he spluttered. 'She's important to me, she's my grand-child!'

'Prove it,' the girl said smoothly. 'You won't find her father's name on the birth certificate, only mine. And she's staying mine. Good day to you.'

Henry was stunned into silence as he followed her out to the top of the stairs, and then he found his voice. 'She's my granddaughter too,' he protested. 'I do have some rights, whatever it says on that bit of paper.' Seeing she made no move to answer he added, 'And I don't even know her name.'

The girl paused on the top step and looked back over her shoulder. 'It's Rose,' she smiled. 'I called her Rose.'

Stunned, he stood watching her as she swept down the stairs. Aaron's tall figure strode across the shop floor to open the door for her, and Henry saw her glance briefly at him as he bowed slightly, and then she swept out. She'd always seemed such a quiet girl when she used to work in his sewing room, thought Henry. He'd even considered making her his overseer after Miss Openshaw left. More went on inside the heads of these quiet ones than you would ever guess.

He watched his son's broad back as he stood in the open doorway. For that brief moment as they passed within touching distance of one another he could almost see them as a couple. Maybe he had played it all wrong. If only Aaron's colourless little wife had half the spark of that girl who had just swept out of the door and, in all probability, out of their lives for ever . . .

Aaron stayed holding the door, watching the woman as she walked away down King Street. There was dignified grace and a kind of delicate purposefulness in her step; she was clearly a woman who knew her own mind.

She must be a valued customer who'd been seeing Father about an order. He must ask him who she was, this lady with the hint of mystery in those cool green eyes. Their gaze had only met for a very brief moment but in that second the enigmatic look in those eyes had taken his breath away and sent ripples of excitement thrilling through his veins.

She turned the corner into Cross Church Street and disappeared from his view. Aaron let the door close and turned away, frowning. Where was it he'd seen eyes like those before?

But try as he might, he could not for the life of him remember . . .

A secret sense of exultation burned in her. Finding it impossible to stand patiently at the tram stop May walked fast along the Manchester road towards home.

She'd fenced with Henry Rose and won. He wasn't going to have Rosie, no matter what he offered. She didn't need him, or his money. She didn't need anybody to make a success of her life. Now she was ready to go out and face the world and nothing was going to stop her.

Just Mother, Cassie, Elsie, Rosie and me – the Turnbull women against the world, and we'll make it. Excitement burned in her, mingled with just a tinge of apprehension, as she hurried home to share the news with her mother.

Will Napier whistled to himself as he packed away his tools and came out of the yard into Cedar Street. He was just in time – May was coming round the corner and he quickened his step to meet her.

'Well?' he asked anxiously. 'What did he want?'

She smiled up at him, and he was aware of the confident glow in her smile. 'Would you believe it, Will – that man wanted to buy my Rosie.'

Will stared. 'He what?'

May began peeling off her gloves as she walked on. 'I told him what he could do. Whatever I have is my own – nothing and nobody is going to take my baby away from me. I'm keeping her, come what may.'

Will could feel the anger beginning to rise inside his chest. 'Bloody cheek,' he muttered. 'She stays with us.'

May glanced up at him. 'Us?' she repeated.

He felt the colour burn his cheeks. He'd no right to say that and he felt embarrassed. 'I knew her before she was born,' he muttered by way of justification, 'when she was just a lump.'

They were back at the archway now. On an impulse he stopped suddenly and seized May's hands in his. 'Look,' he said fiercely, 'what that baby needs is a father . . .'

She withdrew a hand and laid a gentle finger to his lips. 'Maybe, maybe not, but one step at a time. There's things I still want to do, like getting this business off the ground once the strike's over. So let's take it easy, please.'

He let her hands fall. 'I'm sorry,' he muttered awkwardly. 'I don't want to rush you. I just want to see you right.'

He put his hand in his pocket. 'Here,' he said gruffly. 'Here's another one for Rosie.'

She looked down at the polished wooden brick he held out, then closed her hand over it with a smile. 'You're the best friend a woman ever had,' she murmured. 'Let's keep it that way for the time being.' She gave him a mischievous glance. 'But I'll be very happy to walk out with you,' she added softly. 'Will that suit?'

He grinned happily and took her hand in his. 'Right then,' he said, 'let's walk. But first . . .'

With a quick glance around, he drew her gently into the shadow of the archway and whispered into her ear. 'Even best friends are allowed a cuddle.'

Old Mrs Boothroyd trundled slowly down Cedar Street. Somehow the distance between home and the corner shop seemed twice as far when the sun was cracking the flagstones and you'd a laden basket to carry.

It was no use – she'd have to stop for a breather. Stooping stiffly, she laid the basket on the ground and then straightened, rubbing the aching small of her back. Summertime or not, she'd have to rub in a bit of wintergreen tonight.

With a sigh she stooped again to retrieve the basket and as she moved on, past the opening into Jordan's yard, she caught sight of a blur in the shadows under the arch. Well, bless my soul! It was a young couple embracing – in fact, if her fuzzy eyesight didn't deceive her, it was May Turnbull and that good-looking new foreman!

Well, well, thought the old lady as she shuffled on towards home, the affair had got a bit further than just walking down on the towpath, seemingly. Kissing in broad daylight! For the ladylike May Turnbull that must mean something serious. She wasn't a bit like that brazen young sister of hers who'd taken up with a man more than twice her age.

She took out her key and unlocked the front door with a feeling of satisfaction. She'd been right all along about those two. Ada Turnbull might not be able to see what was going on right under her nose, but they couldn't fool me, she thought. Seventy I might be, one foot in the grave and waiting only for Jordan's to carry me out feet-first, but I've not forgotten how it feels to be smitten . . .

May took one last look at Will's broad back as he made off down the yard towards the workshop before she turned and came out into the sunlight. Cassie was striding jauntily down the street towards her.

Her sister's eyes lit up as her gaze flicked over the new outfit. 'Hey,' Cassie murmured admiringly, 'don't you look posh, all dressed up like a dog's dinner! Where did you get them from?'

'Had them made – for your wedding really.'

'So why are you all dolled up today? Where've you been?'

'I had a bit of business to see to, that's all.'

'Private, eh? Been to see a man about a dog?'

'Something like that. Come on, I'm dying for a cup of tea.'

They fell into step together, arm in arm. 'I'll have to look to my laurels now,' said Cassie. 'Can't have you outshining the bride on me wedding day.'

May smiled. 'I'm sure your Harold will see you right. Where is he, by the way?'

'Down the Conservative Club. They've asked him if he'd

427

like to rejoin so he's very happy. I thought I'd pop down and see our Rosie while I've chance. You know, I've never fancied having babies, but she's made me think.'

'Me too,' said May. 'Babies do that to you.'

Cassie cocked her head to one side. 'I wonder if Mam suddenly became more serious when she had us – I mean, do you think she ever had time to have fun?'

'She must have once. When she was courting Dad.'

Cassie looked thoughtful. 'You wouldn't think so to look at her now, would you? She's a widow, nearly forty, and she's struggled all her life. And what's she got out of it?'

'One daughter with an illegitimate child and another living in sin,' laughed May. 'What's she ever done to deserve that?'

She let go of her sister's arm as they reached the house and dug in her bag for the key. Cassie peered in at the window, and then her fingers flew to her mouth.

'I don't believe it,' she gasped. 'Don't look!'

'What? What is it?'

Curious, May leaned over her shoulder and peered through the gaps in the lace curtain. Mam was on her knees in front of the fire, a sponge in her hands, and she was dribbling tracks of creamy lather down Jack Smedley's naked back as he sat in the tin bath. There was a contented smile on her lips as she dipped into the water for another spongeful.

May heard Cassie's deep sigh. 'Well, would you believe it?' she murmured. 'And it's not even Friday night.'

THE END

THE JERICHO YEARS
by Aileen Armitage

Jericho Farm, high in the Pennines, had been in the Hemingway family for generations. Life on the farm was hard, yet the place had a rugged compulsion for those who lived and worked there. But now James Hemingway was thinking of breaking with tradition and selling up. With his wife tragically dead, David, his son, making a separate career as an artist, and his daughter, Ellen, a strange, withdrawn and troubled girl, there seemed little point in staying on at Jericho.

Then David, the beloved and only son, was struck by a fatal illness and with Lisa, the girl he wanted to marry, came back to Jericho, to the house and land that he loved. As the new family coped with fresh tragedy and began to try and weld together once more, so an entirely unexpected and unconventional relationship exploded into their lives, one that offered hope to James, to Lisa, and to Jericho Farm.

0 554 14049 X

ROSY SMITH
by Janet Haslam

It was a terrible tragedy which first brought Rosy Smith to
Derwent House, the grand home of John Hardaker and his
wife Dorothy. The loss of one of their twin baby sons in a
mysterious accident meant that Dorothy no longer found
herself capable of caring for the surviving twin, Nicky – so
Rosy, only sixteen but full of love for the helpless child, had
to step into the breach. As the years went by and Dorothy
became less and less able to deal with life, Rosy's mother
Nell, the housekeeper, watched with trepidation as John
Hardaker's interest in his young nanny became noticeably
warmer.

In time, Rosy became the mistress of Derwent House, but
her new position brought her, not the happiness she longed
for, but unexpected misery and yet more tragedy. The old
family house was to see many changes and revelations before
Rosy could at last find contentment.

0 552 14297 2

THE BRIGHT ONE
by Elvi Rhodes

Molly O'Connor's life was not an easy one. With six children and a husband who earned what he could as a casual farmhand, fisherman, or drover, it was a constant struggle to keep her family fed and raised to be respectable. Of all her children, Breda – the Bright One – was closest to her heart. As, one by one, her other children left Kilbally, Kathleen and Kieran to the Church, Moira to marriage, the twins to war, so Breda, the youngest, was the one who stayed close to her parents. Breda never wanted to leave the West of Ireland. She thought Kilbally was the most beautiful place in the world.

Then tragedy struck the O'Connors and the structure of their family life was irrevocably changed. Reeling from unhappiness and humiliation, Breda decided to make a new life for herself – in Yorkshire with her Aunt Josie's family. There she was to discover a totally different world from the one she had left behind, with new people and new challenges for the future.

0 552 14057 0

A SELECTION OF FINE NOVELS
AVAILABLE FROM CORGI BOOKS

THE PRICES SHOWN BELOW WERE CORRECT AT THE TIME OF GOING
TO PRESS. HOWEVER TRANSWORLD PUBLISHERS RESERVE THE
RIGHT TO SHOW NEW RETAIL PRICES ON COVERS WHICH MAY
DIFFER FROM THOSE PREVIOUSLY ADVERTISED IN THE TEXT OR
ELSEWHERE.

14036 8	MAGGIE MAY	*Lyn Andrews*	£4.99
14058 9	MIST OVER THE MERSEY	*Lyn Andrews*	£4.99
14049 X	THE JERICHO YEARS	*Aileen Armitage*	£4.99
13992 0	LIGHT ME THE MOON	*Angela Arney*	£4.99
14044 9	STARLIGHT	*Louise Brindley*	£4.99
13255 1	GARDEN OF LIES	*Eileen Goudge*	£5.99
13686 7	THE SHOEMAKER'S DAUGHTER	*Iris Gower*	£4.99
14095 3	ARIAN	*Iris Gower*	£4.99
14139 9	THE SEPTEMBER STARLINGS	*Ruth Hamilton*	£4.99
14140 2	A CROOKED MILE	*Ruth Hamilton*	£4.99
13872 X	LEGACY OF LOVE	*Caroline Harvey*	£4.99
14138 0	PROUD HARVEST	*Janet Haslam*	£4.99
14297 2	ROSY SMITH	*Janet Haslam*	£4.99
14220 4	CAPEL BELLS	*Joan Hessayon*	£4.99
14262 X	MARIANA	*Susanna Kearsley*	£4.99
14045 7	THE SUGAR PAVILION	*Rosalind Laker*	£5.99
14331 6	THE SECRET YEARS	*Judith Lennox*	£4.99
14002 3	FOOL'S CURTAIN	*Claire Lorrimer*	£4.99
13737 5	EMERALD	*Elisabeth Luard*	£5.99
13910 6	BLUEBIRD	*Margaret Mayhew*	£4.99
13972 6	LARA'S CHILD	*Alexander Mollin*	£5.99
13904 1	VOICES OF SUMMER	*Diane Pearson*	£4.99
10375 6	CSARDAS	*Diane Pearson*	£5.99
13987 4	ZADRUGA	*Margaret Pemberton*	£4.99
14123 2	THE LONDONERS	*Margaret Pemberton*	£4.99
13870 3	THE RAINBOW THROUGH THE RAIN		
		Elvi Rhodes	£4.99
14057 0	THE BRIGHT ONE	*Elvi Rhodes*	£4.99
14318 9	WATER UNDER THE BRIDGE	*Susan Sallis*	£4.99
14291 3	PRIDE OF WALWORTH	*Mary Jane Staples*	£4.99
14296 4	THE LAND OF NIGHTINGALES	*Sally Stewart*	£4.99
14118 6	THE HUNGRY TIDE	*Valerie Wood*	£4.99